REFRAIN
OF LIFE

REFRAIN OF LIFE

SON OF FLAME
BOOK TWO

J. J. Hutto

Podium

Podium

REFRAIN
OF LIFE

CHAPTER ONE

Starlight's Call

430 years ago
Little Brook—Level N/A

It had happened . . .

Uncle Falls had warned her, but he was always going on about things she could hardly understand. Her existence was simple. She found joy in singing and dancing among the rocks and shoals that had helped form her. Anything else was needlessly complex. This did not mean she was mindless; it just meant she only spent time thinking about what was important. Like finding the smoothest stones, or racing leaves down the current.

Now his warning echoed over and over in her head.

Uncle's roaring bass had come vibrating through the currents that had birthed her. "Careful, Little Brook. Stray too far from the mountain and one day you might find yourself unable to hear the song. The Land moves, child, sometimes in ways we can scarcely predict," he had admonished her as he watched her flow down her length and play further and further down the banks of her father.

If only she had listened . . .

She had wandered down Father's shores, following the call of a lark until it alighted on a nearby hilltop. She had giggled in delight as it began a chittering argument with another male over the perch. She found herself endlessly fascinated by both the simple and the empowered creatures of the plane and could watch them for hours. This was not the first time she had followed some interesting subject back to their home, and it had always turned out fine in the past. Her ability to seamlessly move between her physical form and her water manifestation had made her almost immune to any of the typical dangers near her home. It had just been another endless-sky day in the shadow of the mountains that were her home.

Then, as she watched the birds, the Deep Magic had washed over the Land like a wave, crashing through her form and leaving her disoriented. As she had come back to full awareness, a distinct and novel silence settled over her soul . . . The song was gone. A keening wail of distress warbled up from her throat. The Land had moved, and the portion she was on had been called away, leaving a gaping hole in her core where her connection with her family had once dwelt.

If only she had stayed closer! She would have been kept whole and watched another change wash through the Land with her family. But she had strayed too far when the shift had come to balance out the push and pull of those who thought they could rule this place.

The deep roots that had always tied her closely to her family, to her place in the Land, felt as if they had been ripped from their soil and laid bare before the elements. Her sorrow intensified the pain as she looked back toward where the mighty river, her father, had once cut through the landscape. A bleak marsh now choked the horizon where the mountains once stood. They were gone, and she was alone. Her whole world had changed, and now she was adrift in a current she could not understand.

Day turned to night, night back to day, and the Little Brook wept great tears for the family and home she had lost. The calling of the marsh toads and whine of the crickets only compounded the melodic despair of her cries, giving them a haunting, gut-wrenching quality.

Very few trees had survived the inhospitable marshland, and the wide-open night sky bore witness to the Little Brook's loss and her longing.

Wisdom—Level ???

The stars twinkled angrily down at her, demanding that she change course again.

"Just because you are slightly older does not mean you get to order me around. I understand what you are asking, but I am on a very tight schedule!" she muttered harshly up at the night sky from the seat of her wagon. Her mule cast a baleful eye back at her antics as he continued to trudge along.

A sudden shower of comets cut through the sky, all moving toward the newly arrived marsh.

"It's all well and good for you up there! But some of us must live out our existence down here, and going that way will set me back weeks!" she almost shouted into the empty night.

The mule simply flicked his ears in annoyance as he continued to plod along the barely used cart path running along the outskirts of the marsh.

The expansive sky above them slowly darkened as one by one the stars winked out, leaving behind empty holes of blackness where galaxies once spun.

"None of that now!" she huffed, relaxing the stubborn set of her shoulders, rolling her eyes in exasperation.

"Honestly, if people only knew how dramatic you all can get, I swear . . . But this is the last time! I have my own responsibilities to tend to, and they don't include your every whim," she muttered darkly up at the bright starry night. With a click of her tongue and a slight tug on the reins, she guided her mule onto a path through the marsh that had not been there moments before. While still muttering darkly to herself, her eyes took on a many-hued glow and she peered out into the unremarkable distance, seeing things that no other could see.

She cocked her head and her stare sharpened as she read through the pattern of the Under **Weave** like a familiar book.

"Hmmm, now that is interesting . . . ," she said as her eyes returned to their normal deep brown. She then thoughtfully pulled out some Legendary-grade wool and began to knit calmly with the reins lying in her lap. The mule placidly made his way through the marsh one plodding step at a time.

2 weeks later
Little Brook

She didn't know how long it had been. But she did know that at some point she had stopped her cries.

The tears had simply stopped coming.

She looked down again at her azure form, now almost completely transparent. She was suffering the fate that any of her kind would if they were separated too long from moving water. The stagnant waters of the nearby marsh taunted her. The water in them called to her, but the composition might as well have been poison. She refused to give in to the whispered thought that she should just phase into her water manifestation and become one with the muck and mud before her, losing what was left of herself in the process.

"Come, child, there is no use moping," a voice called from the bottom of the hill. Little Brook whipped her head up to find an old cart being pulled by a mule and driven by a middle-aged woman in dark clothing.

No, that wasn't right . . . Despite being almost all black, the voluminous robes she wore shone faintly with a starry-sky pattern. Little Brook watched in amazement as some of the stars formed a new constellation and shot off out of sight on the robes. It was so delightfully magical and familiar that she couldn't keep herself from laughing, and the tinkling bell of her joy rang out over the marsh.

"Now, now, don't go showing off." The woman frowned down at her clothing. But when she looked up, she wore a faint smile. Brook had always been taught to stay away from those not of the Land, but *she* was different. She wasn't of the

Land. Brook could tell that immediately, but something about the way she got off the wagon while taking care not to step on the thistle growing near the cart path spoke of respect and knowledge deeper than most of her kind held.

Wait . . . That cart path hadn't been there earlier, had it?

The woman in dark starry clothing clucked in sympathy as she approached, noting the near insubstantiality of Little Brook. "You are in a poor state, aren't you? I see why they called," she said as she reached the top of the hill and looked Little Brook up and down.

Just a few moments ago, Brook had been ready to fade away, but something about the sympathy grated on her wild nature and she rushed and babbled back at the woman.

"Yes, well, no need to get upset. I have come to offer you a chance to return to your family," she stated abruptly as she pulled something long and woven from her robe.

Brook tinkled in shock at the woman's words. There was a way home? Through the Land she could feel her home and family, but they were so distant that she couldn't even feel a direction from the faint tug on her core. And even if she could, without moving water she would never survive long enough to make it to them anyway.

The woman seemed to have no trouble understanding her meaning and continued as if they were having a normal conversation.

"In your free form, you perhaps only have a day left before you fade completely. However, I can bind you to this piece of clothing and halt your decay," she said slowly, letting the gravity of Little Brook's situation sink in before continuing.

"If you give up your form to be woven, you will be bound to serve whoever wears this. But I promise you two things. The first is that you will only serve worthy masters. And the second is that one day you will find your way home . . . Do you accept?" She held out the cloth for Little Brook to inspect.

Brook leaned closer to look over the fabric critically and upon closer inspection saw that it was humming with magical energy. She could even feel that it had been a gift of the Land, not taken by force. Brook looked up once more at the mysterious woman.

Considering her limited options, and her longing to see her home again, this would have to do. Besides, something about the stern but careful woman instilled a deep trust in Little Brook. Looking into her eyes reminded Little Brook of the times her father had told her legends of great-grandfather Ocean. She wasn't one of the people, but she understood her place and moved with the flow of the pattern, not against it. This was rarely true of those not of the Land.

Perhaps Brook should have listened to her uncle, but she hadn't and had to face the consequences. But deep in her core, she knew that this was where the flow of the pattern was taking her.

Still meeting the woman's eyes, Little Brook gave a firm and determined nod, to which the woman smiled back graciously before waving her hand in Little Brook's direction. She felt a tug, and then a draining sensation started to pull from her center. She looked down in wonder as the substance that made up her form dissolved and flowed like a tiny stream of water into the grayish fabric, dividing into thousands of tiny strands and integrating with the knit pattern, dyeing it a deep blue. Now alone, the woman gave another, sadder nod to the scarf lying still in her hands.

"Very sensible of you, little one. You have honored me, and now I will honor your trust," she said solemnly before turning smartly around, tucking the scarf into her voluminous sleeves, and heading back down the hill toward her cart.

"I have a friend in the Steppe who will know just what to do with you . . . Balaam! Stop eating that thistle at once! You know it gives you indigestion!" she snapped at the mule, who continued to munch happily on the interestingly textured flower.

CHAPTER TWO

Beginnings

Present day
Jonathan Tillman – Level 18 Son of Flame

Tilly followed the clearly excited lapin out into the street and found it absolutely choked with people industriously moving up and down the thoroughfare, carrying all sorts of goods. Tilly wrinkled his nose at a passing worker coming in from the direction of the docks with a pole over one shoulder and a wicker basket filled with fish hung over the other. They managed to move a little further down the street before both Shuji and Tilly had to stop as a team rolled a pallet of logs ahead of them, taking up nearly the whole width between buildings. The pair squeezed to the side with the other commuters, and the pallet continued toward some empty plots further into the burgeoning city.

Shuji looked over at Tilly, beaming like a proud parent as they both watched the timber continue down the street. "You see, Mr. Tillman, preparations are in full swing! We know not what will happen when we activate the crystal, but we are preparing for any eventuality, whether it be production boosts or even a building gift from Nephesh itself! Whatever the case, we want to be as ready as possible, and the council has been hard at work planning for the most likely eventualities," Shuji confided in a loud voice as the bustle of the growing city increased and the two continued on their way.

As soon as the flow of the crowd resumed in the right direction, Shuji was moving, jostling, and bouncing between people as he merrily made his way to what used to be the valley gates of the village. Tilly had to lean hard into his *Dexterity* to even keep up with the surprisingly graceful lapin. But knowing how fast events could outpace him, he kept asking questions even as they moved through the busy streets.

"So, I get that we don't know the details, but give me the broad strokes, Shuji! How does the crystal help run a faction, besides the starting bonuses you told me about?"

The lapin's ears twitched in response, and he slowed slightly. "Oh, yes, my apologies. It is difficult not to get carried away assuming you know what most do. Crystals offer two powerful options to every seat of power," he expounded loudly, growing slightly out of breath as he spoke but too excited to reduce his pace.

"All races of Nephesh have a basic set of combat and crafting classes available when they come of age, as well as access to one or two classes uniquely suited to their race." He happily continued his lecture even as he adroitly maneuvered his bulk through and around different clumps of mostly lapin people going about the city's preparations. "The lapin people have a class called Peasant, which has the main advantages of rapid procreation and plus twenty percent efficiency when producing any foodstuffs or timber buildings. But with a Sovereign Crystal, you can obtain unique classes specific to the power that owns the Crystal. When we had a Sovereign Crystal of our own, all who met the stat requirements had access to the Ronin and Samurai classes. Something that we lost when our nation fell. The honu have a hereditary class, Tide Caller, which is very powerful but too specialized to allow them to function outside of partnership with other races."

They moved onto the main thoroughfare leading to the now absent main gate and the refugee camp outside. Shuji paused in his explanation, taking in the city-sized camp that now filled the valley on this side of the river with an inscrutable expression. He glanced over at Tilly, who was considering him thoughtfully, and smiled his large-toothed smile before continuing.

"The Thousand Phalanx Empire had a Sovereign Crystal that it kept in the courtyard of the palace. With the legacy of thousands of years and growth behind them, they were old enough to have access to all sorts of rare classes. The most famous of which were of course the Phalanx Infantry and the Bastions. Unique classes are always better than base classes, and it is because of this that our people were denied access to them for generations, apart from a few notable exceptions."

By this point, they had passed through what seemed to serve as the loose perimeter of the tent city that had sprung up to house the close to one hundred thousand refugees that had escaped the empire's fall.

Over on the other side of the river, Tilly could see a much smaller orderly encampment for the honu and the beginnings of miles of fields and pastureland. Things were being built and deconstructed all around him, but there was a certain amount of order to the chaos. He saw that despite the almost endless crowd of tents, they all more or less followed the neat square-like pattern originating from the huge log building going up at the center of the camp. This pattern allowed for easy movement through the tents and there were even a few clearly marked muddy roadways bisecting the sprawling formation. The wide churned roadways had been flagged every few feet to keep them clear of living spaces and were being well used, crowded with workers transporting logs from the mountain and hauling in what seemed to be game and forage from the surrounding forest.

"Ah, I sometimes forget just what a walk we are setting ourselves up for with this location . . . ," Shuji huffed out as they moved down the simple but straight road. Tilly tried to keep his head screwed on straight as it swung back and forth to take in this new mass of races, all ready to create a new home after losing everything. Then a question occurred to him at Shuji's statement.

"Wait, why the Temple? Don't we need to protect the Crystal or something once we establish it? If we do it there, it will be so far from the city."

"Yes, well . . . ," Shuji began between carefully managed breaths. "The agreement was to make this Crystal equally available, and with the threat we see rising, it seemed like a good idea to take on Divine Patronage again. We have not failed to notice how, uh, effective your powerset has been against this enemy, and so the council compromised on this location. Equal access for all, and a defensible fallback location in the event of a catastrophe."

"Divine Patronage? Wait . . . Does that mean you guys are all taking on **Origin** as the god of this kingdom or whatever? I mean, have any of you even heard of **Origin** before? Does anyone know any stories or myths that mention him?" Tilly asked, surprised at how quickly they had decided to partner with a completely unknown power. From what little he had gathered, following a god here wasn't like back home. It seemed to have many more practical requirements and benefits.

"No, Mr. Tillman, none of us had heard mention of this figure before. But oftentimes this can mean the god is very old, and any god who is old enough to be forgotten is powerful indeed if they can still touch the physical plane without worshipers. Also, both you and Ichiro seem to have been chosen to be invested with its power, and typically, the best measure of a god is their followers."

"Wait, Ichiro? What do you mea—" Tilly was cut off by a loud croaking shout directed at him from the line of tents to the side of the road.

"That's him, Edna! Hold on one cherry-picking minute, human!" shouted a voice from within the tent city.

Tilly couldn't help but tense at the sudden attention as many turned to see what was happening. He had never liked crowds and nothing that had occurred the last two weeks had made that discomfort any more bearable. He scanned the faces turning toward him curiously and with unease. He didn't find the owner of the voice in the immediate crowd, but as he looked further back into the tents, he spotted an elderly satyr hobbling around the walls of cloth and poles, waving him down, huffing and puffing with exertion. Tilly arrested his already slowed pace and stopped short, trying to process where he had seen the elderly satyr before. Shuji continued on a few more steps before turning to find Tilly had stopped, his enthusiastic smile dampening.

"Mr. Tillman, they will be left waiting if we don't hurry," Shuji muttered distractedly as he searched for the caller himself before finding the refugee moving toward them through the tents. His eyes flowed over the satyr and moved back to Tilly with barely a pause.

"If we stop here, many will want to speak to you, but we simply don't have time for that sort of thing right now."

Tilly ignored him as he spotted an even smaller satyr woman following a few steps behind the first, who had finally made it through the tents. They both wore rough spun coveralls, and they practically beamed at him between billowing breaths as they looked up and saw he had turned to wait. Identify pinged over both of them.

Level 44, Farmer

"Bless my oats! It is wonderful to see you!" the elderly satyr shouted with a youthful exuberance as he finally caught his breath. "They said none knew if you had made it out of the city, but I knew a tough young man like you wouldn't give up so easily, even if you did take your time coming through that portal. Edna and I have visited every day to see if you made it!" He wheezed triumphantly as he arrived before Tilly. The whirling in Tilly's mind tumbled into place as he finally placed the two.

"That's it! You are the two I carried to the portal right at the end!" Tilly exclaimed.

"Mr. Tillman, the council and perhaps even your god will be kept waiting . . . ," Shuji muttered, standing off to the side as he leaned suggestively toward the mountain. Tilly barely spared Shuji a glance before turning back to the couple, who had both reached out and grabbed his hands in theirs.

"It's great to see you two! I had hoped—" he started but was immediately cut off.

"Oh, hush! No need to pretend you have been thinking about us two old-timers!" the man said with a knowing smile. Then his wife, Edna, cut in.

"What George here means to say is that we are very grateful for all you did, not just for us, but for many here. We have been hearing stories and we wanted to tell you that we don't care what the rumors say! If you and that nice lady are what humans are like, then humans are just fine with us!" she declared resolutely, taking time to look around at the crowd as if daring them to say differently. During her small speech, Tilly felt something being tucked into his hands, and Edna leaned forward to whisper, "I know how hungry you young people get. Here is a little something we scrounged up for you."

"Watch it, young man! If she were any younger, I might be concerned!" George said in a loud voice as if whatever they were doing had to be covered up somehow. He then pulled their hands back from the exchange and gave Tilly a firm nod.

Tilly felt the familiar long-sought warmth that always came with a public acknowledgment and its constant companion, shame. Even here and now, the wheedling fear that he was an imposter somehow wormed into the back of his mind. No matter who these people thought he was, they would never know just how many times he had chosen to hide from his pain instead of face it. He suddenly felt sick as he looked around at the smiling careworn faces watching the interaction. Worry wriggled in his stomach, and he couldn't shake the feeling that despite coming this far, he didn't have what it would take to keep all these people safe . . .

Then his eyes landed back on the wide-open expressions of the elderly couple before him. He considered them a moment as they smiled up at him and his hand felt around the small round gift they had discreetly deposited in his hand. They did not have much to offer, but they offered it nonetheless. There was something firm in their understanding of life, and he couldn't help but remember them crawling hopelessly forward under the weight of an angry god. However vulnerable these two were, they exuded a sturdiness that somehow pushed back all of Tilly's worries. If they could keep fighting, so could he.

"Mr. Tillman, if you would—" Shuji began to interrupt, but Tilly silenced him with a jab of his elbow. Then he put on his best smile and found the most gracious tone he could.

"Thank you both! It means the world to me that you made it through. I don't know much about what is going on yet, but if I don't miss my guess, your skills will be immensely valuable to the city going forward." Both of the elderly farmers straightened from the unconscious stoop that age imparts to all and nodded in affirmation.

"Right you are, young man! Bless my peas! Right you are!" George declared before turning to Edna. "Come on, wife. The boy is right. If we start soon, we might be able to plant another twenty hectares by dark," he said, his face screwed up in determination.

"Yes, dear, I'm sure we will," she said as she moved along with him back toward the river, making sure to turn and send Tilly a wink and a warm smile.

"If you are quite done, Mr. Tillman . . . ," Shuji said, fidgeting in place.

"Oh, don't get your robes in a twist, Shuji! How about we jog the rest of the way to make up time since I have wasted too much of it," Tilly shot back at the Librarian, cutting his harsh tone with a sharp, snarky smile. In response, Shuji's face moved through a range of emotions before landing on a chagrined smile of his own.

"Ah, yes, fair point, I suppose. Let's get on with it." He sighed. Tilly then patted the rotund lapin on the shoulder, feeling lighter than he had in years. He'd gotten a good meal, a good night's sleep, and for the first time since he had arrived, he wasn't running for his life! He honestly had no clue if he could be what these people needed, but that wasn't going to stop him from trying.

He moved off through the crowd and down the road, making his way toward the diminishing tree line at a slow jog. In his right hand he fingered the barely ripe apple and smiled.

It was time to return to the Temple, the place where it had all started.

CHAPTER THREE

The Champion's Mantle

Tilly pushed until Shuji's labored breathing began to get out of hand. Then, as they reached the base of the mountain, he slowed and turned to wait for the large lapin. They had made it to the far end of the valley, where the muddy road narrowed into a small but clear path moving straight up the slope of the mountain.

"Sorry for using up time on those farmers, Shuji, but this run will have gotten us back on track, I think," Tilly shouted over his shoulder pointedly.

There was still a way to go for the already sweating Librarian, but Tilly couldn't keep himself from poking at him one last time for his insensitivity back at the camp. That farmer couple had been so earnest, and Tilly hoped he never got so busy or important that he didn't have time for people like that. He gave the mountain path a long look and let out a low whistle at the incline.

"Ah . . . yes . . . ," Shuji gasped, stumbling to a stop next to him. "Not too much further now . . . I believe."

Tilly snorted in response. "Shuji, I have personally made this trip a couple of times now. If this trail is clear and extends all the way to the Temple entrance, we will get there in two hours at a fast walk."

Shuji began to groan before cutting it off by clearing his throat. "Well, I likely won't have another chance in this lifetime to witness the activation of a Sovereign Crystal, so set the pace, Mr. Tillman. I will keep up if it kills me! They said they would wait until noon, and I'll not chance missing it," he declared, the lines on his face hardening into a pattern of grim determination.

Something about his resolute love of discovery and the previously unmentioned timeline suddenly got Tilly feeling guilty. He realized that Shuji had risked not witnessing something he felt was historic just to make sure Tilly got some answers before being thrust into the middle of events again. There he was, jumping to conclusions before knowing the whole story . . . Aside from the rough start, the lapins had been a huge help to him, and he needed to start giving them the benefit of the doubt.

That reminded him! There was one thing Shuji hadn't finished explaining before the messenger bird had come and they had set off into the city.

"Shuji, really quick before we head up, you said we needed to think about making this place defensible as we activated the Crystal. Why is that? What is coming?"

"Wha—" Shuji jerked, turning from his determined staring match with the mountain. Then the question caught up with him. "Ah, yes. Apologies, Jonathan Tillman! This is a very important concept. When a new nation or power is declared through a Sovereign Crystal, Nephesh itself changes. It is a land that always maintains balance. Nations aligned with the light balance out those allied with darkness. The Isle of Light and headquarters of the Temple of Light are far to the east, just off the coast of the Azure Vasthold. To balance this, the seat of dark influence on the plane is as far west as you can go. There, the sun ends its journey and light never touches the soil. Past the Blasted Lands are the Pits of Despair, where demonic princes rise and fall with the eddies of power.

"The rest of the nations on the endless continent fall in the middle of these two seats of power. They form a complex pattern of checks and balances over the whole, constantly changing yet remaining more or less equal. None but the Cartographers know how to follow the endless shifting of the Land. Most nations just concern themselves with their immediate neighbors and those they have access to through a teleportation network." Shuji had turned back to Tilly now, fully in his lecture mode. Then a bird called from up the path and he jumped before turning to look up the mountain path again.

"I am sorry, Mr. Tillman. There is more to say on the subject, but in short, every time there is a great shift in power, or a new nation emerges, Nephesh itself moves, rearranging borders and topography at the edges of established nations' territories. So, while we are far into the frontier now, we will undoubtedly be moved once we declare ourselves a nation." He was breathless as he concluded his rapid exposition.

"So, this whole area is going to be teleported somewhere else, and we will be bordering completely new neighbors?" Tilly asked, pulling the most immediately important piece of information out of the lecture.

"Yes! That is correct, although it is highly unlikely that we will be near the center of things. Typically, the more powerful you are, the deeper into the heart of conflict you are thrust. Those are the lands of eternal contestation, and at their heart are the unclaimed peaks. It is said that if those peaks are ever taken, the balance will shift and Nephesh will either ascend or descend fully into the hands of its new rulers," he said while turning back and forth from the trail distractedly, like a little boy having to go pee.

"Alright, let's get moving!" Tilly relented, having plenty to chew on after that exchange. Then, softening his tone, he said, "Also, I'm sorry, Shuji. I wouldn't have teased so much if I had understood the timeline you were under. I promise we will make it, even if I have to carry you!"

Shuji chuckled, and his good-natured smile returned as he shifted his robes around his corpulent belly and gave Tilly a sharp nod in response. "I'm ready!"

Tilly led the way up the path, setting a ground-eating pace that he estimated was right on the edge of Shuji's ability. He kept a close watch on both Shuji's physical state and the position of the sun, trying his best to keep them on track.

They marched that way for an hour before Tilly recognized a certain clearing off to the right and did a double take. Shuji was still faithfully puffing behind him with sweat soaking the armpits and collar of his robe. He probably had time for a quick detour. He moved off the path and called over to his companion, "Shuji, keep it up! There is something I need to grab, but I'll meet you nearer to the top, I promise."

The lapin just nodded in response, keeping his eyes straight as he continued to march onward at the steady cadence they had set for the hike. Tilly gave a quick wave before jogging off through the clearing where he had met the Carnonos in an attempt to backtrack his way to the Charmin Tree for the third time.

After a few minutes of tramping through the woods he found the small tree missing two clumps of leaves, but still looking healthy despite the loss.

"Sorry, buddy, last time for a while, I promise," Tilly muttered as he riffled through his fantasy fanny pack and got rid of a few herb bundles that he had forgotten the use of. He did keep the last of the bandages and a metal tin that was filled with something that smelled like Vicks.

Once the enchanted pack had enough room for thirty or forty leaves—supple, pliable leaves—he gathered them as quickly as possible from a variety of low-hanging branches and stuffed them in the pack.

"Until next time." Tilly nodded to the tree while attaching his fanny pack back under his jacket, then turned to go. But after a few steps, he hesitated and called back to the tree over his shoulder, "And thanks. You probably don't understand this, but you have been a small but needed comfort in a world of constant change." Nodding to himself, Tilly continued hurrying off to catch up to Shuji, who was still doggedly pushing himself to keep the pace.

Unnoticed, the small tree's leaves rustled as if blown by a windless breeze.

Tilly caught up with Shuji after about five minutes of jogging and couldn't help but notice pocks and vein-like patterns in the rock and plants around him. They were beginning to reach the area that had been riddled with **Corruption's** influence. Except every sign they passed now had been scoured clean by purifying fire. Now all the plants that had once been infected seemed to be thriving. Tilly's hand unconsciously went to his side, which had an annoying habit of itching every time he thought of it. He hoped that getting rid of it would be that simple . . . once he learned to "Lay it down" as Thunder had said.

Aside from **Herb Lore** sending him notifications that he only bothered to skim, he spent the rest of the hike deep in thought, thinking about the implications of helping to start a new country in this world and the journey he would inevitably have to set out on to get rid of his own **Corruption.**

Before he knew it, the trees cleared and he was stepping through the tree line into the eerily perfect semi-circle clearing marking the opening of the Temple. The roots that had once choked the entrance and fanned out into the surrounding forest were gone, leaving a faint dark-gray ash that covered everything.

Standing at the entrance was the small group they were supposed to meet. The whole group was locked in a discussion, furiously arguing some important point. Well, not the whole group. Two familiar lapins with axes strapped to their backs kept watch on the forest, guarding the council.

Nyuk and Kuro both twitched their ears at his arrival, and Kuro shouted, "Human! Welcome back from your week-long nap!" Which he followed with an enthusiastic wave of his hand.

Typical, Tilly sighed internally.

At his greeting, the others looked up. The group was made up of two elderly honu, whom Tilly vaguely recognized, Linus, now looking a lot older and wearing a lemon-pucker scowl, and next to him was another, shorter satyr with spectacles and a very well-groomed beard. Making up the last pair of the council were Hiro and Ichiro. Hiro gave him a formal nod, while Ichiro smiled brightly as if seeing an old friend.

They all moved forward to meet the approaching pair, one looking apprehensive and the other breathing heavily.

"It is well you have arrived! We are very eager to begin, Mr. Tillman," said the spectacled satyr.

"Yes . . . welcome . . . Have you been . . . briefed?" one of the two honu elders asked. As she spoke, **Identify** began to ping over their heads as it showed Tilly just how far some of them had come.

Level 46, Tide Caller
Level 50, Tide Caller
Level 65, Empire's Bastion
Level 43, Bureaucrat
Level 58, Samurai Lord
Level 42 (25), Samurai Hatamoto

"I'm pretty sure I have a handle on what we are about to do and why, but I don't understand what my place in it will be," Tilly replied, then he turned to the three he didn't know. "Also, my name is Jonathan Tillman, nice to meet you. It's an honor to meet the council members elected by the people! Sorry that I don't yet know your names."

"Ah . . . Yes, that is my fault!" Shuji broke in, putting on his best diplomatic smile, which was more or less ruined by the sweat soaking his robes and face. "These are Elders Kira and Kalea. They were the next oldest in line to survive our escape from the city," he said, gesturing to the two female honu, who nodded along with their names. "This is Pupienus. He was elected, along with Linus, as one of the two most capable leaders for the refugee contingent." Linus only scowled in response, and Pupienus gave a haughty yet wary nod. "The other two you know well. Each faction has the right to appoint two leaders in the manner they choose. The council leader, currently Lord Hiro, has tie-breaking power. We have a charter that outlines a course of growth that has been ratified by all present members." Tilly shivered at the political undertones that he could easily hear in that explanation.

Pupienus's nose drifted higher in the air at the mention of ratification, while Linus's scowl deepened into a full-on "Get off my lawn!" old-man frown at Shuji's words. The others remained more or less impassive, except for Ichiro, who seemed to be looking off into the distance, his milky white eyes following something.

Afraid that they were going to get any deeper into the explanation of the current politics, Tilly quickly moved on. "Got it, sounds like you guys are doing a fantastic job! So, what do you need from me here?"

Hiro humphed and Tilly might have imagined a slight twinkle in his eye as he turned back toward the Temple and answered as he went. "Temples and their effects on surroundings vary greatly and are entirely dependent on the deity. We hope that establishing the nexus of our nation's power here will trigger some sort of boon from your **Origin** and impact the classes we are offered, amongst other things. As the chosen Champion of this deity, we hope you being here to intercede will offer us some agency in this process." With that, he started walking toward the entrance.

"Lord Hiro! Are we sure we have come to a proper agreement on priorities?" the spectacled satyr called after him. Hiro didn't bother to respond, just waving off the question as he walked. Shuji and the rest of the group except Nyuk and Kuro moved to follow.

"You guys aren't coming?" Tilly asked as he passed them.

"We will stand watch out here . . . Typically, being near you when something big is going to happen can be dangerous," Nyuk said drily. Kuro nodded along solemnly at the words.

"Suit yourselves. I hear this is going to be pretty cool," Tilly said, moving past the two and joining the group as they entered the simple stone opening to the Temple.

CHAPTER FOUR

Big Crystal Energy

Tilly hurried to catch up with the others moving through the front entrance of the Temple, carved into the side of the mountain, with hardly a thought for the things he had faced here on his two previous visits . . .

Well, that wasn't exactly true. Some of those grizzly memories tried to surface as they moved down the front passageway and assembled in the anteroom of the Temple. But Tilly kept them tamped down, continually singing "The Final Countdown" under his breath in a semi-successful attempt to distract himself.

The group formed in a half circle in the central chamber, which had become a cafeteria-sized room with a high ceiling and softly glowing walls. Hiro turned away from the center of the room and addressed Tilly in a formal tone.

"Jonathan Tillman, Champion of the god **Origin**. We plan to activate our nation's Sovereign Crystal in this first room. Will this displease the patron of this Temple in any way? Do you not have the ability to speak for your god in this?"

Tilly took in the stares of everyone present, who had all turned to see his answer. He wasn't sure how formal this was or if there was a right answer, but he went with his gut, which hadn't killed him so far. Then again, it had come pretty close . . .

"Honestly, I think he will be fine with this. I'm not sure about other gods, but he doesn't seem to think about this stuff in the same way as the other deities I've heard of. It's not that he doesn't care . . . I think he does, but it's more like he . . . is looking to do good by us. Well, the honest answer is that I don't know. But I do have a good feeling about this," he finished lamely, not really prepared to represent a being that he hardly understood himself.

Hiro bowed formally, acknowledging his answer, and then turned to look deeper into the Temple. After a moment he spoke. "It is with open intentions we seek to tie this nation's fate with yours and enact a Covenant. We will align ourselves with your cause, and in turn, we ask for your blessing and protection in the face of the coming threat. You are unknown to us, but the darkness we face is known well enough. No deity has done as much for our people since our own patron gave up her power to grant us this legacy. We share enemies and allies alike. Let us be bound together in the eyes of Nephesh and all who dwell within it," he intoned formally before bowing again.

His words echoed through the glowing chamber, and nothing seemed to happen. This did not ruffle Hiro, who nodded to Ichiro and stepped aside. His son stepped forward and pulled out a cloth bundle from under the banded sash that held his sword. He unwrapped the bundle carefully and revealed a golf ball-sized Crystal faceted with hundreds of flat planes.

The shape was difficult to pin down and seemed to change as light danced within. Ichiro held it up and a small stream of white energy flowed from the center of his forehead to the Crystal, which took it in and then began to hum. Ichiro slowly pulled his hand away and left the Crystal floating in the center of the room, rotating slowly.

The humming intensified and the glow became brighter as the Crystal began to spin faster. Tilly couldn't help but look over at the others, especially the lapins, who had been planning for this moment for generations. He couldn't imagine what this moment would mean to them, but as he turned his head, he was struck by a sudden deafening silence. The humming had cut off completely. He whipped his head back to the Crystal and found it still shining brightly but completely frozen in place, hovering a few feet off the stone floor.

He turned to the others and found them all frozen in place wearing some mix of awe and trepidation on their unmoving faces. Looks like time was getting weird around him again . . . But at least he wasn't stuck in it, like his second visit to the Temple. Tilly looked around in confusion, trying to figure out what had gone wrong.

Maybe something had tripped the Temple's time-dilation defense? Perhaps he had been wrong about how the magic of the Crystal and **Origin's** power would interact. He walked through the group and around the Crystal and found them to be completely frozen in the grip of time, but otherwise unharmed.

Tilly sighed deeply and moved toward the entrance of the lower hallway. If there was an answer as to why this was happening, he would probably find it in the altar room.

He moved slowly this time, not quite able to summon back the ability to block out the terrifying memories of his first two trips down this hall. Something about time being frozen robbed him of his earlier defense mechanism. No song came easily to mind, and he was once again left alone in this place to face his thoughts. The further he walked, the more his pace slowed as he found himself strangely reluctant to discover whatever waited for him in the central chamber.

The fine dark-gray dust—or, more specifically, ash—did not stir as he stepped slowly into the light of the much larger central chamber. There, silently burning, was the deep blue, almost white, flame. It rested on the rough-hewn stone altar and had tripled in size since he had left it, and it seemed to still be growing.

Tilly hesitantly approached closer as the flame continued to burn higher, its light fierce and everchanging. There was a palpable sense of eagerness emanating from it, as if it was ready to spread, or . . . consume. No, that wasn't it either . . . Destroy? That was closer, but still not quite the word for the desire that was vibrating off the altar . . .

Purify.

That was it. It was kindled and ready, longing to be unleashed on the world to do its work.

The warmth in Tilly's chest bloomed to a full and intense heat in response to his recognition of the feeling radiating off the flame. Except as soon as he recognized the flame's desire, he found a mirror of that desire igniting within himself. He wanted to vent this energy, to consume and destroy that which had poisoned his days so far on the plane. He needed to burn this infection *out!*

The **Corruption** in his side started to writhe painfully, and Tilly coughed down a groan as its tendrils raked disturbingly against the interior of his torso. Tears flooded his eyes from the sudden onslaught of pain. It knew what he was considering, and suddenly, he found it difficult to care about the consequences.

He *hated* this thing.

The anger that was rising in him wasn't the mind-numbing rage that **Corruption's** influence had fed him to incite violence on the streets of the capital. Instead, the discontent that was kindling in his chest wiped away the doubt and fear that constantly buzzed around him like flies. Even in the face of this literal gut-wrenching pain, he knew he was ready to do whatever he had to to get rid of this invader.

The flame inside him howled hungrily at the thought of its wrathful judgement. Tilly would purge it from his limbs, then move out into the world, wiping its taint from the plane.

These thoughts cut through the pain wracking his body with a burning clarity. He couldn't help but laugh, his abs contracting around the sickening contortions writhing under his skin. It was all so clear now. The **Seed** was *scared*. It was scared of *him* and what he was becoming.

He almost vibrated with a need to try cutting himself open again with enflamed strikes from his hatchets. He knew he could do it, and he suddenly didn't care what happened to him. He was tired of letting this thing hide in his body, and he knew he would burn it alive, no matter what it cost.

His hands shook as he reached down to his belt loops, allowing the flame from his chest to flow down his extremities.

"You will destroy it that way . . . but you will die in the process," a voice said quietly from behind him. In shock, he spun as it continued, unconcerned, "A different way has been revealed to you for a reason."

Tilly finished grabbing for one of his hatchets as a handsome woman wearing dark voluminous robes came into view. She was standing in the shadow of the arched entrance with her eyes focused on the altar. The shifting light of the flames highlighted faint reflective motes of white on her otherwise night-black clothing.

"Who are you?" Tilly asked, slowly lowering his weapon. The flame in his chest remained steady, not at all reacting to her presence.

Her eyes hadn't left the flame as she had spoken, and for a moment she seemed to have forgotten he had even asked her a question. Then she spoke again, but this time her words emerged along with a disturbingly deep harmony, causing Tilly's chest to vibrate along with the syllables of her non-answer.

The first lost, buried in time.
The second kept safe in memory's embrace,
and the third perched as a jewel on the crown of the world."

Then her eyes cleared, and she finally looked away from the flame and took in Tilly, looking him up and down as if considering him for the first time.

"When the flame reemerged from the **Weave**, the enemy twisted much to gain a foothold in this area first, mangling its plans in some places to marshal a presence here. I thought I was too late to stop it, and yet here it stands, free of its captor and with a new Champion! The changes allowing you to intervene were so subtle and minute that I missed them at first. Even I forget sometimes who first taught me how to read the threads," she said, with a rueful shake of her head and a small self-deprecating smile that made her sharp, distinctive features less severe.

Great, another mystery power that seems to know exactly what is going on, but only speaks in riddles.

"Hello, I'm Jonathan Tillman, nice to meet you," he said, putting on his most congenial smile. An itch was developing between his shoulder blades, and he felt sure that some sort of calamitous event was going to interrupt the conversation before he could learn anything useful. Whoever she was, she also didn't seem to be affected by the flame's time dilation.

"Of course. Wonderful to meet you, Jonathan Tillman. It has been quite some time since he has had a Champion for this particular Facet. But my counsel stands. Despite its nature, I highly doubt you are meant to let yourself be consumed by fire in order to destroy your infection. There is another way I believe, although that path is unclear to me." She watched him as she spoke, seeming to weigh his reactions as if they could tell her something that he himself didn't know.

"The Flower . . . ," he said with a sigh as he slid the hatchet back into its loop.

"Yes . . . I can see how the Bloom would work. But why are you being sent there?" Her eyes drifted off away from Tilly as if following some sort of pattern.

Then she suddenly winced, and her eyes snapped back to Tilly's face. "It has been a long time since I last saw Thunder. Send him my regards," she said, suddenly ready to leave. The shadows around her began to deepen alarmingly as they mingled with her robes.

"Wait! Who are you, and can you do anything to help us? We are about to get teleported or attacked or something! We could use the help!" he shouted after her fading form. In response, the shadows stopped moving around her, leaving the impression of a floating head, the only part of her body not swathed in the dark robes.

"I am called Wisdom, and you must not fear. Your people have chosen rightly in seeking his aid. He seldom gives what you expect, but it is always what you need. I have already done my part, and after an unexpected detour, I was able to retrieve my gift for your new nation. It will be waiting outside the Temple." Then, with a nod of farewell, the shadows completely enveloped her, and he was alone in the room.

A thunderous crack broke the silence behind him, and he whirled to see words forming out of the flame on the altar.

> *HIDDEN QUEST COMPLETE: RESTORE A NATION*
> *TO THE PATRONAGE OF ORIGIN'S FLAME*
> *COMPLETION REWARDS DISTRIBUTED ACCORDING*
> *TO CONTRIBUTION*

CHAPTER FIVE

Glow Up

Just as Tilly finished reading the fiery text, something snapped the strange stillness of his surrounding environment, and he felt the passage of time reassert itself. He took a deep breath, trying to push down the surprising amount of nausea that shifting in and out of time seemed to always bring. Swallowing down a wet burp, he looked back up to find the words above the altar collapsing in on themselves.

Their forms shivered and devolved back into a floating vortex of fire that was being sucked into a central point above the main flame of the altar. Tilly watched as it compacted into a fist-sized ball of brilliant flame, which continued to pull in on itself. The smaller the compressed point of energy became, the higher the pressure rose in the chamber, and Tilly winced in anticipation as he realized what was happening.

Whatever "Facet" of **Origin** this was, it seemed to have a fondness for explosions.

Instead of continuing to watch it compress to an increasingly small point, he glanced back at the entrance trying to decide if a warning would help anything . . . Nope, no point in trying to outrun this thing.

It had said rewards, right? he thought as he crouched down and covered his face with his arms. Some part of his brain noted with fascination that his armor was already shifting to its yellow salamander form. He wondered idly if that was in reaction to a real environmental danger or his internal anticipation of a coming fire-based threat.

After only a few seconds in the international "brace yourself" position, a huge *WUUMMPPHH* blew past him. The air around him hiccupped inward before exploding back outward, followed by a wall of immense heat.

Tilly winced as it hit him, but, similar to his enflamed state, he comprehended the heat on a sensational level but found the expected pain absent. He hesitantly lifted his head from between his knees and found himself facing a small hovering blue flame with an object floating in its center.

He stared at it dumbly until **Identify** pinged above it, marking it unhelpfully as:

Hidden Quest Reward

His notification log had started blinking, so he pulled it up and found the most recent entry.

> ***Congratulations!*** *You have unlocked and completed a Hidden Quest. Your contribution is graded as A-tier. You have received a Mythic-grade Quest Reward.*

That was it, nothing else in the description. Tilly closed down the log and considered the thing hovering in the flame before him. As he watched, the flames began to dissipate, making the object easier to discern. Then, as he watched, the flames winked out, and Tilly had to snatch the object as it fell to the floor.

Opening his hand, he looked down in wonder at a baseball-sized oblong object, etched with strange moving symbols that formed patterns reminiscent of flames. As Tilly watched, the symbols faded until all that was left was a light-blue oval shape with hard ridges and planes making up its surface. It looked like a many-faceted jewel, but for some reason, Tilly couldn't shake the impression that it was an egg.

A slight tingle started in the back of his mind as he considered it, but he would have to save figuring this thing out for later. Right now he needed to check on the others. The flame hadn't harmed him, but it was a core part of his power. Worry shot through his system as he stuffed the egg-like rock into his fantasy fanny pack and considered the flame on the altar one last time. It crackled merrily, as if satisfied with its work.

Tilly gave it a quick glare, wondering how he had been stuck with the explodey part of **Origin's** nature, before turning to jog back toward the antechamber. As he moved through the passageway, he noted that the stone fittings making up the walls and ceiling were even brighter and more well-made than they had been minutes before.

He sighed in relief as he arrived back at the antechamber, which had become so bright that it was almost like emerging back into the light of day. None of the occupants seemed to have been harmed, and the large room was now dominated by a crystal pillar whose top and bottom were rooted into the floor and ceiling like a strange tree. The Temple itself seemed to be feeding its blue-hued energy into the pillar, while the central portion of the pillar was constantly pushing out a bright white light back into the Temple. The energies seemed to be feeding off each other in a mutually beneficial cycle.

But that wasn't the only thing that had changed in the room. **Identify** pinged new information over almost all the members of the council! Hiro's dark samurai armor with yellow stitching and highlights remained the same, but his previously unadorned head now held an absolutely badass new helmet. On its crest was the yellow sickle of a moon and above his head hung his new class.

Level 58, Daimyo

Both the honu elders wore the same robes but they each had new staffs topped with what looked like sextants formed from shells.

Level 46, Way Finder
Level 50, Way Finder

Linus's face, while still wrinkled, had taken on some indefinable element of dignity, and his class had been changed as well. His armor was unchanged, but instead of looking like an elderly veteran reliving his glory days, he now radiated a feeling of earned glory and competence in the field. On his head, instead of a helmet, was a metal laurel.

Level 65, Consul

Even Ichiro had gotten a new piece of gear. He was seated across the room in a meditative kneeling position, and his eyes were wide in wonder, continually weaving through the room, following some sort of pattern that Tilly could not understand. His light armor had been completely replaced with layered samurai robes that were covered in a many-hued maze, which seemed to move even as Tilly watched. His class was the same, but the level discrepancy was gone, leaving him at the lower level.

Level 25, Samurai Hatamoto

Of all the chamber's occupants, Shuji reacted to his reward with the most emotion. He held a large tome in his shaking hands, looking down at it with tears in his eyes. It was wrapped in dark leather with a glowing blue symbol on its cover, which Tilly could not make out. His class was the same, but judging by the look in his shining eyes, Tilly doubted he cared very much.

Pupienus stood almost as a counterpoint to Shuji's awestruck reaction. He held up a new pair of glasses and eyed them critically as if he was trying to decide if he should even put them on.

The first one to notice Tilly's entrance was Hiro, his eyes looking up from what had to be his character screen and narrowing. He looked back at the position where Tilly had been standing before the time-stop and then back at Tilly, who was now fifty feet away without having moved to get there.

Finding everyone unharmed and with a power-up had Tilly feeling giddy, and he couldn't help but wink at the newly appointed Daimyo. Who cares if all he got was a mystery-box award? It looked like everyone around him had come out pretty well, especially the ones who had seriously contributed to the hidden quest at some point.

Aside from Hiro's puzzled frown at Tilly's strange human eye twitch, everyone else was busy looking at their own notification logs and character sheets. The spectacled satyr jumped as he looked around with his new glasses and found Tilly standing in the entryway on the other side of the antechamber.

"Hum—uh, I mean, Jonathan Tillman, how did you . . ." He trailed off and then cleared his throat. "It seems you were right about the benefits of this alignment . . . But I still do not have access to our city interface. Lord Hiro, if you would be so kind, can you inform us of our position and if these . . . uh, boons have extended to our whole populace?" he asked, in a tone that bordered on patronizing.

Lord Hiro nodded fractionally before turning to the Crystal and lifting his hand as if interacting with another larger screen. The others watched him, waiting patiently, except for Linus, who seemed to be able to see what was happening in front of Hiro even though it was just empty air to Tilly's eyes.

Looking up from what Hiro was doing, Linus explained, "Well, it seems like Hiro and I have received class upgrades that allow us direct access to the interface. Hiro, I'm sure, would have had this with his last class, but faction management is one of the purposes of my new class." As he said "management" his voice stumbled over a growling hitch.

He looked like he was trying to swallow a lemon, and Tilly could only imagine what a class that specifically gave him management abilities would do to his outlook on life. Some people were made for admin work and it made others sick. Tilly gave Linus a nod of solidarity. He was a fighter and would adjust to his new fate with the same grim determination that he had used to face death in the past.

Hiro swiped his hand and dismissed his screen before looking up at the rest of the group. "The system has awarded our new faction a name, something we have not been able to do ourselves," he said, shooting a hard look in the direction of the Bureaucrat. "It refers to us as the 'Three-Fold Alliance.' I am not yet sure of the full significance of this title, but it is certainly related to our new patron deity. There are two points of immediate interest in the establishment section of the city interface. I believe I can share them with you . . ." As he spoke, his eyes flickered as he delivered some mental commands to his HUD.

A green screen appeared in front of Tilly and from the expressions of the others, they each had one of their own as well.

Establishment

***Congratulations**, Three-Fold Alliance! In conjunction
with your starting position and in acknowledgment of the
considerable forces arrayed against your existence, you have been
awarded two city-wide Boons.*

***Origin's Aegis**: Extending out in a 5-mile area of effect, Origin's Flame
will release a reverse time dilation. For every hour outside the area of effect,
24 hours will pass inside the affected area. This effect will last the equivalent
of one day on the outside.*

***Fires of Creation**: For the duration of the Aegis's effect all skills
will experience a 50% increase in efficiency for gaining levels.*

Then at the bottom of the screen, in a completely different script than the notification, was a personal note from **Origin**.

A bond has been struck.

*Nothing that comes against you will triumph
as long as the covenant holds.*

"Much better than we hoped . . . and much worse," one of the honu elders said, looking up from the screen with a hard glint in her eye.

"It seems . . . we will be in . . . conflict . . . almost immediately," the other said, agreeing with her assessment. Their words drew Ichiro from his consideration of the words before him.

"We have been given what we did not think to ask for: time. Let us use it to its full effect. Our food and shelter challenges are not solved, but with new classes available, and a skill leveling bonus, we should be able to integrate our increased population," Ichiro said thoughtfully, his strange white eyes having no problem reading the notification screen in front of him.

"We will have to see what changes have already been wrought on our populace and what opportunities they provide before we form a plan of action. But near the top of the list should be scouting our five-mile allotted area and finding out who our new neighbors are as soon as possible," Linus added, while Pupienus began to mumble about figures and estimates to himself.

Shuji hadn't even looked up from his large book, and Tilly found himself wondering if he had heard any of it.

"Shuji, what have you got there?"

He looked up with puffy red eyes, blinking rapidly as he looked around the room in confusion before focusing on Tilly.

Yep, he had definitely been crying.

"Jonathan Tillman . . . This is an Enchanted Librarian's Codex, linked to me. It stores all the information I gather through any means and indexes it. It does so perfectly, without error, essentially allowing me to copy any book just by reading it. It is a library in itself and will record all that I have ever learned and all that I ever will learn within its pages. The implications are staggering," he said, hiccupping back a sob.

"There is one more thing here," Hiro said, interrupting, "under the advancement tab." He followed the statement by sending them another screen.

Advancement

Current Status of Three-Fold Alliance: *City.*

Next stage of Advancement: *City State [25 miles of influence, wall advancements, access to auction house, and establishment of a standing army.]*

Requirements

Population: *110,000 / 50,000*

Subdue Surrounding Area: *Cleared*

Obtain the Patronage of an Origin Facet: *1/2*

"Jonathan Tillman, what is an '**Origin** Facet'?"

CHAPTER SIX

Wisdom's Gift

Hiro's question lingered in the air, but Tilly didn't answer right away. He took another minute to process the implications of the advancement tab on the screen in front of him while the rest waited on his answer or reread their own screens.

The Three-Fold Alliance had almost everything they needed to advance to a City State, which would give them the ability to field an army and strengthen the walls. Not to mention the twenty additional miles of buffer between them and the "neighbors," whoever they were.

Tilly didn't know what the auction house was, but he had no doubt it would probably be just as important an opportunity for the burgeoning nation as the other upgrades . . . But of course, all of them were dependent on if they could find and obtain the Patronage of another **Origin** Facet.

His mind whirled as he went back over the words Wisdom had spoken in that strange voice in the central chamber. Something about memories and jewels . . . He needed to get his *Intelligence* up.

"Look, I'm only working with bits of information myself, but as far as I understand it, what lies at the center of this Temple is just a piece of **Origin's** nature, hence the name Facet. Honestly, it hasn't once been explained to me, but I am pretty sure I have seen another of these. There is a Flower somewhere that I am being encouraged to find. I saw this other Facet in a . . . vision after the fight in front of the city. I know that it is surrounded by mountains, hiding in a small valley, not unlike us. The more I interact with both of these things, the more I feel like they are more than just objects of power. They feel . . . foundational somehow."

Hiro looked as if he was about to reply when Tilly realized what was behind him leaving out his number one reason for searching out the Facet . . . He had now heard from three sources that the only real way to get rid of his **Corruption** was to find the Flower. As soon as he identified this, the subtle whispers that had been playing at the back of his thoughts surfaced.

Leave it out.

You don't know some of these people.

It's not important.

Tilly's face screwed up in anger and shame as he realized he was going to do it all over again: hide his problems and stick to being a lighthearted hero, not a liability. If he told them about this, would they think he had orchestrated this somehow?

The implications and possibilities were like sludge, slowing down the pace of his thoughts and causing him to retreat into himself instead of revealing any sort of need. Hiro was about to follow up with another question when the truth came rushing up out of Tilly's core, spilling out in a blitz of desperation.

"When I saw the Flower, I met its guardian. He told me that if I wanted to be free of the **Corruption** infecting my own body, I would have to find them again. So, however we choose to pursue this advancement requirement, I have to be involved!" The words came out hot and angry, having narrowly won the inner conflict playing out in his soul.

Hiro took the almost shouted follow-up statement in stride. The others had a wide range of reactions to the news. The honu elders' eyes hardened, while next to them Linus might as well have been told it was going to rain for all the change that came over his expression. Pupienus, however, took the cake. He audibly gasped and took a step back from Tilly as if the infection could be caught by breathing the same air.

"How could this be? I was told you represented the deity at odds with this horrendous substance! They assured me that you can even cure most cases of infection. Explain yourself!" he sputtered, looking around the room as if he had been tricked by all parties present.

"Silence!" Hiro growled as he unleashed his aura and caused everyone in the room to flinch, besides Linus and Ichiro.

Hiro turned the full weight of his flat stare on the Bureaucrat and declared sternly, "He was infected saving the life of my son and is much more an ally to this Alliance than you are. Our goals align, which I doubt is a coincidence, but even if they did not, we would still support him." He turned to the honu elders. "I believe your predecessor was aware of Jonathan's state and decided to trust him. I ask you to do the same. He is not an agent of our enemy, he is simply fighting it internally as we all are externally." Hiro let the pressure of his aura slacken. The elders gave him a long considering look before turning their gaze back to Tilly.

"Be that as it may . . . we still should . . . have been informed . . . It could have . . . impacted our votes," one of them said. Tilly had honestly already forgotten which was which, and at this point, he was too afraid to ask.

Ichiro chose this moment to gently break into the conversation. "Look at what we have gained! We could have remained undeclared and not built up these gains over decades. On Nephesh, stagnancy is death. Knowing what you know now, would you have chosen any differently?"

"Yes!" squeaked the Bureaucrat, but everyone ignored him. Ichiro watched the elders with an expression of relaxed curiosity.

"Our people have forgotten . . . the dream," replied the second elder slowly. As she continued, her voice strengthened as if speaking the words aloud settled it in her mind. "That is what . . . my father said . . . when he met with you . . . That you would help us to . . . remember . . . what we have forgotten . . . We remain committed."

Then everyone turned to Pupienus, and he shrank back under their combined stares.

"Yes, well. We all agreed on this manner of governance, and I am not fool enough to try and violate it right from the beginning. It is decided! We continue," he admitted spitefully.

"WONDERFUL!" Shuji shouted, startling half the room as he slammed his giant book shut. Tilly wasn't sure if he was reacting to what had just transpired or something he had just read from the supernatural backup of his knowledge. Either seemed possible.

"I am sure there is much to catalog and record! These rewards offered to our people seem to be almost unprecedented. There will probably even be new classes!" he said as he tucked the book away God-knows-where and moved back toward the entrance as if everything had been decided.

Ichiro shrugged happily and got to his feet, turning to follow, and all the others except for Linus and Hiro moved along with him. They both looked at each other and moved over toward Tilly.

"However unwilling I was at the time . . . you saved my life," Linus said solemnly, "and most probably the Bastions would just be a memory if not for you. So, know this: as long as I am alive, our armed forces will be for you. You have stepped in for us several times now, and we will do the same for you at a call." He finished formally with a hard military salute knocked against his chest.

Hiro regarded his actions with a ghost of a smile on his face, which disappeared as soon as he noticed Tilly's glance.

"Just let us know when you have any more idea where this Facet is. We cannot lose you as a resource, or as a friend . . . And depending on how hard the fighting will become, we very well could need those advancements as soon as possible, so let me know as soon as you find anything else," Hiro added gruffly. Then he clapped his hand on Tilly's shoulder. Their earnest attempts at reassuring him struck something deep in Tilly. Another blow landed against the stony distance that had insulated him from the opinions and, at times, the caring of others. In the face of their support, he decided to take things one step further and voice his fears along with the challenges he faced.

"That . . . means a lot. You are both extraordinary leaders, and I am glad my journey has brought me alongside you and your people. But I have one other favor to ask," he said, taking a deep breath. "I wish I could say **Corruption** was forcing me to do things, but it isn't like that. It takes whatever darker desires were already inside me and strengthens them, making my decisions seem reasonable in the moment. It is . . . becoming more and more difficult for me to recognize its influence on my mind . . ." He trailed off, trying to find out exactly how to word his request. They both gave him space, not interrupting as he tried to express what he needed.

"I guess what I am asking is, watch out for me. There will probably be a few times when I start acting erratically and I'll need you to step in and stop me. If I can't get back in control, I need you to do *whatever* you have to . . . Don't let me become one of those things. Do you understand?" he finished, gasping out the final lines of his request as the **Corruption** within him began to writhe angrily.

"Worry not, Jonathan Tillman, we will do everything we can to help you. But if we fail, I will not hesitate to end you before you become something else," Hiro replied in a hard voice before clapping him on the shoulder again and turning to go after the others. Linus was nodding along in total agreement. Tilly felt no sense of hesitation or regret in those words, and he stood there in momentarily stunned silence.

He didn't know whether to feel relieved or disappointed with how quickly and confidently Hiro had agreed to kill him if necessary. But an ask was an ask, and it just meant that he *really* needed to find out where this next Facet was, one way or another.

He looked over at the Crystal and it flashed before presenting a green screen in front of him.

Welcome to the Three-Fold Alliance Sovereign Crystal.
Would you like to view available class change options?
Y/N

Out of curiosity, Tilly selected Yes.

Scanning current cla- - - -

- - - -

- - - -
- - - - Error
Son of Flame class incompatible with the current system.
Would you like to begin again at Level 1 with a compatible class?
Y/N

Tilly sighed as he selected No. It was not like he would choose something else, anyway. With his Titles and skills synergizing so well with his current class, it would be foolish at this point. But that didn't change the fact that it felt damn annoying to be railroaded this way.

He left the Crystal behind, hoping that it would be more useful for refugees than it was for him. His walk turned into a run as he heard shouts coming from outside.

"Look, miss! I don't know where you came from, but I don't like being snuck up on!" an outraged Kuro yelled.

"For the last time, you box of rocks, I didn't choose to be here either. Now if you will just point me toward the nearest working teleport hub, I can find my way back on my own!" a melodic female voice shot out in reply, stringing her words together in a rapid but musical cadence.

Tilly emerged out into the front of the Temple to find the entire council standing off to the side, wearing various expressions of concern or suspicion. Apart from them stood a stunning young woman, wearing exquisitely tailored clothing in different shades of green and jewel tones. The layers were cut to form a strange mix between a ball gown and a formal three-piece suit.

Level 86, Ward of the Summer Court

She stood almost butting heads with Kuro, while Nyuk stood just to the side holding a new smaller ax at the ready. Above both of their heads was a brand-new class.

Level 25, Forest Warden
Level 29, Forest Warden

CHAPTER SEVEN

Another Explosion

The whole scene made for an odd standoff, with the leaders of the Alliance on one side and this new lady on the other. Yet despite the numbers imbalance, both parties seemed somewhat equal.

"Madam! Are you from one of our new nearby nations?" Pupienus shouted from behind Linus and Hiro, who wore equally guarded expressions as they considered another new variable in the already complex situation.

"No, you sniveling idiot, my people live nowhere near here!" she shouted before groaning in frustration and saying in a lower, but just as exasperated tone, "Now *please* tell me you have a working teleport platform in this gods-forsaken hick town."

Tilly was surprised to see flowering vines springing up from the ground and spiraling around the woman's legs as her expression grew more desperate.

Shuji cleared his throat and stepped forward, offering up a theatrical bow. "My lady, welcome to the newly christened Three-Fold Alliance. We regret to—" At the word regret, Tilly watched the lady's razor-thin hope of escape snap, along with her composure.

"THAT HAG!" she shouted, interrupting Shuji and stomping one of her feet as the vines around her suddenly sprouted sickle-like thorns. At this display, Nyuk and Kuro started to back away, holding their weapons in a guard position.

"I knew I felt a ripple in the Land! And now you tell me there is no platform here . . . She trick—UUGGHH! That sneaky windbag! She all but told me, and I was too happy to be away to realize the implications! Winter's Night, this is infur—"

"Hey!" Tilly shouted, happy to interrupt the spoiled woman's tirade. "Did somebody named Wisdom drop you off?" As novel as it was, he wasn't going to stand by while some noble lady threw a tantrum. They had too much to do.

Her jaw snapped shut like a sprung bear trap, and before he could register it, she flashed in front of him, moving at a speed completely unreconcilable with her impression of being put-upon. Now, only inches from Tilly's face, her slightly shorter form seemed to tower over him as she leaned in, exuding something not dissimilar to Hiro's killing intent aura.

"Do you know her?" she chewed out through grinding teeth.

"Met her just before she left. She said you would help us . . . and between you and I, she didn't strike me as the kind that would lie," Tilly grunted back, standing upright and drawling out his response in a bored tone out of sheer force of will. Her presence had a certain command to it, pulling on him to obey, to give in, but he staunchly refused. He leaned hard into the seen-it-all expression every firefighter develops after enough time in the field. Her aura of command washed over him like waves against the breakers, and he showed none of it in his vague return stare.

He didn't like his friends being insulted in front of him and he *really* didn't like that she believed they owed her something. His challenge caught her off guard, and she stepped back, considering him again as if she had only just noticed he was there.

"A human? Out in the backside of nowhere? Perhaps something *is* happening here worthy of my time," she said, curiosity shifting her previously commanding tone to something that might have been considered playful in other circumstances. Her eyes flashed green for a moment, and a frown broke her small smile. "And a Champion? Of a deity I have never heard of, no less . . ." Suddenly she was looking at him like an annoying crossword puzzle with too many blanks and not enough clues. "That is quite impossible!" she declared with finality.

Tilly was about to tell her otherwise when she continued, talking over his inhale to interject as if he had ceased to exist, a small crease appearing between her perfect eyebrows. "I know the names of every living divine and only the current Paragons can anoint a new Champion on Nephesh." Then she shifted her attention to the Temple Tilly had just exited, and her eyes flashed green again before widening as she took a step back in shock. "This is old . . . Older perhaps than my moth—just who are you?" she whispered, turning her gaze back toward Tilly with something other than conceit coloring her tone.

"My name is Jonathan Tillman. My friends call me Tilly . . . Well, not yet, but they will eventually, and I just got here a few weeks ago. From day one I have been getting my ass kicked in this lovely plane of yours and I have done a fair bit of ass-kicking myself. Which I understand is fairly normal. What is not normal is what I have been fighting . . . Something called **Corruption**." As soon as the word left his mouth, the skin around her eyes tightened slightly before her expression returned to one of neutral curiosity.

Over her shoulder, Tilly caught a small nod from Hiro to Shuji, who quickly moved forward.

"Madam," Shuji said, stepping into her view again with an even more theatrical bow. Tilly swore that Shuji sometimes had more in common with the ringleader of a circus than a scholar. "If you are here to offer us some aid, we would be most grateful to accept. While we do not have a working teleport platform right now, we do have the ability to repair what we have. We simply lack the resources."

Small budding grasses were springing up around her perfectly pressed pant legs and they seemed to lean in and support her as, all of a sudden, her imperious air deflated. Her haughty features softened into something much younger and out of place. She considered the still bowing lapin and the faces of those in the group standing outside the Temple.

"My name is Erash, and I was brought here on the promise of access to an apolitical Sovereign Crystal. I was told that this Crystal would have a class appropriate to my . . . stature. My current abilities and stat build are unique and something of a secret, and I had thought that my only chance at advancement would be in my home, but *she* assured me there was another way forward . . ." She trailed off as if looking for something more to add.

At her words, Hiro stepped forward, speaking in a respectful but confident tone. "If you promise no harm to my people or our Alliance, we will happily grant you access to our Crystal. Consider it a Home Gift, and if I am not mistaken, your promise and this gift are better than any binding treaty," he said, his eyes watching her carefully.

Her young demeanor vanished at the mention of promises and gifts. Tilly's jaw almost dropped as she seemed to age twenty years into a lady in the prime of her beauty and strength. Her expression firmed into something cold and calculating as she eyed the group imperiously.

"A bargain offered," she said, a sultry smile playing around the edges of full lips. "Very well. In exchange for free access to your Crystal and your teleport platform once it becomes available, I will shed this class and its inherent obligations for one that is beneficial to both parties. In this new role, I will serve you for a year and a day to the best of my abilities. At the completion of my obligation, I will have the right to change classes again or keep the new class as I see fit."

"Done. Agreed and accepted." Hiro's voice rang out in a firm, clear baritone. A strong wind danced through the nearby trees, and Tilly thought he heard a thrum resounding in the air around them.

"Thrice struck . . . Perhaps we are not so far from civilization after all," she purred, looking like a cat who had just been offered warm cream.

"Now, wai—" Pupienus tried to cry out before the air was suddenly knocked from his lungs with a sudden thud. Tilly looked over to see Linus's ever-present frown briefly soften as the Bureaucrat wheezed next to him. Erash turned towards the entrance of the temple, and some of her predatory confidence drained from her expression.

"Best start now, before . . . Well, best to get started," she corrected, then carefully lifted her feet free of the patch of wildflowers that had burst into being around her and moved through the ancient but still intimidating stone opening to the temple.

"I'll find my own way, thank you!" she called back over her shoulder, having moved past Tilly and partially down the hall before anyone could even think to go with her.

As soon as she was gone, Pupienus's reedy voice broke the silence, sounding strained. "Now hold on a minute! You cannot just make commitments for us without a vote!" he complained, stepping away from the Consul while clutching at his midsection, some fire returning to his eyes. "I was elected to represent my constituency and I will not be bullied into a dictatorship!" He seemed like the kind of guy who would rub Tilly the wrong way no matter what plane he was on, but at that moment, watching him square off against the rest of the council, Tilly couldn't help but feel a little respect.

One of the honu elders turned to him and caught his eye. "She was more . . . than she seemed," she said, letting the implication of her words hang in the air for a moment. As a look of confusion settled on the satyr's face, Hiro turned to explain.

"I waited until I was sure, but once I knew what she was, it was imperative that I offer her a gift and a bargain. If I had not, she would have offered us something far less beneficial, and we would have started negotiations on her terms, not ours. Their kind is bound completely by a certain set of rules, and at the same time, utterly unpredictable."

A bargain struck . . . Oh shit! Tilly knew this one!

"She's a fey, isn't she?" Tilly called out, excited to finally not have to ask for once. Hiro and Linus both shot him looks before Linus gestured sharply toward the Temple.

"She is obviously running from something," Linus whispered at Tilly harshly, "otherwise she never would have offered terms that were so generous. We do not want whoever would look for someone like her to find her here. Even speaking of their kind can create ties to them. So from now on we will keep this to ourselves!" Linus was handing out orders to all present as if he were back on the front lines. The other satyr's eyes widened in understanding, and the honu nodded. Tilly bit back his chagrin at having his moment ruined.

The one time I actually know something, he huffed internally.

"Told you we should have left as soon as we dropped them off," Nyuk muttered to Kuro a few feet away from Tilly. Hearing their soft exchange, Tilly turned to them.

"How did she even get here, and when?" he asked the pair.

"We were standing out here keeping watch when Nyuk here swears he hears a cart coming . . . I tell him to stop being an idiot, 'cause no cart can come up this little mountain path we cleared to the Temple, and before we can resolve our dispute, the whole Temple explodes," Kuro said, leveling a flat look at Tilly before continuing, leaning into the story with all the passion of an old drunk at a bar. "So first, we make sure we aren't burning alive. Then, we accept the strangest notification screen I have ever seen, which offers us this new *rare* class, which my lady will love by the way, and then *bam!* There she is, standing right on top of us, muttering to herself like a mad woman."

"That is enough! We will offer no insults to our guest! She will keep this agreement to the letter, and we will accept her help in whatever form it comes," Hiro declared to the group, his tone brooking no response. Then he turned to Tilly, and asked, "Now, who is this Wisdom you met and when did it happen?" Shuji's ears twitched in interest at the posed question.

Before Tilly could answer, a green flash erupted from the mouth of the Temple, followed by a forced opening of his notification log.

Rejoice, Three-Fold Alliance! Your Temple abandoned to Origin's Flame has received a new High Priestess. An order of clergy may be established and full Temple function restored as requirements are met.

Congratulations! Due to the overwhelming qualifications of your new High Priestess, the Three-Fold Alliance will receive an additional Boon! Now all crops, livestock, and wild game will be 20% more productive while under your city's influence.

Tilly cleared away the forced notification screen to see the statues in front of the Temple reforming into large imposing forms of primitive warriors. That wasn't all: the large stone opening to the Temple started to grow elaborate doors set on hinges of stone, which depicted a frieze of burning flame. The others around him looked up from their screens in shock as the newly formed doors opened and Erash strode out, holding a staff with a living blue flame at its top.

Level 86, High Priestess of the Living Flame

"Now, I need someone to tell me who **Origin** is and what his Facets are. We must gather more of them as quickly as possible so my—rather, this Temple's influence may expand."

Tilly was the first to recover from his shock, probably because every day in this world brought new and crazier things than the last for him.

"Wait, you chose to become a priestess for a god you have never heard of? Why?" Tilly demanded.

CHAPTER EIGHT

Marching Orders

She paused there, enjoying her moment, framed in the entryway of the newly regenerated Temple. No doubt she had received the same update they all had about the new overqualified High Priestess.

"This class was the only one available that was an increase in rarity from my last class. According to the system, this deity hasn't had a high priest in three Epochs . . . The requirements didn't seem too difficult, and the gains provided are more than acceptable," she said, turning her nose up slightly, not at all attempting to cover an almost palpable level of satisfaction.

Tilly's fading shock was quickly overtaken by exasperation. *Seems like anyone can walk in and get a job these days!* He let out a self-deprecating laugh. "What a pair of representatives we will make . . . *'Please, sir, what does it mean to follow* **Origin***?' 'Sorry, lad, we just met the guy, we'll let you know when we find out.' 'Although I will warn you, so far it's been mostly explosions.'*" He finished his little monologue and looked around at the others, hoping to lighten the mood.

Unblinking eyes stared back at him, ranging from confusion in the honu to disappointment in Hiro's eyes. Tilly coughed awkwardly at the silence, and Erash stepped forward into it confidently.

"Speak for yourself, human. The Temple has made abundantly clear what it needs to advance its influence, and I can commune for direction once a month as an intermediary for the nation I am representing. You may be lost in your role, but I am clear in mine," she said in a huff before sweeping past him and moving to the council to begin discussing how the Temple could partner in their future efforts.

The embarrassment he felt in the wake of his stupid joke and the haughty reply from the new High Priestess set Tilly's ears buzzing. Her conversation with the council fell into the background as a potent anger attempted to flood his internal levies of emotional control.

Who does she think she is?

It was just a stupid joke . . . Ungrateful bit—

"No," he muttered under his breath as his right arm jerked, throwing a vicious punch into his side.

His clenched fist pounded into the site of the infection, releasing waves of agony from his abdomen. Something about the sudden pain shattered the syrupy sweet spiral of bitterness that had been building. He refused to be the kind of guy who went into a tantrum at every little insult, no matter what this bullshit trying to take his body wanted. The buzzing subsided, and a deep angry ache settled in its place.

"So, what did you get?" Nyuk asked, breaking Tilly's thoughts away from his unnoticed internal conflict by giving him the point of distraction he needed to steer his thoughts toward safer waters.

He turned and shrugged in response to the new Forest Warden as he reached behind his back and fished out the crystal egg, "I don't know what this thing is," he said before tossing it to the inquiring lapin.

"Hey!" Nyuk said in a sudden panic, handling the caught stone like he was playing hot potato. He bounced it between his hands two times before tossing it at Kuro with a wicked grin.

"Watch it, buckteeth!" the other warden shouted back as he caught it in his leather vest, avoiding touching it with his bare hands. He walked carefully back over to a bewildered Tilly, who plucked it from the leather cradle.

"Seriously, guys, right now I don't think it does anything. I'll have to mess with it and figure it out later," he said, holding up the oblong mystery object and handling it with impunity. Both the lapins winced at his cavalier manner.

"I am no master **Identifier**, but even I can see it is rated Mythic," Kuro said, keeping a wary eye on the object in Tilly's hand.

"Knowing you, human, that is a locked ancient-gnomish explosive enchantment that could level this mountain," Nyuk said gravely, stepping back even further.

This kind of ribbing was all too familiar and reminded him warmly of the firehouse. In fact, he almost started telling them about some of the guys he used to work with when he felt a pulse of feeling emerge from the egg. It seemed to have understood the gravity those two were giving it . . . and it felt satisfied. It wanted to be thought of as dangerous.

The chuckle and story died together on Tilly's lips as he slowly turned his head toward what he was holding. Both lapins shared a knowing look and took another generous few steps back, well away from the entrance of the Temple.

Before Tilly could really consider the object in his hands, the others finished their short conference and Hiro began issuing out orders to the group one by one.

"It is decided! We have been given a short window of time to prepare for what is coming and we will not waste a moment of it. Shuji, you are to immediately partner with all scholar-adjacent classes to order and categorize our population. We need to know what classes we have and what they can do. Send any who still desire to pursue a class change up here with advice, where appropriate. Knowledge is the resource we need most right now."

Shuji nodded enthusiastically, jiggling several chins. "I'll coordinate with Pupienus to make sure all are employed appropriately in our coordinated efforts, as well as continue to build out our merit system for temporary compensation," he said, gathering up the much smaller satyr in an uncomfortably brotherly side embrace and moving back toward the mountain path.

"Yes, yes," the satyr said as he disengaged himself from the large lapin's embrace. "I will see that the work on the city expansion continues and issue regular reports to the rest of you. I would appreciate the same," he called over his shoulder with a level look as he dodged another pawing tug by the enthusiastic Librarian.

"Linus, you are still in charge of organizing and training our armed forces. Hopefully, our combat effectiveness has been augmented greatly by whatever changes were affected by the completion of the hidden quest—"

"Ah! So that is what that was! I felt the magic flow down the mountain from here. I have only read a few accounts of such things. To think that one such occurrence has unfolded before my eyes here only confirms my decision to remain," Erash interjected, gesturing with her new staff unconsciously as if she had held it for years instead of minutes.

"High Priestess," Hiro said, rolling with the interruption smoothly, "if you would, there will be a steady stream of those seeking the Crystal and possibly purification from any lingering instances of infection. Please let us know if you need anything else to perform your duties. The honu will be sending all of our agricultural workers this way to receive your Spring's Blessing, which, as we discussed, we hope will stack with the boons. This will see our people fed and, hopefully, stores built up before the boon is exhausted."

She nodded graciously at his softly put request and the small bows of acknowledgment from the elders. The elders started down toward the path as well, nodding respectfully to Tilly and the lapins as they passed, and the High Priestess turned back toward the newly wrought doors. For all her bravado, from his vantage close to the entryway Tilly thought he saw her eyeing the gaping entrance with caution until she noticed his attention and sniffed, then reentered the Temple with her confident mask fully in place.

"Nyuk, Kuro, it seems you have been gifted a combat class. One that looks suited toward scouting and patrols. Am I correct?" Hiro asked, turning to the two standing apart from the rest of the group.

"Yes, Lord," they replied in unison with respectful bows.

"Good, it is well deserved. You are no longer in charge of our timber harvesting. I am appointing you as the first of our ranging forces. Nyuk, you will lead with Kuro as your second. Requisition bows from our depot and meet me at the front gates in an hour. We will scout the limit of our area's influence and see what we find in our new surroundings. Shuji will send others your way when we get back, and you can report to Linus for the next steps."

At the news, both lapins prostrated themselves, and Nyuk said in a loud voice, "You honor us! We will not fail our people." Then they both rose smoothly to their feet, Nyuk wearing a formal and diffident expression and Kuro looking a little dazed. Hiro said nothing further, and Nyuk realized he had to be back in the town and ready to go in an hour. He tugged the slightly dazed Kuro into a loping jog down the mountain.

In the distance, Tilly could have sworn he heard Kuro come to and complain loudly, "Bows! UGH! Nyuk, you know how I feel about bows!"

A slight twitch in the remaining lapin's ears let him know he wasn't the only one to have heard.

"That just leaves me and Ichiro. Are you sure you don't want me to come on the scouting trip? I have a feeling that whatever faction we have been dropped near is probably not **Corruption** free," Tilly asked.

"No, Jonathan Tillman, you will be risking yourself soon enough, but until then, we are going to do what we can to make sure you live through the next year. With this skill bonus we just received, every one of us not urgently needed must commit themselves to training. You will spar with and learn from Ichiro every morning. Before his change, he was one of the best swordsmen in the empire, whether those old goats wanted to admit it or not."

At that, Ichiro nodded serenely.

"Now, however, he still has much work to do if he is to reclaim the full use of his skill levels. You will spend your mornings in routines devised by him and then rotate through different members of the populace in the afternoons and evenings, training what you think will be most valuable going forward. Consult with Ichiro or Shuji on what those skills should be.

"Mr. Tillman, boons like this do not come often, and you must take this chance to advance your skills. I am sure we will be needing you before our twenty-four days are up, but until we do, you must invest this time wisely."

All of this struck a deep chord in Tilly. He had been on his back foot in almost every combat encounter he had had. This was his chance to prepare for what was coming next instead of just reacting to one emergency after another. Not that he knew exactly how he needed to prepare . . .

Lost in thought, Tilly looked out into the mountain range for the first time since emerging from the Temple. From their vantage point near the top of the mountain he remembered being able to see the range go on as far as the eye could see.

That had completely changed. Now the range ended just a few miles past the village and the river snaked past the burgeoning city between several more peaks before pouring out into open, rolling hills, tinged a coppery red.

When he turned back to Hiro and Ichiro, the elder lapin was already gone, his departure marked by a gust of wind. He had moved so quickly and smoothly that Tilly had completely missed it . . . Reminding him just how far he had to go if he wanted to stay alive in these increasingly high-stakes scenarios.

Well, nothing to it but to get started, he thought wryly. He sighed and met eyes with the last member of the group.

"Honestly, it will be my honor to receive your instruction," Tilly opened seriously. "I have heard several times how low my martial skills are and I'm tired of it. It will be great to have you to point me in the right direction!" Tilly was enthusiastic, his mind wandering through some of his favorite movie montages. *Rocky . . . Karate Kid . . . Kickboxer.*

Ichiro's serene expression turned slightly more focused as his eyes moved to watch something playing out off in the distance. Tilly turned to try and catch it but saw only trees and distant peaks.

"It is fraying out there . . . ," Ichiro whispered to himself. But as Tilly turned back toward him, his eyes refocused on the human, and he offered a sad smile. "Perhaps you can tell me more of what you can do as of now and where you feel your greatest weaknesses are," Ichiro stated calmly, acting as if he hadn't said anything foreboding at all.

CHAPTER NINE

Wax On

Mulling over Ichiro's question, Tilly found himself caught between sharing a list of his abilities and their effects or a higher-level summary of how he thought of himself as a combatant. Ichiro registered his hesitation and gestured to a nearby log with a smile. Tilly nodded in appreciation, and they walked over together and settled down facing each other.

Tilly started with a simple run-down of his *Abilities*, but the conversation very quickly hopped the rails of his expectations as Ichiro stopped him at each *Ability* and asked him how and when they first emerged.

Very quickly, this turned into Tilly giving a full summary of his journey through Nephesh, stopping where Ichiro asked for clarification or more details. Through it all, Ichiro's face never wavered from its serene cast.

Whether this was due to his meditative state or a genuine unruffled interest didn't really bother Tilly. Something about just getting it all out put him at ease. As time went on, he found himself sharing much more of the internal conflict he had faced at each crossroads of his journey so far. It's not that he had left this part out in previous explanations. Rather, it was more that Ichiro seemed to be primarily interested in the internal environments that made up the context for each of his *Ability* advancements and failures. He seemed to care very little for the numbers side of things, instead showing a focused and consistent curiosity around Tilly's internal state and motivations as he navigated the challenges he had faced so far in his time on Nephesh.

It was unlike any conversation Tilly had ever had, and despite Ichiro's blank, pupilless stare, he felt seen in a way that lifted a burden he did not know he was carrying . . . He was sure he had made many mistakes, but Ichiro didn't flinch or react as Tilly navigated his choices leading up to this moment.

"When I saw the tree and what it was doing to you and the flame, I just lost it. I went all out in an attack I didn't even fully comprehend, and that was when I first manifested the flames."

"Ah, interesting . . . I wonder, could you tell me more about what you were feeling at that moment when you charged the altar? What do you mean by 'lost it'? And I find myself wondering what exactly you gained in exchange."

"This time he had one of the little kids and was threatening to kill him. I was already furious, but when he shouted out that I was **Corrupted** in front of Amelia and the kid, something snapped—"

"One moment. Do you mind telling me the physical sensations that accompanied this shift, and if you could, any thoughts you remember in the moments leading up to your loss of full conscious control?"

They talked for hours. At one point Ichiro even pulled out rice balls stuffed with some sort of meat for a late lunch and they both ate as they continued the discussion. Ichiro was especially fascinated by Tilly's description of the pattern reaching into eternity and what he saw at the beginning and the end. He asked Tilly to repeat the story several times, pulling out every detail Tilly could remember, and even some descriptions that only occurred to him in retrospect.

Finally, they arrived at Tilly's description of his recent encounter in the inner room of the Temple while outside of time.

"Hmm . . . This Facet of our patron that we host in the Temple continues to display a penchant for affecting time. A very rare power"—there he paused, his look taking on a momentarily heavy cast—"and very dangerous. Perhaps more powerful than the flame *Abilities* you have demonstrated so far by an order of magnitude." As he mused, his expression softened as his gaze drifted from Tilly back to the Temple.

"Ichiro, can you tell me a little more about your eyes?" Tilly asked, his curiosity getting the better of him as he once again tried to understand what exactly the lapin was seeing that others couldn't.

"Ah, of course," he said, dragging his attention back to Tilly. He took a deep breath and explained. "The cleansing you released when you ended **Corruption's** incursion into the Temple hit me while my gaze was frozen open in a captive state." An almost imperceptible shiver ran up his body.

"The clash of forces along with direct contact with the blast resulted in a new title and an accompanying skill that allows me to see not just the physical world, but whatever forces move beneath it. Right now my vision is filled with a sea of interwoven strands of past, present, and future possibilities, along with all the forces acting on the environment around me. It is so complex that I would be at a very real risk of losing my mind if not for my ability to maintain a near-constant meditative state. Even when I am blindfolded and lose all input from the physical world, I am still bombarded with an overwhelming amount of information attempting to convey to me the interwoven nature of space, time, and energy," he said, some of the gravity of what he was enduring leaking into his voice.

"I am learning to limit my focus and filter out the majority of what I am seeing, but it is . . . very difficult. Especially around many people or strong emotions, which both agitate the already incomprehensibly intricate pattern. I am sure I will grow used to it in time, but it has been a great challenge for me to even achieve the ability to walk and talk normally, and our sparring will be as important for me as it will be for you."

"Wait, Ichiro, can you see things before they happen?" Tilly asked, thinking back to a few of the more clairvoyant moments he had experienced with the lapin. At his question, Ichiro's face scrunched up thoughtfully, and he seemed to roll the question around in his head several times before answering slowly.

"I do not believe so. Perhaps one day something like being able to read the pattern to that extent will emerge, but as of now, I cannot understand the vast majority of what I am seeing. What I do know is that every action is preceded by thoughts and emotions. The stronger the instigating internal emotion is, the more affected the pattern around you, even before you physically move to change it. At times I can pick up on that disturbance in the pattern before the physical action is produced, but this has been a rarity so far. Though, I believe our **Origin** wishes me to make progress in this area, and so he has gifted me an item unique to me." He looked down at his new robe and pulled at the lapel absently. Under his gaze, the pattern on the robe actually started to shift, and Tilly suddenly felt himself falling. He blinked a few times and tore his eyes away, meeting Ichiro's suddenly tired expression.

"You might go insane before you get a handle on this, and I might become a monster that will hopefully be consumed in its own flames before I kill a bunch of people . . . Hell of a pair we make, huh?" Tilly asked smiling. Nothing to it but to grin and move through it.

Ichiro's face screwed up in confusion for just a moment before completely releasing its tension in a simple, easy smile,

"Yes, I believe it is this very adversity that destines us for greatness . . . I am sure this time together will be beneficial for both of us. Even in my **Battle Trance**, it is still difficult to focus on my immediate surroundings and emotions. The flow of the strands around me is incredibly difficult to resist," he said, looking down at his lightly furred hands for a moment as if they held some answers he had not yet found. Then he clapped them together and rubbed them vigorously before looking up at Tilly, his face displaying a small level of excitement.

"But, if I may, I believe there is something more than leveling martial skills that I can teach you. Something that will possibly be much more useful in the long run." Ichiro moved from the log to a place ten feet away and pulled his scabbarded sword out of its band and onto his lap. He gestured for Tilly to come join him in a more meditative posture.

This is it! The full Karate Kid *Miyagi montage begins . . .*

"I'll take anything I can get!" Tilly exclaimed as he moved to settle down opposite the lapin. As soon as he had crossed his legs, the lapin began his instruction in an easy droning voice.

"One of several benefits of my condition is the forced meditative state I must maintain if I want to stay in the present. This has increased my already considerable skill level to something I believe may be unique, especially at my reduced over-all level. I want to pass on as much of what I know as I can to you in this short time, and I believe these techniques will do two things for you," he said, then, raising a single finger, he continued.

"First, it will help fortify your mind against **Corruption's** influence without walling yourself off from your emotions. It is essential that you not drift away from the awareness of your emotions, for they will bear fruit whether you are vigilant or not. Better to know yourself and move from a place of honesty than try and outrun what is inevitable."

"Okay, meditation sounds pretty good, and I can definitely use the help in the self-control department, but my understanding of meditation is that it is all about getting rid of your emotions," Tilly said.

"In truth, there are many techniques that do just that. However, the one I will teach you was given to me by my mother. She came from a long line of servants of the Moon Goddess, and they believed that meditation is about taking time to truly experience the full breadth of thought and emotion, integrating them at every level of your soul. If you do this often enough, they will flow through you like a spring instead of damming you up with a series of blockages that will cause you to act in ways you do not control or understand." That one hit a little closer to home than Tilly was comfortable admitting.

"The second thing that leveling this technique will do is allow you to develop the ability to experience the deeper longings of your soul. All emotion is built on a foundation of desire, and it is the strength of your desire that determines how much *will* you leverage in any given action. But this benefit of the technique is not available unless you understand yourself and, on some level, accept who you are."

Tilly winced internally at how much this was beginning to sound like therapy. Even worse, it seemed like this kind of therapy involved him talking to himself . . . about his emotions. For decades he had survived on his ability to stop thinking and just move, and what Ichiro was suggesting was anathema to that.

"Do the job and get out," he had advised rookie after rookie, teaching them the ways to the *job*.

Yet here Ichiro was, challenging his entire way of facing obstacles. Tilly had always prided himself on his ability to shut out the noise and get shit done . . . but he could not deny that outside of many of those high-stress environments, he always felt more like a passenger than the driver of his own life.

"Is that what **Battle Trance** is? You, doing all of that thinking and feeling while fighting, or, I guess at this point, moving? It sounds disorienting."

Ichiro smiled at the question while shaking his head slightly. "**Battle Trance** is something else entirely. The skill is locked until you get a meditation and combat skill past a certain level. Then at some point in true combat, you achieve a moment of clarity, and the two skills birth a new one. However, due to the power of my *will* and my struggle to stay present, I am slowly adapting it to a kind of constant integrated meditation." As the lapin spoke, his smile slipped momentarily, as if explaining the process of his continued struggle intensified it momentarily.

"As great as this all sounds, it feels like it will take years to truly see results. Are you sure it's going to make enough of a difference for me in the next twenty-four days to survive whatever is coming?"

"That entirely depends on how much you trust me," the lapin responded, open-faced and without a hint of guile or ulterior motive.

Tilly thought hard as he ran through the events of the last couple of weeks as he had shared them with Ichiro. So much of it had felt like he had no choice and was just getting pulled along, often by his own knee-jerk reactions. If he was being honest with himself, he hardly ever thought about those reactions or what they could be covering . . . Maybe this wouldn't make a huge difference in his next fight, but if it could somehow help him get a handle on life here on this plane, it had to be worth it.

"Alright, I'm in," Tilly answered, leaning forward with the same roguish grin that had been plastered on his face on the way to many a fire. If he was going to go for this, he would go all in.

"Wonderful!" Ichiro exclaimed, clapping his hands together and creating a surprisingly loud sound with the impact. "We will begin by unlocking the **Meditation** skill. Afterward, we will return to the valley, eat, and then I will test your blades. This cycle of meditation, eating, and combat will continue every morning we are able. Then before lunch, you will meditate again, processing your experiences and solidifying them in your soul.

"It is my goal to set you up to achieve **Battle Trance** in the coming months, which should help you immensely in resisting **Corruption's** growth in the heat of combat. It will also have the added effect of making you far more deadly than your stats suggest." He stood smoothly from his seated position.

"But first, you must understand the power of a truly hardened *will*. You have felt a small amount of what my father can do when he focuses his *will* into a palpable killing intent. This is not all *will* can do. It can empower almost any action to a degree few know possible."

CHAPTER TEN

Heart Power

Ichiro left those words hanging in the air as he walked smoothly to a nearby boulder. Tilly leaned forward, unable to keep himself from being drawn in by whatever Ichiro was about to demonstrate.

The lapin Samurai Hatamoto smoothly drew his sword, his face taking on an almost reverent expression. Tilly realized he had never seen the blade before and noted that where Hiro's blade was made of an onyx-colored metal, Ichiro's blade shone with a silvery light, visible even under the bright sun.

Ichiro extended his sword arm and tapped the edge of the blade against the stone, producing a predictable clang.

"What you are about to see is not due to a high strength stat or an empowering *Ability*. It is the power of my heart alone that I will demonstrate to you. Attend!" He shouted the last, breaking the soft explanatory tone of his speech as he drew back his sword. The motion was slow, almost glacial, and Tilly found his eyes focusing on the blade as the samurai drew it back.

It suddenly felt . . . *weighty*.

Ichiro drew the blade back until it was pointed completely away from the boulder. He slowly bent both legs, crouching slightly as his eyes hardened. Then, moving even slower, he swung the blade forward from his crouched position. His back foot pivoted, and his legs pushed up from the ground perfectly in sync with the diagonal strike. It played out slowly, arduously over long moments pregnant with some unknown promise.

It almost reminded Tilly of tai chi, except for the terrible inevitability beginning to radiate from the strike. Halfway through the swing, something flashed on the edge of the blade, and the deeper places of Tilly's consciousness were impressed with the concept of *sharpness*.

Amazingly, the swing slowed down even further as the sword gathered more of whatever it was building. Tilly could see veins standing out on Ichiro's neck as his look of concentration doubled down into the gritted snarl of extreme effort.

The moment before the blade touched the boulder, it parted. It was almost like the boulder had lost some unseen contest and had given way before the blade even arrived, consigning its defeat. Ichiro's swing sped up and he followed through smoothly before resheathing the blade in a flash, his eyes closed, and his expression returned to complete serenity.

Tilly watched in amazement as a third of the boulder slid off at an angle and crashed to the ground with a rumbling crack. Then, twenty feet away at the tree line beyond the boulder, the sound of snapping limbs popped off like gunshots as several enormous trees toppled, shaking the ground with their impact.

Ichiro calmly turned and walked back to his place in front of Tilly, then settled back down on his knees with the resheathed sword lying across his legs. Tilly felt almost like he had swallowed a frog.

He had seen magic plenty of times at this point, but this was something more . . . This felt like *Authority.*

"Well, then, shall we begin?" the lapin asked calmly, his eyes still closed.

The shock seizing his thoughts finally cleared and Tilly exploded, "HOLY SHIT, ICHIRO!" before clearing his throat in embarrassment at his exclamation and continuing. "I mean, if I'm being honest, after the 'power of my heart' line I wasn't so sure about all this, but that was insane!"

"Mr. Tillman, please . . . ," Ichiro responded, lifting a hand and motioning in the universal sign for "calm down." "*Will* partnered with a deep understanding of a concept can produce incredible power, but none of it is possible without the diligent training of meditation. May we begin?" His voice had taken on the icy calm of a teacher wrangling a class of first graders.

"Yeah . . . absolutely. Where do we start?" Tilly answered, pulling his eyes away from the tall, angled tree stumps.

Ichiro nodded and shifted into a lecturing tone. "When I first started, I sat with my blade drawn for hours, moving through the surface of my soul with the intention to navigate deeper by cutting through the barriers separating my actions, *will*, and emotions. Eventually, I did not need the blade anymore as the concept began to imprint itself on my being. This became my concept, my focus. You must start with a focus, something that you can pour yourself into endlessly, which resonates with your whole being." As he delivered the information, his speech took on a strange cadence, one frequently interrupted by inhales and exhales that remained consistent and rhythmic. Tilly found himself matching the breathing rhythm without consciously choosing to do so as he processed what Ichiro had said.

"I guess for me"—*inhale*—"a flame makes the most sense," Tilly responded with an exhale, attempting to keep the rhythm even as he spoke. It was awkward, but Ichiro nodded in encouragement at his attempts.

"Good, can you call forth a flame in a position that you can easily see?" Ichiro was still smoothly fitting in his words between breaths so that his rhythm was hardly interrupted.

Tilly thought for a moment. He could enflame anything touching his body, but he didn't want to look down at his hands for however long this would take. He wondered just what it would take to keep a flame going away from his body.

In curiosity, he lifted his hand to his navel and felt the heat there and the flame he had started visualizing within his center. He closed his eyes and leaned into the image, doing his best to maintain his breathing. Magical crap was happening all around him, why couldn't there be an actual flame burning in the midst of his organs?

Before he could think about what he was doing, he made a pulling motion with his hand and felt a piece of the flame come free from his center. He opened his eyes in amazement and found a tiny pure-white flame dancing above his palm.

Carefully, as if it would go out at any stray movement, he lifted his hand until it was a foot in front of his chest and then fixed that position in his mind, focusing on that point as the place he wanted the flame to keep burning.

Amazingly the flickering flame stayed in place as he slowly removed his hand, not wanting to disturb whatever was happening. Once it was firmly in place, Tilly tore his eyes away from the flame to find the normally placid lapin with his mouth hanging open. As he caught Tilly's eyes, his features sharpened to an almost vulpine satisfaction.

"Will this work as a focus?" Tilly asked quietly, not sure what would or wouldn't break his connection with the little piece of his core fire floating in front of him.

"This will more than work! The flame you hold before you is more concept than mana, and it is already linked to your *will*. After hearing more of your class and how you grew, I suspected you had already been harnessing this to some extent, but for you to produce something like this with no **Meditation** skill yet activated . . ." He trailed off, a smugness suffusing his voice as his chosen path for Tilly was confirmed almost immediately.

Those eyes and the expectations they had to represent hit Tilly in the abdomen like a brick. *What am I doing that is so special? Can I keep doing it? What if I lose it?*

The flame snuffed out before their eyes, and he fought back a sudden surge of panic. As the flame snuffed out, a shiver shot through his body and some sort of feedback hit his center, racking his body with pain.

"Shit, sorry, Ichiro!" Tilly growled out in frustration, bending over his middle.

"Peace, Mr. Tillman . . . ," Ichiro replied, his face schooling itself to its normal calm. He began to inhale and exhale loudly while giving Tilly a meaningful look, and Tilly responded by doing his best to imitate. Pushing back against the pain, he straightened his back and shoulders until he was sitting upright and rode out the rest of the pain one intentional breath at a time.

Ichiro continued, "This is my fault . . . In my excitement, I departed from the breathing and threw off your inner balance. You are further along than I could have imagined, and as such it is even more important that you train this aspect of your path of ascension. But without learning to walk, every step at a run is an invitation to calamity."

Tilly nodded and did his best to keep up the breathing cadence: deep inhale, hold, full exhale, hold, repeat.

"In time, we will bring back the flame, but for now, I want you to close your eyes and visualize it in the same place it was," Ichiro invited softly, keeping the rhythm of his words between his breaths. Tilly closed his eyes obediently, trying to relax into the motions of his body pulling in and pushing out the environment around him.

"Good, now I want you to understand that everything that you are—your mind, desire, and emotions—can be fuel for your *will*. So with each exhale, I want you to picture your flame gradually growing stronger. Thoughts and feelings will come—*let them*. Experience them, accept them, and in so doing, add them to the flame, where they will not be destroyed but integrated with your whole self. Breathe in . . . hold . . . exhale, and feed the flame."

As Ichiro spoke, Tilly let himself be carried along with the droning monotone of the lapin's voice, picturing the flame exactly as it had been. He took time to think about what Ichiro had said and connected his exhales with the oxygen any fire needed to continue combustion. He treated every exhale like he was blowing on embers at the bottom of a pile of leaves until a new flame sprang up to consume the dry material. As he watched his breaths slowly impact his visualized flame, he realized that each dead leaf was energy trapped in a prison of expended purpose. Then the flame would come and release the dead matter from its locked form and give it new life as light and heat.

With every inhale, the flame would flicker as if disturbed by the passage of air, but as he exhaled, the fire would grow slightly more intense, taking in the conceptual fuel and becoming hotter and more intense.

The noise of the forest faded away as his whole sensory world became the sound of Ichiro and his breathing. The small flame slowly grew larger, every cycle of breathing feeding it as he slowly unlocked the doors of his heart. As the process grew easier, Tilly became aware of the tightness in his chest once again. This time, instead of trying to ignore it, he breathed through it, like you would a cramp in a run. He strained the auxiliary breathing muscles between his ribs against the tightness as it attempted once again to use the fear of failure to constrict his desire to succeed. This internal tension imparted a feeling of claustrophobia, which in turn called to mind his inability to escape his present circumstances. The hopeful faces of everyone in the refugee camp came back to him, crowding in on the darkness of his contemplation.

His breathing hitched, and the flame flickered, suddenly unstable.

He forced himself to stay in rhythm with Ichiro, and instead of moving away from the feeling, he dived deeper into it, following the flow of his emotions, allowing them to intensify with every breath.

So many people are depending on me. But I'm just a grunt who breaks everything he touches . . . What if I fail all over again?

The thoughts rolled through him, accompanied by increasingly strong emotions. Dread and even animal-like panic came to the surface as he searched out his feelings on the new role he held amongst the people of the Alliance. His side squirmed in delight at the delicious brew now steeping in his mind. His chest tightened further, and it felt like he was breathing through a straw as he fought against the need to increase the pace of his breathing.

In the past, seeing something like this hidden in his psyche would have caused him to slam the door on the trail of emotions and seal it with as much apathy as possible. This was the kind of stuff that caused you to hesitate . . . to doubt. Something that he could not afford to do in the kinds of situations he had faced on a daily basis.

I never froze in a burning building . . . but I'm completely stuck now.

Trapped in a cycle of his own making, the emotions he had finally let free were wrapping him in knots of panic and doubt. He wanted to stop. He *needed* to get more air than these slow breaths would allow. Yet the sound of Ichiro's breath echoing his own imparted a feeling of vastness to the darkness behind his closed eyes. The space his flame floated in seemed incomprehensibly large, and yet at the same time intimate. The darkness covered him, hiding him and acting like a balm against his panic.

He wasn't okay . . . but he was *safe*. It was time to stop running from this part of himself.

He opened himself further to the feelings that had lurked in the deep places of his mind for decades. They rushed into him, choking his internal environment.

The dread of failing others who depended on him.

His failure pushing the people around him away.

The panic of being someone's last chance.

The expectation of the crowd once again surrounded him, watching him with misplaced hope, asking him to do something that he couldn't . . . He scrutinized those faces, looking until they shifted from vague, conceptual entities to real people. They were the children from Amelia's shop, the old couple that had slipped him an apple. One by one the faces became real, and that changed something . . .

It changed *everything*.

The thought of failing them still filled him with panic, but to give up on them before trying was far more terrifying.

The flickering flame steadied, tripling in size on his next exhale as he let go of outcomes and leaned into what he was. Their hopes and expectations no longer threatened to crush him . . . They became his strength.

He was their Champion.

Truth crashed into him as some deep part of himself identified with the role that he had thought an arbitrary title from the system. He had always wanted to be a hero. It is what had compelled him to join the fire department out of high school. They were the only figures he could think of that had existed on the edges of his shattered life as beacons of consistent good.

But somewhere along the way, he had lost that. The toll of the job, shift after exhausting shift as life shoveled more and more shit onto him . . . It was a horrible responsibility to hold someone's life in your hands, and under that weight, his cracked foundations had slowly crumbled until he had become a bitter shadow of himself. But Tilly was beginning to believe again, not just in himself, but in the one who had chosen him . . .

The flame was roaring now, not consuming, but integrating his whole being into a state of purpose-filled oneness.

"Jonathan," a steady, strained voice interrupted.

Tilly's eyes flickered open, and the flame winked out of existence. He looked around in sudden confusion to find the sun setting and Ichiro now sitting ten feet away with sweat dripping down his face. This did nothing to dampen the fierce smile playing out over his features. A ring of scorched earth surrounded him, and Tilly's eyes jumped to his notification log, which was blinking with a new alert.

CHAPTER ELEVEN

Montage

With a mental command, the most recent entry into his notification log burst into being,

> **Congratulations!** *You have learned the skill* **Meditation.**
> *Your* **Meditation** *level has increased. Adjusting for previous experience . . .*
>
> **Meditation** *Level 1*
>
> **Meditation** *level up! Level 2 . . .*
>
> **Meditation** *level up! Level 7*

Tilly stared at the notification screen dumbly for a moment, trying to comprehend what he was reading . . . Why would the system have to adjust for previous experience? When had he ever practiced meditation?

Unbidden, memories started to rise to the surface of his consciousness. Countless collective hours of exertion surrounded by smoke and flame. Early in their careers, firefighters become very disciplined in their breathing while using air from their packs, conservation being key. Inhale, pause, exhale had been the formula that had seen him through more than one near miss on a low-air emergency for a fellow firefighter.

He had always loved the breathing discipline, the strange peace he only seemed to be able to find when enmeshed in his gear, breathing through his facepiece and trusting it to protect him in hostile environments. In those moments, overcoming the dangers he had grown to love, he felt . . . *whole.*

Huh.

The lapin stood across from him, wiping sweat from his forehead with the sleeve of his robe.

"Ichiro, what just happened?"

"You began to embody your concept. No actual flame manifested this time, but the deeper you went, the more heat you put off. I cannot imagine what a **Battle Trance** with such a concept will be able to do. But perhaps in the short term you should meditate away from buildings and people," the lapin answered, smiling wryly.

"Ha ha," Tilly mocked in turn, sure Ichiro was exaggerating. Then, as he followed the lapin to his feet, he found the bottom of his pant legs covered with fresh black soot stains. As he wiped at them in vain, they slowly faded away due to his magical leathers. Below his moccasins was a charred imprint of his sitting position. Tilly looked up with a wince.

"Alright, I see your point. Where should I go to meditate if not my room?" he asked.

"Come, it's getting late. I will show you," Ichiro answered, looking up at the evening sky before turning to consider the Temple and frowning. Tilly followed his gaze and thought he saw one of the new doors moving out of the corner of his eye, but as he watched, nothing changed. The front of the Temple remained still, in its primitive but restored state.

"Sounds good. Let's get going," Tilly said distractedly as he pulled his eyes back from the Temple entrance. "Are we still going to spar tonight?"

Ichiro's slight frown disappeared at Tilly's question, replaced by an eager grin.

"Jonathan Tillman, with the current blessing on our skill advancements, we will spar as often as possible," he answered, tucking away his sword into the sash around his waist before continuing. "First, we will test the full limit of your *Endurance* and then see where you stand with your martial skills. We will start with weapons only, then integrate the rest of your skills and *Abilities*."

He turned and started jogging down the mountain. He seemed to be moving at an easy pace, but as he rapidly disappeared from view, Tilly realized his speed would have been an Olympic sprint back on Earth.

Tilly scrambled after, surprised to find the pace only mildly challenging. In fact, with his *Dexterity* he wasn't even encumbered by the changes in terrain and footing that accompanied the forest trail back down the mountain. He was so focused on enjoying his new ability that he didn't notice the small pulse of dissatisfaction from within his fantasy fanny pack as the heat fully dissipated from Tilly's body. The consciousness faded back to sleep with only a minute crack in the gemlike surface to mark the change.

Ichiro led them down to the base of the mountain, passing by several groups of people making their way up to the Temple. They didn't stop to engage, just danced around the groups, moving almost as easily off the path as they did on. They didn't slow until they broke through the tree line and caught a fresh look at the camp.

If Tilly had thought it was busy before, he was floored by the amount of industry displayed by the inhabitants this late into the day. Several more of the huge log buildings had been erected in the center of camp, slowly replacing the tents. The road leading over to the river and the fields on the other side was just as choked with workers as it had been this morning, and Tilly even spotted a large bridge now spanning the stretch of water. The structure sparkled as the evening light refracted off and through it.

"Is that ice?" Tilly exclaimed as he came to a halt.

Ichiro turned and considered the direction that Tilly was staring. "I am not sure, but whoever made it did so alone," he said, squinting toward the simple but enchanting structure. Turning back to Tilly, he shrugged. "I did not know the honu could affect the temperature of their waters . . . Most likely this is one of many surprises we will find after the distribution of the quest rewards."

"Awesome," Tilly breathed, happy to see such gains for people who had lost so much.

"Come, we will move through camp and around what was the village. I believe they were setting up the training yards on the other side of the valley when I left this morning." Ichiro gestured with a "come along" motion and then took off at an even faster pace.

The crowds they passed became a blur as Tilly moved at what must have been the edge of his body's new capability. Ichiro loped ahead of him showing no strain at the increase, but Tilly started to feel his lungs burn. Unhelpfully, his mind pointed out that this must be one of the consequences of such a low *Strength* stat. He would be able to keep up something moderate all day, but he quickly found his limits when pushing his boundaries.

They sprinted through and around clumps of people, jumping over low tents as often as dodging. Before he knew it, they were at the entrance to the lapin village, which was now only marked by two large ditches reaching out in either direction to enclose the buildings within.

To Tilly's chagrin, the lapin increased his pace again and started to pull away, turning right along the edge of the ditch. Tilly poured on everything he had and the burning in his lungs spread to his arms and legs as he kept pumping. They circled the perimeter in less than a hundred seconds, and Tilly almost ran into a stopped Ichiro as he rounded the final bend.

The lapin was standing calmly, drinking water from a trough set up against the perimeter line of the old village. It was one of many and served as the main water source for the thousands of people practicing rudimentary formations and drills. The land on this side of the village was especially flat and the recruits drilling there had already trampled it to dust, forming a dirt square that could have covered several city blocks.

"Whoa . . . ," Tilly said as he gasped for breath.

"Yes," Ichiro replied, looking over the assembly proudly.

"Many started training days ago, anticipating access to a class change. This is a huge opportunity for those who would have otherwise been forced into specific classes by means or resources."

Recruits had been divided up into twelve large groups and were being drilled by some of the Alliance's few experienced soldiers. The nearest group of over two hundred was being harangued very loudly by a striking satyr woman in a form-fitting patchwork of leathers and armor.

Level 38, Flame's Watch Captain

"You bunch of polished Auroch turds! I said *left*! Form up and try again," she shouted after a particularly dismal attempted maneuver. In exasperation, she turned away from her charges and her eyes caught Ichiro and Tilly standing nearby. Something mischievous flashed in her eyes as she registered their presence, and she turned back toward her group and shouted, "At ease! Get some water. We will not sleep or eat until we can move as a unit. I told them I could get you all the **Unit Movement** skill, and by the gods, I will do it!" Then she turned back to Tilly and Ichiro and jogged over. The loose formation behind her practically collapsed before moving as one toward the troughs.

"Greetings, Captain Achillia!" Ichiro called as she approached. Her considering look burst into a smile at his acknowledgment and numerous gold teeth gleamed like beacons beside their natural counterparts.

"Well, Lord Ichiro! I'll be damned to the Pits if you aren't the first to recognize me right off!" she exclaimed.

"I must admit, it was the colorful language and your blade that gave it away." Ichiro was smiling in satisfaction while simultaneously eyeing the invisible pattern unfolding all around her. She turned her intriguing smile on Tilly, and he had to admit that despite the patchwork gear and intermittent gold teeth, she was stunning. The only things that marked her as a satyr were hooved legs starting at the knees and thick curled horns turning back from her forehead, framing dark ringlets of hair.

"Rumor is, you caused all this," she said as she gestured vaguely along her body, smirking as he followed her gesture.

"Um, have we met?" Tilly asked hesitantly, feeling like he was missing something.

"Yeah! Back when I was an old hag, you dolt!" She guffawed.

That was enough to strike his memory, and a vague image of a female guard captain missing teeth came back to him.

"The quest reward made it down here?" Tilly asked, astounded.

"Made it? Gods-damned wall of fire rolled down off the mountain like it was The End itself! Thought it was some old monster until we was hit and the notification popped up."

"Fascinating," Ichiro muttered, looking well past the watch captain to the group drinking from the other troughs, many of whom displayed the newly bestowed Flame's Watch signifier above their heads.

"Any of us who stood against the snakes and the rest got a class change. As for me, 'cause I made sure my whole town made it through that shit show of an invasion, the system said I had a 'Legendary contribution.' Said I had earned me a 'Temporal Renewal,'" she said, emphasizing the syllables of each of the phrases. "All that means is I got everything tightened back up to how it used to be, except the teeth of course . . ." She trailed off and sucked at her gold teeth loudly.

"Excuse me, Captain," Ichiro broke in, "would you speak to the others about reserving this corner for us in the mornings?" He gestured to the now open expanse of parade ground nearest to the group.

"Yes, sir," she said, sketching out a salute before turning to cast a baleful eye over her group. "Almost everyone here was with me on the line. Most got the new class, the rest will head up in the morning. We was told the farmers get first priority . . ."

"Well, it looks like you have this well in hand. Do you mind if we use the space?" Ichiro asked politely.

"Fine by me, as long as you don't mind us watching. They aren't gonna be worth two shits as soon as they realize who you are, anyway. Might as well use it."

"What do you mean, 'use it'?" Tilly asked.

But she was already gone, turning toward the other troughs and bellowing in that impressively loud voice, "Alright, you stumble-footed idiots. Eyes up! Time to see what a couple of our elites can do! This here is the human who is responsible for getting you your fancy new classes, and with him is Lord Hiro's son, who by all accounts might be the best swordsman in this Alliance of ours!"

She gestured grandly at the now-empty section of the field.

CHAPTER TWELVE

That's Not Sparring

Tilly tripped over his own feet as he followed Ichiro out to the middle section of the parade ground. He couldn't help but look back at the group excitedly talking amongst themselves as the captain stood off to the side smiling.

"Are you ready?" Ichiro said as he turned to face Tilly while resting an easy hand on the hilt of his sword. Tilly's eyes were drawn to the casual gesture like a magnet.

"Um, don't we need practice weapons or something?"

"No," Ichiro responded simply, his expression open and honest as he rocked back on his heels in anticipation of the spar. "Simply do your best to attack me. I believe I am more than skilled enough to handle anything you are currently capable of without your *Abilities*." As he spoke, he searched the human's face for the reason behind his hesitation.

Tilly sighed and slowly pulled his hatchets out of their loops. *Of course these guys wouldn't use practice weapons. It's not like this is a HEMA convention.*

"I guess live weapons make the most sense," he grumbled to himself as he stalked forward at a crouched walk, trying not to let the natural fear of being stabbed show in his movements. Tilly had faced death and injury plenty of times. But charging in with adrenaline pumping was one thing. Choosing to get stabbed for . . . practice was something entirely different. He felt like a rookie all over again, nervously shifting his grip on his hatchets as he rushed forward, wanting to get the first exchange over with.

Ichiro's face brightened once he saw Tilly move forward, but otherwise, his stance stayed completely relaxed. With a wince of anticipation, Tilly lunged forward and swung his hatchets from both directions in his signature close-combat opener. He still felt like an imposter when it came to using the weapons, but he had developed a few internal rules over the last couple of weeks. Rule number one: if you have two weapons, try to swing them from two different directions.

Ichiro stepped smoothly to the side, pulled his sword and scabbard out from his sash in one easy motion, and knocked away the hatchet in Tilly's right hand while moving out of range of the other swing. Everything about his expression and seemingly effortless movement convinced Tilly that at least one of them knew what they were doing.

Ichiro's confidence loosened up Tilly's movements, and he spun with the parry hoping to bring the struck hatchet back around toward Ichiro. But his plan was completely interrupted by an explosive blow across his back.

The air burst from his lungs as he face-planted into the churned dirt.

"Shit, Ichiro!" He coughed. "Little harsh," Tilly growled, pushing up from the ground, but he froze in his movement when Ichiro's blade whispered free and slid into the ground next to him, nicking the side of his neck.

"Very sorry, Jonathan Tillman, but your skills will only improve if you face bodily harm. I am afraid that each day we will spar until you're too injured to continue, then break to allow you to regenerate," he said as he pulled the sword away slowly, finally having realized the reason for Tilly's hesitance. He simply didn't know what was required to raise a combat skill.

Tilly could hear some of the men to the side sniggering, and he forced himself to drop into his meditative breathing as his blood began to boil at once again being caught off guard by the rules of this place. It would have been fucking nice to know he was signing up for a beatdown every day. But whatever . . . Better to learn lessons here, where he would only be injured, than out there, where he would be killed for his ignorance.

He groaned as he pushed back up to his feet and turned to face Ichiro, who had once again sheathed his sword.

"Okay. Does this sort of skill leveling involve any pointers?" Tilly asked in a growl, then touched his neck and looked at the blood that stained his hand. He was keeping his cool, and the slightly embarrassed look on Ichiro's face mollified him somewhat.

"Yes, but not tonight. Simply do everything you can to hit me, and you may use your weapons and *Abilities* to their full extent," Ichiro replied, gesturing for them to continue.

Tilly took a few rapid breaths, the anticipation of very real pain and injury spiking his chemical balance. He had thought he was pretty acclimated to how things were going to be here on Nephesh. But the juxtaposition of acceptable risk here versus back home was staggering. He had done endless live fire training evolutions where safety was king. Training in this world was more of a "learn by doing" approach with only a modicum of thought for safety. Then again, with most injuries able to heal up in an hour or two, it made sense in an unfortunate way.

Well, time to nut up or shut up.

If he was going to get his ass beaten, he might as well give it his all.

His grip tightened on both the handles of his weapons before he whipped both hatchets at Ichiro as hard as he could, the close quarters only allowing them a single revolution before they each clanged against Ichiro's reflexively loosed sword.

Tilly spun with the revolution of his second throw and called back the hatchets almost as soon as he heard the clanging parries. At this point, his ax-throwing skill was sufficient to allow him to immediately release again as he came around, no longer needing to consciously aim.

Ichiro had not seen him do anything like this before and was kept momentarily busy deflecting the surprising follow-up throws. Hoping for this, Tilly was already diving forward after his fourth consecutive release, trying to squeeze his surprise opener for all it was worth.

Ichiro's movements stayed smooth throughout, and his blade seemed to be in two places at once as he deflected both follow-up throws and brought his blade forward to ward off the charge. But it was just a fraction too slow as Tilly crashed into him. The blade bit into his shoulder, but through the pain, Tilly was already punching his right hand with his recalled hatchet into Ichiro's ribs.

The lapin folded over the thrust, dropping his elbow down on the blade and knocking it out of Tilly's hand. Then the world rotated on its axis and Tilly was flying through the air, blood spraying from his shoulder.

Ichiro had rolled back with the tackle, lifting his leg simultaneously to kick Tilly's chest in. He crashed to the ground and rolled over a few times, his weapons lost in the maneuver.

Tilly moaned in pain as he attempted to get back to his feet while guarding both his chest and his actively bleeding shoulder.

"Very good!" Ichiro exclaimed happily while wiping his blade clean of Tilly's blood, then sheathed it. Even with his eyes hooded against the pain, Tilly spotted a small cut on the lapin's right elbow where he had knocked aside Tilly's weapon. A fierce smile slashed through the pain on Tilly's face.

"I aim to plea—*ugh!*" Tilly winced as he felt a vice squeeze down on his chest.

"Savage, with an uncanny feel for timing. With such little finesse and almost zero knowledge of the use of your weapons, you still managed to find some impressively effective combinations! You seem to favor throttling the initiative, forcing the conflict to go at your pace . . . This is good. It is no fluke that you have survived to this point," Ichiro said, ticking off the points on his lightly furred fingers as he considered Tilly's downed form with a look of appreciation on his face.

"Looks like our human knows how to take a lick or two, boys!" Captain Achillia shouted good-naturedly from the troughs.

"Careful, Captain," a new voice called from the other side of their section of parade ground. "I have seen him deliver a 'lick or two' of his own. Most of us would probably fair the same against the Lord Ichiro, here."

Tilly looked over to find Threstus approaching. His gait and posture remained unchanged, oozing feline grace and menace. His class, however, showed a surprising new feature.

Level 48, Three-Fold Bastion Commander

"Oh, I was only joking, Commander, and you know it! I just want this lot to see that no matter how good you are, leveling skills involves a beating or two!" the captain shouted back in mock outrage. Threstus nodded back at the reply and then waved the men at the troughs off, command evident in the gesture.

Captain Achillia moved seamlessly with the implied command. "Alright, scum sacks! Back on the field and in formation! You will never learn to fight if you can't even walk right!" she shouted, easily transitioning from spectator to officer. While she gathered up her group, Threstus finished approaching Ichiro and Tilly.

"Just received word through Shuji from Lord Hiro. They have done a circuit and most of our boundary remains unchanged, except a new mouth at the other end of this valley where the river lets out," he said, gesturing along the path of the river to the new break in the surrounding mountains.

"What does that change?" Tilly grunted through bruised ribs.

"They have spotted some combatants milling in the open landscape beyond the border of our protections. Currently, they seem to be moving very slowly toward our boundary to investigate. Hiro is going to leave the boon area for as short a time as possible to collect intel on the probable enemy. In anticipation of his findings, we are directing fifty percent of our building efforts to the gap. It must be defensible as soon as possible." He spoke as if listing off what they were going to eat for dinner.

"Whoa, I knew it would be happening fast, but a possible war so soon? This place is nuts." Tilly sighed.

"Such is Nephesh. Stagnancy is death, and the system regulates the balance to make sure everything is always in flux. The whole plane has evolved Epoch after Epoch, moving toward something. What that thing is . . . not even the scholars know," Ichiro added gravely, eyeing Tilly with consideration.

"Nonetheless, your mornings will remain unchanged, Tillman, although you will be sparring with others in addition to Ichiro as soon as we can get the priestess down from the mountain. Perhaps in a few days. Not everyone can be as gentle as the young lord and you will need her healing as sparring progresses . . . as will others in this ragtag bunch soon," Threstus said, eyeing Tilly's injuries critically, the barest hint of a smile playing around his eyes.

"Oh, fuck off!" Tilly growled swiping at the commander with one of his hatchets. Threstus didn't move as the blade cut the air half an inch in front of his face, only allowing his smile to burst forth unrestrained.

"Remember your spirit later this week when I show you what true dual wielding looks like." He winked before turning and jogging off to catch another group commander to update them.

"He's the new Bastion commander, huh? And I see the Bastions didn't change much after the quest reward," Tilly said as he turned back to Ichiro, who was watching the new opening to the valley thoughtfully.

"When Linus appointed him earlier this week, they almost came to blows . . . But it seems he is settling into the role. The Bastions will be essential as our flagship elite class. I am sure there are some significant internal changes, but it is good for our people that they will be able to keep the name," he replied without turning his gaze away from the gap, his eyes roving all over the area, tracing patterns no one else could see.

While the lapin was still thinking, Tilly considered his health and mana.

Health: 76%
Mana: 88%

"Ichiro, I have more in the tank if you are ready to keep going," he ground out reluctantly, the bleeding from his shoulder already slowing.

"Yes, I have a good feel for your initial style, and I imagine not much changes when you include your powers. Use your ranged attacks as you close distance and then inflict as much damage as you can while attempting to soak up any return damage," he said, only giving Tilly half his attention.

"Uh . . . yeah. That sounds like what I have been doing so far," Tilly answered, his face screwed up at the brief description of all his "tricks." At his tone, the lapin finally looked away from where his father had set off and offered a conciliatory smile at Tilly.

"Do not worry. Effective and complicated are rarely synonymous. We will begin again tomorrow, and I will help you refine what you have already begun to develop. Variation can come after you master your typical combinations. You are not a duelist, facing countless skilled opponents one-on-one. We will focus on keeping you alive and then build out your combat role from there."

Ichiro eyed the sky, now colored in rich shades of pink and purple while the surrounding mountains cast long dark shadows on the valley and its inhabitants.

"Come, we will meditate, then eat, and you will rest again, even if you are not tired. Shuji has cited important studies time after time to me that even though we can endure tiredness and hunger much better with increased stats, there are still consequences. Returns begin to diminish past a certain point, especially when we are cultivating something like *will*. Today has offered us more than enough to consider.

"The longer you live here, the more you will come to find that most combat is much more than numbers. You will meet some combatants that have barely mastered their *Abilities*, while others squeeze out every bit of potential from their builds. For warriors like them, levels can be extremely deceptive," he said, then looked back from the darkening sky and into Tilly's eyes, the sudden ferocity of his stare slightly off-putting.

"You will be one such warrior before we are through, Jonathan Tillman, mark my words."

CHAPTER THIRTEEN

Padawan

Tilly finished out that evening's training by meditating. Well, he tried to meditate.

As he tried to find that same state of calm he had had up on the mountain, he discovered that meditation on the edge of a parade ground hosting thousands of drilling recruits wasn't nearly as productive as the conditions of his first attempt had been. He spent most of the time trying to maintain his breathing while chewing through the Alliance's chances as a new faction versus whatever the system was about to throw at them.

Ichiro eventually called it a night once he noticed Tilly's face devolving from focused to disgruntled. He reached out to help Tilly up off the ground as he tried not to scowl over at the noisy training, which looked like it would continue well into the night.

"Meditating in such environments will assist you in gaining the **Battle Trance** skill, despite the short-term challenge it offers," Ichiro said, patting Tilly on the shoulder as he tried to shake off his dismal performance.

"After earlier, I thought I could dive right back into it," Tilly replied sheepishly.

"I highly doubt you will ever be a man who finds much comfort in silence . . . So instead of training in seclusion, we will lean into your nature as a strength. Do not fight against your environment. Instead, let it wash through you, and as it passes, only quiet will remain."

With meditation out of the way, they grabbed dinner and Tilly found his small shack newly sandwiched between two large timber walls. They now supported structures that dwarfed his room, yet no one had touched the spot that the lapins had reserved for him. With a rueful shake of his head, Tilly entered his new home and collapsed in bed, barely remembering to shut the door behind him. He had pushed himself through another day of radical changes, demanding that his battered psyche adapt once again as the stakes around him were raised to new heights.

Lying there fully clothed, he desperately reached for unconsciousness, but some part of him stubbornly lingered in that place between waking and dreaming for a few more rebellious moments. He was changing, transforming into something totally different from what he had been, and too much of that change was happening beyond the boundaries of his comprehension.

He floated in that in-between, where time spirals and space returns to its beginning. As he transitioned out of wakefulness, his whole consciousness joined together, allowing belief and identity to supersede flesh and blood for a moment. A faint musical note echoed through the space, ringing over him, marking his progress and sealing it over him.

As his deeper consciousness rose to the surface, it attempted to follow the note to its source and saw a riot of color continuously bursting forth into wild patterns, reaching out to and through all things. Yet this song did not expand endlessly; it was surrounded by a crashing, hungry silence.

Tilly's deepest self watched as the screeching of a broken record twisted at the edges of the song, attempting to unravel it from the outside in, just as it consumed him from the inside out.

8 hours later

Tilly awoke to the industrious sounds of sawing and hammering just outside his thin walls. He rolled over, swallowing through the dryness in his mouth, and grinned as he found water and a simple meal of rice and eggs on a tray next to his bed.

He chowed down and guzzled the water before slipping out into the early morning to find that he was once again far from the first one up in the city. Everywhere he looked he saw people hurrying, but not in the same way he had seen in the capital during its final hours. The people he saw moving through the slowly filling streets walked with purpose. Their slack looks of hopelessness had been replaced by determination, and in some cases, Tilly even saw eagerness to attack the day's work.

Carpenters were shouting at masons to hurry and lay stone for foundations, while behind them fishermen hauled in early morning catches in heavily laden baskets. It was clear that the entirety of the Three-Fold Alliance knew about the boons and was intent on getting as much out of them as possible.

He hopped into the stream of people and headed through the burgeoning city to the parade ground. His pace increased to a jog almost subconsciously as the energy of the surrounding populace lightened his steps. Minutes later he arrived at the agreed corner of the parade ground to find Ichiro already kneeling in meditation. Tilly's face unknowingly turned down in a frown as he hurried over to take a position opposite the lapin in the dawning light of the day.

Ichiro's breathing remained unchanged, but a small smile tweaked the corners of his mouth as Tilly studiously got into the breathing pattern and began to focus intently on his visualized flame.

Soldiers trickled onto the field around them, clanking along in unfamiliar gear. They cursed their own clumsiness and teased each other in turn, preparing for another intense day of training. Tilly breathed in their presence and breathed it out again. Taking Ichiro's words to heart, he tried letting all the sensory input he was receiving move through him instead of trying to wall it out.

Commanders began bellowing out orders and harassing any stragglers. Formations were established and drills began. Nearby someone tripped and the sound of a dusty *thunk* reached Tilly. His right leg began to cramp, and the annoying muscular pinch demanded his attention for a few long minutes.

All these things and more flooded Tilly's senses, and he did his best to take them in and let them go again, trying to find that deeper place he had touched in front of the Temple. But his flickering flame had only grown a small amount by the time Ichiro broke their meditation.

"That is enough for now, Jonathan Tillman. I can tell you are improving tremendously."

"Yeah, not sure about that," Tilly snarked as he got to his feet and shook out his sleeping lower extremities.

"What was found can be found again. Do not be disappointed that all of your progress is not blindingly fast," the lapin admonished, his stern expression looking out of place on his relatively young face. Or maybe he just looked young when Tilly compared him to his father, who seemed to be made out of granite marked by the long lines of the burden of leadership.

The younger lapin's stern look, however, remained until Tilly relented. "Oh, alright! I just hate the thought that I'm doing less than I could be." Tilly sighed and rolled his shoulders, loosening his back.

The lapin nodded in solemn understanding before stepping back a few feet and clearing his throat.

"Now, as your skill advances, your footing, hand placement, and form will all improve incrementally. Our best understanding of skill leveling is that as you take steps toward improving your natural capability in an area, the system supplements that improvement. So, for every level you advance a skill, you must take a significant step forward on your own, and the system adds to that improvement with a portion of its vast store of experiential knowledge. Knowledge gathered throughout the many Epochs this Land has seen." Ichiro was lecturing, clearly reciting much of this by rote, and if Tilly didn't miss his guess, he knew exactly who Ichiro's tutor had been.

Tilly broke into the lecture with what he hoped was a clarifying question. "But that is not the whole story with martial skills. The system will not 'supplement' improvements there without you facing serious risk. Why is that?"

"Excellent question! It is actually for our benefit," Ichiro answered excitedly, choosing not to pick up on the slight whine that may or may not have entered Tilly's voice at the tail end of the question.

"Can you imagine what the truly powerful would be able to do if they could advance such skills in the safety of their strongholds? Power would be perpetuated endlessly without challenge or change. No, even the inheritors and great powers of this world must put themselves at risk to advance. In fact, the kind of training we are doing here would not typically be enough to significantly grow your skills, due to your knowledge of the non-lethality of our encounters. But with the boon in place, this loss is balanced out, giving us the luxury of advancing our capability as combatants without risking our lives."

At this point, Ichiro's expression was so enthusiastic that Tilly almost felt bad about the dread that was once again building internally at the thought of being cut and stabbed for a couple of hours.

"The only thing that will not improve with this training is your sense of what will be effective against different enemies. In this, you already have good instincts, but we will sharpen you as much as possible over the next weeks until you are operating at the full potential of your build." Ichiro's gaze grew more serious as his hand moved to rest ominously on his sword. "Now, I want you to try the same opening strike you used against me initially yesterday. I will respond by countering exactly how I did last time. Anticipate my movements and see if you can't produce a different result."

The rest of the morning was a slog of painful repetition as Tilly grew familiar with just how fast and capable Ichiro was with his sword, drawn or sheathed. They moved through the same close combat opener and his method for closing the gap on any enemy who had a counter for his ranged throws.

Ichiro struck Tilly with numerous painful but superficial cuts, stabbed him a few times, and even broke Tilly's hip. Every injury was a shock to Tilly's system and kept him on a razor's edge every time he reset to face the calm swordsman. Every couple of exchanges, Ichiro would send Tilly to rest for ten to twenty minutes, or until he was capable of full range of motion.

Even with Ichiro's occasional slips into distracted, far-off staring, it was still a brutal lesson in combat. The lapin's inborn battle reflexes were more than enough to match Tilly, even when he was disadvantaged by his condition. In one of these exchanges, when Ichiro's face suddenly went slack, Tilly swore Ichiro's sword jerked the lapin's arm into a fanning block that intercepted both of his strikes without its wielder even realizing what had happened.

By the end of the session, Tilly found himself unable to repeat his feat of surprise from yesterday. Hundreds of blows taken and not a single one given in return . . .

It was grueling, both mentally and physically.

It reminded Tilly of some of the hardest gear workouts he had ever done; seventy-five pounds of wet protective equipment doing its best to drag him into the ground as he carried dummies, climbed stairs, and advanced a charged hose. *That* level of physicality, but with the abrasive mental element of facing constant injury from a violent opponent. Tilly's fight-or-flight instinct took a beating along with his body, suffering from decades of peacetime living.

Even his close familiarity with the pressures of a life-and-death profession fell far short of what he needed to develop to survive in this world of subsonic sword strikes and fists that could break through stone walls.

When Ichiro called an end to the spar, Tilly was unconsciously flinching away any time Ichiro brought his sword around to bear, his battered subconscious barely coping with the trauma.

With the sun sitting high in the sky, Ichiro considered his student's state carefully, measuring opportunities for further progress against risk.

"That is enough for today. I believe continuing will do more harm than good," he finally said, then sheathed his sword and bowed to Tilly. "You have shown incredible resilience for one new to this world. I am honored by your courage." He came up from his bow with something more solemn replacing his typical serene expression.

"Thanks . . . That means a lot, actually," Tilly replied, attempting to slide his hatchets into their loops several times before actually getting them in.

"Make sure to drink some water before you start meditating. I want you to take time to feel your way around the mental and emotional obstacles you are facing," Ichiro said, his eyes softening even as his tone remained heavy.

Tilly nodded along absently as he moved slowly toward the water troughs, a limp in his right leg gradually resolving itself, the pain fading but its memory still affecting his movements mentally.

He absently cupped the water in his hands and splashed it over his face and sweat-soaked hair. As his mental fog began to clear, he opened his blinking notification log to a sea of detailed injury logs. Wincing, he mentally invoked the damage notification filter once again, leaving only the numeric evidence of his progress.

***Beginner Hatchet** Level 12 > Level 14*

***Dual-Wielding (Hatchets)** Level 8 > Level 11*

***Ax Throwing** Level 15 > Level 16*

A thrum of satisfaction reverberated through the numbness that accompanied continuous trauma. The whispers telling him to give up, to ask for a break, or even to run away were ruthlessly smothered by the proof of some sort of improvement. If he could show similar gains over the next weeks of training, he would more than double his current martial skill levels.

It wasn't just his skill levels going up: he felt himself gaining a better understanding of the flow of combat itself. Sure, he hadn't been able to come up with meaningful counters to the lapin's speed or skill, but over the course of the morning, he had slowly developed a certain feel for where to attack. Instead of mindlessly following his skills' guidance, he found himself actively looking for the most effective places to push and mentally noting where it would be pointless to attempt a strike.

As those three notifications glowed in front of him, he squeezed every bit of hope and encouragement he could from them. He would do this again tomorrow . . . and the day after . . . However many days it took, he would do what he had to. They all had to become stronger if they wanted to survive.

He had to survive, and he had to get the Seed of Corruption out of him.

Whatever it took.

CHAPTER FOURTEEN

To Fight Death

S et ablaze with proof that all this was making a difference, he took a few steps away from the troughs and settled into his meditative pose. Anchoring his thoughts on Ichiro's guidance from the day before, he began to accept the input trickling in from his surroundings. After a while, the input from his senses fuzzed into white noise and he shifted to accepting whatever emotions began to rise up in the space of his quieting mind.

Everything he had endured and everything he had yet to face . . . It was all fuel.

Its passing would change him, form him into something new, and he did not know exactly what it was that he was becoming . . . but he accepted that too. While he did not sink any deeper into his consciousness, something that Ichiro had said earlier pinged at the back of his mind, and he gently unfolded the morning's events, replaying the two combat scenarios Ichiro had led them through.

The events came to him with startling clarity, and he found himself once again thrust into the visceral realities of combat as he allowed the memories to wash over him. At some points, he couldn't help but flinch as his mind relived each strike and thrust in terrifying detail. It had to be the system augmenting whatever it thought Tilly's seven levels in **Meditation** were worth.

Refusing to miss the chance this new ability afforded, he forced himself to experience the whole morning again, step by step. He needed to understand what was happening in their combat exchanges on a deeper level. He didn't have time to put thousands of hours into learning the intimacy of combat, so he needed to squeeze every drop out of the opportunities he had.

Each time the memory of a painful strike tried to scatter his focus, he fought not to pull away, attempting to learn from the pain that was in every lesson.

Several cuts along his right shoulder made clear in great detail that he was overreaching with his right-handed attacks. Brutal strikes against his turned back told him that spinning in front of a faster opponent was idiotic.

Slowly, the painfully immersive review of his morning training session deepened his understanding of the advantages and shortcomings of his combat style. Right now, he was "shock and awe": take the initiative with surprise and depend on the bonuses from his Mantle of Champion to try to out-damage his target. Trying to go toe to toe with an experienced opponent over any length of time, especially one who was not **Corrupted**, would be suicide for him without a party.

These truths became crystal clear to him, even as he slowly purged the trauma from his psyche. He was so focused on squeezing out these insights that he didn't even notice the flame before him anymore. Yet every pain accepted and every lesson learned was fed unconsciously into that fire, causing it to grow more intense. Even as he did something as simple as replaying a recent memory, the deeper places of his consciousness slowly dragged him down out of time and into the realities of the building blocks of his soul.

In, hold, out, hold.

He was learning to be deeply present as his external and internal worlds were slowly experienced, processed, and integrated. Breath by breath, the morning's painful, and at times traumatic, lessons were integrated into the underpinnings of consciousness, slowly solidifying his undiscovered core beliefs.

At some point in the process, even the sharp memories of the morning training session faded away, and there was only the flame and his *will*, growing incrementally more intense as he sunk deeper.

He didn't have to tough this training out. He didn't have to ignore the physical and mental toll such a grueling regimen inevitably took on his mind. That is what old Tilly would have done. He had spent a lifetime running from pain, shoving down fear, and moving forward. Doing so had demanded insidiously little of him in the moment and exacted a terrible price over a lifetime.

Get a little harder.

Get in, do your job, get out.

Don't stop moving, don't let it catch up.

He was beginning to understand the enormity of the trauma he had held back over the decades. It was like an ocean that threatened to drown him, held back by the cinder blocks of his own slowly calcifying heart.

To feel was to crumble, and behind that wall, swimming in his ocean of pain like a shark, was **Corruption**.

What could he do?

To destroy the wall was to lose control, to invite in the beast.

To his shock, he even began to see cracks where facing his demons internally had begun to let some of that fear and pain through—

A voice shattered his focus, tearing through the parade ground in panic. "HUMAN! Where is the human!" it demanded as Tilly's eyes snapped open, looking for its source.

"Lord Hiro is hurt and needs the human now!" the voice continued to call.

Ichiro was already looking toward the messenger, deep concern written all over his face. Tilly followed his eyes to look for a panicked guardsman in the nearest drilling formation that was facing their direction. Then Ichiro's eyes flicked back to a space near Tilly only to have Threstus arrive there in a blur, skidding to a stop in the spot Ichiro had anticipated.

His face was grim.

"I just got the news, and I'm heading to get the priestess. Lord Hiro returned covered in wounds, and many of them are infested with **Corruption**." As soon as Ichiro nodded in acknowledgment, Threstus blurred off again.

Tilly didn't wait but leaped to his feet and ran toward the messenger, who caught his approach, turned to lead and, running ahead, said, "Come! The Wardens sent me. He is at the other end of the parade ground!"

Groups of soldiers quickly moved aside as the guardsman and Tilly ran through. Ichiro pulled ahead of them in the first ten seconds and was already kneeling next to Nyuk and Kuro when Tilly and the guardsman arrived less than half a minute later.

Tilly slid, baseball-style, next to Ichiro as Kuro explained in a rush, "There were already *things* coming to investigate us by the time we arrived at the gap with Lord Hiro last night. Their ability to move seemed slow to our augmented perception, but there was a group of at least thirty—"

"They were called **Corrupted** Strigoi, all around level thirty-five, and they were led by a level seventy-five Strigoi Consumer," Nyuk cut in.

"They would have been able to enter the boon area before we could have returned with more forces. So Lord Hiro commanded us to watch and report whatever happened while he went out to meet them."

"Lord Hiro was incredible!" Kuro shouted before looking down and choking out a sob.

"He unleashed some attacks unlike anything I have ever seen at the bastards, and many never even made it to him. Then the leader turned and tried to flee, but Lord Hiro chased, taking many wounds to make sure no word of our disposition left the field. The rest of the smaller ones mobbed him as he chased the Consumer and cut him down," Nyuk continued.

While they had been talking, Ichiro had removed much of his father's armor, revealing numerous bites and tears on the lapin's body. Far too many of the areas showed the familiar black veiny signs of **Corruption**. Hiro's breathing was shallow and had slowed down to less than five breaths a minute. This was worse than what they had seen from the naga's poison in the city.

Even as his mind cataloged the wounds, Tilly began to kindle his **Flame's Renewal** *Ability* deep in his chest. As it activated, he fought to hold it back and build the intensity of the flame even further. Tilly didn't know if the limits placed on the *Ability* were for the target's protection or not, but he did know what an imminent death looked like.

Lord Hiro only had a few minutes left.

He held his breath as he fought to increase the intensity of the *Ability* without changing its nature. Then, just before he felt it start to deform into something different entirely, he exhaled explosively and swept the trajectory of his breath down the length of Hiro's body, making sure to leave no wound unaccounted for.

As the invisible magic of **Flame's Renewal** left Tilly's lungs, it immediately burst into blue and white flames, showering Hiro's form. At the sight of the white flame, Ichiro's eyes flicked up to Tilly before he nodded in thanks and focused back on his father.

Tilly began to wince, as, unlike in its typical iteration, the *Ability* began to burn across the surface of the lapin's skin and cause physical damage. Damage that the lapin could hardly afford. The tongues of flame flickered and danced as they homed in on the infected wounds and began to sink into the putrefying flesh, hungrily chasing and rooting out the infection.

The sizzling pop of seared meat rose from the wounds, and they all watched as **Corruption** and flame spent themselves in mutual destruction. By the time it was through, the wounds were completely cleared of infection, but the lapin's skin was left molted and rippling in the places where the flame had rested. Perhaps most disturbingly of all, Hiro hadn't reacted once as his body was set temporarily aflame.

"Doesn't anyone have a health potion?" Tilly whispered out through his scorched throat with a cough.

"No, Jonathan Tillman. We never had many and those that we did have were all used in the fighting to protect our people's escape," Ichiro whispered back, searching the air around his father for some sign of hope as Hiro's breathing slowed to intermittent shallow gasps.

Tilly reached over to the lapin's wrist and felt for a pulse.

Radial pulse absent.

Hiro suddenly took a long shuddering breath and then stilled.

"Oh, goddess!" Kuro moaned.

Tilly immediately slid into position near Hiro's chest, putting a hand to the carotid and watching for any signs of chest rise . . .

Nothing and nothing.

"Ichiro, I don't know if this will work in this world, but we are going to try," Tilly said forcefully through his parched throat. "When I say so, close your father's nose and breathe deeply into his mouth, twice."

The lapin's head whipped around to him and nodded swiftly before shuffling into a ready position near his father's head.

Tilly doubled up his palms over the base of Hiro's sternum and began to pump his chest. As rote as these motions were in Tilly's muscle memory, he was immediately thrown off by the inflexibility of Hiro's ribs.

Of course, this tough motherfucker must have a bunch of points in Endurance.

Tilly bore down with all of his *Strength* and finally felt Hiro's sternum and bottom few ribs pop out of place. After that, with much more force than normal, Tilly was able to get into rhythm and compress Hiro's heart. At thirty compressions, he called for Ichiro to breathe; the lapin complied immediately while more and more soldiers crowded around the scene.

Tilly kept pumping until he hit another thirty, at this point covered in sweat from the effort of attempting to compress the lapin's heart through the tough protection of his magically enhanced bone structure.

"Breath again, Ichiro, and everyone else, shut UP!" Tilly yelled at the murmuring crowd.

Ichiro puffed two full breaths into his father's mouth, and Tilly confirmed the chest rising along with lung movement before he reached up and felt for a pulse.

He held his breath . . . *Nothing.*

"Ichiro, I have seen someone come back after fifteen rounds of this back on my plane! We are not going to giv—"

BOOM!

An explosion ripped open the space behind Tilly, flinging him forward and scattering the crowd behind him in all directions. Tilly rolled with the force of the blast and came to his knees as he turned to face whatever had just hit them from behind, both hands holding his hatchets.

Standing there, wreathed in blue flames, was Erash. Tilly didn't know how she had gotten there so fast, but he sagged in relief when her eyes zeroed in on Hiro's prone form and she rushed forward, bringing her staff to bear.

Her eyes flashed and she muttered an incantation as blue flame flowed from her staff and washed over the lapin's body. When nothing changed, she cursed under her breath and started again, this time her voice carrying something far deeper.

The words were incomprehensible to Tilly, but just hearing them caused his teeth to ache and his eyes to water. The air surrounding the priestess and Hiro began to thrum with power as the flame on her staff flashed in rhythm with the heavy syllables of her words. Ichiro ignored all of it, still watching his father with fierce concentration.

Then there was a green flash and the packed ground under Hiro loosened, turning darker and richer. It shook and moved like a living thing, reaching up and pulling the lapin into its embrace, fully covering him in fresh loamy soil, which immediately sprouted wildflowers.

All eyes went to the priestess, who sagged against her staff, her spell finished.

CHAPTER FIFTEEN

Drastic Decisions

A stunned silence choked the area around where Hiro had been lying just moments before. Almost everyone stared down in shock at what now looked disturbingly like a well-kept grave. Even the whispered questions of those at the edges of the crowd who couldn't quite see hushed as the weight of the moment settled over the parade ground.

For her part, Erash continued to gasp in lungfuls of air, like a swimmer coming up after a long dive. Her hands clutched her staff, white-knuckled, and lines creased around her eyes as she watched the mound of freshly turned dirt.

Then Threstus arrived in a blur to stand next to the priestess, obviously only now catching up to her. "Wow, you can really move when you want—" he started before breaking off as he took in the surrounding mood. "What did I miss?" he asked, his voice turning serious as his eyes inevitably found the mound of dirt.

The shock was broken by the question, and the surrounding crowd started yelling in outrage and confusion. In response, Ichiro shot to his feet in a smooth dangerous motion, his hand on his sword as his eyes followed all sorts of unseen paths entering in and out of the dirt mound. Something powerful was happening there, and Tilly gasped an inhale of his own as he realized he had been holding his breath in anticipation of . . . something.

Voices yelled out through the angry milling crowd.

"WHAT DID SHE DO!"

"WHAT HAPPENED TO LORD HIRO?"

"ARE WE UNDER ATTACK?"

"Calm yourselves!" Ichiro shouted in a low, intense voice, his eyes continuing to trace patterns leading off in multiple directions from his father's mound. "This woman is one of us! She is the new High Priestess of the god of the mountain. He is the one many of you have to thank for your new classes!" He finally looked up from tracing the almost manic pattern his eyes had been absorbed in. The crowd quieted in response to his command, and Ichiro turned toward the priestess and stated in a calm, respectful voice, "I see that he yet remains with us. But as I watch, his core pattern is being altered. Please explain what is happening."

The immutable peace of Ichiro's deep meditative state lent a gentle and polite tone to his voice, but Tilly didn't miss the fact that his hand had remained resting on his sword when he turned to the priestess.

Erash looked up from her vigil, almost as if she had not heard any of the voices until this point. Her face somehow took on a gravity and maturity far beyond its youthful beauty as she considered Ichiro's question. The weight surrounding the pair suddenly doubled as their eyes met before dissipating just as quickly as it had come.

Erash nodded in acknowledgment of whatever had just passed between them and answered, "Hiro was facing a stacking debuff called **Corrupted Vampiric Infection**. I have never seen it in person, but it simultaneously removes a target's regen and 'turns' the target once they reach zero health. This debuff is not unheard of, but it was far more powerful than it should have been at this level. The **Corruption** had been cleared, but the rest of the effects of the debuff refused to be cleansed . . ." She trailed off, looking back down at the grave before continuing.

"When I got here and read his recent damage log, I saw that almost all of the infection had been cleared and that his health had moved up and down between a quarter of a percent and half a percent for over ninety cycles." Her eyes rose to Tilly from the dirt mound, sharpening in interest once again.

"I immediately cleansed the remainder of the debuffs and attempted healing, but something blocked my attempt at regeneration. It felt to me like trying to heal someone who had already passed beyond our plane . . . Something I cannot yet accomplish. So, with no options left and a patient on the brink of death, I chose to do something . . . drastic." At this point in her explanation, her words flowed forth more hesitantly as the lines on her face softened back to something younger and less self-assured. Tilly was left with the impression that he was listening to a teenager explain why they had broken curfew instead of to the highest-leveled entity in the Alliance.

Ichiro nodded along, unsurprised at the state his father had been in when she arrived. "This drastic choice . . . It is better than death, yes? I see much of what makes up my father still there, but there are significant things being added as well," he said, encouraging her to continue.

"Yes, I hesitate to speak of this because it is part of my people's inheritance. But I chose this course, and I will see it through; In my lands, when a warrior makes a sacrifice of sufficient substance to protect the Land, they become eligible for a very particular ritual. I saw it as I was looking for anything else I could do to halt Hiro's decline. The ritual called to me—"

"A moment please," Threstus interrupted politely before turning to the crowd, many of whom were straining to hear. "Lord Hiro will be just fine! Our priestess took care of it. Now, off with you! All unit commanders gather your groups and return to drilling! We begin line work and combat forms today whether you are ready or not!" His sudden loud shouting hit and dispersed the surrounding soldiers like magic. Kuro and Nyuk remained behind, sitting back on their haunches at a respectful distance, watching for any change in their lord.

Once the whole of the audience had dispersed, Tilly followed Ichiro to his feet and reinstigated the conversation. "So, whatever you did, it kept him from dying. That has to be good, right?" Tilly inquired, brushing the dirt from his knees.

"That is correct . . . ," she answered, still struggling to find a way to describe the ritual in terms that were honest but not too revealing. "I have seen my . . . mother perform this same ritual once, for an Entkin who had fought back an ogre incursion at the mouth of a canyon on our borders. He held until our forces arrived and was little less than a husk by the end of the battle. My mother arrived in time to perform a version of what I just did, and the Entkin was restored, even advancing a tier in the process. But there is a price . . ." She looked down from Ichiro's face to the ground where the Land had taken Hiro into its embrace. "Hiro is currently undergoing a transformation into a guardian entity for this faction's portion of the Land. So, yes, he will still be alive, but not in the same way he was before. He will never sire any other children, nor will he need to eat or sleep." Her voice dropped as she revealed the cost of the ritual.

"Will his mind be altered?" Ichiro spoke a little more sharply than his previous inquiry.

"No, though he will be tied deeply to this portion of the Land and invested in its growth. He will no longer be able to level. Instead, his *Abilities* will compound as this faction and its influence increase. His power is now directly tied to the weight your nation has on the spiritual fabric of Nephesh. Finally, as long as your nation's Sovereign Crystal remains intact, no wound can kill him—defeat will only place him in a slumber until the damage is restored." She sighed. "At least, I suspect this will be the case. I did not anticipate the change my own powers have undergone with my new class and obligations. It does not feel like any negative alterations were added to the ritual, but it was not the same one I learned under my mother's tutelage."

Ichiro took the news with a thoughtful frown while Threstus processed the costs and benefits in a more pragmatic manner. "Ichiro, forgive me if I am overstepping. But this sounds like something your father would have chosen for himself if given the chance. It gives us one more edge in protecting our emergence into the conflict of Nephesh, which seems to have become more perilous than ever before," he said softly, finding the lapin's eyes and showing none of his characteristic sarcasm.

Ichiro took a deep breath at Threstus's statements and nodded in thanks to the Bastion commander.

"A similar thought had crossed my mind as well," he said slowly, seeming to come to terms with the turn of events, which none of them could have anticipated happening this early in the process of their faction's establishment.

Throughout Erash's explanation, a war of emotions had moved through Tilly. When faced with the prospect of Hiro's death, he had moved back into the toolset he had employed thousands of times in his old life. It had all come back to him so easily, and while it hadn't "worked," it had seemed to have made enough of a difference that they wouldn't be losing the leathering old samurai any time soon.

Then the whole conversation was interrupted as Linus arrived at a jog, having just received the news. Some minutes were spent catching him up, and all four of them immediately started planning the next steps to secure the gap and await Hiro's return. Instead of joining in, Tilly's eyes wandered to his flashing notification log.

Congratulations! *You have just averted a fatal debuff without using any mana or Abilities!*

*You have learned the skill **First Aid**.*

First Aid *- Using a combination of your knowledge of the internal composition of living beings, medical techniques, and basic aid supplies, you are able to neutralize or even clear negative debuffs. Your interventions add a +n% multiplier to your target's inherent healing ability,*
"n" being your level in this skill.

*Your **First Aid** level has increased! Adjusting for previous experience . . .*

First Aid *Level 1*

First Aid *level up! Level 2 . . .*

First Aid *level up! Level 35*

It may have been childish, but the validation of such a high skill level given for what had been a career that spanned decades filled him with satisfaction. He might not be able to heal, but hell if he was going to let someone around him die if he could help it. In fact, the similarity between this skill and his old career actually imparted a level of comfort with the prospect of playing that sort of role in parties when necessary. Maybe this could be a key to rounding out his build when he ran out of mana—something more akin to a specialized paladin than a pure tank or mage DPS.

There were some things he couldn't do anything about. But to have this tool back in his belt and acknowledged by the system meant a lot to Tilly. His vision may even have begun to grow blurry before he wiped the stray speck of dust from his eye and brought his attention back to the matters at hand. Tilly's moment went unnoticed as the four in the background finalized the temporary plans in light of recent events.

"I'll dispatch half the Bastions to the gap now to guard the work party we have heading that way this afternoon. We need a trench as soon as possible, and stone behind that over the course of the next weeks. Our small community of dwarves reported another strange encounter with that woman in black yesterday as she left our land. She pointed them to an ancient collapsed quarry and mine on the other side of the mountain. We should be able to move that stone to the gap using the river starting as early as tomorrow. I know the dwarves are ecstatic to get moving," Linus listed out, summarizing their next steps.

Tilly continued to only half listen to the logistical details as he watched a breeze stir the grasses and flowers sprouting in the spot Hiro now lay.

Then he realized that he hadn't felt any air moving as he watched the plants begin to sway.

"Guys!" he called over. "Something is happening!"

The other four came over in a flash as the freshly turned dirt began to move along with the plants, shivering and swaying. Then, like the classic scene from any first act of a zombie movie, Hiro's hand burst forth from the ground, reaching up to the sky in a grasping motion.

CHAPTER SIXTEEN

Preparations

Ichiro was there in a flash, grasping his father's hand and heaving him out of the ground. The elder samurai-turned-guardian exploded up in a shower of dirt and stumbled forward into the arms of his son. Ichiro held him there for a long second before Hiro pulled away gently and looked around at the small audience. As he met their eyes, the dirt shivered off from him all at once, revealing the same figure they had just seen buried with one main difference.

Guardian Daimyo of the Three-Fold Alliance

Hiro's armor and sword remained untouched as did his characteristic hard-eyed stare. Except now it was more than just a facial expression. That flat look was now augmented by eyes formed from the same green gemlike substance that made up the Sovereign Crystal's structure. They were intense, glowing with an internal light that was visible even under the cloudless afternoon sky. Because of them, it took Tilly a moment to notice the other, more subtle change. The parts of his lightly furred skin that weren't covered in armor now displayed an intricate network of markings that depicted dancing flames.

Hiro looked down at his hands before making a gesture and taking on that distant middle look of someone checking their screens. They all watched him, wanting to give him time to adjust to his new reality. The silence, however, stretched slightly too long, and Tilly couldn't help but try and break the tension.

"Looks good on you, Hiro!" he said cheerily, gesturing up and down at the lapin's body and interrupting his reading.

The samurai stared back at him implacably for a long uncomfortable moment, but Tilly might have caught a glint in those crystalline eyes at his gratingly awkward joke.

"Father, how are you feeling?" Ichiro asked in the wake of Tilly's interruption.

The newly christened Guardian Daimyo flicked his eyes down in a dismissal of his screens and turned formally to the priestess. His voice at last emerged in all its baritone glory.

"I owe you a debt. I spent my life willingly to buy time for my people and you have given it back to us along with a great gift," he said, emphasizing his words of appreciation with a deep bow.

She surprised Tilly by bowing even deeper in return.

"The Land has chosen you. May the ground beneath your feet grow rich with the blood of our enemies, Guardian," she replied with equal gravity, her response ringing with some small portion of the power that had echoed through her voice when she had cast the ritual earlier.

Hiro nodded, finding the words a fitting response, and turned back to Ichiro and Tilly, his crystalline stare contrasting oddly with Ichiro's all-white gaze.

"Thank you both," he said, gesturing down at the ground where he had recently lain. "I was not taken against my will. The . . . Land offered me a choice: my bond for some of its power. I accepted eagerly. This is another chance to see my duty to my people fulfilled, and I refuse to let it pass me by."

"Are you still . . . yourself?" Ichiro asked in a low, concerned voice.

"The bond I have taken is rooted in my desire to protect this place at all costs. I can never again leave the boundary of our people. In exchange, I will persist as long as they do, growing in power along with the Alliance." Then, taking special care to look Ichiro in his equally off-putting eyes, he continued, "I am Hiro Matsumoto, Fourth Lord in Exile, and now Guardian Daimyo of the Three-Fold Alliance. She has laid no additional bond on me. I do not think the power she now channels would have allowed it even if she wanted."

"He is correct," Erash broke in, pulling their eyes over to her. "I lost access to several of my more 'suggestive' *Abilities* when I took this office. In their place, much of my remaining build has been empowered and geared toward purification and renewal. While in this role, my power keeps me from laying any geas."

At her words, Ichiro nodded to himself and Threstus laid a friendly hand on Linus's shoulder, and quipped, "Thank the gods you are still fit for duty, Hiro. I don't think our Consul here can take any more paperwork."

Linus's thoughtful frown turned into a stormy scowl as he struck out like lightning, swinging a closed fist at the offending arm like he meant it. Threstus snatched his arm back a mite too slowly, rolling with the blow but not avoiding it altogether.

Then, continuing as if nothing had happened, Linus returned to verbally walking them through the plan of attack. "Lord Hiro, the stone should start arriving tomorrow, and half our workforce is shifting to the wall project starting this afternoon. The commander, here, will hold half the Bastions back to continue training our forces. I want to send the other half with you to hold the pass until we have fortifications in place. We can send regular updates on other progress, but this seems paramount."

"That is acceptable. I will leave Nyuk and Kuro here to gather any volunteers for the Rangers and begin their training under Threstus. None of our enemies escaped our first encounter, but they know there has been a shift as well as we, and when none return from their first investigative party, more will come. With the boon, we have a chance to be ready, but I expect some sort of response in the coming hours. Once our presence is confirmed, if they mean to come against us in force, then we will undoubtedly be facing a fully mobilized force when the boon expires."

"What about me? Does this change what I should be doing?" Tilly asked, ready to post up with Hiro and rain down fire on the new foes.

"Jonathan Tillman, your task remains the same. Increase your survivability and do what you can to find the next **Origin** Facet," Hiro said curtly before turning to Ichiro. "We need to be sending patrols along the mountains and forests on the rest of our border. I am sending you to oversee this. We will rotate in others for sparring, as duty allows, to offer Jonathan Tillman a variety of challenges. I trust you have laid a sufficient foundation."

At that, Ichiro smiled. "He has done very well, and consider it done."

"Oh, I have the perfect starting partner for him!" Threstus broke in, still rubbing his shoulder where Linus had struck a glancing blow. "He isn't much use in the beginning parts of training anyway," he continued, eyeing Tilly with a shit-eating grin.

Tilly winked at him in response, doing his best to cover up the sudden shiver that ran up his spine at the ominous proclamation.

"Sounds like I should start spending the mornings down here?" Erash asked with a quirk of her manicured eyebrow.

"That would be our preference. Your services will be needed soon," Linus answered respectfully. "We have some interested in testing themselves at the Crystal to see if they qualify for any priest classes. If any are accepted by the Sovereign Crystal and our new patron, we would like you to see to their training as well."

"I look forward to it, Consul," she said, adding only the slightest emphasis on the class name, before turning and walking away.

"Well, if that's all, I have a mess of unruly candidates here that need to at least know how to hold a weapon before another war gets well and truly started," Threstus stated crisply before turning in the opposite direction of the High Priestess and moving back toward the drilling soldiers.

At that, as if by some unspoken signal, the others nodded, waved, or simply turned, all moving toward their separate duties and Tilly found himself standing alone, looking around the parade ground like he had missed something.

"So, no training advice, huh?" he asked the empty air.

Then, not wanting to seem lost, he rested his hands on his weapons and wandered over to the water troughs to do some thinking.

Part of him appreciated the freedom that they were entrusting to him. But if he was being honest, another part of him found being wholly in charge of his time daunting. In some ways, he had spent his whole life moving from one emergency to another; now he was being invited to prepare in whatever way he thought was best. He was sure there would be a follow-up threat to the border soon. But until then, he wanted to put in as much time as possible into strengthening skills he already had.

He pulled up the skills list and gave it a hard look, trying to decide what would increase survivability and what was just novel fluff for now.

> ***Skills:***
>
> *-**Forestcraft** level 12*
>
> *-**Identify** level 17*
>
> *-**Cooking** level 12*
>
> *-**Beginner Hatchet** level 14*
>
> *-**Animal Processing** level 9*
>
> *-**Stealth** level 7*
>
> *-**Herb Lore** level 3*
>
> *-**Ax Throwing** level 16*
>
> *-**Dual-Wielding (Hatchets)** level 11*
>
> *-**Spirit Walk** level 14*
>
> *-**Meditation** level 7*
>
> *-**First Aid** level 35*

Well, he could throw out the active combat skills, he was already training those. He could also throw out the quality-of-life skills. Those were important over time, but they wouldn't do much against **Corrupted** Vampires.

That left **Stealth**, **Identify**, and **Forestcraft** as his best bets for increasing his chances of survival outside of combat. He needed to be able to spot and avoid trouble when possible, not to mention the benefit to his general ability to survive if he was ever caught out on his own.

After sparring tomorrow, Tilly decided he would find Ichiro and join up with the patrol force, perhaps even join in some Ranger training while he was at it.

That still left him the rest of today . . . He looked back at the walls, the camps, and the fields beyond. Shit was about to hit the fan all over again, he could feel it. So, before he threw himself into preparations, he decided to try and find the few people he hadn't seen since the fall of the empire's capital. Who knew when he would next get the chance to connect?

Tilly wandered back through the city; his progress was stopped by a massive group of laborers heading toward the parade ground, and probably the gap in the mountains beyond. They all carried a variety of tools for dirt-moving and construction and their classes varied. Tilly saw everything from Masons to Foremen present in the crowd.

Once through the city, he made his way over to the new bridge and was pleased to find at least one of the objects of his search almost immediately. If he got the chance, he had decided to thank the honu who had done so much to cover his back right before their escape.

Franklin stood on the banks of the river, casting an ice-aspected *Ability* over the flowing water. Tilly watched as he targeted the bridge's supports one by one and recast. As soon as the cloud of frost produced by his mana hit the supports, he would move his hands around in concentration, as if shaping clay. Then the cloud would move on, leaving a slightly reinforced and more ornate structure behind.

He had also exchanged the more typical honu robes for something thicker and fur-lined, most likely because his new class had not come with any innate elemental resistances. One thing that had remained was the same brilliant blue scarf Tilly had noticed on their first encounter. It fluttered in the wind over the collar of his new jacket, not much more in sync with his look. With all the changes he had already seen, Tilly was happy but not surprised to see a new class identifier over his head.

Level 35, Tundra Caller

"Franklin! How are you doing?"

"Very well! Thank you for asking, Mr. Tillman."

"Please, I don't think I stand a chance to convince the lapins, but call me Tilly. I'm glad I found you!"

"Very well . . . Tilly," he said, his speech showing some of the honu propensity for slowness for the first time. "I heard you had returned mysteriously and the elders briefed us on a coming change, but I could not imagine something like this," he said, gesturing happily to the ice structure he had been producing.

It was crude but sturdy and made an almost constant stream of traffic back and forth from the agricultural lands to the population centers possible.

"Yeah, I saw you put some of it up yesterday. Amazing! How often do you have to maintain it?"

"Every four hours or so, but along with the ice augment to my water *Abilities*, I gained a skill called **Sculpt Element**. At higher levels it will allow me to form complex shapes out of ice. Every time I reinforce the bridge, I am advancing this skill," he said excitedly, then a log bumped against his structure from upstream and a worker grabbed at it with a hooked pole, shouting for another. Franklin finished reinforcing his last support and turned fully toward Tilly.

"They tell me my bridge will be replaced by tomorrow and I'll be moving to the wall project," he said, pointing over to the pile of logs on the bank a little further upriver. "I can only assume this means we are already facing outside pressure," he added, a shadow falling across his features.

"Yeah, we had a pretty close call at our new border earlier today. Hiro barely stopped it. We have the Bastions moving up that way to secure it while some sort of fortification is built. But even with all that happening, it felt important to me to find and thank you. Without you, I wouldn't have made it out. You kicked some serious ass back there," Tilly said as he clapped the honu on the jacket covering his shell.

He didn't know him terribly well, but Franklin had fought by his side and covered him during the last fight, and that meant a lot. The honu people had paid the highest price for everyone to escape, losing Kihei and the other four elders . . . Tilly sincerely hoped others had acknowledged their sacrifice in some way.

Franklin received the strange physical interaction and the offer of thanks with a polite if confused smile. He looked Tilly in the eyes and slowly reached around to his back and gave it a few pats of his own.

"I am glad you made it, Tilly. Too many didn't. We have been offered a chance to rebuild and perhaps, one day, even fulfill the dream of my ancestors," he said, the lines of heaviness around his eyes easing slightly as a small smile softened his serious expression.

CHAPTER SEVENTEEN

Catching Up

Tilly spoke with Franklin for a while longer, not really saying much, just making a point to show the honu that he was thought of and appreciated. In the follow-up chatter, he learned that Amelia was just over the bridge, helping to oversee the initial setup of the agricultural zone.

Nodding to Franklin and promising to find him on the wall, Tilly jogged off across the bridge and moved into the miles of valley lying on the other side of the river. He had only seen this part of their settlement from a distance and had been interested in getting a closer look anyway. Aside from the private settlement the honu had started, this whole side of the valley was being aggressively converted into agricultural plots.

He saw miles of pasture with a surprising number of animals already grazing peacefully within hastily constructed fence lines. Even at this distance, he could tell that none of the animals were quite what he would expect from domesticated livestock. Instead of being drawn to the interesting agricultural questions of fantasy farming, he turned to move deeper into the already thriving food-producing plots. He skirted the flooded rice fields already being harvested by farmhands and walked a small dirt path between several huge gardens of impressive variety.

Past them he saw miles of grainfields that showed crazy amounts of growth for only a week's cultivation . . . Everywhere he looked, workers were busy. None seemed to be in a rush, but Tilly also couldn't spot a single person sitting or relaxing. They all seemed to be diligently pursuing their tasks with focus.

Then again, with the boon and the bonus from gaining a nature-aspected High Priestess, Tilly could imagine that everyone wanted to work around the clock to produce as much as possible before any bonuses ran out. Plus, it was probably pretty awesome for any class-related skills they were training, especially if those skills were leveled by the volume of food produced.

"Young man!" shouted a warbly voice from deep within one of the garden rows.

Tilly looked over and spotted a familiar old satyr shuffling toward him with surprisingly sprightly steps. He couldn't help but smile as a brand-new class identifier appeared over George's bobbing head.

Level 58, Agriculturalist

"What can I do for you? You must be hungry! I knew they wouldn't feed you enough." He shot through the three sentences between billowing breaths of exertion.

"No, sir! They are feeding me plenty, and I'm sure that's due to all your hard work producing enough food for all these new hungry mouths," Tilly replied gamely.

At that George's face brightened even further and his eyes took on a clever gleam. "I'm sure you had nothing at all to do with the wall of fire that offered Edna and me this incredible opportunity," he declared happily, leaning in and raising his eyebrows suggestively. "Because of these new classes, we have gained four levels in the last twenty-four hours!" He was almost shouting, punctuating his words with jabs of his fingers into Tilly's chest. "Edna's a dang Arborist now! Our orchard is almost exploding with fruit, and the loggers have taken her out to the camp. Apparently, with her along they produce fifty percent more high-quality timber!"

"No less than you two deserve, I'm sure!" Tilly replied, warmed by the capricious glow emanating from the enthusiastic old satyr.

"Son, I don't think you understand," George said, leaning in as if sharing a secret. "The prerequisite for this class is to have overseen over a hundred acres of agriculturally converted land and successfully produced two hundred percent of its base potential . . . And I was just offered it! Somehow, the system seems to think I had a part in all this happening. Declared my contribution 'Rare.'" He gestured around grandly with a slight tinge of awe coloring his voice.

"George," Tilly said as he laid a hand on the Agriculturalist's shoulder and gently turned him back around. "You are as much a part of this as anyone. Seriously, thank you for your diligence so far. I'm sure the system knows what it is doing." Tilly was surprised to see tears begin to pool at the edges of George's heavily wrinkled eyes.

"Son, even the empire didn't employ an Agriculturalist . . . Every crop I handle in some way increases yield by thirty percent. And I gain *experience* every time any worker under me gains a level . . . I am almost a boon unto myself," he choked out between emerging sobs.

At that moment, Tilly didn't really know what to do. George had probably been a Farmer for longer than Tilly had been alive, never dreaming of such a chance for him and his wife. Tilly's heart went out to the genuine courage this couple had shown, and he felt a deep gratitude welling in his chest that he had been there at the right moment in time to make sure these two had made it through the portal.

Tilly had spent a lifetime working in emergency response, his most consistent kind of patient being the elderly. In all that time, he had learned that there were only really two kinds of old people. By far the most common kind of elderly person was the one who was just a shadow of their younger self, living most of their remaining years looking back in sorrow, bitterness, or both. Society had told them that they were a burden, a drain on a system to which they no longer had anything to offer.

Then there was the much rarer second kind of elderly person. The one who still seemed to want to give as much as they could to their surroundings. However it was gained, the humility and thankfulness evident in their final years always caused them to shine like beacons amidst their surroundings.

George and Edna were probably always going to do whatever they could for those around them . . . And here he was, sobbing before Tilly, overcome by the chance to be able to do even more.

Before Tilly even registered what he was doing, he had wrapped his arms around the much smaller satyr, and George's crying redoubled. He clung to Tilly like a buoy in a storm, and inexplicably, Tilly felt tears welling in his own eyes.

"You're a good boy, you hear!" George's muffled voice emerged from Tilly's furred jacket. For some reason, that did it. A baseball-sized lump rose in Tilly's throat, and no matter how hard he tried, he couldn't swallow it back down. His chest began to shake with the effort, and before he knew it, he was the one crying, leaning into the surprisingly strong satyr's arms.

They stayed like that for a while longer, until the swells of emotion had subsided. George stepped away, wiping his eyes and smiling at Tilly's bemused expression.

"Now, young man, don't tell me you are one of those who think tears aren't manly! A man who can't cry, can't offer his strength to the world around him, he only knows how to hold it all to himself and watch as those weaker than him fail . . . You aren't that kind of man."

Tilly nodded, unable to find any words to respond to George's firm declaration.

"George! There you a—oh, Mr. Tillman . . . I didn't expect to see you here," came a cultured female voice from off to the side. Tilly looked over to find Amelia emerging from the same garden that George had just come from.

"Ah! Mrs. Cooper! I believe this young man was looking for you! I'll go check on the children's progress and see if they need anything while you two catch up," he said, shooting Tilly a wink as he turned to go.

Amelia's eyes narrowed at George as he turned to walk away. Then she swept her gaze over Tilly and took in his red puffy eyes and ruddy cheeks . . .

"You wanted to see me?" she asked, quirking an eyebrow. Despite her outfit being a strange mix between laboratory assistant and safari guide, Tilly couldn't help but notice how at ease she seemed surrounded by growing things. Her simple white blouse was slightly askew under her multipocketed coat and a smear of dirt smudged her nose, but the tension that had characterized her on their first encounter seemed to have been drained away.

"Uh, yeah . . . I, uh, wanted to check on you and . . . ," Tilly said, looking around, a little lost at the sudden shift in conversation. He had come to find Amelia and clear the air, but he hadn't thought through what he was going to say. Sweeping his gaze over the garden, he had to bite back a smile as he spotted George peeking out from around a corner and giving him the universal "get on with it" motion.

Amelia turned her head to spot what had drawn Tilly's attention, but the old man had already disappeared like a ghost.

"Apologize! I wanted to apologize again," he blurted.

A conflicted look crossed her face at his words as she turned back to him. She stuffed her hands in a pair of her many pockets and blew out a long breath through pursed lips. Then after a thoughtful moment, she replied, "No, Jonathan . . . I'm the one who owes you an apology."

"What! No, you saved our lives and almost—"

"Stop! Please," she interrupted, holding up her hands to forestall any objections. "I have only met three other humans in my time here, and all three turned out to be twisted in some disturbing way. When I first met you, part of me was looking for betrayal from the outset . . . Then when it turned out that you were **Corrupted**, well, that was all I needed to write you off."

"No, Amelia. I should have told you. I should have told everyone . . . but I didn't, because I was scared," Tilly confessed in a rush, afraid that if he didn't get it all out, his compromised internal thought process would twist this into some sort of self-righteous pity party.

She wrapped her arms around herself as she struggled to get her own words out the way she wanted them. "Look. I heard how you got infected. It clearly wasn't your fault. Now that I feel it inside of me, nibbling at the edges of my being . . . I can't imagine what it would be like to fight something like this while trying to adjust to an entirely new world. I was scared out of my mind for months when I first arrived, hiding in the caravan, afraid of almost everything I saw. If it wasn't for Grandmother Weaver . . ." She trailed off with a sigh of exasperation, looking off into the distant past.

"Amelia," Tilly said, calling her eyes back to his.

"I get it. You were in an impossible situation, and you didn't need to be dealing with my problems on top of everything else," he said, finding himself inexplicably angry that she didn't seem to understand what he was trying to say. He was trying to apologize! He had been wrong, whatever his excuses were. He had still chosen to hide his situation for selfish reasons. Why couldn't she just accept his apology and they could move on, giving him a chance to prove he could be better?

She continued to stand there, holding herself and staring into his eyes. Whatever she saw there caused her eyes to grow stormy in response.

"'On top of everything else'?" she quoted, the lines of her face compressing into a scowl. "George and Edna told me how you risked your chance at reaching the portal by trying to carry them to safety, *on top of everything else!*" Her anger was now in full display across her features. "If you won't accept my apology, that's fine. But please, try not to be so hypocritical about it!" she spat, then turned on her heels and marched off, leaving Tilly standing there at a complete loss for words.

What just happened?

Eventually, he wandered back through the fields and gardens until he found the bridge again, this time without Franklin. The building crew, however, was already hard at work using the current structure as a support to sink the logs in at spaced intervals for the new wooden bridge. There was another honu there who was splitting the current each time they dropped a new log in, allowing a smaller gnome to be lowered in first to dig out a hole for the foundation of each one.

Tilly watched for a while in silence, trying to process everything he was thinking and feeling as the sun began to set in the distance. Torches were stuck in the ground and along the edges of the bridge so that the crew could keep working, and Tilly crossed the bridge after a while and started walking along the edge of the camp.

He didn't know how he had expected that to go . . . but he had hoped that apologizing again would clear things up, maybe even allow him to ask her some questions about what this world was like from her perspective. But, somehow, he had made things even worse.

Then again, that was how it had always gone with the women in Tilly's life. Why would this be any different? A lifetime of failed conversations flashed through his mind as he gloomily moved through the fog of memories from his marriage.

He continued to stroll around the edge of the camp, not yet ready to head back to his room. In the last glimmer of sunlight, he idly pulled out the gemlike egg from his fantasy fanny pack. He rubbed along its smooth multifaceted surface, wondering again what he was supposed to do with it.

His thumb hitched on something as he passed it back and forth between his hands. Curious, he ran his finger over the spot again and again, confirming a definite break in the smooth finish. Holding it up close to his eyes, he couldn't quite make out what was responsible for the change in sensation.

So, without really thinking about it, he enflamed his left hand and held it up to the gem, trying to get a better look.

CHAPTER EIGHTEEN

Kindle Unlimited

The glow from his enflamed left hand lit up the gem in a thousand iridescent fractals. The effect of the flickering firelight on the object was so mesmerizing that it took Tilly several moments to notice a pulling sensation on the flame around his hand.

Tearing his eyes from the glowing gem, he saw the flame surrounding his hand straining toward it, like iron filings to a magnet.

"What the—" he muttered as he tried to cut off the flow of his mana to his hand.

It didn't work.

He actually felt the flame in his chest stoking higher in response to the pull on his mana. Whatever this was, his flame-aspected mana wanted to connect. As he pushed harder, he realized he could cut off his mana flow, but the mana itself seemed . . . reluctant. The straining flame's wispy edges stretched as hard as they could, falling just short of the gem's surface.

Well, the fire inside me hasn't steered me wrong so far, and this was a quest reward . . .

Tilly's wince of concern softened as he felt something from the gem that reminded him of the mewling noise a kitten would make when it was looking for its mother.

Hunger?

Mystified, Tilly slowly moved his hand closer until the flame's edge touched on the surface of the gem. Upon contact, it was sucked into the tiny crack on the gem's gleaming face. The pull on Tilly's mana pathways did not lessen—if anything, it increased—and he couldn't help but glance up at his mana bar as the gem continued to pull on his flame hungrily.

Tilly watched as his mana ticked down to 80 percent. The glare from the gem had grown noticeably brighter, and it occurred to him that he didn't want anyone coming by to ask what was going on. So, looking around, he hunched over the now happily shining object and started to move away from the tents.

"Man, I hope Nyuk was wrong about you . . . If you look like you are going to explode, I'm jumping into the river, I swear!" he muttered urgently at the object he was trying unsuccessfully to hide under his jacket.

The gem continued to glow brighter, and heaven help him, Tilly found himself smiling at the contented burble it released into his mind as the pull suddenly cut off. Tilly looked around suspiciously at his surroundings, but the far edge of the camp he had wandered through was quiet. At this point, the gem—no, the *egg* had grown as bright as a bonfire. Sapphire-hued light danced through its many facets.

Tilly moved away from the edge of the camp toward the bank of the river, tucking the thing under his leathers. Another contented burble sounded off in his mind, and he shot off a quick plea to **Origin** that this wasn't some sort of cute, sentient bomb.

Once his moccasins hit the sandy edge of the riverbank, he hunkered down and took the gem back out, shielding as much of the light as he could with his body.

"What exactly are you?" he whispered to it.

In response, it started to thrum, then vibrate as the light emerging from its center brightened. Tilly's expression of wonder broke down into a cringe of worry as the small crack burst with an even greater light and began to spread across the surface in a network of fine fractures.

"Please, please, please don't be a bomb," he hissed at the object as the vibrations it was producing built into a crescendo.

Tilly felt? Understood? Heard? He didn't really know how to describe it, but a tiny exultant cry emerged from the back of his mind as the surface of the crystalline egg shattered into a million motes of light.

Blinking his eyes rapidly to try and clear the sudden blindness, he rubbed at them with his other hand.

"*Peep?*"

As his sight returned, he was surprised to find something that looked a lot like a chick standing on his hand, no bigger than a baseball.

"*Peep?*" it said again, giving him that side-cocked one-eyed look that only birds could give. Its down coat was completely white instead of yellow, and its little feet sported surprisingly sharp talons for a newborn.

"What are you?" he asked again.

Then, as if the system had finally decided to throw him a bone, an identifier pinged above its head.

Bonded Newborn Phoenix

No level, but he guessed he would have to figure that out later. For now, he was struck by how unbelievably adorable the little thing was.

"You are way better than some fancy new class, aren't you?" he cooed at the chick as it began to scratch and peck at his hand. Tilly immediately got the impression it was asking for more . . . *food*. Especially since the little talons only mimicked the scratching motion and didn't break the surface of his skin.

Without thinking, he enflamed the hand it was standing on in response to its unspoken request. It chirped happily at finding itself surrounded by the blue fire and began to peck in earnest at the flames dancing around it. Tilly perceived the heat being pulled from around his hand, up into his palm, and then disappearing as the phoenix consumed it.

"What do I call you, little thing?" he asked in delight.

Without breaking off its happy pecking, Tilly felt a complex series of images and sensations move through his mind.

He saw an infinite flat expanse. It was completely dark and cold with nothing to break up its features. Then something changed far in the distance, the darkness lost its heaviness, and the smallest blush of light burst forth. The light wasn't powerful or overwhelming, but in the context of the endless dark expanse, it held a whole universe of meaning.

The chick broke off its pecking as the flame sputtered out, another 10 percent of Tilly's mana gone. It then settled down happily onto his palm.

"Any chance you have a nickname? I don't think that will translate very well into regular speech."

"*Peep!*" the chick trilled offendedly as it cocked its head at him in consternation, then settled down into a seated position to preen itself.

Before he could make any suggestions, he felt its awareness begin to move through his memories like a light illuminating the page of a book. After a few minutes, the chick shook its little head and ruffled its down feathers before tucking its head into its shoulder.

The awareness faded from his mind, and Tilly heard a faint whisper dance at the edge of his consciousness.

She Who Kindles the Dawn.

Then she was asleep, nestled in the palm of his hand, and he couldn't help but smile. He could feel the little creature's complete trust in him as she drifted off. He had been given charge of something helpless and adorable, and as inconvenient as it might turn out to be, he felt her unconditional trust eroding some of his self-doubt.

"Thanks for working so hard to simplify it for me, little one. How about I call you Kindle out loud, but between us, I'll use your full name," he whispered.

The little phoenix didn't reply, and Tilly watched the minute expansion and contraction of her little chest as she settled into a deep rhythmic sleep. Watching her like that called Tilly's attention to his own bone-deep weariness. He had been beaten like a drum, done CPR, and walked all over the Alliance trying to reconnect with the few people he hadn't seen on this side of the portal.

Tucking her into the crook of his arm, slightly out of sight, Tilly headed back to his small one-room shack. He arrived almost an hour after sunset, and he slid open the unlocked door to his small house. As he closed the door on the ever-changing city landscape outside, he wondered for a moment why his small building had remained untouched.

Shrugging to himself, he moved into the room in almost pitch-black darkness and kicked the edge of his bed in the process. He grunted in frustration and Kindle ruffled up her feathers before resettling absently in his hand.

Not wanting to disturb her any further, he crawled into bed and set her against the warm exposed skin of his neck. She chirped sleepily and moved in closer until a light but very noticeable pressure started to expand and contract in the space between his shoulders and his chin. Without further thought or worry, he, too, drifted off to sleep, dreaming about the breaking of dawn and the beginning of things.

The next morning, he awoke to a jabbing in his neck. He jerked back, afraid he was being bitten by a bug.

"Gah!" he gasped as he scrambled sleepily from his bed. A small cry of outrage followed him as he moved from his original position.

"*Peep!*"

Coming completely to wakefulness, the full breadth of yesterday's events hit him, and he looked down at the little phoenix in awe . . .

She looked him dead in the eye and slowly mimed scratching and pecking.

"Oh! Of course. You are hungry!" he said, his eyes wandering around the room and finding his typical breakfast tray and pitcher of water. Man, they were good. How did they always have this ready before he woke?

Kindle followed his glance around the room and found nothing of interest. She peeped at him again to grab his attention and mimed eating, trying to help him understand what she wanted.

"Yeah, yeah! I get it. But we can't just feed you off the heat my flames produce. I can only assume your appetite will grow, so we need to figure out a better system." She eyed him critically, unimpressed by his excuses. "Besides, no way am I going to feed you inside a wooded building. Meals will happen strictly outside!" he said firmly.

Tilly moved over and began to scarf down his food to the outraged sound of more than a few chirped complaints from his new companion. The injustice of his act was clearly more than she could bear. As quickly as he could, he scrambled out the door with Kindle insisting that she should now ride on his shoulder.

When he placed her there, her little claws locked into the material of his jacket and no matter how he moved she stayed happily perched in place. And so, he emerged out into the street with an all-white chick riding on his shoulder like some sort of wannabe pirate.

On his way to the parade ground, he stopped a group of carpenters and asked what they did with their waste pieces of lumber. One of them, a lapin, replied that they were sent into the camp and added to the firewood supply. When Tilly inquired if he could have some delivered to the parade ground each day, the lapin bowed and went off to speak with some of the other workers.

Reassuring Kindle that he did, in fact, have a plan to feed her, he jogged to the parade ground, having realized that the phoenix was not at all bothered by his movements. By the time he arrived, the drilling had already begun, and he could tell he was later than he had been yesterday.

"Baby-Man! Where have you been? Are you scared to fight Gorock?" a booming voice called from beyond the water troughs.

Tilly winced and cleared his throat to try and ease the sudden nervous warmth that rose from his stomach at the thought of several hours with the giant warrior.

"Am I looking forward to it? No," he called as he turned to square up to the Bastion, who, of course, had also received a new class in the aftermath of the quest reward. Except his was different from his companions.

Level 48, Wall Breaker

Gorock stood there, almost twice as tall as Tilly, and looked down at him with a sadistic grin on his goat face . . . or not—Tilly still couldn't read Gorock's expressions. But if he had any money, he would put it all on "sadistic grin."

CHAPTER NINETEEN

Training Day

Kindle ruffled her feathers on Tilly's shoulder.

"*Cheep!*" she cried in anger, eyeing the giant towering above her.

Gorock's eyes shifted in confusion and dilated at the sight of the little chick. He identified the creature and then his goat scowl—smile?—returned in full force.

"You will be very fierce, I think, burning one . . . but not for a while yet!" he answered before bellowing out a laugh that was completely unrestrained by the lack of any discernible humor. Tilly turned his head at the creaking sound of a cart and saw a laborer wheeling a mountain of wooden scraps over to the end of the troughs. He dumped them out with quick, economic movements before turning to go back the way he came.

"Just a second, Gorock," Tilly called as he rushed over to the pile. The still-laughing Wall Breaker just waved him on, winding down from his amusement. Tilly called a thanks over to the laborer, but if he heard, he didn't turn from his route back to the bustling construction going on all over the valley.

Tilly used his foot to shift over a campfire-sized bunch of wood, then enflamed his foot and shoved it into the pile on the packed dirt of the grounds. It took about ten seconds before it was burning merrily.

"Don't take too long playing with your fire, Baby-Man! Gorock is very busy," his booming voice called from the sparring area. "I have many bones to break today."

"Here you go, little lady. This should hold you over while I . . . practice fighting," Tilly whispered, plucking the chick from his shoulder and lowering her into the fire.

As he reached down, Kindle eyed him and Tilly felt the image of her little claws float to the top of his mind.

"No thanks, girl. I'll be fine. It may not look like it, but I am almost one hundred percent sure that guy over there is a friend," he answered. He was surprised to feel his hands begin to burn as they interacted with fire not produced by his mana, but his armor quickly responded by covering his hands with gloves of Sun Salamander hide.

Neat.

Kindle, however, had no problem with the different source of heat, fluffing her down coat and beginning to preen happily as flames licked all around her form. She scratched a little circle before settling down amidst the burning wood.

"Baby-Man!" Gorock called again, his voice having moved from amused to frustrated faster than a toddler denied their snack.

"Just call over if you need something," Tilly said hurriedly before turning around and jogging toward his "teacher" for the day. "Keep your pants on, Gorock! And don't give me any more shit about being busy! I bet if you weren't here, they would send you to carry stone at the wall build," Tilly called as he approached before pulling loose his hatchets and twirling them with all the bravado he did not feel.

This is going to suck. Might as well charge into it blades out.

"GOOD!" Gorock boomed as he laid aside his shield and weapons and gestured an invitation to Tilly with open hands before assuming a boxer stance.

"Come at me, Baby-Man. Use all your tricks and fire and we will see who gives the healer a harder time!" He finished with another burst of disturbing goat laughter. The combination brought to mind a deep human baritone and the sound of a screaming goat.

The weapons lying on the ground at Gorock's feet screamed of supreme confidence . . . and Tilly just shrugged. He was man enough to understand that he would need every advantage he could get, and if this was what the others thought would help him advance the fastest . . . he would give it his all.

Without further hesitation, he set alight and launched both hatchets, then charged almost immediately behind them to the sound of Gorock's bellow of excitement.

Twenty minutes later, both combatants lay on the ground surrounded by charred dirt and splattered blood. Tilly groaned as he tried to take another breath, and the now familiar feeling of fractured ribs grated excruciatingly against his lungs. On top of that, he was pretty sure one of his forearms was shattered. Oh, and his ankle was swollen beyond recognition.

Gorock lay a few feet away, taking short breaths interspersed with giggling fits. His body was covered in burns and he sported several already closing shallow wounds from Tilly's hatchets. He sat up, wiping his eyes as tears of laughter threatened to pool and spill down from his large oblong-iris eyes.

"Baby-Man, that was the most fun I've had in weeks! Are you ready to keep going?" he said, his monstrous constitution already undoing the waxy edges of his biggest patches of burned skin.

Tilly groaned in answer as he looked up at his mana and health.

Health: 42%
Mana: 3%

"No—ugh. Not going to be . . . ready for a while."

Tilly rolled his head over painfully and spotted Kindle fast asleep in the smoldering ashes of the campfire he had made her. Despite everything, he smiled. At least someone was having a good time this morning.

"Now, young one, you take the big stupid one. I'll handle the smaller, slightly less stupid one," a voice called from outside Tilly's range of vision. It took a second, but the cultured voice and clipped tone of disapproval keyed him into the owner just before a cascade of healing fire washed over him.

A comforting warmth suffused his form, concentrated on the places he was most injured. There the warmth heated until it was just south of painful, like slipping into a hot tub on a cold day. A stinging sensation accompanied the reknitting of his bones and the restoration of bruised flesh, and he watched in fascination as his health rapidly climbed back to 100 percent.

With a moan of relief, he sat up just as the priestess cast another *Ability* on him and the slow refilling of his mana started to ramp up to a flood. Before he knew it, he was completely topped off.

But all of that faded out of his immediate attention as his eyes fell on a strikingly familiar young satyr woman casting over Gorock. She had to be in her mid-teens and something about her face tickled Tilly's memory like a mental itch. Yet he couldn't recall meeting a girl of that age in any of his travels so far on Nephesh.

She was wearing priestess robes of a much simpler quality than Erash's and held a plain scepter in her hands.

Level 3, Priestess of Origin's Flame

He continued to stare in muddled confusion, and the young priestess looked up from her focused casting on Gorock to catch him watching. A rosy blush started on her neck and crept up her cheeks as she quickly looked back down. Then in a quiet voice, she said, "Hello again, Mr. Tillman."

Tilly cocked his head, her face maddeningly familiar, and yet he could not recall meeting anyone li—

"A phoenix!" Erash shouted, then rushed over to the still-sleeping bird before turning back toward Tilly incredulously.

"And bonded at that? Human, how did you get your hands on a Mythic elemental?"

Tilly had torn his eyes away from the girl to answer Erash's question when Gorock spoke over him while climbing to his feet.

"The fire loves our little human! You should see what a glorious bomb he makes. It is obviously a gift from our fire god, healer. Now, no more questions! I am teaching him how real warriors fight!" Gorock shook out his arms in readiness.

Looking back and forth between the girl, Gorock, and Erash, Tilly got to his feet as well, dusting off his now fully healed limbs.

"Yeah. That is pretty much it, I think," Tilly muttered before turning back to the young priestess. "I'm sorry, have we met?"

The girl's blush grew brighter as she attempted to stutter out a response. "I saw—you healed—when—"

"Oh, come on, girl!" Erash interjected in frustration. "You are the only one this deity has chosen as a full priestess. Please try and act like you have some backbone." Then, turning toward Tilly, she said, "It is my understanding that you purified this girl, and in doing so, you unlocked an *Ability* by whatever means your class and mantle possess. It is my theory that this imbued her with enough potential to qualify as a candidate." She hurried through this explanation, then, turning back to the fire, she slowed her speech to a more thoughtful pace. "As to the elemental—"

"Her name is Kindle," Tilly interrupted absently, staring at the girl as the pieces came together.

"Yes, well, as to Kindle, you will continue to feed her as much heat and flame as she asks for. Then report to me on her stages of growth. This is an unprecedented opportunity to learn about the—"

"Sorry, ma'am, but I'm not reporting shit to you," he interrupted again, looking back at the priestess in frustration. Then, looking Erash in the eyes, he growled, "I appreciate what you did for Hiro yesterday, and if you have any questions, feel free to ask. But if you expect me to jump at your every demand, it's going to be a long year of service."

Somewhere behind him, Gorock let out an explosive sigh and dropped his arms in disappointment at what was obviously going to be more talking and less fighting.

Tilly continued to stare as Erash bit back a scathing response and looked down at the phoenix with something that might have been envy.

"Very well. I will be checking in on both of you when I see you each morning. This is an immense privilege you have been given, Mr. Tillman. I hope you take it seriously."

Before Tilly could respond, a small voice interrupted from Gorock's side. "Mr. Tillman, I snuck up to the Temple last night. I know I am too young to get a class, but I wanted to help. I hoped that the one who had given you the power to save me would be able to do something," she said hesitantly, and as she looked up and saw that he was listening, she went on. "I was offered something called a Covenant. I gave up the rest of my childhood and the possibility of ever taking another class. In return, I am the only other member of the Alliance who has been offered anything above the rank of acolyte to the Temple," she concluded, having grown bolder as she finished telling her story.

"Why would y—" Tilly tried to ask, but Gorock had had enough.

"Gah! Talk later. Now we fight!" he bellowed, then stomped his foot and lifted his fists into a boxing stance once again.

The young priestess immediately began to back away from the sparring area, to Erash's side, but even as she retreated, she called over, "Don't worry about me, Mr. Tillman. It was my choice, and now I have a Rare class with the possibility of even greater opportunities in the future. Plus, I think we both know that my childhood ended before I met you . . . At least now I have a chance to do something to help those I care about."

Sorrow welled up in him as he watched Erash put a hand on the girl's shoulder and lead her to other sparring areas. There was no doubt that what she was doing was incredibly brave . . . But the small part of his heart that had been a father ached at the thought of the little girl giving up the rest of her childhood.

Channeling the heady mix of feelings into resolve, he turned back to Gorock. In the face of her determination, he couldn't do anything but his best.

"Alright, you big goat! All I have been hearing from you is whining. That's real funny considering you keep calling me a baby!" he called out as he summoned his hatchets back into his hands and wreathed his whole body with flame.

"HA!" Gorock shouted in delight before charging forward in response.

CHAPTER TWENTY

Boot Camp

The rest of that morning was every bit as brutal as Tilly imagined it would be. Erash had to stop by a couple more times to put him back together, but by the end of the morning, Tilly entered into meditation with a lot to process and even more understanding about the shortcomings and potential of his build. Ideas that had begun to form over the couple of sparring sessions with Ichiro solidified as he smashed them against the massive brick house that was Gorock.

Against swarm and mob-type enemies, he ended up filling more of a DPS role, using his flames and especially his bonus against **Corruption** to devastating effect. However, the dynamic needed to completely change if he was facing a single, much stronger opponent. That was doubly true for his sparring partners, who were affected by his fire as if it was just normal flame, negating the bonus that he had come to take for granted.

That's not to say that his flames had no effect. Over the course of the morning, Tilly started to see the power of the stacking aspect of his *Ability* against an opponent who had more of a tendency to tank his hits than to dodge them. By the end of their final session, Gorock was covered by smaller but still smoldering wounds that continued to damage him long after Tilly was incapacitated.

Of course, all of this was only possible against a weaponless Gorock. That was okay with Tilly, though; he doubted he was expected to be able to beat the Wall Breaker, especially this early in his training. Rather, this pairing was probably chosen to force him to adapt his style to the other end of the spectrum of opponents he might face.

Against an opponent like Gorock, he would have to move more into a dodge or tank role. He wasn't nearly fast enough to fulfill the role yet, but leaning into his flame *Abilities* to distract and wound rather than dealing big hits seemed to be what would work best.

Eventually, as he grew, his *Dexterity* would begin to stand out, but until then, he would have to be extra tricky to stay alive. Along that line of thought, he had even started popping random flashes of flame on other parts of his body during combat to try and make his movements more confusing to follow. For his trouble he had eaten a couple of thick knuckle sandwiches, but not before causing Gorock to flinch one or two times. Against such an experienced combatant, he would take that as a win.

Tilly returned to the field after meditation and lunch, which he made sure included a fresh stack of burning wood for the hungry phoenix chick. She was definitely in her infant stage of development and seemed content to eat and sleep as much as possible. But when the next patrol of Ranger trainees gathered, Kindle peeped excitedly and settled onto Tilly's shoulder for the next portion of the training.

Nyuk met the group and explained that Kuro had been out all morning patrolling and that Ichiro would lead another group out that night. The squad Tilly was standing with had all once owned a class that involved either a ranged weapon or spending a lot of time in the forest. When news came that new classes were available to those who had not been offered them initially, they had all made the journey to the Temple.

This, however, meant that everyone, including Nyuk, was missing some key aspects of a Ranger tool set. Nyuk explained that he knew the forest well, but his ranged weapon skill was barely half of what Tilly had on his sheet. This meant that, instead of instructing, Nyuk simply participated as others from the group demonstrated essential skills for the Ranger build. He assigned a trapper to teach the basics of stealth and a hunter to instruct on ranged weapon basics.

The close combat, however, he led himself, highlighting the differences between fighting a humanoid opponent with a weapon and facing down one of the denizens of the forest. He had numerous stories from his time in the logging camp, and Tilly began to realize that the two Hiro had selected to join him on his suicide mission had actually been the best suited in the village to see him to the **Corrupted** Temple and back again.

After the basics, but before they left for the forest, they moved through the newly constructed obstacle course, made at the edges of the grounds for dexterity-focused builds. Some of the challenges in the course would have been impossible for any normal human without any additional variables. But Nyuk insisted they navigate the course while carrying their weapons at the ready. Even the ex-hunter of the group had trouble scaling the wall and crawling through tunnels while keeping his bow in hand.

Once everyone made it through the course, Nyuk informed them that in a couple of days, they would advance to attempting the course while being fired upon by the other Ranger trainees. Then, mid-course, they would have to pinpoint the threat and fire back while still navigating obstacles. This would increase several skills at once, and while it sounded like another way to gain puncture wounds, Tilly couldn't help but look forward to it. At level sixteen, his **Ax Throwing** skill was the third highest in the group, and he was the only one used to releasing projectiles on the move.

Tilly found himself enjoying this aspect of training much more than he expected as he pushed his new body and stats to the limits of speed and fluidity while keeping one of his hatchets in hand. In fact, the only one who seemed to enjoy the course more than Tilly was Kindle, who trilled in excitement, clinging to Tilly as he moved over, under, and through the obstacles at increasing speeds.

When Nyuk announced it was time to leave, she let out a peep of disappointment before being hushed by Tilly. They picked up rations on the way out and moved off to the edge of the valley, then entered the forest and hiked another mile to the boundary of their territory.

This was the first time Tilly got to see the edge of the boon's effect himself. Goosebumps ridged the skin on his forearms as he watched a breeze move through the trees around him only to stop at an invisible line twenty feet further up the mountain. Past that point, everything seemed frozen . . .

Well, not *frozen*, exactly. Tilly caught sight of a branch falling in the distance and watched in fascination as it descended to the ground as if slowly lowered on a rope. Looking up, Tilly caught sight of a tan-furred squirrel the size of a dog slowly arcing through the air away from where the branch had just fallen.

"To them, we are moving at twenty-four times our normal speed. Our voices sound like a high-pitched whine, and as long as we keep moving, our forms will be blurred with speed. But for our purposes, none of that matters. We will spread out in pairs and follow this border toward the sunset. You are to stay completely hidden from the rest of the patrol as we move, and in the future, all patrols will move in pairs.

"The goal is to train **Stealth** and get you as familiar with this forest and mountain range as possible. Tomorrow we will have the night shift and set up camp."

Tilly collapsed into bed that night only to get up and do it all again the next day. His days were a blur of pain, exhaustion, and slowly increasing skills. Through it all, he squeezed his proportionally high *Endurance* for all it was worth, training under or against people two or three times his level and milking the skill-leveling bonus for all it was worth. His crazily proportioned *Endurance* stat showed its mettle the first time Tilly took an arrow from a distant patrolling Ranger trainee.

It felt like he had taken a moderate punch from a small fist, but the arrowhead didn't even break the skin. Compared to a swing from Gorock or a blade strike from Ichiro, the attack seemed almost laughable. That was until Kuro chewed him out loudly, telling him the point of the exercise was to be unseen, not to become a "smiling-idiot-target." He punctuated his point with several bow shots, hitting Tilly's back with considerably more force. These blows against his back felt much stronger but still didn't break his skin. The ex-logger was considerably stronger than the other trainees, but until his **Archery** skill improved, he wouldn't be able to leverage it very much.

Each morning they would pair him up with a sparring partner, or partners, and have him fight with different limitations. Sometimes he was up against a group of twenty of the new soldiers, evading being cornered and taking as many out of the fight as possible before he was incapacitated. In these matches, it was more about anticipating group dynamics and causing maximum chaos than it was about avoiding hits, most of which could no longer hurt him from the lower-level combatants.

On other mornings, he would be paired against one or two much more skilled opponents. These sessions focused more on adapting to different combat styles and an overall sharpening of his combat senses than his ability to deal damage against a mob. When it came to the Bastion veterans or a few of the other elites of their force, Tilly was still taking grievous wounds after each sparring session.

Erash or Aurelia—the young priestess who had been supernaturally aged into her class—would inevitably have to stop by his sparring area three or four times before the morning was done. Each time they made sure Tilly's health was topped off and he had plenty of mana to keep going.

He couldn't say it got any easier, but he did experience his mind slowly hardening to the pain and shock of what would have been debilitating injuries in his old life. In this world, a single broken extremity was barely an excuse to rest. Instead, he found that with his *Endurance,* even when his mind was screaming at him to stop, he could push his body far past what it should be capable of, especially in instances of injury or exhaustion.

The meditation helped with this immensely, and he found his *will* intervening for him in times of immense duress more and more often. With it, he was able to leap forward to capitalize on an opening even with a shattered femur or turn away strikes that should have demolished his guard. His *Strength* was dismal and he avoided direct contests in the stat whenever possible, but having one more option to shore it up in combat was a welcome surprise.

He didn't see the white flame again, but he could feel himself becoming a much more dangerous combatant as his hard limits became malleable through the combination of his emerging combat instinct and his disproportionate *Endurance.* He also found his skill levels advancing at an astonishing rate, even with the boon accounted for, and when he had taken Ichiro aside to ask him about it, the lapin had just winked. Clearly, there was more to this meditation style than just a "family technique."

His patrols with the Rangers pushed his non-combat skills hard as well. They began moving in long lines along the border, separated by twenty or thirty feet, and tried just as hard to spot each other as they did any threats to the Alliance. This was made even more harrowing by the live-fire policy the instructors had put in place. This boosted their distance combat skills and **Stealth** gains immensely, but it also resulted in Tilly frequently putting his new **First Aid** skill to use. Most unempowered distance attacks did little against his *Endurance,* but for other trainees they were devastating. Tilly found himself carrying an entire extra bag of bandages and supplies when they went out to compensate. Not that he could heal anyone, but he was slowly coming to terms with the fact that it didn't really matter on Nephesh. His skill level was high enough to cancel any normal active debuff besides **Internal Bleeding**, and once the ongoing damage was taken care of, he found his patients recovering enough to walk in an hour at most.

But injury didn't change the exercise. Nyuk, Kuro, and Ichiro insisted on continuing even while carrying the injured. In fact, they would frequently elect the best at stealth or distance attacks to carry the wounded, further handicapping them and pushing their skill gains even higher.

After twenty grueling days of almost non-stop training, Tilly's skills had skyrocketed.

---

*-**Forestcraft** level 12 > 18*

*-**Identify** level 17 > 19*

*-**Cooking** level 12*

*-**Beginner Hatchet** level 14 > 28*

*-**Animal Processing** level 9*

*-**Stealth** level 7 > 18*

*-**Herb Lore** level 3 > 5*

*-**Ax Throwing** level 16 > 30*

*-**Dual-Wielding (Hatchets)** level 11 > 24*

*-**Spirit Walk** level 14*

*-**Meditation** level 7 > 12*

*-**First Aid** level 35 > 38*

CHAPTER TWENTY-ONE

A Dark Horizon

Tilly wasn't the only one with impressive gains during this time. The few thousand refugees and lapins that had chosen the Flame's Watch class drilled relentlessly. They kept an intense rolling schedule of eight-hour shifts around the clock: eight hours of training, eight of rest, and eight guarding the wall construction in the gap.

There, Hiro stood vigil against the eventual reprisal of the enemy, but thankfully, only occasional groups of **Corrupted** Strigoi were spotted from the new fortification over the first twenty days of the boon. No further elites were spotted. Whatever hierarchy existed in this new faction, it needed more than a dozen hours to organize the next investigation into the Alliance's territory.

After the first ten days, and almost eighty hours of training, the one hundred fighter units could almost seamlessly move between several of the formations Tilly had seen the Bastions employ in defense of the front gates of the capital. Then they began sparring drills in earnest along with mock battles, turning the practice area outside the city into a proving ground of sweat and blood.

The "mock" battles between units pushed the few Acolytes of Flame to their limits and frequently required Erash's intervention to restore a unit to full health so they could continue training. Most units had a Bastion veteran at their head, with the ten best soldiers in the unit elected as squad leaders. The unit instructors were brutal in their training, inflicting wounds as often as yelling at those they felt needed discipline.

Yet even this was mild compared to the rotations where Gorock faced off against one of the units himself. The Wall Breaker proved his name over and over, shattering shields and formations alike. He held nothing back, nearly killing many of his opponents despite the close supervision of Erash.

Nothing impressed on Tilly just how abnormal his *Endurance* was for his level more than watching Gorock shatter every bone in the body of a level twenty-one

Flame's Watch soldier who hesitated in bringing up his shield before a sudden charge by the Wall Breaker. Erash had been called over to another sparring field, and the acolytes simply weren't strong enough to reverse the damage before he bled out, leaving the soldier to shudder out a few last weak, gasping breaths.

Tilly had rushed over, but even at level thirty-eight, **First Aid** was completely useless against so many damaged internal organs. This small tragedy didn't impede the mock battle at all. The whole unit continued to try and wound Gorock to end the exercise. This was not to say that they were unaware; Tilly observed with hard eyes that none of the others failed to bring their shield to bear in the following attacks from the Wall Breaker.

Tilly thought about saying something to the Bastion in the heat of the moment, but he was finally learning some restraint. Conditions like this would have been atrocious back home, but here, facing extinction, it was just seen as a necessary loss in the process of survival. Tilly didn't have to like it, but he was done dying on small hills when they clearly faced a far greater enemy.

This intense preparation almost immediately began to show its worth as the frequency of enemy appearances beyond the wall began to increase. A leaderless group of **Corrupted** Strigoi were more like beasts than any sort of sentient social group. As soon as they spotted the wall being built in the distance, they would immediately sprint toward it and attack the closest living beings with abandon. Shuji postulated that at lower levels this class was driven by an insatiable hunger and was not capable of normal intelligence. This caused them to disregard numbers and fortifications each time they charged, howling in glee, their maws slathered with black-flecked drool at the appearance of new prey.

Hiro treated these groups as intense leveling opportunities for the units stationed with him at the wall. He refused to intervene in the fights if the group of Strigoi was less than ten strong, and even then he would only intervene if a soldier's life was on the line. Each Strigoi was more than a match for three or four of the Alliance's new soldiers, but this only pushed their unit tactics and skills to new levels as they faced a dire threat together. The **Corrupted** vampiric race was freakishly strong despite their emaciated forms, and black ichor oozed from their claws and mouths like venom, making any strike a threat to life.

A priestess was always called after these fights to cleanse the **Corruption** left in wounds now that every strike taken from an enemy resulted in infection. Thankfully, the new Flame's Watch class came with some inherent resistance to the infection, which slowed its spread noticeably, and very few soldiers came close to full consumption before the priestess's arrival.

After the twenty days of brutal rotation of battle and training, the Three-Fold Alliance could field a force much more combat-hardened than any commander on Earth could have ever dreamed of. The new Ranger force averaged level twenty, but this number was intentionally deceptive due to the uncommonly high skill levels each member of the new Ranger corps hid behind their low level. The average Flame's Watch soldier had a more balanced power display, averaging level thirty-two, and the benefit of *experience* gains from real combat at the wall construction site.

Even Kindle had started growing lustrous azure and white feathers. She couldn't yet glide, but she could now light the fire of her own meals. Tilly had to keep a close eye on her after she had decided to have a midnight snack in his little room around day eight of training.

As hopeful as the population had been at the onset of building a new home, the reality of Nephesh's nature was not lost on any of them. While many were still working toward the development of logistical necessities for a population of their size, the evidence of preparation for war was everywhere.

Everyone who had even the barest skill in smithing was working around the clock to equip the new force with some sort of consistent kit. The quarry with a mine in its depths was alive day and night with the sound of workers swinging away to loosen more of the Land's precious bounty. Car-sized blocks of stone were transported as soon as they were cut by groups of a special class called Teamsters. Masons would receive a new block and get it into place, making sure it fit seamlessly with the design.

Franklin was based at the wall around the clock diverting the river and assisting with ice-constructed scaffolding whenever they started on a new section. Tilly even spotted Amelia a few times on patrol, doing something at the boon's boundary. She was wielding a new staff with a green crystal on its end and channeling what felt to be impressive amounts of mana into the plants lining the invisible barrier.

He thought about breaking protocol to go speak to her, but almost as if he could read minds, Ichiro slid up next to him and asked him not to interfere.

"The High Priestess and Mrs. Cooper have devised a very clever protection for our unwalled boundary, which should give us time to respond if anything tries to approach from a more circumspect angle. But from my understanding, it is very difficult. Perhaps it would be best if you let her continue."

They only had two days left on the boon when the enemy's true reprisal appeared on the horizon. The disappearance of what had added up to over a thousand Strigoi had not gone unnoticed. By the time the sun set outside the boundary on the twenty-second hour of outer time, the enemy's full response had materialized. Training was called to a halt, and Tilly, along with the rest of the elites of the Three-Fold Alliance, was called to the wall for an emergency conference.

Meeting on top of the seventy-foot fortification, they surveyed the enemy in grim silence. The wall had nearly been completed: twenty feet thick with a four-foot layer of ice coating the enemy-facing surface of the structure. The field in front of them was choked with a muddy delta as the aptly named Silver River poured out its contents endlessly from under the wall into the down-sloped fields of withered grass and sparse, stunted trees.

The only things left to be constructed were the stairs leading off the back. In his old life, Tilly would have considered this an impregnable fortification. But now, facing a horizon that had turned as dark as a stormy sea, it didn't seem like nearly enough. Even Tilly knew he could scale the walls with the heads of his hatchets, given a little time. He doubted it would be able to do anything but slow down any warriors fielded by the vampiric faction. The wall would be an impediment, nothing more, but one he would much rather have than not.

"Shuji, is there anything else you can tell us?" Hiro asked in a quiet but intense voice.

"I'm afraid not. With our teleport still down, we are cut off from any information networks I might use, and without a base of one of the larger continent-spanning factions . . . we are limited in our abilities to gain any further knowledge of our foe."

"Erash, have your people faced anything like them?" Linus asked as he turned to face the grim High Priestess, who was muttering under her breath and watching the distant army like a coiled snake. She answered Linus without turning from their dark ranks.

"No, Consul. My nation is a special case, balanced within ourselves and constantly at war with each other. If not for my education in the various magics, I would not have heard of vampirism at all . . . But perhaps there is something I can do." She looked thoughtful, then lifted her staff and began to mutter under her breath again as the air in front of the group shivered just beyond the edge of the wall.

Then, raising her voice with a final authoritative declaration, she thumped her staff on the ground and the blurriness in front of them snapped into clarity; a huge lens of air now focused in on the enemy line ten or twenty miles away like it was only a hundred feet.

"Do not try to **Identify**, it will give away the scrying. Instead, wait a moment and I will display what my *Abilities* tell me," she said hurriedly as the seemingly endless horde of enemies gradually came into sharp relief.

Tilly had to fight to turn off his now almost unconscious use of the skill that had become so central to his life on Nephesh. Before him, masses of enemies came into view, and at first, Tilly thought the makeup of the force thundering toward them in slow motion was arrayed at random.

But as Erash panned the view to survey the force, a pattern started to emerge, one that was only confirmed by the slowly populating identifiers that appeared within the circle over the different warrior class types.

The most numerous were the same kind of creatures they had already been facing in sporadic attacks on the wall. But as he focused in to look at one in particular, a line of information popped up next to the identifier, and Tilly's eyes widened at what must have been Erash's high-level skills and *Abilities* at work.

Level 35, Strigoi—Base soldier of the Ravenous Horde—Used as scouts or fodder

As the view continued to pan, Tilly began to spot another kind of soldier. For about every fifty of the standard emaciated bald nightmares, there was a huge, bloated caricature of the same creature, standing alone in a little island of emptiness. Tilly wondered why until one of them snatched up a normal Strigoi that had wandered too close. It shoved the struggling creature into its oversized mouth and chomped down ferociously.

Level 47, Strigoi Flesh Bag—Base shock troops of the Ravenous Horde, protected by thick layers of putrefied flesh—Used for damage absorption

Then there were the stringy-haired elites Nyuk had mentioned, the first of the horde Tilly had seen wearing any sort of armor.

Level 75, Strigoi Consumer—Elite troops of the Ravenous Horde, typically charged with commanding one to five hundred base members of the horde—Used as unit command and mage search and destroy

Then, suddenly, the slow panning by Erash's ability hit a huge break in the formation and moved along empty land for a hundred or so yards before stopping at two figures. As it beheld them, the ability started to strain and bend under the pressure exuded by the targets.

The first figure was a giant version of the Flesh Bags. It towered a story and a half over the second figure, almost as wide as it was tall, and was glacially lumbering forward on elephantine legs draped with grotesque layers of still-bleeding flesh. Its huge maw crammed full of teeth was even more disturbing for its proportional largeness in comparison with the rest of the body.

Level 98, Dimitrov the All-Consuming – ???

The second figure was almost human in size and skeletal, but it was difficult to tell due to the layers of black tattered cloth it had draped itself in.

Level 84, Vamp—

Tilly watched as the populating text suddenly stopped and, chillingly, even bound to one twenty-fourth the speed of normal existence, the figure's head whipped up to stare right at them.

Its face was wrapped with what looked to be blood-soaked bandages, but its eyes and mouth were left visible. Seeming to somehow spot their little group, its thin lips parted in a horrifying parody of a smile, revealing two-inch-long teeth set in double rows. Dead, fishlike eyes glittered in amusement, and Tilly's feet were suddenly stuck to the stone as those eyes started to glow red and screaming started to crash into Tilly's consciousness. He felt twin trails of wetness cutting down his cheeks and his throat grew raw.

The figure's presence pushed through Erash's *Ability*, and some sort of mental connection was formed between the observers and the observed. The blue and green runes forming the outer edge of the spell started to warp and twist as a rust-colored energy filled them. Tilly hardly saw any of this as the force of the figure's stare continued to slam into him, drowning his consciousness with a *will* unlike anything he had ever felt.

The **Corruption** in Tilly's side writhed in glee as all of Tilly's hard-fought mental defenses crumbled and a despair as deep as the ocean drowned Tilly's mind in an animal-like panic. Its tendrils began to encircle his heart and lungs, reaching into his extremities, eager to take control. Those eyes took in the group on the wall and found them wanting as the bandaged figure poured all of its hatred and terrible hunger into their minds and hearts.

Then another voice rose above the screaming. Harsh words filled with a potent mix of defiance and authority hit the spell circle, which had almost entirely shifted to a muddy reddish color, and shredded it, breaking the magical connection. Tilly collapsed onto the floor, his figure not the only one to have found a boneless relief on the cold surface of quiet stone.

CHAPTER TWENTY-TWO

Whispering Eye

Asoft muttering filled his consciousness like a pleasant conversation overheard from the next room, and the darkness receded. Tilly's eyes flickered open to find Erash standing over him, looking concerned, her perfect features marred by two red stains running from her tear ducts past her chin and down her neck. The pleasant feeling left him as her magic returned to the flame on top of her staff, leaving his mind feeling black and somehow twisted in on itself. Even flashes of what had just happened to him left him feeling like a used garbage bag.

Kindle ruffled her almost complete coat of feathers in concern and cooed questioningly near his face, her bright blue eyes looking deeply into his. She sent an impression of a predator and taking shelter. Honestly, Tilly couldn't agree more in that moment.

"Jonathan Tillman, are you alright?" Erash called, and Tilly realized this was not the first time she had asked. He noticed she still stood above him with her staff ready.

Tilly struggled for an answer, his thoughts slow and thick. Eventually, he focused on his HUD and his blood froze in his veins.

Corruption's Influence: 34%

Shit. Shit. Shit. Tilly's mind seemed stuck on a horrified loop as the reality of his situation tried and failed to sink in. Kindle trilled in concern, rubbing her head into his hair in an abortive attempt at comfort, but Tilly was too dazed to take it in.

All of his meditation, all his work, trampled by that . . . thing. Ten percent of his agency gone in an instant. He mutely lifted his hand to the wetness running down his face from his eyes, nose, and ears. Whatever that was, it had fucked him up good.

"I'm still me . . . if that is what you are asking," he groaned out slowly, looking at the red smeared across his palm after his unsuccessful attempt to wipe some of it away.

Erash nodded in relief, then straightened up and looked around at the others, who, with the exception of Hiro, seemed to have undergone a similar if less intense trial.

"That was mind magic on a level I have never experienced, and that is saying something. I am sorry for not anticipating this reprisal. This failure is unacceptable," she uttered with a slightly lost look in her eyes as she addressed the group in apology. "I could ha—"

"We needed more information, and you gave us much more than we could have hoped. I would rather face an attack like this now than in the coming battle with no warning," Hiro interrupted gruffly, hand on his sword as he stood at the edge of the wall observing the coming enemy.

"Well, whatever that thing was, **Corruption's** influence over me increased by another ten percent," Tilly spat bitterly as he got to his feet and pulled up his stats and new debuff and buff numbers.

Status Effects:

Minor Corruption [Hidden] *-24% Wisdom +16% Strength*

That put his *Strength* at 15.8 and his *Wisdom* at 13.68.

He swung his arms around gingerly, feeling the new coiled strength that the interwoven tendrils had added to his shoulders and thighs. The network had begun to stretch into his extremities and lend its unwanted power to his movements. At the same time, he could feel the increased drain on his mana regen as the infection arduously took and converted a portion of Tilly's power to continue its invasive growth.

Ichiro turned toward the group as if just now noticing them, having been lost in his thoughts and whatever his eyes were showing him above the coming battlefield. "I am afraid that whatever power that creature is wielding, it is melded almost perfectly with the Abomination's taint. I could see the **Weave** itself unraveling as its influence touched us," he said as he wiped the blood from his face.

"Well . . . what is . . . our plan?" one of the honu elders asked, her voice heavy with the weight of what they faced, her lined face showing only the faintest evidence of the mental attack.

Hiro considered their words, still looking out over the wall at the far distant horde, slowed to a crawl by the magical haste of the boon.

"With this new information, we have a chance to structure our defense and maximize our advantages. The fact that they have a class dedicated as 'fodder' tells me that they will spend their superior numbers to weaken us and then strike with their elites to take out any magical support we have. They outnumber us ten to one. But with the time **Origin's** boon has bought us, we have gained a far superior position," he said, then turned from the edge of the wall and looked back at Tilly. "None of this changes the ultimate outcome of this fight. We will fight defensively and be ground down by their least valuable troops until they can break us wide open. As it stands now, without support from other parts of the continent, without the ability to resupply, and without the bonus of a standing army, there is no chance for victory." His hard eyes bored into Tilly. "We need that Facet, Jonathan Tillman. Is there not anything else you can do to locate it?"

"I have tried playing through the memories of my encounter with it during meditation but found nothing there. I think I have seen it a few more times in my dreams, but I can't remember any of them when I wake. I have even gone to the Temple a few times, but all that I get is the same flame and altar experience as everyone else . . . I'm sorry, but I don't think I have made any progress on that front."

Then Ichiro's eyes snapped up.

"Did you not say that after the explosion in the battle before the capital gates, you gained a spiritual skill? Have you tried it since arriving here?"

"No, I have been so focused on combat and survival that it didn't—" Then Tilly smacked his bloody hand on his forehead. "The threads! The last time I activated **Spirit Walk**, I was able to follow a thread to the Facet's location. But it disappeared after the nexus closed. I should have thought of this earlier." He growled in frustration and settled back down into a seated position while Kindle hopped around him curiously.

"*Cheep?*"

The whole group was focused on him now, and as he started to deepen his breathing, he explained, "I'm going to meditate and then activate the skill. Hopefully, those two will synergize and I will be able to get you more information. I'm going to try and find whatever connection I stumbled upon last time I was in my spirit form."

His breathing fell into the rhythm that had become almost second nature after hours of daily practice over the last weeks. He fell deeper into his meditative state and the group around him began to split off, planning for the coming assault. Their words drifted in and out of his consciousness as he settled himself into a state of acceptance and calm.

"Food is no longer a problem, but we will need to establish a supply depot . . ."

"We will rotate two units at a time at the edge of the wall, three deep, and hold the Bastions in reserve for any breaks, along with two of the three squads of Rangers . . ."

Inhale. Hold.

Exhale. Hold.

Finally, when he was fully settled into his environment and had worked through accepting his body and the changes it had just experienced, he activated **Spirit Walk**.

The disjointed feeling of moving *sideways* through physical space to enter into something parallel but not the same still somehow felt nauseating. Nonetheless, Tilly's spirit detached from his body and looked down to find the thread connecting him back to his physical form had grown much thicker. It now looked to be a complicated braid of fibers made up of . . . well, himself.

Or at least whatever he was made up of in his spirit form. He looked down at his ghostly body and found that, unlike the tether back to his body, his spirit form had not improved since the battle. But it seemed that the meditation had helped him ground his spirit form to his physical state more securely. He knew instinctively that the added strength of this connection would make the return to his body much faster if he ever needed to cross great distances in his spirit form again.

He raised his spirit eyes from his bodily connection and looked around, finding everyone but Ichiro still engaged in planning as if nothing had changed. Ichiro was looking in Tilly's general direction with a middle-distance look in his eyes, and Tilly wondered how much he was seeing . . . He waved at the lapin but got no response before turning to the advancing enemy.

Tilly saw a dark chaotic cloud of writhing static accompanying their advance, like a storm head rolling over the endless sky of the Midwest, in the United States. It was pure chaos . . . Unlike the feel of the blood ritual from the nagas, which had been malignant but consistent in form, this felt . . . broken. Like it had once held its own pattern, but that pattern had dissolved and left behind a corrosive momentum of *undoing*. It gave the impression of the snapping of strings or the rusting of metal, moving through the existing order and unmaking it. If Tilly could have shivered, he would have as he realized that in his spirit form, he was just another pattern to be unwoven in the face of that cloud's momentum.

Thankfully, at this distance he couldn't pick out any specific signatures or forms in the advancing force and was glad he didn't have to face the spiritual reflection of the owner of those insane red eyes.

He shook his insubstantial head to try to focus and assumed his meditative pose again, floating a couple of feet above his body. He couldn't breathe in this form, but something about sitting like this helped him concentrate. He also realized that closing his eyes did nothing to reduce the input of his surrounding environment. Nonetheless, he allowed himself to drift, taking in his surroundings without fighting them. A steady feeling of rightness was flowing past him from behind the wall, washing all the land in its presence. Tilly could tell the feeling originated from the flame in the mountain. It felt warm, bright, and steady. Now that he noticed it, he had a hard time imagining what this place would be like without its presence. Almost as real as the wall under their feet, the formation of energy coming from the Temple felt sturdy and ready to face the coming threat.

He let the feeling of that strength wash over and through him as his senses sharpened, and he detected a glowing thread of light between him and the flame. His awareness of the connection faded in and out; Tilly found it impossible to focus on it specifically, like a figure you could see out of the corner of your eye but was gone when you turned to look.

This was made even more difficult by the ripples of corrosive force that emanated from the vampiric horde. Even at this distance, he could feel it trying to eat away at the boundaries of the Alliance's area of influence.

Tilly floated there as he tried to find a hint of something, anything that could lead them to the next Facet, another piece of **Origin's** influence on the plane. The longer he sat there, the more nuanced and layered his understanding of the effects of the environment on his spiritual self became. With the added benefit of his meditative introspection, he took in the spiritual realm around him, slowly gaining greater insights as his environment met the boundaries of his spiritual self.

This form of him held no shadow of **Corruption**, which was encouraging, but as he focused on his physical body, he could feel the force of its anchor-like hold there. It was a sentient tumor, constantly broadcasting a tooth-grinding hatred paired with a bottomless hunger, which even now was attempting to gnaw away at the edges of his body and soul.

His awareness sank deeper into his spirit self until he felt like he was observing the skin of his spirit form on a micro level. From his magnified perspective, he saw that the boundary layer of his spirit was woven from millions of tiny fibers, and he understood that the tighter the weave, the more resistant to outside influence he would become.

This became clear to him as he watched different parts of the woven structure begin to unravel before the external pressures of the chaotic environment, then be renewed and firmed by another force. Every section that was undone and then restored was strengthened minutely, and he wondered if he was actively watching as his skill progressed in real time.

The source of this restorative force had an unmistakable feel of otherness to it. Unlike the pressure of the coming cloud of chaos and undoing, this energy washed over him subtly, on a different wavelength altogether. It kept fading before he could sense it directly, but Tilly continued to observe, undaunted, as his spirit form was assaulted and then remade in a thousand minute battles of influence.

At some point he entered a dreamlike state of awareness, and the part of him that was only awake while he slept realized that these encounters were not random but were happening in sequence with a strange sort of rhythm. It was wild and almost unpredictable, but at the same time familiar. Tilly's spirit eyes popped open, and he smiled. He had finally realized what he was seeing, or more specifically, *hearing.*

Then, as if his realization turned on a switch, he was suddenly able to hear the music faintly surrounding him all over again. It called him to grow, thrive, and flourish. It was the very same melody that had perfused the hidden valley and drawn him to the Flower in his encounter weeks ago.

Tilly stopped trying to actively observe and instead started to *listen,* letting the effect of the restorative music wash over him. After an indeterminate amount of time enjoying the song, he realized he had begun leaning forward toward it.

Toward it!

He could feel the direction it was coming from! Yet as soon as that fact sunk in, another crashed in with it, shattering his concentration and deafening his perception of the song.

It was coming from directly behind the force arrayed against them, leading straight into the middle of the horde's lands.

CHAPTER TWENTY-THREE

Putting a Team Together

Like stepping into a cold shower, the realization that he would have to head straight into enemy lands to find another Facet of **Origin** shocked him free of his meditative state. Before he knew it, he slammed back into his body and sat up retching as the sensations of the physical world momentarily overlapped with his spiritual perceptions.

Kindle squawked in protest, having settled to sleep on his warm chest during the break. She quickly relocated to his shoulder as he tried to collect himself. The notification icon had started flashing as he came to, and he opened it to try and get his mind off his rolling stomach.

Congratulations! *You have uncovered significant truths of the spiritual realm.*

Spirit Walk *level up! Level 15 . . .*

Spirit Walk *level up! Level 17*

It was good to see his work in **Meditation** have such an immediate impact on another skill. Tilly cleared the screen, mulling over just how complicated cleansing his infection had become, let alone giving the Alliance a chance to survive. The group standing nearby had thinned considerably while he had been out, and Tilly was surprised to note from the position of the sun that it was now early afternoon, much of the next day having already passed. Ichiro, Hiro, and now Franklin headed over when they saw he was back with them.

"Sorry, that took longer than I expected," Tilly croaked, swallowing down another wet burp, then offered Kindle a few comforting strokes before getting to his feet. Touching her felt like touching a silk sheet fresh from the dryer: it was all smooth warmth, and he couldn't help but stroke her feathers every time she perched on him.

"I can see you have an answer for us. What is it?" Hiro asked, his inscrutable crystalline gaze resting on Tilly as he collected his thoughts.

"Good news and bad news," Tilly answered slowly, nodding a greeting to Franklin as the new addition joined the discussion. "I figured out how to pick up a directional heading for **Origin's Bloom**. It took a while, but I am pretty sure I could do it much faster if I had to try again, effectively giving me directional feedback for its location. It feels close . . . Not just over the horizon or anything, but much closer than it was when we were back at the capital."

"Good, our planning had reached an impasse until we could find a way to navigate for the party we are assembling for this quest," Hiro replied.

"Well, that was the good news. The bad news is"—he hitched his thumb over his shoulder, toward the army of infected bloodsucking death slowly spilling over the far end of the plains—"our objective is behind them."

Hiro's face didn't change at the announcement, and Ichiro limited himself to a slight tightening of his eyes. Good old Franklin, on the other hand, stared wide-eyed over Tilly's shoulder as if struggling to process the implications of this news. The most sensible reaction of the three.

"Great Ancestor help us . . . ," he uttered, his wide green jaw slowly clenching down in a nervous frown.

"Pretty much how I feel, Franklin. Well, anyone got any ideas on how to get past them?" Tilly asked, turning from Franklin to the two stoic lapins, who took a moment to share a look at his question.

While waiting for their reply, Tilly looked up and examined the sky over the wall in detail. The line dividing the two areas of influence over the Land was clearly demarcated by a distinct difference in hues. Somewhere slightly beyond the wall, the two different skies mingled, and Tilly guessed that was where the boon's influence ended.

The sky inside the barrier had blurred once the boon activated, still moving between night and day, but in a vague sort of way, without showing any of the particular or peculiar celestial bodies that could be found on Nephesh. On his patrols, he had always been in the forest under a canopy when they skirted the barrier and he had not been able to look up at the meeting place between the two skies.

On the edge of their territory, without any trees or mountains blocking the view, Tilly noticed two things. First, the hue of the sky beyond the wall was a bruised purplish color and clouds covered the sky. The Land there also still seemed to be moving between day and night, but the cloud cover was thick and persistent, and Tilly realized that in all his visits to the wall, he had never seen anything but a cloud-covered sky over the distant rust-brown plains.

Second, as he followed the path of the sky to the still distant force, he saw the clouds progressively get darker and more menacing until they were the steely gray of a pregnant and angry storm.

"We had hoped to be sending you away from the conflict, but preparations have already been made in case of this eventuality," Ichiro finally said, his face so placid that he might as well have been talking about the weather. "We always knew you would have to set out to find the last piece of the advancement requirement for our faction. So the question has been, who would we send with you? Father knew we needed to give this mission its best chance of success without weakening our defense too much to hold until you succeeded, and it was a tricky balance to strike."

"And now that we know it's a strike into enemy territory, it is even more complicated," Tilly said, finishing Ichiro's thought. "Who were you thinking of sending with me? We need to be able to move fast, survive, and hide if we are going to make it to the Facet. Then we need to obtain its patronage somehow and get me cured while we are at it . . ."

Ichiro nodded along with Tilly's examination of the party requirements. "The only thing you didn't mention is that the ideal party would have a healer. Unfortunately, none of the ones we can spare will survive the trip, and the only one we know would survive is bound to serve the Temple for a year." He sighed. "So, we opted for a utility build over a specified role build for this mission's party. No party member will fill any role perfectly, but each will make up for it with lateral skills and *Abilities*. Am I correct in assuming that Honored Kindle will soon be able to sustain flight?" He turned to face Tilly's shoulder, which may as well have held an empress for the way she preened at the lapin's respectful term of address.

"*Cheep*," she replied proudly, ruffling her now almost complete coat of azure feathers.

"By that she means she can glide, but no flying yet. Though, she assures me that she will be fully capable of flight whenever it is *actually needed*," Tilly said, bumping the side of his head against her warm form playfully.

She pecked him lightly in return, and Ichiro's thoughtful expression turned up in a slight grin.

"Good, along with our combined **Stealth** *Abilities*, that should cover scouting. I say we go ahead with the team as planned, Father."

"Agreed. Franklin, I assume you now know why we called you up here?"

"Yes. And I accept. I have obligations of my own calling me beyond our borders, though I had hoped they would wait until our people were more settled. It would be my honor to join in this mission," he replied, readjusting his vibrant blue scarf.

"Great!" Tilly exclaimed, clapping the honu on the back of the shell. "No one else I would rather have on the team. I'm sure that new ice of yours will be all kinds of useful out there."

"Aside from Mr. Franklin and I—" Ichiro continued.

"Wait, you? Won't you be needed on the wall?" Tilly interrupted.

"While I would make some difference, our family style is much more suited to open-field combat than defense. For obvious reasons, my father must stay, but I am free to add my humble ability to this team. Plus, with my condition, we thought I would add unique utility in perception and detection. It is also why I have joined you in training with the Rangers."

"Okay, who's left?" Tilly asked, turning back to Hiro.

"Two others. We have asked Gorock, who is much better outside of a formation than within one, not that he agrees with that assessment. However, when we offered him the opportunity to 'go find other enemies to fight' he was . . . enthusiastic in his acceptance."

"So, that gives us two front liners, one a tank and the other a melee damage dealer. We have two ranged options that double as magic attack, and I can close if I need to. I assume that leaves someone in the support-slash-area-effect role. I'm guessing Amel—I mean Mrs. Cooper would be the best choice out of the options I can think of."

"Correct. She is finishing her work on the boundary now, and we will send her to meet you and your Ranger escort a mile east of here at sunset. We do not know if the time of day affects the enemy's perception capabilities or not. So far there is not much observable difference between night and day past the wall. Nonetheless, that is when your party will head out," Hiro replied, his stoic expression giving nothing away about what he thought their odds of success were.

"Very well. The elders said they had something to pass on to me, so I will see you shortly, Tilly," Franklin said, then nodded to the other two before hustling off at his characteristic un-honu speed.

"See ya in a bit, Franklin!" Tilly squawked embarrassingly after him, his nervousness at the coming mission causing his tone to shift into something slightly goofier than expected. He cleared his throat and turned back to the two lapins.

"Hiro, thanks for putting together one hell of a team. I hope you can hold this pile of blocks without us," Tilly continued, attempting to ground himself in the reality of his words. He looked the elder samurai in the eyes as he continued to avert his gaze from the darkening horizon and their near-suicidal mission beyond. The sudden advancement of his **Corruption** had shaken him pretty badly, and he found himself unable to shake the anxious energy that wanted to animate his interactions.

"We will hold as long as we must," Hiro answered, unbowed by the challenge. Then his gruff voice somehow took on a lighter tone without changing inflection. "The system sets no hopeless tasks. This is possible; it will simply be very difficult. That being said, don't take too long, human. This is the second time we stand together on a wall with me sending you off on an impossible task. The first time you returned in a day. I would appreciate something similar here."

"Speaking of our timeframe, I have several things to see to before we leave tonight," Ichiro added, his soft smile back in full as he moved to leave, bowing to both of them. Hiro offered him a small but genuine smile in return along with the most meaningful sentence Tilly had ever heard him speak.

"Son, I am proud of you. I am sorry I do not say it more often."

Ichiro's serene smile flattened and some of his constant calm melted away before the implacable gaze of his father. He bowed again, this time much lower.

"We have both made mistakes. But I am deeply honored to be your son. We will return," he answered before straightening and turning to leave. His smooth, effortless motions made his speed seem almost impossible as he descended the large stairway still being constructed behind them.

Then it was just the two of them left up on the wall, an island of silence in the midst of a sea of soldiers and workers rushing everywhere to prepare for the coming attack. Tilly knew he needed to leave and collect supplies for his journey like the others, but something held him up there a little longer, and he stood on the wall watching the enemy's approach with the samurai-turned-guardian.

"Do you really think we have a chance?" Tilly finally asked, his voice low amidst the background roar of shouts and preparations.

Hiro didn't look at him or even acknowledge his question, and Tilly began to wonder if the lapin had heard him when he finally responded. "My people have a better chance at freedom now than they have had in the last four hundred years. It will be a difficult fight, but that was always going to be the case. What we face now, we face together. I have put my trust in your god, and I think you should begin to do the same."

Tilly stood there a while longer, thinking over what was ahead of them and what it meant to once again be heading into danger far beyond his ability and level. After a while, with a nod of thanks to Hiro for the company, he left the wall to head back to the city. He needed to find a pack and stuff to put in it.

Send Me on My Way

Tilly made it to his room a little while later, choosing to take the trip at a light run. Kindle took turns launching herself from his shoulder and gliding back down to practice navigating the air at speed. As he looked up, he could tell she still had some trouble gaining altitude, but her maneuvering was looking more natural every day.

"*Cheeeeeep!*" she trilled, then sent him the image of several predators pouncing on prey as her talons locked on his shoulder, arresting her most recent dive. Soon she would be too large to sit on his shoulder; the thought of her no longer being able to perch on him was accompanied by a small pinch of nostalgia at her rapid growth. However, in the face of her fierce pride, he couldn't help but play along.

"AAARRGGH!" he shouted and pretended to stumble as if a great weight had just crashed into him from above. Those last stumbling steps brought him around the corner to the front of his building, and to his surprise, he found some-one waiting for him.

"Good afternoon, Jonathan. A little birdie told us an hour ago that you were leaving, so George and I got this together for your trip," she said, hefting a pack the size of an ambitious middle schooler's backpack.

"*Cheep?*" Kindle replied, not liking being implicated by a woman she hardly knew. She blasted out a mental image of a flock of birds exploding from a small tree, which Tilly took to be a denial of any involvement. He did his best to ignore the byplay and beamed at the Arborist.

"Wow, Edna, thank you! I was about to head to the supply depot to see if I had any contribution points to spend to prepare. Believe it or not, I hadn't gotten around to checking to see what my balance is, or if I even have an official position with the Alliance."

The Three-Fold Alliance's fledgling economy was underpinned by a currency they called "contribution points," something Shuji assured Tilly was very normal in these sorts of situations. Until they established contact with the outside world, no conversion to other currencies was offered or necessary. Everyone in the city was issued a stipend according to their experience, class, and position within the structure of the Alliance, along with additional points assigned to certain tasks and goods produced.

For example, Edna had told him that they would be able to build a nice house after the war with all the points she and George had received for their classes and the amount of food they were able to produce.

Tilly, however, hadn't needed any contribution points to buy any equipment so far. His Legendary gear covered his weapons and armor, and the med kit they had outfitted him with upon request had never come with a price attached. On top of that, the food and lodging seemed to be covered for him as well, or at least no one had said anything so far . . . He was not sure this was true for anyone else in the Alliance, and he wasn't sure how he felt about the special treatment, but he had been training so hard that he hadn't really thought about it too much until now.

"Oh, don't you go worrying about things like that!" Edna said, snapping him out of his sheepish guilt spiral with a surprisingly quick tap on his forehead. "Concentrate on keeping us moving forward! You take care of us, young man, and we take care of you. That being said, I think you will have a fair number of points whenever you get around to checking." A mischievous smile peeked out from her comically stern visage.

"Well, I appreciate it a lot, Edna. Anything else I'll need to grab? I was just swinging by to pick up my med bag."

"That is already packed and restocked at the top of this," she said as she held up the bag for him to put on. "I hope you don't mind. Amelia's coat will make sure you all have plenty of fresh fruit and vegetables. The others will each carry some essentials for the team, including a pot and some dry goods. With your self-repairing equipment and fire abilities, it wasn't too hard to get together what you needed. Just a cloak colored to help you blend in with the environment and a few small essentials."

Something about her holding up the full pack as Tilly shrugged it on reminded him of his first day at school, decades ago. Not that he had had anyone to pack his bag for him . . . But as he had looked at the other kids with lunch boxes and notes from their parents, he had wondered what it would be like to be taken care of in that way.

Tilly cleared his throat and shook away the memories as he turned around to face the tiny woman. "Tell George that I am so thankful for you two. It's the little things like this that keep me moving forward."

"Oh, nonsense! He regretted not being here, but he's been working with Amelia on our boundary. Now I want you to do something for me . . . ," she said, trailing off before surprising Tilly by pulling his shoulders down to her height and planting a quick kiss on his cheek. Then, holding his head down level with hers, she leaned back and looked him straight in the eyes, her expression taking on a much more serious cast.

"No more worrying about us. George and I never got the chance to have children of our own, and for better or worse, you have taken that place in our hearts, young man. We won't ask you to stay safe, but don't take on any more than you have to . . . Too many young people die thinking the world lies on their shoulders. Your effort isn't the beginning or the end of this story."

Looking into her eyes, Tilly realized that even though he had only known them for a few weeks, he couldn't imagine life on Nephesh without their warm support. As the safety of their steadfast care attempted to flood his heart, old panic began to rise up in resistance.

I don't deserve this.

I'll just fail them, like I've failed everyone else.

. . . They'll leave in the end. They always do.

All of that and more crackled at the back of his mind as the white noise of his ever-present anxiety rose in volume. He could feel the newly thickened ichor of the **Corruption's** presence wheedling its way into his buoyed emotions and dragging them back down into the mud of hopelessness.

Through it all, unaware of the secret war raging in Tilly's heart, Edna stood there. She was three-quarters Tilly's height, yet she looked into his eyes with all the confidence of a person completely at peace with their place in the world. At that moment, secure in her belief and trust, she seemed immovable.

Even amid his internal triggers, that expression and the choice it represented pulled words from the deeper places of Tilly's soul. Somewhere beyond that wall, deep in the ocean of his trauma, where his doom lurked, a bright light appeared.

"Thanks, Edna . . . ," he started in a croak. "Honestly, I didn't have much in the way of parents either, so I guess that makes us about perfect for each other."

Silence hung between them as she offered him a small smile and shining eyes. She gave him a motherly pat on his shoulder and rubbed it reassuringly, sealing the moment.

"You better get going, or else you will have this old lady blubbering all over you, and I'm sure you don't have time for that." Tilly nodded gratefully, not so sure that she would be doing all the blubbering.

"I'll see you when I get back. Until then, you two stay safe! Look after those kids for me, alright?" he answered, then shouldered his pack and turned away.

Kindle turned back toward Edna and called, *"Cheep!"*

"I will! And little lady, if anything tries to get our boy, you burn it to a crisp, you hear?" she replied fiercely to the phoenix.

"CHEEP," Kindle affirmed.

Tilly was faintly able to pick up images of forest fires and burning villages whispering by the edges of his mind, and he was sure he was not the intended target.

Wait . . . Kindle, can you talk to others?

After a few more quick stops, Tilly found himself at the eastern edge of the parade ground.

He had made sure to visit the nearest outhouse building and take his time clearing out his system. He had a pretty good idea of what a long trip through enemy territory would be like, and he imagined this would be the last really good dump he would be able to take for a while. The shack he had first visited had grown to a complex of twenty or thirty cubicles, all taking advantage of the building's semi-indoor plumbing, rigged by a few honu craftsmen.

He helped himself to a few *generous* handfuls of leaves from the new Charmin Trees on his way out. Edna had cultivated them on either side of the street near the building, and with her skill level, they had grown almost to maturity in days. Then he visited the supply depot to double-check his med bag and get it stocked to his specific standards.

Never trust a medic who isn't anal about his bag.

After a quick inventory, he grabbed a free attendant and they hurried off to locate the few missing supplies. He saw others verifying their identities on tablets and seeming to go through monetary transactions, but Tilly wasn't asked for anything of that sort; he was starting to get worried about being late, so he decided to check when he got back.

Then he was on his way out of the city. By the time he reached the far edge of the parade ground, the evening Ranger patrol had already formed. Franklin was there waiting with Gorock, who carried his proportionally large pack with ease. Ichiro arrived behind him, moving at a deceptively easy pace, yet somehow appearing out of nowhere.

"Alright, is everyone ready? Mrs. Cooper will be meeting us at the boundary. My understanding is that she will be finishing her work at our departure point." The Rangers all saluted in response, something that had spread through the Alliance's forces from the Bastion's influence. A closed right fist knocked lightly against the chest. Gorock's resounded much more loudly than necessary, and the Wall Breaker looked to be shivering in anticipation.

With that, they moved out, the rear being taken up by Tilly and Franklin. Tilly once again noticed that Franklin had no trouble keeping up with the rest of the group, showing none of the characteristic slowness that his people consistently demonstrated in most situations.

"Hey, Franklin, how come you don't . . . you know, move like the others of your kind?" Tilly asked as they moved through the grass to the tree line at a double-time march.

"Are you asking why I am so different from the other honu you have met?" he responded, shooting an easy glance in Tilly's direction to let him know he wasn't offended.

"Yeah, that."

"My great uncle sent me away from the clan when I received my class. I joined the caravans, gaining experience and levels away from the imperial army and their crooked politics. I had just returned after a seven-year stint when the cult started to truly press the empire. Then a few months later, you arrived.

"My people don't have to move slowly, it is just a cultural habit. There is a class in my people's history called 'Wave Runner' that is built around *Dexterity*. We are by nature a thoughtful and careful race, but often, in my experience, too slow when it counts. I'm sure Great Uncle knew this and that is why he sent me off to the caravans in the first place. During my travels, I saw many people and cities, and eventually, I acclimated to my surroundings. Now I am comfortable at either pace, although I don't think anyone would ever accuse me of being speedy." He chuckled.

"Thanks for being cool about that. It can get frustrating here sometimes when I am faced with a million things I don't know, and I end up making mistakes out of ignorance. It is hard to know which questions are inappropriate and which ones are essential for my survival."

Franklin nodded along with Tilly's words.

"I felt quite the same way my first year on the Steppe. Do not worry yourself on my behalf. If you have any questions, especially about magic and mana-based abilities, I would be happy to share what I know with you. However, I do not imagine there will be much time for talking on this trip . . ."

"I'll keep that in mind. One more thing. Is it okay if I call you Frank? I've always been pretty big on nicknames, and it kills me that almost everyone here refers to me by my full name. I get that it is cultural and a sign of respect, but it feels like I'm back in grade school. Well, except for Gorock . . . He seems perfectly comfortable using a nickname for me."

"Not a problem . . . Tilly."

He smiled, ducking his head under the thickening foliage as they continued through the forest. The Ranger patrol fell back into the habit of full noise discipline and Tilly followed their example.

After a few minutes more, Tilly could see the boundary just ahead of their line. He shifted the pack on his shoulders and settled in his mind that training was over. It was time to see if all the grueling hours he had put in would keep him alive out in the wide world.

CHAPTER TWENTY-FIVE

Gilly Gilly

Hold," Ichiro called back down the line in a whisper. The formation froze a few yards short of the boundary and crouched down. Tilly was still surprised to see how difficult it was to keep track of the unit's location as they melded into the surrounding forest. Even Gorock seemed to have a few levels in **Stealth**. He had watched the others actively train this skill for weeks, and still had to suppress goosebumps at the sight of a whole group of people basically disappearing.

Despite the supernatural elements incorporated in the skill, it still necessitated real-world knowledge and practice. Being careless and snapping a twig would result in a far greater probability of being noticed. But that didn't mean there wasn't magic at work. Quiet footsteps and carefully chosen clothing didn't account for what Tilly had just witnessed from the entire Ranger squad. Aside from Ichiro, who still stood in plain sight looking down the line of the boundary, the rest of the squad had just evaporated.

Tilly recalled the first day of Ranger training, when one of the former hunters had shown them what level thirty-five **Stealth** looked like in different environments. First, he had activated the skill standing in an open field while they watched. To Tilly, it looked like the edges of his profile had blurred slightly before firming back up.

Then the hunter had asked them to look away, and when they had looked back, it seemed like he had disappeared . . . for just a moment. Then something in Tilly's mind adjusted and he was able to spot the hunter lying completely still in the dirt. The muted color choice of his outfit and his skill had somehow caused him to blend in extremely well with the rusty brown ground. There was magic at play, but it didn't come from the user's own mana well. The hunter described moments when his skill had advanced greatly in the past, and how much more the Land itself actively helped him hide now.

At even a moderate level in **Stealth**, an obstruction-rich environment was more than enough to render the user almost completely invisible. After several demonstrations in the tree line, the hunter assured them that high enough levels in **Stealth** were indistinguishable from full invisibility. The downside to the skill was its vulnerability to real physical variables. Some races used scent as their primary sense, and few **Stealth** users took adequate precautions against such detection methods.

Tilly reviewed everything he had learned one last time as he tried to get mentally ready for this next mission. His semi-meditative state was interrupted by two figures advancing slowly through the forest along the boundary. One wore a long trench coat with a green crystal-tipped staff and was casting something silently on the plants along the boundary. Tilly watched from his stealthy position as green-hued energy flooded into one plant after another, settling invisibly into the still normal-looking foliage. The other slightly shorter figure followed along, touching any plant that the first waved her staff over.

"Clear." The call came whispering down the line.

The formation stepped out of cover one by one until a line of Rangers stood waiting for the pair to arrive. The pair paid no mind to the Rangers and continued working right up until they reached the formation.

"Is this the correct location?" Ichiro asked Amelia.

In response, a tired Amelia looked up from her last plant and lifted her staff. A line of foliage running parallel to the border of the boon in both directions moved along with the wave of her staff. She allowed herself a grim but satisfied smile as she lowered her new magical implement and turned to her companion. "Did you get them all, George?"

"Yes, ma'am, all of them have been registered by my *Ability* in the eyes of the system. Now these are just another bunch of my crops, albeit a strange one. I'll know if any harm comes to them," he said with a reassuring smile.

"Good. Even when the boon ends, these plants will continue to grow into one another until they form an unbroken wall. Anyone free of **Corruption** will be able to pass, but with the High Priestess's twist on my *Ability*, they have been keyed to detect and attack **Corruption** if it comes within range." Then she looked directly into the satyr's eyes to emphasize her next point. "Please remember that, should any of our people claim they were attacked 'by mistake,'" she finished darkly.

"Yes, you told me this hours ago," George replied, waving away her warning. "I'll take care of them, and with my bonuses, they will continue to grow well past normal, even without your mana. Now, you take care of yourself and stop worrying about us. You will have plenty to worry about as is." Throughout George's admonishment, Amelia's serious expression softened into a smile.

"Very well, George, point taken. I'll see you soon." She offered him a quick embrace before turning to the group. "Are we ready?"

"Yes, Mrs. Cooper, I believe we are," Ichiro answered warmly, gesturing for the others to come forward. Tilly exchanged a look with George, who mouthed "Good luck" as if Tilly was trying to land a big part in the community theater play. The humor cut through Tilly's mental cramming, and he couldn't help but grin and shoot George a thumbs up before joining the others near the boundary.

The Ranger squad moved to continue the patrol while Ichiro, Franklin, Gorock, Tilly, and Amelia formed a small circle at the edge of the boon. Tilly couldn't help but eye the nearby mana-imbued plants nervously as they huddled up.

"Oh, stop it," Amelia said, catching his look and heaving an exasperated sigh. "You and I are both infected . . . Of course I would have thought of that when I designed this enchantment. Anything with a hint of **Origin's** Flame is keyed to pass."

Tilly smiled sheepishly and shrugged as Ichiro broke in, "Everyone, please. We have a simple goal: find the next Facet. We will avoid enemy engagement where possible." At this, Gorock snorted in derision. "And we will move as quickly and quietly as possible. My father is the only one who has been far enough past the boundary to see where the Land has stitched our two areas together, but he informed me that, except for the pass where we have built the wall, many of the mountains were cut in half by the move and now present sheer cliff faces to the enemy.

"He and the High Priestess are working on building a distraction for the approaching army to cover our descent from any watchers. Once we reach the Deadlands, we will depend on our cloaks and **Stealth** to avoid the enemy scouts. Any questions?"

"Not a question, but depending on what we find at the bottom of the cliffs, I have an idea that should make our movements even more opaque to the enemy," Amelia responded, looking around at the others.

Tilly just unslung his pack and asked Kindle to hop off the bag after he pulled out his reddish-tan cloak. He flung it over the pack and his kit and gestured for Kindle to hop back on. It may have been his imagination, but he thought he felt his armor wriggling in disgust as the normal quality cloak settled over it.

The others followed suit, each nodding toward Ichiro once they were ready. Tilly took one last look at each member of the group, noting just how different their levels and classes were.

Level 48, Wall Breaker
Level 35, Tundra Caller
Level 38, Botanist Surveyor
Level 25, Samurai Hatamoto

And finally, him, a level eighteen Son of Flame. The lowest-tier enemies they faced averaged level thirty-five . . .

God, I am so in over my head.

Sensing the general shape of his thoughts, Kindle pecked at him irritably as she settled back on his shoulder. She sent him an image of a smoldering ember surrounded by damp foliage. It slowly dried out its surroundings, unbowed by the greatness of the trees towering over it. It was in the ember's nature to burn and burn it would, no matter how insurmountable its chosen fuel.

He absently reached up and stroked her feathered back in thanks before deciding to speak up to the group as they made final preparations.

"I know we each have our reasons for going on this mission, but this is as personal for me as it gets. So, I wanted to take this chance before we start to thank each of you for coming," he said, some of the emotion of the sentiment lending a gravelly tone to his words.

"You are the only one with high hopes for this mission," Amelia said with a snort, her hand drifting to touch her midriff under her pocketed trench coat. Tilly winced as he suppressed the memory of her skin burning as he did his best to remove the fatal poison. He swung his gaze around, catching an absent nod from Franklin as he fiddled with his scarf.

Gorock either sneered or smiled reassuringly at Tilly's pronouncement . . . Probably the former. Tilly's gaze came back around to Ichiro.

"It is my honor to accompany you, Jonathan Tillman. Your path will bring great change, and I will walk with you as long as I am able," he replied simply before nodding to each of the others and turning to move through the barrier.

They all followed, feeling nothing as they moved through the shift in the time dilation. But when Tilly looked back, he found the Ranger patrol and George had already gone from the places they had occupied thirty seconds ago.

The group moved through the trees uphill until they reached a gap and came to the edge of a cliff hundreds of feet high. Tilly held on to a tree and leaned out slightly to see just how dramatic the unnatural fortification was.

Even though the system had thrown them almost immediately to the wolves, it had not done so without some favorable factors on their side. Tilly was sure that the impossibly smooth cliffs could be scaled, but he doubted it would be chosen by any significant number of enemies over a direct assault on the wall.

To his right, Amelia had just finished whispering with Ichiro, who was taking turns looking far into the distance at the closing force and then shifting his gaze back to the sky above the boundary, where something was roiling and building in the hazy sky within the boon. Amelia turned to address the others.

"I have a cutting of a certain vine that should work to descend this cliff face, and as a plus, it will wither in a few hours. So, we will go as soon as the storm strikes," she said, holding a thick root cutting with hundreds of feeler-like twigs growing off of it. She placed it on the ground at the edge of the cliff and touched the tip of her new staff to the plant, which started to wriggle and squirm as she channeled mana into it.

New growth exploded out, shooting over the side and snaking down the cliff, sinking its continuously growing appendages into the side of the cliff as it descended. Tilly's head shot up as a crack of thunder sounded from the barrier, and a storm head surged over the boundary toward the rolling hills of the Deadlands beyond.

"That is our signal, gentlemen. It's time to move," she said, then grabbed onto the initial root and kicked out over the side before beginning to descend as the vine grew just ahead of her descent. Tilly watched as she took advantage of the intentional back and forth curves in the growth for hand and foot holds.

The rest followed after her, each taking looks, when able, at the sudden and violent storm surging toward the enemy. It had started to pour sheets of water on the mouth of the mountain pass, adding tons of water to the river delta choking the pass's entrance. Thunder sounded angrily like the clanging of a gong as the force of nature moved toward enemy lines.

"How did they do this?" Tilly called to Ichiro as the outer edges of the storm started to soak them with rain, removing any visibility they had of the area.

"It was Lady Erash," he called back down over the sound of the storm. "She is able to do this in partnership with my father in his role as a guardian. They called it a 'domain ritual.' Though, I am afraid it will not rain for months in our valley as a consequence."

Even in the rain, the millipede vine provided an almost ladderlike descent down the cliff, and after ten minutes, Tilly's moccasins landed in the rusty tan grass that covered the lands of their enemy.

He looked around as the rain started to lighten near their area and saw Amelia doing something with the grass while the others adjusted their tan cloaks and packs. She carefully dug up a clump of the ground cover and placed it in one of her pockets before lifting another and laying it on the sleeve of her trench coat. She waved her staff over it, and the grass started to multiply rapidly, springing up in clumps all over her jacket, breaking up her shape and lending the majority of her form an impressive camouflage.

"Do not worry, Baby-Man, I am sure her explosions are nowhere near as impressive as yours." Gorock chuckled from behind Tilly, causing him to jump.

Amelia looked up from her newly covered form and gestured silently for the rest of them to come forward. She started growing each of their cloaks a covering like a sort of ghillie suit and explained in a low voice, "This plant is called Blood Weed. If you are injured while wearing this cloak, get it off quickly. I might not have time to keep it from burrowing into your wound. But in its inert state, it will provide excellent cover for us as we move."

Tilly stepped forward last, but as she started to cover his cloak in the vampire grass, his Legendary armor underneath started to writhe once again, and this time Tilly knew he was not imagining things. It felt . . . *outraged*.

Tilly was about to call out a warning when his grass-covered cloak exploded all around him, causing Amelia to shout in surprise.

CHAPTER TWENTY-SIX

Inexorable Advance

Igor – Level 84 Vampiric Mesmer

Igor smacked his lips in anticipation, not bothering to rub away the drool that ran down his chin and mingled with the sticky brown bandages covering every inch of his face.

The life energy emanating from this tiny faction was delicious. Behind this pitiful storm and one of those laughable piles of stone the cattle seemed so fond of, something bright burned. It felt old, and somehow, at the same time, it expressed a vibrancy that Igor had never tasted.

He hadn't salivated like this since the **Hunger** first graced the Bloodwells at their nation's heart. Only a few of Father's favorite children had been allowed to drink from the newly enriched treasure, and Igor had not been one of them.

On that day, Igor had watched, salivating, as that fat pig Dimitrov had guzzled from the ruby fount flecked with squirming, succulent darkness. Aside from his eldest, Father had chosen two others to partake, having already taken his fill, of course. At first, Igor had thought there must be some mistake—no one had been as faithful as him in carrying out his father's will! But as he had stood there watching the two others approach the Bloodwell, an insatiable desire had welled up, gnawing up from the pit of his stomach and battering his already tenuous hold on sanity.

He leaped from his kneeling position at the entrance of the caverns, ravenous and desperate enough to risk everything for a taste of the new power flowing from the wells. A multi-octave cacophony had issued from his raw throat as he used **Maddening Screech** to draw the favored pair's attention toward him. Once they had each met his eyes, he knew he had them. They would not be as susceptible as blood bags, but Igor had not risen to this rank by accident.

He stacked **Mesmerize** and **Enrage**, draining all of his mana and half his health as he overcharged both of them with **Blood Sacrifice**.

Anastasiya and Ivan froze mid-crouch, their faces both sporting a rictus of hatred and rage as they were caught in the power of his gaze. He could not hold them for long, but he poured all of his starved ambition into his *will* and mentally thundered his command.

DEVOUR EACH OTHER.

They responded immediately, claws and fangs flashing before the dark ichor of Blood Essence began to splatter all over the cave. Not wanting to waste a second, Igor had shot forward, making use of every bit of his blood-empowered body to reach the Bloodwells and their sensuous whisperings of new dark power.

Then *he* was there.

Igor hadn't even made it halfway before Father had intervened. He had stood before Igor holding his two squabbling children by the necks. His pale sinuous form flanked by two dark-gray wings formed of perfect gray flesh and beautiful angular bones seemed to fill the whole cavern. His eyes twinkled feverishly, shining yellow with new flecks of black wriggling like tiny worms around his pupils. Igor both hated him for his power and loved him for his beauty.

Those eyes seized Igor's soul and would have stilled any mortal creature's beating heart as his voice exploded into Igor's mind.

You dare defy me in my place of power?

The voice raked Igor's mind with pain even as he shuddered in ecstasy at his master's attention. Attention that had killed many of his lesser brethren. But in this, madness gave him strength, and the gnawing hole that was his soul cried out for the new power the wells offered, even in the face of his destruction.

"Benevolent Father, Drinker of Souls, have you not taught us that there are but two laws?" Igor mewed in terror, hating his voice and the weakness of his position before the others. Dimitrov's beady dark eyes danced with mirth between the endless folds of fat that framed his brow.

"I must drink from the Bloodwell, Father! I have proven my power over these two. I beg of you, allow me this honor. I will not fail you!" Igor cried, bowing deeply to the patriarch of the horde and biting his lip in urgent need as dark-flecked blood continued to gush up from the wells just beyond his father's talons.

A rich velvety laughter filled the room as the patriarch tossed aside the other two and opened his arms wide.

I applaud your ambition. Truly I do, but we cannot allow such an act go unpunished, now, can we? he asked, his posture one of a loving father inviting his child into a warm embrace. *I will allow you to drink . . . But you will pay my price.*

Igor straightened and was unable to restrain the moan of horror that slipped from his throat. Still gripped in Father's mental grasp, he moved forward until he was a breath away from the Prime Dirge of the Twilight Lands.

His eyes rolled in his sockets as the visible striations of Father's muscular form parted in hundreds of places to display salivating mouths bristling with needle-like teeth.

It is said that the screaming had been heard by every member of the horde in the planes and that it had lasted over an hour.

Igor's eye twitched at the memory, and he unconsciously shifted one of the flesh bandages a shaman had given him to staunch some of the endless bleeding. The wounds had not healed, even weeks later, and if he did not constantly feed, the bleeding debuff would slowly kill him. But none of it mattered to Igor now. He had been rewarded richly for his boldness.

At the first achingly sweet swallow of the ruby liquid, he had felt his power begin to grow horrendously. His *Intelligence* had doubled while his *Wisdom* had been reduced to almost nothing. Yet the **Hunger** had not left him without a way to regain mana. It had gifted him a new *Ability*, **Mana Siphon**. Now he could draw the mana from any target creature's blood, giving him an endless supply as long as he was willing to take it from those around him. The cattle that surrounded him, pathetic in their weakness, were now his new mana well. Igor abandoned *Wisdom* as he gave himself completely over to the laws of hunger and power.

His sopping wet bandages continued to weep dark ichor down the sides of his face as his eyes shone with insatiable red hunger. His new power demanded to be fed, and it keened from the back of his mind as he used his **Mesmeric Sight** to watch the defenders run up and down the wall in preparation for an assault.

First, they would use this new little morsel of a nation to cull the weak from the horde. Then the strong would remain, rewarded with the chance to crack open this egg and enjoy the gooey softness of this prize. The pretenders to the east would do nothing unless pressed, holding back like the weaklings they were. The fools thought that the horde had given up on its conquest of their lands . . . They didn't know that it would only be days until they saw the light of Father's teachings and joined the horde.

Then all would join Father on his glorious crusade to finally crush the disgusting bloodless, who had hidden away in their precious city for far too long.

Run, little piggies! he thought gleefully as the snacks continued to prepare themselves for the meal up on their pile of stones.

We will fatten you on our weakest, as has always been done. Then the butcher will come calling and rip apart your pitiful force, sinew and joint. And while King-Piggy Dimitrov is gorging himself, I will find the source of this sweet burning power and swallow it whole.

Aurelia – Level 12 Priestess of Origin's Flame

Aurelia could barely stand, yet somehow, she found the strength to continue and shuffled over to the next pile of javelin tips and arrowheads, which the smiths had been producing night and day. Just yesterday, she had been called to the forge compound to cast **Fiery Will** on another exhausted group, giving them the ability to press on.

The *Ability* allowed the target to ignore one debuff for twenty-four hours, and the smiths as well as many of the other essential laborers had been requesting it whenever she was free to clear their **Exhaustion**.

It was no longer a matter of taking full advantage of the huge skill-leveling bonus. By now, everyone knew what was coming, and anyone who could contribute did. Even the rest of the orphans had taken to running meals from the cafetorium to the different labor groups.

The rest of the orphans . . . , she thought hesitantly. She hadn't really seen them much since that night she had snuck away. But she knew that they were working as hard as anyone to prepare for what was coming. All of them had lost their homes and families, and they would do everything they could to keep that from happening again.

She was the oldest now, and it was up to her to lead by example!

The flame had chosen her for a reason. Or at least that is what she kept telling herself as she struggled to follow Erash's vague instructions in her new class. Her training had been a whirlwind of urgent needs and long repetitive hours of casting, giving her no time to process her new, more mature state.

She had purified hundreds of soldiers from **Corruption**, healed four times that many injured, and now she was casting **Ignus's Blessing** on as many projectiles as possible to give the under-leveled forces a fighting chance against the new superior enemy.

The High Priestess could bless thousands of weapons at once with such a simple *Ability*, and she had, but now she was completely spent and there were still more instruments of war being produced. Lady Erash had exhausted herself unleashing that storm . . . Gods, it had been terrifying to watch it build above them, pulling wind from the mountains and water from the river as Lord Hiro and Lady Erash invested it with all the *will* and mana they could muster in partnership with the Land.

They had said it would slow the enemy's approach to the wall and kill hundreds of combatants in the process. Perhaps one day she would be capable of such incredible feats of faith and power. Until then, she had blessings to bestow.

Early on, they had found that a simple iron tip on a spear or arrow blessed with Aurelia's *Ability* would reproduce a weaker version of Mr. Tillman's powerful fire strike. So, they had filled every moment she wasn't needed somewhere else with blessing duty.

She cast again, imbuing another pile of twenty iron heads with **Origin's** power. Her lower lip trembled at the burning in her throat and the aching in her arms. Twenty blue sparks shot from her hands and settled into the iron of her targets. They each took on an almost invisible bluish sheen in response, and the blessing would last for over a week. As she finished casting the *Ability*, her arms dropped and she bit her lip to still its trembling, doggedly moving over to the next pile.

All around her, workers shouted, preparing last-minute logistics to make sure those on the wall were well supplied. Commanders shouted out instructions to formations of new soldiers, whose feet shuffled nervously in place. All present stole glances up at the wall, waiting. Then the alarm call began to echo as spotters up on the cliffs marked the approach of the enemy.

The storm was spent, and the enemy was almost upon them. The boon would be over in a few hours, and then the sickening creatures would come. She suppressed a shiver as she lifted her hands to bless another batch.

Before she could begin, a notification popped up, and she scanned it carefully, still not entirely used to having access to something that had been years away only a few weeks ago.

Congratulations! *You have spent your entire mana pool on blessing objects more than 48 times in 24 hours.*
For your effort, you have earned the Title:
[Bestower of Providence]

[Bestower of Providence]: *You have pushed your mind and body far past its young threshold to channel a deity's power for the protection of your people. This has imbued your call on **Origin's** power with a unique significance.*

+100% on the effectiveness of your blessings on objects.
You gain 0.01% of any experience earned with the use of an object you have blessed.

Aurelia had to read it a few more times to understand the implications, but it finally sank in. Not only would her work here be even more effective, but it would allow her to grow faster, and she *had* to grow as fast as she could if she was going to protect the others.

"I was chosen for a reason," she muttered stubbornly under her breath as she lifted her arms above the next pile and began to cast with renewed passion.

CHAPTER TWENTY-SEVEN

So I Creep

Jonathan Tillman – Level 18 Son of Flame

Amelia flinched away, crying out at the sudden and unexpected magical reaction. For Tilly, however, time seemed to slow down. He didn't know if it was due to **Origin's** influence, but everything slowed to a crawl as he watched scattered tan fabric and clumps of freshly grown Blood Weed dissolve in the air all around him. The material was broken down into energy, leaving behind motes of tan and rust-colored mana that were then sucked back into Tilly's armor.

The Legendary armor set forcefully broke the surrounding material into its base state and then pulled it back in, using the energy to transform. The normally invisible script running up and down the fur and leather pieces that made up his armor flared brightly and began to change.

Fur and leather shifted to something light and dry, looking disturbingly like mummified skin, and then sprouted the Blood Weed everywhere. A hood grew up out of the collar, and he was left wearing what looked like a special forces-style fantasy ghillie suit.

Time snapped back to normal, and while Tilly had gotten to witness his armor transformation process at one-tenth the speed, the others had only seen an explosion of material and Amelia flinch back. Ichiro and Gorock charged forward, and Tilly quickly raised his hands to forestall their advance. Gorock already had his large "shortsword" raised, and Tilly had no idea how he thought he was going to help whatever situation he imagined was taking place.

"It's okay, guys! It's just my armor. It spontaneously transforms . . . sometimes," he called out, realizing halfway through the sentence that he hadn't thought nearly enough about the mechanics of these transformations. He turned to Amelia, who was straightening up, both hands stuffed threateningly in her pockets.

"I had no clue that would happen, I swear," he said waving placatingly while pulling up his flashing notification log.

> ***Congratulations!*** *You have activated a hidden prerequisite and catalyzed an armor transformation. Your armor has taken on characteristics of the Blood Mound Shambler.*
> *+270% to any **Stealth**-related activities while out of combat in the Twilight Lands.*
> *+50% bonus to first strike from **Stealth**.*

"I believe you . . . and somehow I am convinced that this is not the last time something explosive will happen in your company," Amelia said with a sigh, her face softening as she wearily pulled empty hands from her pockets.

"Well, if it's any consolation, this set now gives me a huge bonus to **Stealth**, along with a bonus to my first strike from hiding. It should be a game changer as we move through this area."

Ichiro's face brightened at the news while Gorock's dropped in disappointment as he reluctantly sheathed his sword and turned away, mumbling.

"Very good, Mr. Tillman. This solidifies your position as our scout. We must move before the storm dissipates," Ichiro said, gesturing opposite the cliff face and away from the approaching force. "Gorock, you will guard our rear. Mr. Tillman, you take point. We will move in a staggered line at double time. Keep spacing at about fifty paces. Except for you, Mr. Tillman, you range ahead at two hundred paces. Kindle, if you would accompany me, I will inform you if we need Mr. Tillman, and he can let you know if we need to halt. We will move at a double patrol pace for now. Is everyone clear?" he asked, issuing out the commands in a cool professional tone.

They all responded in the affirmative. Even Kindle responded with a *cheep* before hopping off Tilly's shoulder and fluttering over to Ichiro and settling onto his small pack. She scanned the plains with her sharp all-blue eyes before sending Tilly a word of advice for his mission.

Hide, she sent stoically, accompanied by images of a small creature moving through the underbrush. Then she looked over to him away from the plains and added, *I protect,* accompanied by the image of a mother bird spreading her wings over the nest.

He sent back, *I know you will, girl. I'll be careful, and you do the same.* Then he turned to her new perch, the serene samurai. Tilly was impressed but not surprised at Ichiro's tactical prowess and only had one question about the initial plan.

"What do I do if I am spotted?"

"Immediate and overwhelming use of force. Do not hold anything back, there can be no report of our presence moving through this land," Ichiro responded without hesitation, his calm expression untouched by the intense subject matter.

"Finally!" Gorock whispered in a tone that very much failed to be private.

"We will run as long as we are able and make camp only when we must. Time is no longer working with us . . . Is everyone ready to move?"

Tilly fought down the familiar feeling of being an imposter as he observed the expressions of professional detachment that settled on the others' faces.

Looks like life-or-death quests are par for the course around here . . .

Choosing not to dwell on his scant qualifications in scouting, Tilly shook out his shoulders and drew his weapons. Everyone else shifted to similar states of readiness, and without further preamble, Tilly turned and started moving at a steady jog. His steps ate up the ground and he once again marveled at the fact that he was easily maintaining what would have been his full sprint in his old life. In fact, the state of his body seemed entirely unaffected by the change from standing to running, and he felt like he could keep this pace for an entire day if needed.

After a few yards of finding his pace, he activated **Stealth** and felt the skill settle over him. However, he immediately noticed a difference in how quickly and thoroughly he felt his form become indistinct. He had been told that as long as the skill remained active, he would feel less . . . physically present and that this sensation was often, but not always, a good indicator that he remained unobserved by hostile forces.

As soon as he activated the skill, he felt a flash of alarm from Kindle, who immediately sent, *Where?* accompanied by a memory of his departure from her perspective.

The memory was jarring enough to cause Tilly to stumble mid-stride as he adjusted to the entirely different way she saw the world. All the physical features of the landscape were unchanged if not outlined in a much higher resolution, but superimposed over them was a gray-white haze. Somehow the haze did not diminish her ability to make out even minute details, but it did overlay everything with a confusing extra layer of information.

Tilly asked her to send the image again, and she complied. This time Tilly was able to pick his own form out from the endless sea of grass, partially because he was moving, but also because the haze was markedly whiter around his form. He realized that she had an innate heat sense built into her vision, which made sense considering what she ate.

After a few seconds, he watched himself disappear in the memory, the haze fading to uniform gray right where he had been. Tilly couldn't help but smile at the sight of his huge jump in the skill from his new armor transformation.

He sent back the same image she had sent him along with the word, *Hide*. She answered with a mental *chirp* that was layered with so much attitude that it would have been an eye roll on a human teenager.

As tough as Nephesh had been on him, some of the things he had experienced were undeniably cool. Being able to fade into nothingness was definitely one of those things. He leaned a little more into his pace and started to scan the area in front of him.

The plains were a reddish-tan sea of low rolling hills broken by long swathes of flat land, which interrupted the hills like ripples in a pond. Breaking this expanse was the storm wall, now directly in front of the enemy forces, blocking their line of sight. Tilly continued to move at a forty-five-degree angle away from the cliff wall with the storm and the enemy it obscured to his left.

He kept moving until they had gained about five miles of distance between their group and the pass, keeping his eyes peeled for anything out of place in the monotonous dead grasslands. Cresting a relatively large hill, he crouched low and turned back toward the wall to find that the clouds had cleared, marking the end of the supernatural storm. Tilly was able to barely make out an indistinct gray mass flowing toward the flooded delta before the walls.

As that tide of furious, hungry flesh hit the waters, it slowed significantly, meaning their inhumanly fast sprint was relegated to a jog. Tilly watched for a few moments more as the mass was broken up and reduced on its approach to the base of the wall. His sight failed him in the specifics, but he understood enough to know that the wall would likely hold through the first charge if nothing changed.

Hold on, guys . . . The only thing I can do for you now is keep moving, he thought to himself as he duck-walked to the downslope and started to move again. Just because he couldn't make out individual shapes at this distance didn't mean the enemy had the same limits. Even with his bonus in **Stealth**, he refused to tempt fate by making a silhouette on any of the high points in the hills. He sent back his observation to Kindle, trusting her to convey the update to Ichiro.

He continued along the direction they had set, occasionally sending back an image of a stunted tree or odd boulder to make sure they didn't lose his line of travel. Without any real change in the moody gray skies between day and night, it was difficult to track the passage of time. So it might have been thirty minutes or two hours before he encountered the first scout.

He had been sticking to the lower paths through the low hills, winding his way further and further to the side of the horde when he felt a shiver pass through this **Stealth**. On instinct he dropped, then, achingly slowly, he craned his neck to peer at his surroundings from deep within the cowl of his grassy hood.

Once he had turned his head almost completely to the right, he spotted the source of his unease. A figure crouched on top of a hill just past the one he had been skirting. Tilly watched, barely breathing, as the creature continued to scan the area. Some part of its predator instinct clearly pushed it to search the hills carefully, even though there seemed to be nothing.

Level 37, Strigoi

Tilly sent back an image of the scout to Kindle from his hiding place. She sent back a *cheep* of concern, but also sent along a picture of the rest of the group crouching down and hunkering under their cloaks, becoming little more than misshapen features of the same endless rust and tan grasslands. She even looked down at herself to show a new piece of fabric extending out of the pack below her and covering her blue form.

Finally, the scout stood, giving up its search, and turned back to head away from Tilly and the others. It released a short sharp screech that echoed through the hills and another screech answered the call a few hundred yards closer to the enemy force. That was the moment Tilly realized that these creatures were far less mindless than he first assumed. He didn't know how far this screen of scouts spread from the horde, but he hoped they would get through them soon.

Once he was sure the scout was gone, he sent back an all clear to the others and started moving again. As he loped forward, keeping his form slightly crouched, he carefully scanned each approaching hilltop.

One enemy avoided, thousands more to go.

CHAPTER TWENTY-EIGHT

Overwhelming Force

Over the next several hours he avoided three more scouts as they moved through the screen of eyes and ears the enemy army had this far out from its main force. As they continued to move away from the conflict, scout encounters became rare until Tilly was almost sure he had seen the last of them.

He was really glad they hadn't encountered this screen of scouts when they first tried to escape. Another mile or two closer to the army and the scouts would have probably been too close together to move through with their whole group.

It had been a good while since he had seen the last scout, and Tilly was about to signal back to the others to regroup and set a new heading when he heard a sniffing sound just around the hill in front of him. He scrambled part way up the incline and dived to the ground, then stilled completely as the small figure came into view. This one was slightly smaller than the others, and his **Identify** pinged with the reason a moment later.

Level 28, Strigoi Juvenile

Tilly sent back what he was seeing as the creature continued to wander forward, obviously less focused than the others in fulfilling its duty. Occasionally it would stop and scratch the ground, sniffing at what it found there, then move on. As it came within feet of Tilly, he noticed other differences in its features. Unlike the other hairless gray adults, this one seemed to still have patchy hair covering its head, and a few loose rags hung from its gaunt frame. Its skin displayed black vein-like patterns, connoting a heavy **Corruption** presence.

As it passed, a realization hit Tilly and he had to fight down the gorge rising in his throat. The hair . . . the rags . . . This creature had been something else once. It was a juvenile because it had not shed all of the features of its previous race.

It continued to wander past Tilly, and he was trying to hastily warn the others to scatter from the line he had been setting when a coughing bark sounded from just ahead. The juvenile froze in place and then turned slowly back toward the sound. Tilly followed its gaze, making sure to keep his movements achingly slow to maintain **Stealth**.

Another coughing bark sounded, this time more forcefully, and the juvenile scrambled back past Tilly, looking chastised. Tilly's hood finally cleared from his line of sight, and he saw it.

Level 72, Strigoi Consumer

It had eight or nine other juveniles milling about its feet, all hunched over in subservience, and it was looking down at the stray with fury smoldering in its lifeless eyes. Like the others Tilly had seen, it wore a mix of different armor and several weapons. Up close, Tilly noticed that its gray skin was tinged the slightest purple and it also had a spidery network of heavy **Corruption** burrowing through its skin. The juvenile scrambled up the hill and skidded to a halt just before the Consumer, who issued a vicious kick for its trouble.

Tilly's whole body tensed at the sight of such a large group so close. His joints began to ache with the strain as his knuckles whitened around the handles of his hatchets. The chances of his group being able to take this one without the element of surprise were slim. One misstep by him here and it would all be over. Even if they survived the encounter, there was no way they would be able to keep any from escaping to spread news of their presence . . .

He urgently sent back a command to stop and take cover. Kindle answered with concern and an affirmative that she had passed along the situation. Tilly kept his eyes glued on the Consumer, who seemed to have been assigned babysitting duty. Were there more juveniles wandering around? Sweat began to run down Tilly's face as the lay there, frozen, while the Consumer surveyed the hills before it.

Then screeching sounded from behind the group of Strigoi, echoed by other voices further away. The group's heads snapped back the way they had come at the sound. The Consumer issued a few barking commands before shooting off. The juveniles scrambled after, their gangly limbs hardly reducing the terrifying quickness of their four-legged sprint.

The screeching continued, joined by this group and others. They had found something. Something that had merited a full response.

Kindle sent, *We come*, as soon as Tilly issued the all clear.

For his part, Tilly cautiously moved forward, cresting the hill slowly, and watched as the distant group that had almost discovered him was joined by other individuals. They converged on a spot a few hundred yards in the distance, just out of Tilly's sight behind another set of hills.

A forceful shout rang out from the area, followed closely by a flash of pink light. The group of creatures pursuing the sound went wild, howling as they increased pace. The pink light continued to shine from behind the hill as the creatures arrived at the unseen source en masse.

"Mr. Tillman, what do you see?" Ichiro whispered urgently from the bottom of the hill.

Tilly backed down from the rise and turned to find the others arriving with Gorock pulling up the rear, shield and sword ready.

"Something drew the attention of every creature in this area with some sort of magic. The voice sounded humanoid, and whatever it was, it didn't seem like the Strigoi were rushing over to say, 'Hi,'" he replied.

Then the sound of a truck colliding with a wall thundered back over the hills from the confrontation, and echoing screeches of fury rose from the surroundings, pulling even more Strigoi into the conflict. There had to be twenty to thirty scouts there by now. Ichiro closed his eyes and listened for things the rest of them couldn't hear. After ten seconds, his milky eyes flicked open, and he drew his sword.

"There is, in fact, a battle in play, and the ones opposing the Strigoi seem to be from another faction," Ichiro said, then dropped his pack and let Kindle loose. "We will move to assist, our goals being the destruction of the enemy force in the area and favorable contact with possible allies in the region. They are swarming, and I doubt they have sent any messages back to the main force yet. Jonathan, you take point. Strike first, strike hard."

"Done and done," Tilly said while dropping his pack, mirroring the others, who were loosening gear and readying weapons for battle.

"Franklin and Mrs. Cooper, you are on containment. As soon as we engage, your main priority is to lock down the area, no one in or out. Gorock, we will move in and capitalize on Mr. Tillman's primary strike. Everyone clear?"

Everyone made some version of a nonverbal acknowledgment. Gorock barely contained his giggling delight, and Tilly shook his head in amazement at the Wall Breaker's battle lust. He turned to his bonded, suddenly overtaken with worry that she wouldn't know what to do.

Kindle, you are on overwatch. Only engage if you have an easy win, Tilly sent to the phoenix, trying to give her a role that felt significant without endangering her too much.

She eyed him and sent back contempt, along with a significant amount of confidence in her own abilities. She then turned away, shook out her wings, and took off into the air, not waiting for any further instructions.

"Shit! Alright, I'll see you guys on the other side. Be careful," he whispered hurriedly before running after her toward the sounds of confrontation. He heard the others move after him, but none overtook his position, and Kindle began to send flashes of the scenario ahead of them from the air.

Through Kindle's aerial perspective, he managed to gain a basic understanding of the conflict before him as he ran forward at a good clip. They faced a mass of thirty or so juveniles and two Consumers. Three more of the juveniles littered the ground like abandoned rag dolls, and one of the Consumers was missing an arm.

The group had been whipped into a fury as they attempted to tear through a glowing pink dome that was somehow managing to withstand their attacks. The two Consumers stood back and watched, seeming to be content to let the younger minions wear down the caster.

The barrier was already showing cracks, and through Kindle's eyes, Tilly could barely make out two figures through the glowing pink surface of the magic. One seemed to be a huge knight, decked out in full plate with his face completely covered. The other was significantly smaller, wearing bright multicolored robes and holding his hands splayed before him in an obvious attempt to maintain the barrier against the ferocity of the juveniles.

Tilly slowed his approach as he crested the last hill. He centered himself fully back in his own senses and made sure his **Stealth** was still in place before peeking over the crest. The scene was just as Kindle had shown him, but with his more familiar vantage, his attention was especially drawn to how closely grouped the majority of the juveniles were in front of the barrier.

He took one last scan of the field, looking for the most effective place to strike and tip the scales. He quickly discarded the idea of going after one of the elites, even the injured one. That would be a waste of his initial bonus if he wasn't able to effectively remove it from the fight with the first blow, and against something of that level, he would only have one shot. His eyes went back to the crowd of juveniles ranging from nine to fourteen levels above his measly level of eighteen.

If this were a video game, their grouping would be screaming at him to stack his bonus to a first strike from **Stealth** with an area-of-effect *Ability*. But this wasn't a game, and [Resolute] would only block one strike . . . To fail here would ruin everything.

Fuck it. He had a job to do, and he would do it to the best of his abilities. Some of his old competence rose to the surface as he considered this problem just like he would a burning structure. His two worlds merged and the old feeling of being on a razor's edge that he had used to get going into a burning building slid into place.

Weeks of diving into certain pain and dismemberment paid dividends, and even in the face of possible death, he found himself creeping forward and leaving behind his momentary hesitation.

The **Corruption** wriggled within him, egging him on to abandon all fear and give in to the call of battle pouring off the scene in front of him. The Strigoi seemed to have no fear, throwing themselves at the barrier in mindless fury, and he couldn't deny the pull their frenzy had on him. The freedom it offered was almost intoxicating in its promise of release from his worldly cares . . .

He acknowledged his desire to give in and accepted it with a deep breath. Then he held it, feeling its power weaken against his acceptance. He pulled the temptation close, not denying it but letting it be a part of the tapestry of pain and hope that made up his soul. Then he released it along with his breath. His breathing pattern settled into place, and he stoked the fire within him as he steeled himself against **Corruption's** influence for what now seemed like the thousandth time.

Endurance, don't fail me now, he thought as he crept forward the last few yards toward the ongoing conflict.

Cracks now spiderwebbed the barrier around the ferocious knot of gray teeth and claws that was the pack of juveniles attempting to breach it. Beyond the failing wall of magic was the armored figure, coolly holding its mace at the ready.

Tilly army crawled past the two Consumers, who he was sure would have spotted him even in his Blood Mound Shambler gear if not for the distraction of the conflict playing out right in front of them.

As he neared the back of the frenzied group, Strigoi Juveniles began to howl in glee as they shoved their heads and appendages through the widening weak points in the barrier. The knight calmly shifted his stance and hefted the massive mace, ready to meet the first to break through. Tilly drew in the flames at his center, compacted them, then set **Flame Expulsion** to activate a foot or two behind the mob.

A second later, the roaring crackle of a conflagration exploded out from Tilly's center, and he felt the moment his **Stealth** failed. A screeching bellow of outrage sounded off to the side of the injured Consumer as blue fire shot out from Tilly's position in all directions and engulfed the nearby juveniles.

A flash of intuition shot through Tilly like lightning, and he activated [Resolute] right as a gaunt one-armed figure exploded through the wall of fire and clawed out his throat.

Or that's what should have happened. Instead, Tilly felt the blow land against his exposed neck before his eyes even had a chance to register the Consumer's attack. He was launched forty feet away from the shattered barrier, his throat thankfully intact as he flew away from the conflict.

CHAPTER TWENTY-NINE

The Lost Boys

Tilly impacted the side of the hill and took a few percentage points of damage right as his allies crashed into the confused and injured group of Strigoi. The blast had also been the final straw for the barrier, and as soon as it collapsed, the knight on the other end rushed through the mob toward the uninjured Consumer. This left the colorfully clothed magic user to collapse.

Tilly climbed back to his feet, taking in the scene before him. The mob of juveniles had been scattered with roughly a third of them badly burned and the rest moderately to lightly wounded. Amelia and Franklin had stepped up to the top of the hill to start picking up targets on the edges of the fight, mostly focusing on crowd control and damage over time.

Meanwhile, Gorock and Ichiro had made full use of Tilly's distraction and were engaging the one-armed Consumer who had just tried to remove Tilly's throat. The outer edge of **Flame Expulsion** had barely left it singed, and it seemed to have no trouble facing both the new combatants at once, even with one arm. Gorock's shield was taking a beating as he soaked up a few lightning strikes from the creature's clawed hand. Ichiro was successfully landing hits from behind Gorock's guard. Unfortunately, even with his blade glowing silver, none of the strikes were causing any significant damage to the far superior foe.

The knight was the only one on the field who seemed to hold any advantage, having instantly charged the undamaged Consumer. His monstrous mace blurred through the air, raining down blows on the creature, who wielded a serrated sword with far less grace. The knight was only slightly slower, and that allowed the Consumer to barely evade or parry the vast majority of the blows, but seconds into the fight, it was already flagging.

Tilly's mind went into overdrive taking all of this in. He measured the field of battle, getting a sense of where he was most needed, his intensive training allowing him to commit to a course of action in half a second. He ignored the elites completely in favor of drawing the attention of the much weaker juveniles and keeping them out of the other fights for as long as possible.

The immortal words of Bonnie Raitt started to play through his mind as he charged forward with an animalistic scream, only slightly tinged with panic.

Let's give them something to talk about—

The center group of juveniles turned to his challenge as he sprinted back into the fight, and he activated **Wrath's Shroud**, covering himself in blue flames. This immediately drew the attention of the rest of the juveniles, who howled and shrieked as they recognized the attacker as the one who had just exploded in their midst. They charged to meet him, undaunted by the blaze of blue fire surrounding his form.

Right before they would have crashed into each other, Tilly leaped over the front line of the mob and landed in their midst, then rolled to his feet and hamstrung the juveniles to either side of him with enflamed strikes. The group he had passed over whirled while the back of the group pulled up, confused at his sudden appearance in their midst. He was behaving like no prey they had ever faced, and he kept them on their toes, tackling the nearest Strigoi even as they tried to dogpile him.

He had spent weeks sharpening his combat sense, and he felt the effects of his training regime now as he shot from one vicious attack to another, wasting no movement and never staying in place for more than a second, turning his enemy's advantage in numbers into a hindrance.

Needlelike teeth clamped onto his shoulder in retaliation for another tackle as the blue flames roaring all over the surface of his body melted the offending creature. He pulled the charred teeth with him as he rolled over the now waxy mass of gray flesh, taking several claw swipes on his back and legs as he continued to evade being locked down.

With each swing of his weapons acting as **Flame Strikes**, he punished the **Corruption**-riddled opponents with his huge 200 percent attack damage bonus. His movement through the unorganized mob could be traced by severe lingering burns and smoldering ax wounds. His strategy would have never worked against a more organized force, but the juveniles were new to their existence, and they continued to dive in gleefully over the ruined bodies of their allies, unmindful of the flames wreathing Tilly's body.

This was not to say that Tilly moved unencumbered through the sea of snapping maws and swiping claws. For the duration of his frenetic rampage, what should have been deadly blows were reduced to shallow wounds and bruises by his ridiculous *Endurance.* That, along with the constant damage output from his flames, turned what should have been a near-instant suicidal charge into a war of attrition. He swept through a dozen of the higher-level opponents, landing vicious blows, as he felt his lifeblood draining from his body's accumulating injuries.

He ducked a suicidal tackle from an already burned juvenile but caught a ripping swipe of the creature's clawed hand on his forehead. His blood dried instantly in the heat of **Wrath's Shroud**, and he barreled forward into the next target. To stop moving was to die, and he was doing everything he could to match the mob's ferocity with his own.

But after downing ten of his opponents, he was flagging, and more of the remaining juveniles' attacks were connecting. A blur of blue and white feathers crashed into the head of a creature to his left and caused it to burst into flames as a furious screeching *cheep* resounded in his mind.

A tangle of vines impacted several juveniles behind him, bursting in supernatural growth to snare the Strigoi. They had been about to pounce on Tilly from behind, and he stumbled forward, free from their attack, and swung a dual diagonal chop into two more juveniles in front of him even as his mana dipped below 5 percent.

The juvenile on his left stepped into his swing, taking the head of his hatchet to the shoulder in exchange for biting a chunk out of Tilly's bicep. The juvenile on his right took the hatchet in the side of its ribcage and grabbed onto Tilly's arm as it burned alive, pulling forward to bite at his neck. Tilly slammed his bleeding forehead into the mouth of the one on his right while yanking his arm free of the other and kicking it away.

Tilly's health dropped dangerously as he noticed several **Minor Bleeding** notifications stacked below his falling health. He jumped away from the two dead foes in front of him and whirled to face his remaining attackers as his *Ability* flickered out, leaving him with 13 percent health and zero mana.

Utterly spent, he lifted his two weapons weakly and faced the handful of injured foes that still encircled him. Ice speared a Strigoi directly in front of him and a profusely bleeding Gorock battered aside another two on his left, just as the fourth jumped on him from his right. Before Tilly could react to the enemy trying to bite his face off, its neck burst outward in a spray of black ichor, and Tilly exhaustedly pushed the body off of him to find a bloody Ichiro turning to face their temporary allies, flicking the ichor off his sword.

The knight moved from standing over the body of the Consumer that Gorock and Ichiro had been facing to assist the colorful magic user to his feet. Now that he wasn't looking through a magical barrier, Tilly's **Identify** pinged for both the figures.

Level 72, Knight of the Sanguine Order
Level 43, Bloodline Wizard's Apprentice

Tilly reflexively swept his gaze around the rest of the area to find Franklin and Amelia had made it through with only a few superficial wounds. They jogged down the hill to join the others. Tilly collapsed to his knees, numbness setting into his leaden extremities. He looked over to find Gorock had already collapsed onto the ground nearby, bleeding profusely onto the reddish-tan grass.

It was then that Tilly saw Blood Weed earn its name. As soon as any of the plants were splashed with blood, their reddish undertones burst forth in vibrant color and the skinny bladelike stalks began to grow, straining toward the source of the liquid.

"None of that now!" Amelia growled down at the plants as she jogged up and knelt by Gorock's side, then sent a shock wave of her mana throughout the nearby ground to force the plants back to their dormant state. Tilly's head felt fuzzy, and he saw a **Blood Loss** debuff appear below his still-dropping health.

"Um . . . bag . . . ," he muttered as Amelia pulled out large purplish leaves from her pockets and started wrapping them around Gorock's most severe wounds, which were already festering with **Corruption**. The others didn't seem to have heard his request, and Tilly swallowed dryly to try and speak again.

I'm coming! shouted a mental voice, clearing some of the fog from Tilly's mind. He looked back over the hill and caught sight of Kindle, laboriously carrying his med bag in her talons, barely able to keep aloft.

She dropped it next to him a few seconds later, and Tilly collapsed over it, then fumbled into the side pocket where he kept all the bandages in three four-foot rolls. He grabbed one and immediately began wrapping it around his worst injury, on the inside of his thigh, to stop it from pumping arterial blood down his pant leg. The bleeding had been slightly staunched when he had been consumed by flames, but now he was leaking everywhere.

Kindle hovered over him in concern while Amelia fought to stem the decline of Gorock's health. Ichiro and Franklin moved to stand between their injured party members, and the knight, who had helped up the wizard's apprentice, turned to approach.

"Well met, strangers. We do not recognize your like from these lands . . . Did you arrive with the . . . recent shift in the Land, perchance?" the colorfully dressed apprentice asked groggily, still leaning heavily on the knight's support.

"A moment please. We must see to our wounded," Ichiro said, sword drawn in a protective stance before the group. Tilly wrapped several rolls of bandages around his chest and back while trying to keep an eye on the exchange. As soon as he tied off the bandage, he felt **First Aid** kick in again and sighed in relief as the **Bleeding** and **Blood Loss** debuffs disappeared from his HUD.

His health stopped dropping at 7.5 percent and slowly began ticking up as he crawled over to Amelia and Gorock. She had finished tying off the large purple leaves with little strands of elongated grass and was now reaching into her pockets. She was muttering plant names to herself as she found and shoved some kind of root into Gorock's mouth.

Tilly scanned the edges of Gorock's wounds and found them red and puffy. The spidery black growth of a **Corruption** infection was starting to reach beyond the coverage of the purple leaves. Tilly winced up at his pitiful mana bar. It had barely reached 4 percent since the fight.

Amelia shoved a hand into another pocket and handed him a Shaman's Casting Aid. She tossed the bundle of herbs his way without looking, mostly focused as she was on working Gorock's jaw to chew on the root she had placed between his teeth.

"Yes, of course!" the apprentice said, peering over Ichiro's and Franklin's forms to watch as Amelia and Tilly worked. "Would that I could offer assistance, but I am afraid my skills in the healing arts are poor at best, and certainly not up to the task of whatever new foul blackness has tainted this cursed race."

He continued droning as Tilly took a deep inhale of the herb bundle and felt its effects flush through his respiratory system as he fell into his breathing technique.

Tilly didn't have any way to see Gorock's health, but his giant chest was still rising and falling, and the bleeding had slowed to a trickle after the application of the large purple leaves. The **Corruption** was still spreading, but Tilly's mana was almost back up to 10 percent with the assistance of the shaman's aid.

"I am loathe to interfere, but if you are new here, you may not have encountered this substance before . . . It is not like any poison status effect I have ever seen, and we have yet to find a cure for it," the apprentice continued in concern. The knight stood silently to his side, facepiece down.

None of Tilly's party bothered answering as Tilly watched his mana tick above 10 percent, and as soon as it did, he activated a full-powered **Flame's Renewal**.

CHAPTER THIRTY

The Other Kind of Vampire

The whole group turned and watched in concern as Tilly released his mana-infused breath *Ability*. The magic struck Gorock like a physical blow, causing his whole body to flinch and then go rigid. He released a deep groan, and all of his wounds began to seep again, despite the presence of the living bandages.

But the viscous substance that was being ejected from the wounds was much darker than blood. It flowed in tiny rivulets, attempting to join one another as they poured from Gorock's body. Amelia let out an annoyed hiss and imbued the Blood Weed all around Gorock with her mana to take control of the plants directly. The blades of grass bloomed back to life and consumed the black ichor as it hit the ground, before it could form a cohesive whole. The **Corruption** was absorbed and spread out amongst the interconnected plants, like wine on a tablecloth with Gorock at its center. Once it was all out, Amelia clenched her fist and the infected plants withered, trapping the **Corruption** within their husks.

Gorock's body slowly relaxed, and he let out an involuntary sigh of relief as color returned to his waxy gray cheeks.

"By the Sanguine Heart! What *Ability* is this? Human, how did you achieve what even our greatest have been unable to accomplish?" the apprentice barked, aghast.

Tilly looked up to answer him and finally got a clear view of his features. His face was angular and pale, contrasting painfully with his colorful assortment of layered clothing. But it was his mouth hanging open in shock that yanked Tilly's attention to the defining feature of the apprentice's face. Reaching almost to his bottom lip were two elongated canines.

More vampires?

Tilly's hand fell to his weapons, and the motivation behind Ichiro's stance and caution suddenly became clear. He fumbled for an answer to the apprentice's shocked question.

"I got this *Ability* as much by dumb luck as anything else. But you should know that this 'new blackness,' as you call it, is not just affecting your region. It is seeping up through the cracks of reality everywhere on Nephesh, offering its dark promises to any who are willing to give up their souls," he said hotly, the adrenaline from the battle and another near-death experience still pumping through his system.

"Dumb luck, you say . . . ," the vampire answered thoughtfully, his eyes sharpening. A hungry gleam came over his features as he considered the group anew. Suddenly the stance of the hulking knight next to him seemed to take on an even more threatening cast. The dull sheen of his metallic face plate glinted ominously in the light of several still-smoldering corpses.

"I am quite impressed by how effective your power set is against the Strigoi, especially in their newly empowered state," the vampire continued, licking his lips unconsciously.

"Excuse me. My name is Ichiro Matsumoto. We are on a mission from a newly integrated nation on the border of these lands. Who are you, and if you don't mind, why should we trust you?" Ichiro broke in, calling the distracted vampire's attention back to him.

"Yes, of course, how rude of me! I am Hilbert Ferrier, the last apprentice to the Bloodline Sorcerer Merllyn and a member of the low court of Camelot. This is Sir Michael, Knight of the Sanguine Order. He currently holds a seat at the High Table," the vampire answered formally.

"Merllyn . . . Camelot? Wait, are you guys vampire versions of the Knights of the Round Table?" Tilly burst out, unable to hold his excitement at recognizing some of the possible myths represented by this faction.

Hilbert's face fell slightly at Tilly's words. "Ah, you have heard of us . . . I am afraid some of your information is out of date. I know not what you mean by 'vampire version,' but I would be happy to share the history of my people after we are away from this location. More will come from further afield, even if I reactivate my warding."

"How much longer do you think we have?" Ichiro asked as Gorock groaned and sat up, looking much better after only a few minutes rest. The veiny **Corruption** was gone and his bleeding had almost ceased.

His Constitution has to be insane, Tilly thought, staring down at the Wall Breaker with renewed respect. He had just gone toe to toe with something almost twice his level and survived long enough for the others to finish it. After a moment of consideration, Hilbert answered Ichiro's question.

"We should be fine for a few minutes more. They would never have found us at all if I had not tried to scry the newly formed horde," the apprentice answered sheepishly, and the statuesque Sir Michael moved for the first time to turn his blank face plate down at him. "Yes, yes," Hilbert said, waving away the look with a weak dismissal. "How could I have known they would have such a powerful counter to divination? That has never been a strength of the horde's before! Of course, much has changed in the last few months . . . but that is why we are here, isn't it." Then he turned to the group. "We, too, are on a mission from our order—"

Tilly didn't see the knight move, but his armor creaked as he continued to watch the apprentice. Hilbert stuttered and cleared his throat before continuing. "Ah, well, what I mean to say is, we are on a mission *for* our order. They do not know we have come, and they would perhaps be against our reaching out if they knew—"

"So, you have no power to broker an alliance?" Ichiro asked, disappointment seeping in at the edges of his formal tone.

"Ah, our order is not what it once was. We still present a strong martial presence in the region, but we are . . . declining. The horde has consumed the Jiangshi to the west and the twilight elves, who used to possess the marshes to the south. Now all of those lands have been converted to barren grasslands. You need to understand, each enemy the horde consumes converts to a juvenile of their own race. It has left them with an unsustainable force that has grown exponentially and will consume itself if it does not continue to expand—"

A barking screech sounded in the distance, drawing the eyes of the whole group toward the distant noise. Hilbert's head snapped back to the group.

"I can hide us, but we need to be away from here. On our honor, we will not harm you and yours unless you try and do the same to us," he whispered urgently, gesturing more or less in the direction they had already been traveling.

The smoldering corpses had moved into the visual background of Tilly's mind during the conversation, but at the interruption of the call of more scouts, he had noticed Kindle settling into the largest pile of corpses like a nest. In her presence, the blue embers had reignited and were merrily consuming the bodies. The blaze was so hot that it was producing complete combustion, creating only colorless heat without a hint of smoke. Tilly watched in astonishment as her physical form visibly matured in the presence of the fire and the fuel it consumed.

"We will accompany you for a few hours, but our mission is urgent, and we have little time to spare. Even now, our people are besieged by this new horde, and we must pursue our own objectives here in the Twilight Lands. Come with us to pick up our gear, and then we will hear you out in a different location," Ichiro answered, sheathing his sword.

A call sounded again, closer to the group.

"The initial direction does not matter. I can cast the attention ward anywhere, but it will not stand up to the scrutiny such a scene will bring," Hilbert answered while gesturing at the bodies.

Gorock was helped to his feet, and he shook off his still-healing injuries as he eyed the knight, who was only slightly shorter than him. With that, the group moved back the way they had come. Accompanied by their two new members, they rounded the hill at a jog, heading back to pick up their dropped gear. Tilly moved to follow, calling mentally back through his bond as he ran.

Kindle, leave the rest, we have to go!

The coming gray ones cannot fly. I will be away before they arrive. Worry not, Tilly, she answered in a warm, confident voice. Some of her words carried hints of the wild scenes that had shaped most of her messages in the past, but the majority of the mental communication he had just received used human language. Tilly stumbled and turned in shock to look at the phoenix, who was sitting calmly in the midst of the growing blaze.

I must grow stronger if I am to help you in your task. This is how my kind grows, she sent calmly. Another set of screeching howls sounded from only a few hilltops away.

Now go, silly human. I will be fine.

You better be! he mentally growled back as he sprinted off after the others, not at all liking how fast things were changing with her. A few days ago, she was just mastering flight, and now she was using full sentences.

Once their group arrived at the dropped packs, Amelia made sure their cloaks were covered in Blood Weed, which earned an appreciative look from Hilbert, and they kept moving. Tilly kept looking back anxiously but felt nothing but determination from his bond as the scouting calls converged on their old position.

They continued to run, skirting around the small valley they had just fought within and putting distance between them and the site of the battle. Hilbert slid up next to Tilly and spoke in a low but audible tone. "If that creature of yours is spotted and gets away, it will be blamed for the destruction. My skills gave me no level identifier with its tag, so they will be unable to know if it was capable of such a thing or not."

"What about the wounds caused by weapons?"

"Ah . . . yes," he answered, then thought for a second. "That will depend on whether they have a Consumer nearby or not. If the juveniles are not specifically forbidden, they will eat anything, even their own dead. They are ravenous, all of them, and this land has long been empty of anything they could eat besides each other."

Tilly nodded absently at that, looking back and sending a worried mental inquiry.

Kindle, where are you? It's been too long.

In response, Tilly received a strong feeling of exultation through their bond, accompanied by a recent memory from Kindle's point of view. This time the overlay of her memory barely caused him to skip a step as he kept running. She had packaged it in such a way that as soon as he touched it with his mind, it unfolded and streamed into his consciousness in a far less attention-demanding form. Instead of trying to watch it like a mental video, he simply let the memory sink in, gaining far more from the scene than he had when they had last shared points of view.

She watched as the first scout and then the second crested the hill, charging up to the pile of burning bodies and pulling up in confusion, unable to make out the figure in the midst of the stoked flames. Then she did something Tilly could feel but did not quite understand, and the extra energy-rich heat she had been unable to absorb suddenly exploded in a frontal cone and completely enveloped the two juveniles. The blast also set the two Consumer bodies alight, and she took off in flight as more juveniles crested the hill. A few howled angrily after her, but she had already gained significant altitude.

Then there was a blur from over the hill, and she twisted on instinct as a chipped ax whipped by, end over end, flying at an extraordinary velocity. She whirled around to find a Consumer watching her, its hatred palpable even from this distance.

The memory broke off as she headed away from Tilly's direction, planning to circle around out of sight. She would not lead them to her human.

Good girl, he sent back with the image of a high five, not sure if the satisfaction he felt was his own or the lingering echo of her fierce exultation at her first solo victory.

CHAPTER THIRTY-ONE

Horchata

Kindle rejoined the moving group half an hour later. They had fully skirted the site of the battle and continued moving in the direction Ichiro indicated. None of them had forgotten the pressure the Alliance was facing, and they pushed forward relentlessly, even after the intensity of their last encounter.

The two new vampiric additions to the group seemed content with the direction Ichiro had chosen and moved along easily with the group. Tilly was shocked at how little sound the knight made as he moved; the intricate plate mail that covered his form seemed to flow like water and was easily the finest example of metalwork Tilly had yet seen on Nephesh.

Once the calls of the Strigoi were inaudible to Tilly's ears, Hilbert motioned for them to stop. They had been moving through what probably used to be a creek bed but was now little more than a dusty winding path.

"This is a good place for us to come to some sort of agreement," Hilbert said, looking around and nodding to himself.

"Agreed. Everyone, break out water and rations. We will get the most we can out of this stop," Ichiro called out as he moved to stand opposite the two vampires and dropped his pack.

Tilly mirrored his actions and moved to stand beside the lapin, then reached into his pack to grab some of the food Edna and George had packed for him. The knight had moved to lean against the steeper incline of the hill, going completely still as soon as he achieved a position that seemed vaguely relaxed. It was not lost on Tilly that he had left his right arm and weapon completely free.

Hilbert pulled out a few things from his robes and moved around the group, facing outward, as he did something at the four cardinal points around their position. Tilly took a long swig of his water and checked on the others.

Amelia's short hair was mussed, and her complexion had grown waxy and pale. She was barely breathing hard, but the blouse she wore under her coat was soaked in sweat, and as she looked his way, he quickly continued his scan. Franklin was even sweatier and breathing the hardest of anyone in the group as he held his hands laced above his head. Tilly was amazed at the pace the honu had been able to keep so far and realized that he probably couldn't go nearly as long as the rest. But Tilly doubted he would ask them to slow down on his account. He was just as determined as the rest of the group to accomplish the mission. Yet despite the strength of their determination, Amelia and Franklin clearly had the lowest *Endurance* stat by far, and in a situation like this, it was beginning to show.

On the other hand, Gorock had splayed out on the other bank of the creek bed and was tearing into a large shank of dried meat. Tilly could only assume it had come from his bag and wondered how much of that pack was weighed down by meat. The Wall Breaker kept casting baleful looks at the knight between bites, and Tilly wondered what could possibly be going through his mind.

At the final cardinal point, Hilbert whispered something in a harsh language, and the four points began to glow with the same pinkish hue that had accompanied his magic before. The light faded and the world outside their little group took on a shimmery quality. Kindle let out a *cheep* of interest, looking at the ward with one eye and then the other as she examined it in a uniquely avian fashion.

"This will keep anyone who does not already know our location from finding us and make any search oriented toward us overlook this position. Now, you said you had your own mission . . . What are your intentions in this land? Maybe we can offer assistance," Hilbert said, leaning toward the group eagerly.

"Very sorry, but seeing as we rescued you from that attack, perhaps you could finish telling us about your Sanguine Order and what your interest in our party is," Ichiro responded blandly, his meditative state radiating peace in an almost aggressive show of control as he beheld the two vampires with his milky-white eyes.

"Rescue is something of an overstatement—" Hilbert started, but then the Knight turned his head in the apprentice's direction. He stuttered to a stop, then went on, "But fair enough, especially in the spirit of your actions. I would be happy to tell you more about our people. As your knowledgeable companion stated"—he gestured appreciatively at Tilly—"we started as a kingdom on the rise, led by a truly noble king named Arthur Pendragon . . . With my master as his advisor, we unseated the corrupt monarchies that surrounded us and ushered in a new era of peace and prosperity for all of the Aos Si. Then my master's first apprentice betrayed us, attacking and deposing a neighboring faction that had signed a peace treaty with us.

"Her name was Morgana, and she had been pushing for a continued expansion of our power for some time. My master understood the importance of balance and had advised against it, but with this move, our order ascended to the next echelon of power. This destabilized our region and cast our order and area of influence into the hands of the system. We were sent here, to the Twilight Lands, to bring balance, with a quest to end the expansion of the horde and bring stability to this region.

"Their numbers and strength were much greater than they are now, and thus began the Blood Wars. This was hundreds of years ago, before I was born, but the short of it is that we lost our king in the fighting, and the order had to make terrible sacrifices to survive in this new land against such an unrelenting enemy.

"To ensure our survival, Merllyn took the Blood Oath and fundamentally changed the nature of the curse of vampirism into something our people could carry without it consuming them. Now, we are a society led by dhampires and vampires, who protect the rest of our people and contain the horde all along our western border while trading and accepting tribute from the lands to the east. We became the Sanguine Order and have maintained balance in this region for the last hundred and fifty years. I was taken as my master's last apprentice a few years before he was . . . called away," Hilbert finished quietly, his pale features eerily blank despite the emotion coloring his tone.

"With Merllyn gone and the king dead, who leads your order?" Tilly asked.

Hilbert pulled his focus away from whatever memory had tugged at his mind. "Ah, that would be Queen Guinevere. She leads the order as our Sorceress Superior. After King Arthur passed, my master began training her and several other apprentices to try and increase our chances of survival. Unfortunately, none of the others have survived, but Queen Guinevere continues to lead the order to this day," he answered, his voice curt. Tilly didn't have to connect many dots to guess that she was the one who had been against them striking out into horde territory and trying to contact the new nation.

Ichiro's cool demeanor remained unchanged, but his eyes sharpened as he watched the pair intently. A thought occurred to Tilly that could possibly bridge the needs of both groups.

"You said you guys haven't been able to cure any cases of **Corruption** in your people. We know how much of a problem that can become without quick intervention. If we agreed to clear out the most important cases in your order, do you think your queen would agree to a temporary alliance with us and attack the forces sieging our faction? If we succeeded, we could eliminate an enemy army from the field and strengthen your position."

The apprentice's eyes narrowed in thought, and he turned to the knight, who had not moved the entire time they had been speaking. Something passed between them, and Hilbert turned back smiling, his fangs on full display.

"This plan holds several risks for both of us, but it aligns with our goals. We will bring you to the order and gain you an audience with the queen . . . She will, of course, be furious with us, but this is exactly why we set out."

"Swear to us on your power that you mean us no harm," Ichiro cut in.

The vampire's smile turned downwards slightly, but not in a way that seemed overly suspicious. "I can see how such a thing would go far in assuaging any fears you may have, due to our similarity with our shared enemy . . . Very well, I will do it." He turned toward the lapin and looked him full in the eyes as he produced a dagger from his robes and cut a complicated symbol into his forearm. *"By the power in my blood, I pronounce full guest rites over you as representatives of your faction. No harm will come to you and yours as long as you do not betray this trust,"* he whispered, his forehead beading with sweat as the glyph he carved into his flesh flashed pink and disappeared.

Ichiro nodded in approval and gestured back to Tilly to continue. Tilly knew that the faction upgrade quest offered to the Alliance was essential to its survival. Not that he understood all the details, but gaining an allied force on the field was too good an opportunity to pass up even if it would slow them down in the short run.

"Hilbert, what direction would you say Camelot is in, and how long do you think it will take us to get there?" Tilly asked, settling into a meditative pose.

Hilbert gestured slightly more to the east, taking them off of their original heading by about twenty degrees. "At our current pace, we could reach it in a day with a little assistance. Does this have to do with your mission?" he asked in an innocent, curious tone.

"Yep. But before I tell you more, I need to check something," Tilly answered, then began to breathe in rhythm. From what he had seen of the valley and the Facet's guardian, he felt it was unlikely that they were within the order's lands, but it wouldn't hurt to check. At the very least he would have a good idea where they needed to head after they met with the queen.

He continued to breathe, letting his surroundings in and out, allowing them to wash through him without fighting or trying to impose his will on them. He was doing all he could, and that had to be enough. The others continued to talk and rest while his world became the darkness of his mind and the movement of his breath.

As soon as he felt himself fully settle, he activated **Spirit Walk** and rose up from his body. Hilbert was watching him curiously but did not track the movement of his spirit as it separated from his body. Ichiro's face did not reflect any change as Tilly rose, but his ear twitched when Tilly turned his attention onto the lapin.

All the others were recovering in their own way within the ward. Amelia was brewing some tea and offered it to Franklin, while Gorock lay passed out nearby, clutching the now clean bone like it was a stuffed animal.

Tilly cleared his head and let go of distraction, allowing himself to float there and experience his surroundings on a spiritual level. Slowly but surely, he felt the presence of the myriad threads that wove through all things. He could not see them, but their effects made themselves known in millions of little contact points around the edges of his spirit form. Some threads were a part of him, some attempted to invade, and others touched and strengthened him.

After a while, he found the Flower's music. It may have been his imagination, but it felt slightly easier to discern this time, almost as if it had become fractionally louder. As soon as he had the direction, he shot back to his body, unsure of how much time he had spent in that state.

His eyes flicked open to find Amelia, Franklin, and Hilbert locked in some sort of conversation while Ichiro rested and Gorock stood alert nearby. The knight, however, had not moved from his position, watching the group, and a chill ran up Tilly's spine at just how still the figure had remained. It was completely unnatural.

Amelia was the first to see his opened eyes. "He is back," she said simply as she put away the notebook she had been using while Hilbert spoke.

"Back? Interesting choice of words. Is it some type of scrying *Ability*? I must warn you, they have develop—"

"Yeah, we know about that guy, he absolutely sucks. And no, it's not a scrying *Ability*—at least, I don't think it is," Tilly answered absently as he turned to Ichiro, who had awoken and turned to watch him curiously. Tilly gestured in the direction Hilbert had shown them, then moved his hand twenty degrees further westward. "It is still more or less in the right direction, so going with them would take us off course, but not by much."

Ichiro nodded and turned to the two vampires. "We will accompany you to your order's headquarters and give what aid we can. Then we will continue on. Our Sovereign Crystal has issued us a quest, and the object of our mission is in that direction," he said, pointing where Tilly had just indicated.

Hilbert and the knight shared another look.

CHAPTER THIRTY-TWO

Enemy at the Gates

Linus – Level 65 Consul

Not for the first time, Linus cursed his new class. It was an inefficient mix of political leadership and limited martial *Abilities*. To make matters worse, all of the *Abilities* were limited to buffing forces that the system classified as "standing armies."

Flame's Watch was extremely powerful for what it was, a guardsman class. But without unlocking true martial classes, their utility would be limited. Especially in frontline warfare. The newly minted soldiers were doing an admirable job holding up against the constant onslaught of the enemy. *Abilities* like **Call the Guard** and **Riot Wall** were working so far as a stopgap. **Call the Guard** filled any breaks in the line holding the wall by summoning designated reserves directly to the needed spot. When a member of the Watch was summoned this way, they gained a slew of buffs for the next sixty breaths and a minor gap-closing movement *Ability*. **Riot Wall** was serving as a lesser version of any military unit's shield-push skill. It was meant to be used against citizens and prioritized defense and displacement. Unlike a military equivalent, it offered no multipliers to damage or forward movement.

Aside from some weapon and armor proficiency bonuses . . . that was it. That was what they had to work with as a faction of their size. Despite this, the men and women rotating in to hold the line were some of the finest initial recruits Linus had ever seen. He had risen through the ranks of the empire's military structure until he had gained the highest nonpolitical placement, and he had never seen a more determined group of new soldiers.

They faced waves of enemies, sometimes three times their level, and none broke or wavered. In fact, perhaps because of the lack of unit *Abilities*, which often turned a group of soldiers into a singular, much more powerful entity, skill leveling and *experience* gains had shown to be astronomical. Sometimes powerful unit *Abilities* became a crutch that the average soldier leaned on while ignoring the fundamentals. But with this group . . . the fundamentals were all they had.

All of this he understood, and yet his skin continued to itch as he watched the ongoing combat.

"Justice's Pit-cursed blind eyes!" Linus snarled again under his breath as the most recent wave of enemies retreated reluctantly. The thousand or so enemy combatants had suffered incredible losses—as much as 60 to 70 percent of the attacking wave had perished—while the Alliance forces had lost maybe one in every twenty men.

This pattern had repeated itself over and over for the last day. Each time the Strigoi horde really began to press the forces on the wall, the enemy would call a retreat and move back to their lines. They crashed against their fortified position time after time, taking huge losses in the charge, yet they always pulled back, like dark waves slowly eroding sand from the shore.

When the retreat sounded, Consumers and Flesh Bags that were still standing snatched any soldier they could and retreated with the rest of their forces. Sometimes the man or woman in question was still alive and their screams tore through morale like tissue paper. It was humiliating. Linus could literally feel the Bastions chomping at the bit to get in the fight . . . but they had to be kept in reserve.

As the loose braying mob of gray flesh exited bow range, healers were called in and a changing of the units was ordered by the commanders on the wall.

They are playing with us . . . Gods dammit. An expensive game to be sure, but one that we most assuredly cannot win.

Linus kicked the nearby stone stair in frustration. "These tactics don't make any Justice-damned sense!" he whispered harshly under his breath, then schooled his expression as the replacement unit passed by, their faces grim with determination and, in some cases, resignation.

Most thought they were holding, driving back the enemy time after time . . . Linus hoped none of them realized the truth.

"What troubles you, Consul?" a voice asked quietly from over Linus's shoulder. He spun away from the battlements to find Erash, standing in all her regal beauty, leaning lightly on her staff. Linus knew even that was not as it seemed, and he wondered darkly for a moment how long she would be able to stand without swaying if she didn't have that crutch to lean on.

"Truthfully?" he asked, looking for any hint of sarcasm or mockery in her features.

"Yes. We have moved through a full day with minimal losses or use of resources. Should we not be more optimistic?" she asked, arching one perfect eyebrow at him as if she knew more than she let on. She seemed to be looking for something, and the unspoken implications irritated him further.

He stepped forward aggressively, lowering his voice into a harsh whisper. "You know good and well what troubles me. The same thing that has kept you from resting since the attacks started!" He almost spat in frustration. "This is a farce. They are playing with us, and while I see that their numeric advantage is more than enough to defeat us *eventually* using this strategy, I cannot for the life of me understand why they do not try to sweep us away. If even one of their leaders took the field, I am hard-pressed to see how we could hold against such a meaningful show of force. Yet they wait! Tossing their weakest at us as if we are some sort of idle entertainment," he finished, deflating.

When he looked back up to meet the High Priestess's eyes, he found something bright there. It was sharp, and it was angry. The eyes took on a glow and scanned the ranks on the battlements before returning to Linus.

No, that wasn't quite right; she was staring at a spot right above Linus's head, as if she could see something there.

"Freeze the blood in that bastard's bones! How have I missed this?" she hissed.

"What?" Linus asked, suddenly at a loss.

"That damned mesmer! He has covered the whole tundra-blasted field in a *Malaise*! One so subtle that it has escaped my detection . . ." She trailed off, bringing one of her manicured nails to her mouth and chewing on it in furious thought. "But how do I combat it without waking a reprisal?" she muttered to herself, looking back over the battlements.

"*Malaise*? What are you talking about?" Linus demanded, his sense sharpening to high alert as he looked back at the enemy line in suspicion.

"It is an extremely malicious and subtle area-of-effect spell. It does nothing the first few hours, but after a day, all who spend time in its presence feel defeated, depressed, and confused. After a few days, suspicion and jealousy set in . . . Inevitably, we would start to attack each other, breaking our own defense without them having to do anything but train up their young." She huffed, her eyes shifting back and forth as she went through her mental options. Then she turned to wander away, starting to mutter to herself, "I need some sort of mental purifying effect . . . but it has to be ongoing. One that I don't have to refresh every few hours . . ."

"Wait, are you saying I am under the effects of mind magic?" Linus almost shouted as she turned her back to him.

"We all are, Consul. Just give me a few hours. I can counter this, but I need to do so in a way that does not draw out an immediate confrontation. Ideally, I want them to think it is still working for days yet. Every hour gained is a victory for us, do not forget that, Linus," she said over her shoulder before moving away quickly toward the healing tent and her base of operations.

A few moments later, Hiro arrived, coming down the rear stairs and catching Linus's gaze with a questioning look.

"The men said you were shouting at the High Priestess . . . I imagine you would not do so without reason," he stated as he neared Linus's position at the base of the stairs.

"We were speaking of the enemy's tactics, and somehow, through the discussion, she discovered some sort of large-scale mental magic at play. She headed off to counter it . . . I may have overreacted, which is not typical of me, and perhaps evidence of her point. Gods, I hate mind magic."

Hiro nodded, his crystalline gaze missing nothing. "The honu have a saying: 'A shark's hunger undoes his brother and protects us all.' They use it to describe a creature of their oceans whose young devour each other until only the strongest remain. It is in their nature to sacrifice the weak so that the strong may rise. I think we are facing something similar here. They see us as a leveling aid . . . and meal opportunity. They rightly believe us to be harmless to them on any scale that matters.

"The ones that escape back to their lines have fed, to some degree, on our men, and who knows what level of significance that has in their culture. If not for our purifying capabilities, this tactic would have already destroyed us by nature of the **Corruption** they are attempting to infect us with. But now, it is working in our favor. Each day they give us is a gift: we grow stronger and our people gain the time they need to accomplish their quest. None of this will be easy, but we would not have been thrust into this conflict if there was not a way through.

"I had lost hope the first time I met that human, yet through him our people have obtained more than they could have ever dreamed . . . There is a way through this, friend, we just have to hold on." As the elderly samurai finished, something like kindness glittered in his hard green eyes.

Relevus – Level 22 Butcher

He'd had the dream again . . .

This time he had woken up outside the camp near the forest covered in blood.

Blood was nothing new for Relevus, but the portly satyr was used to it happening in the back of his shop. He had especially loved when the farmers would deliver live animals, and he—

But that was all over now. The slimy Scale-bellies had taken everything from him. He'd had to leave behind almost everything except a few of his favorite knives, and now he was stuck in this frontier refugee camp, surrounded by idiots who pretended like the fools in charge were some sort of saviors.

He had gotten sick with many of the others while living in the squalor of the capital city, but he hadn't gone begging for some handout like a weakling. He had toughed it out, like he always had, and the strange black rash had slowly faded from his skin, leaving him feeling better than ever.

Then the dreams had started.

Dreams where he was wistfully taken back to his old shop. There he would relive the memories of the best days. Slaughter days, when he could end another living being with nothing but the strength of his hands and the edges of his knives.

He smiled as he thought of the dream again before looking down and remembering he had blood all over his hands. He wiped at some new wetness dribbling from his mouth and created a red streak down his forearm.

Huh.

He didn't know exactly what was happening, and as long as he didn't get caught, he didn't really care. The dreams made him feel strong. They gave him that feeling of control that he missed so much from the back of his shop.

Through the darkness, he stumbled over to the river's edge and washed off the blood as best he could before heading back to the camp. There were hardly any Watch around with the attacks happening on the other side of the valley. The misstep of a foolishly early activation of the Sovereign Crystal was just another example of the ineptitude of these new leaders. The food and shelter problems they claimed to have solved would have only taken the weak, leaving the strong majority secure.

They are going to get us all killed, just like the idiots in charge of the empire tried to do . . .

"Relevus," a voice whispered from the shadows of a tent as he entered the camp.

The Butcher's head whipped around until he found a gaunt figure wrapped in robes so that nothing but his elderly face showed. He had what might once have been dignified features, now lined and worn by the elements. But his eyes were still sharp, glittering with intensity from their shadowy cowl.

"Who are you? How do you know me?" the Butcher asked in outrage, barely covering over his rising panic.

Have I been discovered? Will I have to end this old man? he thought hurriedly as he reached for his knife below his dirty leather apron. For some reason, the motion sent a thrill through him, and he felt a strange but pleasurable sensation from the area of his body that had recovered from the rash.

"Worry not. I am not one to deny a man his simple pleasures," the robed figure said as he waved placatingly. "I am here because I see greatness in you." He showed a row of sharp teeth. "You are not the only wolf penned in with the sheep."

CHAPTER THIRTY-THREE

Next Stop, Camelot

The wizard's apprentice met Tilly's eyes after sharing a look with his silent companion, a complex expression on his face.

"I am afraid we most assuredly know where your quest objective is. That way lies the city of Requiem. It is the seat of power for the Whytes. They are a faction formed of incredibly strong imprints left by those who have passed beyond the veil of this plane. For a long time, they remained neutral in this region, but now they face a siege many times greater than your own. Last reports place the majority of the horde's forces outside their gates, attacking relentlessly."

"That makes them allies, correct?" Ichiro asked.

"Now, yes. In times past they stayed completely contained behind their nigh impregnable walls and sheer mountains. The horde seems to have turned out in full force to break the city, which is another mystery in itself of this recent shift in power . . .

"They call the Whytes 'Bloodless' because, while the strength of their supernatural presence creates a corporeal body, they have no life force from which the Strigoi, or even we, could benefit. This has positioned them to stand apart from the conflict that has always marked these lands. In fact, unless one had access to a prohibitive amount of wealth with which to trade, one would hardly be worth their notice. And even in that case, they only allow non-Whytes to do business outside the walls.

"However," the vampire said in a stage whisper, then gestured theatrically at the knight, who remained completely frozen against the berm. "I do know of one living being that has both entered and exited the city. He doesn't speak much about the experience, but don't hold that against him.

"I present to you Sir Michael. His story is his own, but suffice it to say, if you wanted to make it into the city, there would be no better guide, and he is not bad in a fight either, which you will probably need if you want to make it past the siege," he finished with a flourish, obviously smug that he had something to weigh down his side of the scale.

The statuesque knight slowly moved to look over at Hilbert, who looked back after his presentation and shrugged, unashamed. Finding what he was looking for in that motion, Sir Michael nodded once and then returned to complete stillness.

"And so, we are prepared to offer terms!" Hilbert said, clapping his hands together. "Come with us to Camelot and render the aid we so desperately need. I cannot make any promises or predictions on behalf of our leader, but afterward, no matter what, Sir Michael and I will accompany you to Requiem and do everything we can to get you into the city."

Ichiro turned and looked to the others, not questioningly but clearly opening the floor for input.

"It seems to me that the possible advantages outweigh the delay," Amelia chimed in. Franklin nodded in agreement, and Gorock wasn't even looking at the group. He had sat through the conversation looking longingly back the way they had come, as if reminiscing on the recently fought battle.

Ichiro then turned to Tilly, who considered the two before him with narrow eyes. There was more going on than the apprentice had admitted, and the mysterious silent knight obviously had more to him than stage fright . . . This could very well turn into a huge time suck with no gained advantage for their people.

Hilbert, as if sensing Tilly's reserve, smiled reassuringly, once again putting his two elongated canines on full display.

Yeah, that's not helping, dude, Tilly thought sardonically before deciding to ask one final question.

"Okay, so the leadership of your order are all vampires and dhampires . . . How much blood do you have to drink to survive, and how do you obtain it?" he asked, interested to see how the apprentice would handle such a broad question about his society. The vampire's smile dampened.

"Yes, I can see why you would want to understand this before entering into an agreement with us. I will be brief. First, as to how much we must drink, it entirely depends on our level of activity. We may enter into periods of rest for decades and not drink for the whole duration. However, Sir Michael and I, with our heightened activity, will need to drink before we continue to Camelot. And likely again once we arrive in the city."

As soon as he mentioned needing to drink, Tilly and several other members tensed, wondering if they had just discovered a trap.

"Do not worry, friends!" Hilbert waved placatingly, showing his empty hands. "We would never embark on such a mission without our own supplies," he said, then slowly reached into his robe and produced a silvery flask. He then looked over at Sir Michael and motioned for him to do the same. The knight moved slowly, so as not to startle anyone, and touched his right thigh below his mace, then came away with an elaborate syringe-looking object that differed greatly from Hilbert's flask. It had been seamlessly integrated with his armor, and Tilly had not noticed it at all until the knight pulled it away with the click of a metallic release.

Hilbert held eye contact with the group as he opened the flask and took a long drink before capping it. The runes along the side glowed for a moment before showing a circle that was a little less than half full of ruby light.

The knight beside him lifted the syringe to his forearm and placed its now glowing tip against his armor. The metal folded back briefly, and a hissing sound shot out from the object as it touched the bare skin underneath. The normally stoic knight experienced an involuntary full-body shudder at the injection and then quickly put the object away before Tilly could get a better look at its composition. It snapped back into place under his mace and out of view.

"As for how we obtain this precious resource," Hilbert continued, drawing the attention away from his companion and back to himself, "we do so just like any political entity: through tax and trade. To enter our city, you will be taxed. We call it the 'gift.' Through an enchanted object, you will donate a small portion of your life's blood. In return, you are promised basic rights in the city and a measure of protection. All citizens and allies of our order have the choice to pay either the blood price or its equivalent in Standard gold. Many do not mind temporarily giving up some portion of their health in exchange for what the order has to offer.

"We try to keep the number of turned citizens as low as possible, to remain sustainable, but with the increased pressure from the horde . . . Things are not as balanced as they once were," he finished, biting off the last words as if reluctant to part with them.

Tilly turned to Ichiro, whose expression remained unreadable.

"I think I agree with Amelia. There are certainly risks, and we are gambling with precious time, but the possible upside is too good to pass up," he said quietly. He knew everyone could hear him, but he still wanted to signal that he was only talking to Ichiro. The lapin's face remained unchanged as he took in the last of the group's input and turned to face the vampiric duo.

"As a representative of the Alliance's ruling council, I formally accept your offer. We look forward to a possible partnership between our peoples . . . But be warned: do not be fooled by our level disparity. As you have already seen, we have much else to bring to bear besides simple stat superiority. So, deal with us honestly and we will do the same with you."

Before Hilbert could answer, the knight stood and moved forward. Ichiro responded gracefully and without hesitation, rising to his feet to face Sir Michael. The imposing figure thrust out his hand and Ichiro looked down at it for a moment before clasping it firmly, shaking once, and then stepping away and bowing. The knight awkwardly mirrored his movements and then straightened.

"Well, this turned out wonderfully. Just wait until we see the look on Mallytza's face!" Hibert exclaimed excitedly. The whole group looked at him questioningly. "Ah . . . well . . . She is an ally we have in the court. She didn't think this was a good idea and is the only one who knows exactly where we went," he said, his face becoming even paler, if that was possible.

Is that the vampire version of blushing? Tilly thought to himself as Ichiro turned to face the group.

"Collect your things and prepare for another run. We will not stop until we make Camelot, and we will be leaving shortly."

Tilly reached for his bag and absently began to wonder how he would get his armor to turn back into its Blood Mound Shambler form when the flashing icon at the top of his HUD finally got his attention. In all his worry about Kindle, the two vampires, and his **Spirit Walk**, he had forgotten about leveling! He glanced up sheepishly at the flashing notification icon and the log appeared in front of him.

He filtered through the damage indicators, asking the system to summarize the net gains of the battle.

Congratulations! You have defeated 18 Strigoi Juveniles in combat and assisted in the destruction of another 7.
Due to level disparity, an experience multiplier has been applied to your gains.

Congratulations! You are now level 19.

Congratulations! You are now level 20 . . .

Congratulations! You are now level 23.
1.3 million exp until the next level.

You have 25 unspent stat points.

Whoa, five levels! Not bullshitting around with a mana feedback loop is awesome! Now, if only I could find the time to grind . . . , he thought, quickly running through the math he needed to maintain [Resolute], which had once again saved his life. Despite the high cost, there was no way he could get rid of something that so consistently saved his life.

Okay, so from five levels, I gained forty stat points total, ten of which automatically went into Endurance, *and five of which went to* Dexterity, *one point for each new level. I'm going to need to double those ten points if I want to keep* Endurance *higher than the other stats combined.*

He dropped another ten stat points into *Endurance.*

The feeling was immediate; though not as intense as it had been in the moments before he had dived into the fiery cave so many weeks ago, it was still significant. It felt like his physical form had become more substantial . . . No, that wasn't it. More dense?

He looked up at the others, who were almost ready to go, and pushed off the musing for later. He still had fifteen more stat points to assign. He pulled up and looked over his stat sheet critically.

Stats:

Constitution: 18

Endurance: 121 (133.1)

Dexterity: 40 (44)

Strength: 13 (15.8)

Wisdom: 18 (13.68)

Intelligence: 16

Okay, he was still taking a serious hit on *Wisdom*, which had absolutely established itself as the bottleneck in his ability to output damage . . . And if he was being honest with himself, even though his crazy *Endurance* was soaking up a lot of damage up front, his fighting style was still taking him far too close to death for it to be sustainable. So *Constitution* couldn't be ignored either.

Everyone around him stood and shouldered their pack as Tilly made his decision. Ten in *Wisdom*, bringing it to twenty-eight base, and five in *Constitution*, taking it up to twenty-three. He then hopped to his feet and shouldered his pack before moving forward with the others as Hilbert whispered some arcane words, and the glowing symbols hemming in the group faded away.

Next stop, Camelot.

CHAPTER THIRTY-FOUR

Running up That Hill

They set off at a ground-eating pace with Hilbert leading the way, following some sort of magical compass. The group stayed mostly silent as they ran, but Tilly found that he was a long way from feeling any exhaustion after the break they had just taken. His *Endurance* had just gone up another twenty points, and he felt like he could probably run at this pace for the next twenty-four hours and barely be winded at their destination.

The effortless feeling that marked his movements during moderate physical activity contrasted greatly with how quickly he had felt depleted near the end of the fight. It seemed like his abysmal *Strength* stat was holding him back whenever he operated at the leading edge of his physical ability. However, if he kept himself to moderate output, he had the sense he could go on for a ridiculous amount of time.

That being said, when he thought back to the recent battle, he couldn't help but smile in grim satisfaction. He might not have been a paragon of grace, but he more than held his own in the fight. All of the practice scenarios and the brutal skill leveling he had done over the last month had really transformed his combat ability. Sure, his power advantage over **Corrupted** opponents was the only reason he had survived that last encounter, but it had not been the only factor . . . He had also kicked some significant monster ass.

And he wasn't the only one! Kindle had demonstrated a dramatic increase in capability after the fight. Tilly could only imagine how having access to this new sort of fuel allowed her to advance. Instead of riding on Tilly's pack, she had taken to the air, gliding as an almost invisible spot high above them. She was now more at ease in the air than perched on his shoulder. A change that he wasn't sure he liked. He loved her increased survivability, but not being needed quite as much stung a little.

Are you sure you don't need a rest? I think Hilbert has some sort of tracker that lets him avoid scouting parties, so you don't have to keep watch all the time, he sent again, marveling at their ability to suddenly converse in complete sentences.

We just rescued that peacock from a pack of the gray flightless. With your permission, I would like to remain above as another set of eyes, she replied with only a hint of exasperation, then he felt something like affection thrum through their bond. *But I promise, I will tell you if I need a rest. I can sense how strange my growth seems to you. But this is my nature. I cannot remember them, but I can feel hundreds of my previous lives reaching back through time. This is the way my kind grow.*

Tilly tried to dampen down his sadness at how much she had changed in such a short time, knowing that she could feel it as clearly as he could feel her concern.

Well, I am excited for you to continue to advance . . . I saw that flame attack you did at the end. What's next? he asked, unable to keep from sending images of mythological phoenixes he had read about in the past. Creatures that were the living embodiment of flame. Symbols of immortality and resilience.

She considered the images he sent, and replied hesitantly, *Some of that feels correct, but I know for certain that I can and will die. It feels like an essential part of my cycle, and when the time comes, I will know how to best leverage my end. Also, I don't think I have ever been bonded before, and I feel there will be unique options for us going forward as we both grow. Things that none of my kind have ever experienced.*

On the tail end of that thought, Tilly caught the barest hint of a concept. Something that she couldn't put into words. It felt sort of like a future invitation to become a whole that was greater than the sum of their separate parts. He wanted to ask more but got the sense that she was already pondering over the same questions, and he realized how jarring it must be for her to advance in leaps like this. Catching hints of what had been and yet being forced to remain in ignorance until reaching a future unknown threshold of power had to be difficult to balance.

So, he released their connection and smiled as he felt her return to the newfound joy of untethered flight. She may have been maturing rapidly, but there was something innocent and captivating about her exultant emotions at rediscovering her chief domain. She was a creature of air and fire and today's events had allowed her to discover a much greater portion of herself.

He left her to it, deciding instead to catch up to Ichiro, who whether by coincidence or intention had maintained the first position behind the two vampires who were leading their group through the twisting lowlands that wound between the hills.

As Tilly pulled up beside him, he noted that while the lapin didn't seem as fully at ease as Tilly, he looked like he also would have no trouble keeping this pace for hours on end.

"Ichiro, can I ask you something personal?" Tilly spoke in a low tone, hoping that they were far enough away from the vampires that they wouldn't be overheard.

"Please, Jonathan Tillman, feel free to do so. I will let you know if I think it unwise to continue in our discourse," he answered with a quick but pointed look at the two ahead of them.

"As you and Shuji both know, my build is maxed around *Endurance*, and while I think I understand both the benefits and costs of my stat layout, I am not sure I fully understand the context of my numbers," Tilly laid out hesitantly in a whisper, trying to form his ideas into a cohesive question. "Shuji told me that if my stat score numerically matched my level, then I would be around the average for someone at my stage of power. He then explained that most builds only double or, rarely, triple their level score in a single stat and that each multiplicative threshold I pass produces some sort of unmeasured but noticeable impact. But now, my *Endurance* is more than five times my level and I'm not sure I really understand the implications. How does it square up against something like a level seventy-five Consumer, for example?"

Tilly watched as Ichiro considered the question and for the first time noticed that the lapin wasn't breathing in rhythm with his steps. Instead, he was maintaining a double-speed version of the meditative breathing he had taught Tilly a month ago.

Then it hit Tilly . . . Ichiro was meditating. He never stopped meditating. In the recent fight, while he was running, even while he talked, he fit every one of his moments and actions into the cadence of his meditation. Tilly couldn't imagine what his skill level must be at this point.

Ichiro's calm and measured answer interrupted Tilly's musings.

"A very popular theory in this area is that your *Endurance* and an opponent's *Strength* are measured against each other by the system in every martial exchange. If the stats are equal, then there are no unseen stat modifiers affecting the blow. However, if your opponent has twice as much *Strength* as you have *Endurance*, then they might gain something like a plus-fifty-percent modifier to their damage output. But the reason this is only a theory is that these exchanges are also affected by armor, positioning of the blow, and racial and skill boosts to attacks and defense. In fact, there are even more theoretical factors than the ones I am mentioning."

"The exact numerical advantage of having such a high *Endurance* is not known, but doubling or tripling your opponent's *Strength* score will make their *Strength*-modified attacks significantly weaker against you. The same is true for magical attacks and *Intelligence*, as well as environmental damage against your physical body. *Endurance*, essentially, is the measurement of your body's ability to persist in its ideal physical state no matter the opposition. It does not, however, help you with spiritual and mental attacks . . . That is where *Wisdom* comes in, and it is the area of your build I have been most concerned about."

"Yeah, I can see that. Especially with **Corruption** eroding my mental defenses. The attack from the red-eyes guy more than demonstrated that . . ." Tilly trailed off, losing himself as he considered Ichiro's answer while mindlessly following the group through the hills at an easy jog.

He had achieved some measure of mental defense against the surges of dark desires that were leveled against him in times of extreme stress, but that wouldn't help him when it came to resisting the powers of the forces arrayed against him. Ichiro watched the conflicting emotions play out across Tilly's face and lapsed easily into silence, content to give his companion space to process.

The Wisdom *bottleneck is where the min-maxing of my build takes its toll. But honestly, [Resolute] has saved my life so many times, I can't imagine going forward without it, and without the increase to my survivability that* Endurance *has given me, I wouldn't have made it through half of the fights I have faced so far. So, I'm pretty much committed . . . Just got to keep moving forward and look for some alternative way to shore up my weaknesses besides stat dumping. At least until I finally rip this thing out of me.*

They continued on their run for hours, letting Hilbert lead them around enemy hot spots well in advance of actually seeing them. After a while, Tilly moved up to ask him about the compass object he held, and he explained that it was keyed into the vampirism variant that infected the Strigoi. It was something his master had left him as a parting gift years ago.

Otherwise, they made great time through the Twilight Lands, something that Hilbert said would normally be much more difficult if the horde wasn't so concentrated on both fronts of attack. During one of their short breaks, he shared with the group that the order still patrolled the edges of the horde lands on their border and typically kept covert resources invested in tracking horde movements. Yet every major horde aggression over the last few months had been so far away from the order's lands that intervention had seemed like a foolish risk to the queen, who thought each attack was a feint to lure them away from protecting their supply lines.

However, the consequences of this non-interventionalist policy had driven a very small number of their order to seek out alternatives. The horde continued to expand at an alarming rate, and Hilbert, Sir Michael, and a few others thought that their continued expansion had to be stopped at all costs.

The group kept their breaks short, and after what seemed like seven or eight hours, even Tilly was starting to develop a sheen of sweat under his Blood Mound Shambler armor. Franklin and Amelia were in much worse shape. They barely kept pace and relied on different herbal concoctions from Amelia's never-ending stock to keep moving. Even though they had not uttered a word of complaint, Tilly was beginning to grow worried for the pair.

"There it is, one of our outposts!" Hilbert's voice interrupted Tilly in the middle of another worried glace back at the two who were now struggling not to fall behind. "We shall vouch for you and hopefully secure better transport for the rest of the trip to our order's capital," he said, looking back at the last members of the group lathered in sweat and grime. They did not reply to his comment or even look up as he gestured to what Tilly could see was a small military structure on the horizon. The two vampires didn't seem winded at all for the effort, but a darker part of Tilly was glad to see that they still did have to breathe to function.

He had been thinking a lot about what had happened back with the ancient cave bear and was sure there were another couple of tricks he had up his sleeve, even in open-air environments, that would multiply his group's attack power by an order of magnitude . . .

They approached the rest of the way to the outpost at a walk, and as they drew near, Tilly saw that it was a squat medieval-style fortress, surrounded by a wall two stories high. The moment they came within view of the fortress towers, a cry went up, and soon after, a group of ten riders emerged from the gate to meet their group out in the open.

CHAPTER THIRTY-FIVE

Team Edward

Their approach didn't seem initially hostile, but Tilly couldn't help but notice that each rider held their weapons at the ready as their formation rode out to meet his group. Once they got within range, Tilly's **Identify** pinged, and he learned several interesting things.

Nine of the ten riders had the class Dhampire Cavalry, with levels ranging from the low forties to the mid-fifties.

The warrior at the head of the formation was a painfully handsome vampire with long blond hair streaked gray at the temples. He was decked out in traditional plate mail and held his open helm under one arm and his reins in the other.

Level 74, Knight of the Sanguine Order

He held the same class as Sir Michael, but his armor was much less . . . otherworldly. Sir Michael's armor had no gaps and no discernable straps or joints, whereas this knight wore something more like what Tilly would expect from the Middle Ages. It was ornate to be sure, marked along its edges with runes that glowed faintly, but it didn't hold a candle to the intricacy of Sir Michael's. This knight also rode out with his face uncovered, his vampiric nature on full display.

All of these details fell to the background as the cavalry's mounts came into full view. Each one seemed to be a nightmarish combination of horse and skeletal hunger. They all varied in some way, some showing the grayish hairless skin of the Strigoi, some with a plump purplish hue. But all had an equine head with sharp fangs reaching down past their lower lip.

Vampiric Nightmare [Mount]

"Ho, there! I recognize you, young Hilbert . . . And Sir Michael, I am surprised to see you away from your duty in the capital . . . Who are these that accompany you, and what is your business past our borders?" the knight called authoritatively.

Sir Michael offered a simple salute in response, not overly enthusiastic and probably keeping within the boundaries of decorum. Hilbert, however, threw on a huge smile at the knight's approach.

"Sir Cador! My, it is good to see you! We are on a very important errand and would love your assistance." He waved warmly.

The knight pulled up the formation and looked down on them, confusion slowly souring to suspicion as he took in the others in the group.

"Errand, you say? How is it I have heard nothing of this from the queen? I gave her my report this morning, and she spoke naught of you or of a group of foreigners passing into our lands . . . especially from enemy territory."

"Report this morning . . . Of course you did," Hilbert muttered darkly through the side of his mouth before continuing in a loud voice. "Yes, well, there is a chance she doesn't know about this particular . . . errand."

At that, the knight's face hardened and the eerily silent mounts shifted foot to foot.

"You can't expect me to allow you to pass. There is a reason I am trusted with this post. At the very least, I will need to hold you in the fort until I can get in contact with the queen," he said in a weary voice.

"That is not acceptable," Ichiro said, stepping forward to address the group.

"At this point, you don't have much of a choice, traveler," Sir Cador said as his hand dropped to the pommel of his sword.

"Well, now! Hold on a minute! Sir Cador, this is not what it seems, and we really are in quite a hurry!" Hilbert said as he stepped between the two groups, appealing to the commander of the fort.

The cavalry looked ready to ignore the wizard's apprentice, and Tilly rested his hands on the handles of his hatchets, not willing to be intimidated. Then Gorock took it way too far and drew his weapon, snarling. Ichiro turned on him and made a fierce negative motion with his hand while Hilbert stepped even closer to the knight's group, whose mounts danced around him.

Sir Cador's eyes were hard as his companions reached for weapons.

"Wait! We are from the newly integrated faction currently under siege by the horde!" Tilly shouted over the din of weapons being loosened.

"Yes! Sir Cador! If I can just have your attention for a moment more! Our business is with the queen and it is urgent. The horde expansion continues unchecked, and these . . . ambassadors hold the key to our continued survival!" Hilbert shrilled with both his hands in the air, urging calm.

Gorock reluctantly sheathed his sword and Ichiro turned back to the group as Sir Cador's eyes narrowed further.

"Continued survival? I never thought to hear such weak-willed mewling from one of Merllyn's apprentices. Since our excursion two months ago into the heart of the Deadlands, we haven't seen a single Strigoi within ten miles of our border. They are scared, *apprentice* . . . The border is secure, and we are under no obligation to intervene in distant conflicts!" he said with a stubborn flintiness gleaming in his eyes.

At those words, Hilbert completely dropped the Mr. Nice Guy act. A fierce snarl put his fangs on full display, and runic circles started to dance around his upraised hands. Which suddenly seemed much more threatening.

"You bull-headed idiot! Would you just listen for a moment!" His voice boomed, releasing a concussive blast that whipped back everyone's clothing.

"Was your son not one of the ones injured in the 'excursion,' as you call it? It has been painted as a victory, but half of the High Table came back with that debuff, and we have yet to find a way to cleanse it. He and the others now lie entombed, perhaps never to wake, and still you cling blindly to this foolish non-interventionist idea! Just who is the mewling weakling here?"

There was a sound like a crack of thunder and before Tilly's eye could register what had happened, Sir Michael stood before Hilbert with his mace out, catching a blow that would have cleaved the apprentice in half. Sir Cador's reluctant but dutiful mask was gone as he pushed down against Sir Michael's weapon with animalistic fury.

"Don't you dare sully my son's sacrifice, peasant!" the wild-eyed knight screamed, spittle flying from his fanged mouth.

Hilbert's magic winked out, and he stepped right into the path of the blocked blade so that it was only a hair away from cutting his neck. The cavalry behind the enraged knight milled about in uncertainty, and Ichiro signaled everyone to wait, his eyes watching the conflict, seeing more than the rest of them could.

In a voice barely above a whisper, Hilbert answered, "I told you, Sir Cador . . . *They* hold the key. I have seen them clear the infection with only a breath. We need to get to Camelot, and we need to get there fast."

The wild flickering in the knight's eyes slowly dimmed, and he looked at the group as if seeing them for the first time. "They can cure it?"

"Yes, they have even offered to help in exchange for an alliance. Something that we need desperately. It is not enough for you to let us pass . . . I need some of your mounts to be temporarily bound to this party. I have seen the horde at their gates. They will finish the winnowing in a day and attack in earnest soon after. If they break through, we will all be out of time."

At that, Tilly saw Ichiro's ears twitch, and Tilly shared his surprise at the previously unrevealed intel.

The knight seemed to be on the brink of relenting before the emotion on his face drained away, reverting to its previous mask. Tilly watched as the commander thought through the risk and made his conclusion before stepping away from Sir Michael and lowering his weapon.

His expression took on that reluctant, dutiful cast that Tilly had seen in leadership hundreds of times. The face of someone unwilling to stick their neck out doing the right thing. That cowardly mask had been responsible for the deaths of more than a few people in Tilly's past life. When life-saving action butted up against protocol, professional reputations got laid on the line . . . and that's when you would find the cowards hiding behind rules and regulations.

That couldn't happen here. Over one hundred thousand people were depending on them to make something happen, and Tilly wasn't going to let their mission get caught up in stupid red tape. Every hour meant more deaths on the wall, let alone whatever Hilbert had just said about the "winnowing."

Tilly stepped right into the knight's face as he was about to open his mouth, forcing eye contact, and said, "You don't know me, Sir Cador, but I have been marked by the same force that has infected the horde. The same thing that now has your son. The Strigoi think they have found a new form of power, but by now, they are most likely almost completely under its control. It will not stop until it consumes everything it can reach. We can and will help your son. Our nation needs you as much as you seem to need us. *Don't delay us here.*"

The knight looked Tilly up and down, taking in his strange armor and low level, as he considered his words. Then a complicated series of emotions crossed his features, ending in a hard-eyed resolve. He sheathed his sword and swore softly to himself, casting an accusatory glance at Sir Michael and Hilbert.

"How is it that you two are always in the midst of trouble? If I send you on and you are unable to deliver on this promise, I will beat you to death myself, if it is the last thing I do."

"Thank you, Sir Cador! You won't regret this, we promise!" Hilbert answered exuberantly, before adding, "Now, I know you have a command to maintain here, but we need mounts for these five if we are going to make it to Camelot at speed."

Sir Cador looked at the wizard's apprentice like he was pushing it, but then he looked back at Amelia and Franklin struggling to remain standing.

"Can you not leave a few behind?"

"No," Ichiro and Tilly answered at the same time.

"We cannot risk our true objective by splitting the party," Ichiro added.

"And what objective is that?" the knight replied, suspicion rekindling in his tone.

"They seek the city of Requiem," Hilbert cut in. "Sir Cador, we only need you to temporarily offer up five of your mounts for the trip to the capital, nothing more. The sooner we get there, the sooner we can make our attempt to restore Constantine and the others who slumber."

Sir Cador let out a long exasperated sigh and turned to his men.

"Oh, alright. Rich, Ed, Thaddeus, and Erec, dismount. Blood is short all across the kingdom, so your companions will be paying their own blood price. My men and I will dismiss our mounts in six hours. That is more than enough time for you to make it to the capital," he said as he moved toward his freakish horse creature and took down his weapons. After he had them in his arms, and his men had reluctantly obeyed, he turned back to the group. "Sir Michael, I do not like what you are, but I respect your place at the Table. Do not give me cause to regret this." Sir Michael saluted him formally and reached for something at his neck.

Hilbert turned to the rest of them as Ichiro moved closer to whisper, "You said nothing of mounts. How far away is Camelot, and why did you not speak of this winnowing earlier?"

Hilbert had the good sense to at least look chagrined as he answered, "It will be less than the six hours they are giving us. As far as the mounts are concerned, I don't like them any more than you, but they are necessary to complete both of our missions. The time frame does not change the fact that we still need each other," he explained as the soldiers led their Nightmares close to the group.

"You five will need to allow them to partake of your blood. This will form a temporary bond with the Nightmare and it will let you ride it as long as the bond-holders maintain the manifestation," Sir Cador explained to the group, a pitiless smirk on his pale face.

Just how much else has Hilbert been holding back? Tilly wondered to himself as his own gray-fleshed, fanged Nightmare approached, led by a sour-faced cavalryman.

CHAPTER THIRTY-SIX

Blood Bank

After a brief explanation by Hilbert on what exactly Nightmares were and an unpleasant ritual involving the summoned mount clamping its fanged mouth onto their forearms, they were ready to go, each having given up about 10 percent of their blood to the bond.

Hilbert explained that summoning a Nightmare was a unique *Ability* pioneered by Merllyn. Because he had basically invented a racial transformation, he had some effect on the *Abilities* allowed to the new vampiric variants. This hybrid racial trait-*Ability* allowed the user to summon an equine manifestation of their greatest fears and use it as a mount. It cost them life energy to maintain—or life's blood, for any not of the vampire race.

After they completed the ritual, they all received some version of the status notification:

> *You have ritually enacted a Blood Bond. For the duration of this bond,*
> *your health will be capped at 90% and the other 10%*
> *of your life energy will go toward your blood-bound*
> *manifestation as tribute.*

Sir Cador warned them that they would be dismissing the borrowed mounts in six hours, at which time the Nightmares, and the debuffs, would disappear. Most of the mounts didn't change as they took on new riders, maintaining the shapes of their owners' fears, which seemed to universally revolve around hunger and devolving into their more beastly enemies.

Their guides, however, were both exceptions to this rule. Hilbert's summoning had resulted in a mount that was a strange cross between a spider and a horse, with eight legs on an elongated equine torso and a set of arachnid eyes. Hilbert audibly gagged as he approached the obedient creature and shivered as he mounted it.

Sir. Michael's summoning resulted in something that echoed the more Strigoi-like mounts of the cavalry but had a deep purple tint to its skin and was incredibly sleek and muscular, as opposed to the uniformly skeletal, hungry look of the others.

Once all the mounts were present, they climbed into the saddles, which were another part of the spell, each adjusting to their rider magically. With a final admonishment from Sir Cador that he would be notifying the queen of their meeting, they had set off at a gallop. They rode past the border fort and followed the road behind it into the Sanguine Order's lands.

The mounts were completely metaphysical in nature, not true living creatures, and this made riding them much easier than it should have been. Tilly had never gotten a chance to ride a horse in his past life but found the experience with the Nightmare mounts to be eerily smooth. A rhythmic staccato of hoof beats marked out their mile-eating pace as they moved through the countryside at speed.

He could feel an invisible tether attaching himself to the creature. It started from the spot of the creature's bite and ended in the center of its mass. Tilly guessed that was the active cost of the *Ability* being channeled through the **Blood Bond** debuff. As soon as they were out of sight of the fort, Kindle dived back down to fly parallel with the group, complaining about the "animated parasites" the group were now riding. Tilly asked if she sensed anything evil from them, and she answered in the negative but maintained a strong feeling of distaste throughout their mental conversation.

Tilly wasn't sure, but he thought it had more to do with him having another kind of bond than any dislike she had for a summoning of this type. After a while, she ascended and promised to let him know if she spotted anything out of the ordinary.

An hour or two into their journey, the climate had almost completely reverted to something that felt much more alive than the endless reddish tan of the Deadlands. The ground became covered in green grass and was characterized by intermittent stands of trees and rolling moors. Eventually, they even started to pass small villages and farms.

The architectural style of these settlements ranged from typical medieval village, with thatched roofs and dirt roads, to human-sized hobbit-hole structures, which Tilly was able to **Identify** as "Aos Si Barrows." Some of the ones they passed as they got deeper into the order's lands were absurdly large hill-covered structures that looked like they could fit fifty to a hundred people.

The people Tilly spotted from the road were remarkably ordinary at first glance.

Level 22, Farmer
Level 15, Peasant

They all shared distinctive creamy porcelain skin and glinting eyes like you would see on a cat in low light. He did not spot any other vampires on their trip but did see occasional groups of dhampire infantry posted in some of the larger settlements.

Overall, the journey was remarkably smooth, and while the Nightmares were creepy as hell, whatever magic had created this summoning *Ability* had made it almost idiotproof. Tilly could constantly feel the mount responding to his intent and any movement he made with the reins seemed almost redundant. In fact, as soon as he had set it in his mind that he was following the two vampires in the lead, the Nightmare he was riding had simply continued in that vein with little or no input from Tilly.

The mounts never slowed from the cantering pace that was set at the beginning of their journey. This probably had something to do with the fact that they didn't seem to breathe, each one tirelessly bearing its rider for the low, low price of their life energy.

Tilly would have loved to use the journey to ask more questions, but the noise of a group of hooves constantly hitting dirt and stone roads was prohibitive. So instead, he just kept an eye on his surroundings, trying to learn as much as he could about their new neighbors. He also took the opportunity to break out some provisions and get in a meal while he could.

With the Alliance under siege, he didn't think there would be much time for eating, drinking, or . . . any other essential bodily function during this quest. Luckily for him, the stress had tightened everything right up, and he doubted he would be *going* any time soon. He eventually looked back to find Amelia and Franklin asleep in their saddles and was glad they had found some time to recuperate. Gorock still held the rear of the formation, looking comically large on his horse-sized mount. This more than anything told Tilly that normal physics didn't apply, as Gorcok's skeletal Nightmare didn't look any more tired than the rest.

Then it occurred to Tilly that Gorock's *Constitution* was probably also the highest in the group, so the 10 percent the creature was gaining from the **Blood Bond** was probably more than enough to offset the extra effort.

Tilly, I see your destination ahead . . . It is not what you are expecting, Kindle sent through their bond, accompanied by her view of the city.

From her aerial perspective, the city was dominated by a structure that appeared to be a large stone castle, half sunken into the hill upon which it was built. That hill was surrounded by three rings of stone walls, making the approach to the central structure extremely secure.

As Tilly continued to examine the image, he realized two things were off from his initial perspective. First, he had vastly underestimated the scale. Kindle focused in on a figure the size of an ant patrolling the top of the outer wall, and Tilly realized that the central ring wall was twice as large as the one they had built at the mouth of the valley.

The second thing he realized was that the hill was a part of the structure itself, mirroring the barrow style of building that he had seen throughout the countryside. Stairs and gates were set directly into the side of the grass-covered dirt and led into a settlement-sized structure within.

Even with all of this, Camelot was still smaller than the Thousand Phalanx Empire's capital, both in geographic footprint and population. But what it lacked in size, it more than made up for in defensibility. The whole city layout was clearly designed with a militaristic purpose in mind.

"We should see the city once we top the next rise," Hilbert shouted over the sound of the galloping Nightmares. The rest of the group perked up at the news, and Tilly glanced back to catch Amelia blearily rubbing her eyes in the saddle and Franklin stretching in his. Hilbert pulled up at the top of the gentle hill and waited for the rest of the group to catch up. No one gasped as the city came into view, but you could tell that everyone was impressed by the sight of the valley below and the huge hill fortress that dominated it.

From the ground view, Tilly got an even better sense of the scale. The hill that the castle was sunken into was probably the size of ten or fifteen city blocks, and it rose more than a hundred feet off the ground. The only reason Tilly didn't feel like it qualified as a small mountain was that it looked like it was made up of dirt, not stone.

Every inch of the hill not supporting an opening to the interior or a cobblestone road was covered in grass and cultivated plant life. About fifteen feet out from the base of the giant barrow was the innermost of the three walls, with one main gate leading out of the fortress and into a more traditional medieval settlement with stone and timber buildings and slate roofs.

This more familiar cityscape filled all the space between the second and third walls. Outside of the second wall stood some of the settlement-style architecture of the inner section but also displayed were larger, more impressive structures, some of which broke with the medieval theme. Tilly spotted a large timber arena and several buildings that could have been temples, including two that he thought he recognized from his time sneaking into the Temple of Light.

It looked like the space between the first and second walls was for commercial ventures, while the space between the second and innermost walls was reserved for residential areas and smaller businesses.

Overall, the city was incredible and made it crystal clear to Tilly the differences between the factions in higher and lower-level areas. Even the land around the city felt . . . denser. Richer in some indescribable way that made its potential apparent.

"And he will build a great city . . . where all will know peace and prosperity," Hilbert said almost to himself as they all looked out over the seat of power for the Sanguine Order. Then the dreamy expression on his face hardened into something more serious, and he turned to the rest of the group. "There is a tax to enter the city. I do not know if you carry any Standard currency, but the price can also be paid in blood. Almost everything in the city can be bought with blood if you are willing to pay. The blood tax, once paid, typically results in a ten percent *Constitution* debuff, and it lasts for five to ten hours, depending on your race. Once we reach the gates, I will banish your mounts, and the **Blood Bond** will be removed."

Ichiro frowned in thought, and Tilly wondered about money for the first time. Did they have currency? What was the "Standard"? How was that handled between factions?

"How is the tax collected?" Amelia asked, staring down at the city with a considering look.

"What do you mean?" Then realization dawned on Hilbert's features. "Oh, gods! No one bites you or anything, we have magical devices that collect and store the payment to an exact degree," he answered. "The devices are certified by the Commerce Guild itself and cannot be tampered with by any except guild workers. The city has a long-standing agreement with them to make our non-traditional economy work, and it has been safely in place for hundreds of years. That being said, never give blood to someone looking to circumvent the system. It is in place for a reason, and exchanging blood outside of its bounds is illegal in our lands," he finished sternly, clearly proud of the system that governed those in power.

At his explanation, Ichiro nodded slowly. "We do have some meager funds if a need arises, but I would prefer we save them. Is everyone willing to pay the tax?" he asked as he turned toward the rest of them.

CHAPTER THIRTY-SEVEN

Taxation Without Representation

Under Ichiro's open gaze, no one hesitated in affirming their willingness to take on a *Constitution* debuff for the benefit of the mission. With that settled, he turned toward the two vampires and gestured forward.

"We are ready and in your care. We need to see your queen as quickly as possible and will do whatever we can for those who are infected. After that, we must continue on, perhaps stopping for some specific supplies on the way out."

"Of course. We will do whatever we must to gain an audience immediately," Hilbert said heavily, rubbing at his forearm where he had cut his oath before kicking his mount into a canter. The group followed Hilbert as he set off, and Tilly once again marveled at how smoothly the summoned mount responded to his intentions.

They covered the rest of the distance to the first gate relatively quickly, and as they approached, Tilly called up to Kindle, *Hey girl, we are headed into an unknown here, and I honestly don't know if it would be safer for you to stay out of the city or ride in with us . . . So I'm going to let you decide.*

I am coming now. I will move with you into the city and make it harder for any to dismiss your words. Only fools would take my presence lightly.

Till looked up and watched as her blue speck slowly grew larger, falling from the sky, and then she fanned out her wings at the last second to halt her dive. Her talons touched the top of Tilly's pack almost gently, and she fluffed her feathers, not quite hiding her pleasure at such a smooth landing.

Impressive! I can't believe how fast you have improved, Tilly sent, not having to lean into the compliment at all. It was still jarring to watch her grow in leaps and bounds like this.

It is less improvement and more remembrance. I regain myself as I grow stronger. I do not yet know my full capabilities, but I know they are far greater than what I have discovered so far, she sent back, preening.

As they drew near the gates, they found a small line of people actively moving through the taxation process and a large group of wagons off to the side, waiting their turn before entering the city.

Tilly curiously eyed the different cargos as they passed, spotting normal goods, like produce and textiles, but also seeing things that he couldn't figure out in a glance, even with **Identify** active.

There was a large chunk of silver crystal roped down on a wagon bed that the system labeled as "Silverite." There was also a train of wagons protected by surly-looking one-eyed guards.

Level 48, Cyclopic Brawlers

On the backs of their wagons were large urns lashed upright by numerous ropes. The urns were covered in a red glowing script, reminiscent of what Tilly had seen on the blood repositories Hilbert and Sir Michael had shown them. But the script looked sloppy, as if it had been carelessly scrawled instead of meticulously crafted. Tilly couldn't help but get a queasy feeling as he stared at them.

Then Hilbert's voice interrupted Tilly's gawking. "Ho, the gate! Good morning, gentlemen, how goes the watch?" he called cheerfully as he bypassed the other individuals waiting in line and moved right to the guards and official running the tax and entry checkpoint.

There was some grumbling as they passed the others on foot and in wagon, but everyone quieted once they saw the Nightmares. It would make sense that the mounts typically marked a higher station in the city, and Tilly realized it was probably one of the reasons Hilbert had angled for their whole group to borrow the creatures.

At Hilbert's greeting, all the dhampire guards and the vampire official looked up at the approaching group, wearing many shades of the same frown. None seemed interested in matching Hilbert's cheerful tone.

Then, from within the shadow of the gate, an elegant-looking knight with dark hair and even darker eyes stepped forward, a sneer evident on his face.

Level 68, Knight of the Sanguine Order

"Ah, the stable boy has returned . . . Imagine my surprise when I was called from standing vigil over my brothers to fetch our little lost lamb."

"Sir Accolon, of course . . . It's you," Hilbert replied in surprise at the sudden appearance of the knight, his tone slipping into a higher octave.

At his false cheer, the dark-eyed knight's sneer turned further downward into a snarl.

"You've finally done it, you filthy upstart. She is ready to set you cleaning Dagonet's cage for the next century. And you!" he said, turning on Sir Michael. "You call yourself one of us, but we all know what you are. Some of the others may be fooled, but after abandoning your post, they will see what I do to an imposter." He finished his accusation by spitting on the ground at the feet of the Nightmare.

Sir Michael didn't even flinch at the insult, while Hilbert looked . . . mildly nauseous.

Ichiro moved his horse slightly forward and attempted to salvage the situation. "Sir, we are here as official emissaries from the new faction grafted into these lands. We request an audience with—"

"I know what you claim. Cador sent in the report hours ago. We don't believe in good fortune or miracles around here, and that old buffoon must be getting desperate to make such a misstep," he said dismissively, barely glancing in Ichiro's direction. "Pay the tax and dismiss those mounts you have sullied. You are to come with me, and the queen will see you at her earliest convenience." He sighed as the sneer settled back into place, his anger turning to exasperation.

"We have seen it with our own eyes, Accolon," Hilbert started to explain, but he was cut off by a furious hiss from the knight.

"How dare you refuse me my title!" he barked as his fury blazed back to life in an instant. "Do not waste any more of my time on this farce. Remove yourselves from those mounts and pay the tax!" His eyes glinted dangerously.

Hilbert nodded stiffly in reply and complied. He dismounted his eight-legged Nightmare, careful to avoid looking at the creature, and Sir Michael mirrored him, seeming completely at ease even in the face of the tense exchange. The rest of the group followed suit, and Hilbert muttered something under his breath to his mount, which caused it to fade away like fog before a noonday sun.

He then moved toward the rest of the mounts, muttering an incantation before each one and laying a glowing hand on their withers. At the glowing touch of his magic, they each faded away. In less than a minute, all of the Nightmares were gone and they stood before the uncomfortable-looking official and the contingent of guards, who didn't want to be caught in the middle of whatever was playing out between the knights and the wizard's apprentice.

"Arms, please, gentlemen," the official asked the two vampires, who moved with rote compliance to stretch out their right forearms. The official pulled out what looked like a large enchanted monocle and peered down at the appendages for a moment before waving them through. Whatever the device checked, it seemed unaffected by the armor Sir Michael wore or Hilbert's colorful robes. Then the rest of the group moved up and the official droned, "Blood or Standard? Blood tax is currently set at one point three-two pints. Standard is seven silver, four coppers today."

"We will pay in blood," Ichiro responded coolly as he moved to present his arm first.

The official marked something in his ledgers and lifted another object from the table. It was a dull gray metal tube marked with arcane symbols, and as he held one end to Ichiro's arm, the symbols started to glow red.

Blood Extraction Tube, Rare [Commerce Guild Certified]

The light of the tube was matched by a large container behind the table that was also covered in the now glowing symbols.

Blood Vessel, Epic [Commerce Guild Certified]

They must be linked, Tilly thought as the red glow died simultaneously on the vessel and the extraction tube. The guards' positions flanking the official now took on new meaning as Tilly realized that they were probably there as much to guard the Blood Vessel as the gate.

Ichiro filed past, looking no worse for the experience, and Tilly moved up next, holding up his arm and pulling back his sleeve without a word. The official made another mark in his ledger and placed the end of the tube against his skin, activating its ruby glow.

The device sputtered and flashed red before going dark, and the official sighed, "Traveler, please deactivate any defensive *Abilities*. This is not designed to hurt you."

"Uh, I don't have any defensive *Abilities*," Tilly replied, confused.

"Sir," the official said with a flat look, "we have been doing this for a long time, you are not the first one to think of such things . . . but you will not be entering the city without paying, either in blood or coin."

"I'm telling you, I don't have anything active at all right now. It's a problem with your stick thing."

"Excuse me, I believe I may understand the problem," Amelia said as she stepped up from behind Tilly in line. "I do not know what the device is rated for in regard to *Endurance*, but despite his displayed level"—Amelia gestured vaguely above Tilly's head—"he is probably well above the threshold for that device."

"Preposterous!" the official sputtered. "The enchantment is rated through the second tier of *Endurance*."

"Wow, really?" Amelia answered looking over at Tilly with a shocked smile.

"You really doubled down on *Endurance*, huh?" She continued trying, unsuccessfully, to push down her grin.

"I have very good reasons for my build. I got it approved by Shuji and everything!" Tilly replied in mock offense, while the official looked on aghast.

"I'm sorry, but you can't be serious. To do such a thing would be to cripple any possibility of balance . . . ," he cut in incredulously. At his statement, Tilly winced, his small smile at Amelia's teasing disappearing, and he turned back to the official.

"I said I have my reasons. Now, can I pay this tax or not?"

"Ah, yes, of course, my mistake . . ." The official shuffled around behind the checkpoint before pulling out a new metal tube with the same markings. The only difference seemed to be that this one was made up entirely of silver. Tilly held his arm up again and the official pressed the end against it, then activated the enchanted object.

Blood Extraction Tube, Epic [Commerce Guild Certified]

The symbols roared to life instantly, and Tilly felt a rushing sensation as something was pulled out of his center through his arm and into the devices. He couldn't understand how Ichiro had endured the feeling so calmly. It felt like he was being sucked dry, and as the device winked out, Tilly struggled to stay on his feet, swaying in place.

The official frowned as he turned and watched the glowing symbols on the Blood Vessel stay lit for another three seconds. "That can't be correct," he muttered to himself. A new debuff flashed at the top of Tilly's HUD as he attempted to steady himself against the table.

Blood Loss:

You have lost over 30% of your blood in a short amount of time.
-30% to your Constitution for 5 hours.

"Uh . . . ," Tilly said shakily. "My math may not be perfect, but this thing took way more than one point three-two pints from my body."

CHAPTER THIRTY-EIGHT

Don't Stop Me Now

Tilly experienced a strange combination of nausea and sleepiness before he managed to fully steady himself against the checkpoint table. Losing that much blood without a wound was a surreal experience and it took a moment for him to get his bearings.

The official was busy turning back and forth between the device and the vessel behind him, repeatedly muttering under his breath. The dark-eyed knight cleared his voice noisily from the shadow of the gate, and the official jumped, startled by the interruption to his musings.

"Ah. Very sorry . . . Sir, this is quite irregular, I do apologize. I don't think the device was calibrated to be able to factor in what could be—do pardon me for saying this—an unforeseeable ratio between *Endurance* and *Constitution*. Nonetheless, the error is ours, and while we cannot issue you your blood back," he said as he pulled out a special sheet of paper with gilded edges and started to fill it out, "I can issue you this notice of refund along with a small damage payment from the Commerce Guild. Their backing comes with an insurance policy of sorts. Turn it in and they will issue you a payment in either Standard or local currency." He signed the paper with a flourish and handed it over to Tilly.

Notice of Refund

[This document can no longer be altered. It has been sealed with an official skill.]

*This notice of device failure may be turned in by Jonathan Tillman
to be exchanged for fiat currency at any Commerce Guild location.
Item cannot be lost or stolen.*

"Thanks." Tilly smiled weakly, then rolled up the sheet and stuffed it in his pack.

"Villers! If you take any longer, I will leave them here to find their own way to the keep and I will give the queen your name when she demands why!" Sir Accolon shouted in impatience.

The official fumbled with the original extractor and laid it against Amelia's arm as she stepped up smoothly behind Tilly.

"It's never easy with you, is it?" she whispered conspiratorially to him as the device lit up along with the vessel. She didn't flinch as the blood extraction finished, then moved past to join the others. Tilly didn't bother to restrain a woozy smile at her antics. It was kind of nice to be able to joke around a little bit, even if it only seemed to be possible in the middle of a life-or-death mission.

The last members of their group made it through without a hitch and they all moved past the checkpoint. They were passing under the foreboding portcullises and murder holes when Accolon stepped in front of them, sneering for all he was worth.

"Gods, I can already tell you are going to be a chore. Come, Her Majesty waits for no one," he declared curtly before turning on his heels and moving through to the light on the other side of the gate passage. The group hurried after and found a small escort of six Dhampire Guardsmen waiting for them. They were each dressed in fine livery and carried polearms.

Level 42, Dhampire Guardsman

At the arrival of their leader, the group of guardsmen spread out to encompass the group and began their march through the city with Sir Accolon at the head, followed by a slightly reluctant Hilbert and a silent Sir Michael.

The escort moved through the city at a quick walk, and Tilly was struck by the differences between it and the empire's capital, the only other city he had encountered so far on Nephesh. The streets were cobbled, and the outer district held large medieval-style buildings. This was completely different from the sandstone-paved streets and heavily Roman-influenced architecture of the empire. Both had felt established, but Tilly thought there was a good chance that this faction was younger by a significant margin, despite its higher tier of power. He couldn't begin to guess the ages of some of the vampiric figures Hilbert had told them about in his short recounting of their faction's history, but he doubted the faction as a whole was more than five hundred years old.

Tilly mulled over the nature of the rising and falling of power on Nephesh as they passed a side street leading to the arena, several large inns, and a theater. He did note that there were no beggars on the streets, or any signs of poverty for that matter. In fact, on the whole, the streets were far less crowded than either the Alliance's new capital or the empire's before it.

Not to say that there wasn't a constant buzz of activity thrumming through the city, but while there was traffic, there were no choke points on the roads, and while there was the murmur and chatter that accompanied any population center, Tilly didn't catch any of the shouting that he would expect from hawkers.

A variety of peoples and races could be seen on the main road, but everyone seemed subdued—not cowed, per se, but something indefinable was missing . . . Soon enough they were through the first section of the city and had passed another gate, this one manned by guards who seemed much less impressed by the knights in their company. Both knights and Hilbert had to present their arms again, and a writ was requested from Sir Accolon to prove permission for "outsiders" to gain admittance to the inner city.

Once they were through to the inner city, any hint of outside architectural influence disappeared. The population was reduced again by a significant factor, and they were almost all of the Aos Si race. A pale, beautiful people, who all carried the same air of aloofness. There were some businesses in this section of the city, but most of the buildings were residential in nature.

The trip through this area was much shorter than the last and with only a few looks of interest from the residents. The escort proceeded to the main gate of the keep, a solid intimidating structure that looked like it was about to be swallowed whole by the giant barrow that engulfed it. The stone fortifications jutted from the manicured grass and landscape of the hill they were built into, and the opening yawned wide, leading into the significantly darker interior of the keep.

This checkpoint was manned by two knights who wore their entire plate, and while their armor didn't obscure their faces like Sir Michael's, they seemed just as uninterested in talking. Both hardly moved as they watched the procession pass through the security checks and gain admittance to the keep. Sir Accolon fought fire with fire and leaned into ignoring their presence as fully as possible as he passed by. Sir Michael, on the other hand, offered them a formal salute before continuing into the keep.

Once inside the structure, strange pinkish lights began to illuminate the cavernous hallway, and numerous servants became visible, moving about the passage, busily attending to whatever duties their stations demanded. All of them were Aos Si. As Sir Accolon continued to lead them forward confidently, Hilbert looked around and slowed his pace, allowing him to fall in with the group. He flicked his hands and subtly cast something that muted the air around them.

Without looking at them he muttered, "This is both going better and worse than I thought. As long as you are able to clear the infection, everything should be fine. I am afraid that due to the way we have . . . gained Her Majesty's attention, your welcome will not be very warm. Whatever happens to Sir Michael and me, do not get involved. Maintain your positions as emissaries and be insistent that you be allowed a demonstration of your claims."

At this point, most of the group seemed unsurprised by the complicated nature of their reception but they all nodded along with the explanation. Except for Gorock. Tilly wasn't even sure he had heard. The giant had found a piece of jerky from somewhere and was noisily chewing it with his eyes glazed over in pleasure.

Hilbert dismissed his small spell and picked up his pace to rejoin Michael's side, a small popping sound accompanying his movement away from the group. Tilly cast a sideways glance at the guards, who appeared not to have noticed anything, and found himself impressed by the apprentice's sneakiness. They had entered a huge underground hall floored with a beautiful mosaic, which was too large for Tilly to gain an understanding of while walking on it. At the end of the hall was a giant staircase leading up to a set of double doors flanked by numerous smaller entrances.

In the distance, Tilly saw a group being let into the double doors and faintly heard a crier announcing the group to whoever was on the other side. He had difficulty making it out over the clattering of their footfalls on the mosaic. Sir Accolon reached the base of the stairs and leaped up them two at a time, obviously ready to be done with his fetching duty, and the rest of them had to jog to keep up.

As they topped the stairway, a servant in an ornate uniform moved forward from one of the side doors and stepped in close to speak with Sir Accolon. The knight nodded along in annoyance at whatever he was hearing, and as soon as the servant stepped away, Sir Accolon turned and smiled, showing the full length of his fangs.

"And so, my duty is fulfilled. Stable boy, you and this hulking imposter are to be tried before the High Table for disobeying orders and dereliction of duty. As for your friends," he said, turning his toothy smile on them, "they will receive their chance to beg of the queen's mercy. But know this: she is much less patient with fools than she once was. So do not waste the Table's time. Be quick about your business. You will be called in as soon as the current filth is shown out. Apparently, it is a day of vagrants and swindlers," he finished, his smile curling into its typical sneer. Then he turned and walked down the hallway to another, much nicer, side entrance.

At his apparent dismissal, the guards backed away to the top of the stairs to keep watch on the group, seemingly labeling them as no threat. Hilbert moved to the benches flanking the large door and collapsed into one of them looking exhausted, leaving Sir Michael to remain stoically standing watch in front of the large doors.

Tilly was moving toward the slouching apprentice, hoping to get as much information as possible about what they would face in the chamber, when another side door, opposite of the one Sir Accolon had moved through, opened. A lady in an ornate dress rushed out of it, then closed the door behind her carefully to reduce any noise.

Level 32, Lady in Waiting

She wore a beautiful dress that was cinched tightly around the bodice and flowed outward at the hips, and her hair was piled atop her head in a complex configuration of braids and ribbons. As soon as she turned from the door, her pale, beautiful face took on a look of such exasperated disbelief that Tilly couldn't help but feel ashamed by association, even though the look was entirely directed at Hilbert.

"How could you?" she sputtered at the apprentice, who opened his eyes wearily before registering the owner of the voice. As soon as he saw her, he sprang up, ramrod straight.

"Mallytza! My dearest! What news of the court?"

"Don't 'What news of the court' me!" she almost shouted before looking around and schooling her voice. "After your display in front of the High Table, you were expressly forbidden from pursuing your plan. Not only did you ignore a command from the queen, you pulled away one of those called to stand vigil!" she whisper-shouted, then turned to the statuesque Sir Michael, who somehow managed to look chagrined without moving a muscle. "And you! You know full well your standing at the Table! Half think you should have never been admitted in the first place. With this, you will lose your seat for certain, if not worse! What have you to say for yourselves?"

Hilbert stood and shot a quick look at Sir Michael before holding up pleading hands. "Mallytza, my moon and stars. We did it! We have found a cure to the Blood Darkness," he said, gesturing vaguely in Tilly's direction like he was some sort of commodity. "It will be a simple matter to negotiate terms and see all those who are laid low restored!"

At his words, the Lady in Waiting turned to consider the outsiders for the first time.

CHAPTER THIRTY-NINE

Court Crashers

The Lady in Waiting considered the group for a moment as she processed Hilbert's words.

"Can you do it?" she asked, cutting straight to the point.

"Yes, ma'am. I can clear up anything but the worst cases. If they are too far gone for me, then it is probably too late for them anyway," Tilly answered solemnly. Kindle took the opportunity to fluff up her feathers while sitting on his pack, drawing the lady's eyes for a brief moment.

Nice, he sent to her with the image of a thumbs-up.

"Well," she said, turning back to Hilbert and Sir Michael before lowering her voice even further, "the shortage has gotten worse since you left, and with the new levies, we are coming perilously close to our emergency reserves." She had leaned in closer to Hilbert so that Tilly was barely able to hear what she was saying.

"I thought the entry tax was higher than I remembered," Hilbert muttered.

"She has already raised those taxes twice, but with many of our trading partners turtling up against the rising threat and the residents hitting their life-energy limit we are at our lowest level in decades."

"I thought we carefully monitored the residential life-energy limit!"

"We do! But what other options do we have? The Weasel somehow heard about our predicament, and it is a sign of the times that the queen has even given him an audience."

"I wondered about the shoddy blood magic I saw coming in. She can't be considering it! The last time he . . ."

Tilly had been so focused on listening to the whispered conversation that he had missed the entry of another group to the main hall. But as they approached the base of the large stairway, the clamor of their footfalls made the rest of the exchange impossible for him to hear. Tilly turned and saw a group of guards escorting some of the Cyclopic Brawlers from the strange caravan they had passed earlier. Two pairs of the one-eyed brawlers were each carrying a stave that ran through a handle on a large clay urn covered in angry red symbols.

Cyclopic Brawler must have been a *Strength*-based class because they had no trouble carrying the urn, which looked like it could hold over four hundred gallons of liquid. They marched along with their dhampire escort, not hesitating as they reached the stairs and started climbing.

Once again, Tilly got a sickly feeling at the sight of the urn, and as the guards approached holding it, his gut churned. The lingering nausea from the blood loss and the heady feeling emanating from the urn and the four brawlers combined to make his vision swim for just a moment as they passed him at the top of the stairs.

To his left, the large double doors swung open, and a rich velvety voice echoed from within, "There they are now, Your Majesty. Once you see my product, you will understand that this opportunity is exactly what your order needs in such trying times."

Then the door swung shut, and Tilly's vision refocused. Mallytza, Ichiro, and Hilbert were now whispering furiously behind him, but their words were lost in the background as he clutched his stomach. Amelia approached him, her eyes following the path of the urn with as much concern as he felt.

"I don't like the feeling of that magic. It's too close to the nagas', with a similar . . . taint," she muttered as she turned toward him, then noticed his discomfort for the first time. Kindle chirped in agreement, watching the closing door with a sharp gleam in her eye.

As the doors finished closing, Tilly straightened, pulled his arms away from his center, and came fully back to himself as his mind finally parsed the different sensations that had rolled through his body. Some were new, but the sudden writhing he had felt reverberating up his side was not. An awful clarity washed over him, and he looked over at his companions in momentary shock.

"Those warriors are **Corrupted** . . . And whatever they say is in that urn, it's a lie. Something terrible is waiting inside."

Amelia's eyes narrowed considerably. "Are you sure? I felt something from my infection, but it is faint, and it is not the first time I have felt such things over the last month," she asked, her intensity trailing off with the reminder of her internal struggle with **Corruption**.

The wriggling and twisting through Tilly's torso was beginning to subside, like the wringing of nervous hands. As he thought back to the other times he had felt this sensation, he was reminded of the first time he had confronted Titus.

"No, I'm sure. We have to do something about this now, before it's too late!" he growled, the reality of the situation settling on him with its full force. He turned and rushed to the trio behind him, and Amelia followed, mirroring his urgency. The three looked up at his approach.

"We have a serious problem. Whatever is in those urns is **Corrupted**," Tilly announced in a heavy whisper. Ichiro's eyes sharpened immediately and then glazed over as he looked through the door at the hall beyond with his sight *Ability*. The Lady in Waiting didn't register the meaning of his words, but Hilbert's face fell at the announcement.

"**Corrupted** . . . That is how you refer to the Blood Darkness, isn't it. You mean to say that it's some sort of trap?" he asked anxiously.

"Absolutely." A sudden breeze to Tilly's right marked Sir Michael's arrival. "We need to get in there and stop whatever is about to happen."

Hilbert's face fell even further, and if it could have gotten any paler, it would have. "Gods above, I hope you are right . . . Wait, no, I—"

"Hilbert, what is happening?" Mallytza demanded. "Darling, whatever the Weasel just brought into the High Chamber will be disastrous for our order if it is not contained."

At that, her confusion melted away to deadly focus, and Ichiro's distant gaze centered back on the group. "A very large shift is coming. Threads are already fraying," he said.

"Alright, alright!" Hilbert said, waving in frustration. "We need to get in, and I am afraid these guards will not allow that on a simple hunch . . . I have a fairly illegal mind-magic spell I can use, but I have to be completely outside of their attention to use it."

"Distraction, got it," Tilly answered resolutely. By this time their huddle had been joined by Franklin and Gorock, the latter of whom was now smiling hungrily at the break in the boredom.

"I will return to the queen's side as quickly as possible. She must know," Mallytza said, then produced a pair of daggers from nowhere and laid them against the flats of her forearms as she glided back to the servant's door with a sudden feline grace.

"I will stay here. The rest of you move over to the doors, and be ready to move as soon as the guards are down—the spell will only last for about ten breaths," Hilbert muttered, already forming arcane gestures with his hands.

The group quickly moved to the space before the double doors, having already attracted the attention of the majority of the guards with their furious whispering. Tilly immediately began belligerently shouting, not wanting any of them to glance over at Hilbert, who had remained in the shadow of the closing servant's door.

"Listen, you hose-wearing peacocks! I am tired of waiting. We have something very important to share with your queen. I won't be kept out here like some errand boy!" Tilly yelled, putting on his best impression of a drunk looking for trouble. He didn't know why that was what came to him in the moment, but the guards ate it up and moved toward him with polearms at the ready.

"Sir, you will await the queen's pleasure!" one of the guards shouted back as they approached from their positions around the top of the hall. As soon as the last guard passed Hilbert's position, the wizard's apprentice raised his hands.

"I honestly don't give a shit"—Tilly dropped his pack as Kindle took to the air above the group—"about your queen's pleasure." Then he drew his hatchets and painted a manic grin on his face at the cautious approach of the guards.

At that insult, the group of guards pulled back their lips in snarls, showing fangs and giving voice to their outrage. Just before they could charge, Hilbert completed the spell, and a pink flash ripped through the hall. Tilly's vision cleared, and he found the guards frozen in a tight half circle around him, having begun a charge but now wearing vague expressions of confusion on their slack faces.

"Move! Ten breaths!" Hilbert shouted, rushing toward the doors. The group had all drawn weapons, and Gorock and Sir Michael flung open the doors, releasing the last sentence of the conversation that had been going on within.

". . . inspect this sample for yourself, Your Majesty, it will more than assuage your concerns," the velvety voice promised.

Time seemed to freeze as everyone within the large chamber looked up at the unexpected interruption. In that momentary confusion, both groups sized each other up.

The chamber was large and circular. The outer edge was taken up by large stone columns, and a table sat just in front of the columns, wrapping around the whole space in a circular strip of elaborately carved wood. There must have been over a hundred seats around the table, but about four-fifths sat empty. Three seats directly across from the opening were more ornate than any of the others. The largest seat in the chamber was empty, as was the one to its right. But the one to its left held a hauntingly beautiful pale vampire in a rich red dress. Her eyes were two ruby orbs that shifted their narrow suspicious gaze from the center of the chamber to the entrance.

Level ???, Sanguine Sorceress Superior

The center of the chamber was open and currently held the four Cyclopic Brawlers, who had dropped their burden, and a hooked-nosed man, who must have been the owner of the velvety voice. He had just passed off a goblet of something to one of the two knights standing guard before the queen, and at their interruption, his face had screwed up into a rictus of rage.

Level 59, Black Market Trafficker

Tilly was shocked to see his third human in his time on Nephesh.

"You dare enter this chamber unannounced?" the queen shouted as she rose to her feet.

"Your Majesty, if you could give us a moment to explain!" Hilbert shouted, rushing in behind Tilly with the sound of outraged guards coming to their senses echoing from outside.

Tilly's eyes had become hyper-focused on the other human in the room, whose face had immediately schooled to calm. He started walking toward the urn at the center of the room as if nothing was amiss. Tilly's gut twisted in on itself, and he knew without a shadow of a doubt he had to stop this man.

"Hilbert—" the queen started before being interrupted by Tilly's shout ringing through the chamber.

"Stop him from reaching the urn!"

As if his words broke the fragile glass of stillness in the room, everyone started moving at once. One of the two knights protecting the queen drew his weapon and rushed forward, passing the trafficker and charging Tilly's group, and the other remained motionless, looking down at the cup in his hands. The rest of the knights surrounding the chamber exploded to their feet, but few had weapons in hand, and even fewer still were wearing their full plate. Tilly's whole group charged forward toward the urn and the Cyclopic Brawlers, while the trafficker dropped his pretense of calm and sprinted toward the center of the room.

"I demand to know the mean—" The queen's voice carried through the hall before cutting off as the knight in front of her, the one who had received the cup, groaned and dropped it, looking down at his arm in horror. It began to bulge and deform under his armor. "What—"

Her voice fell just as Mallytza arrived at her side, weapons drawn.

CHAPTER FORTY

A Bloody Mess

Too much was happening for Tilly to keep up with events as they unfolded around him in a flurry of chaos and conflict. He didn't get a magical 360-degree slow-mo breakdown of the fight as it happened step by step. Instead, his whole attention zeroed in on the narrow band of obstacles and objectives that lay before him.

Sir Michael exploded past the rest of the charging group to crash into the brawlers while Ichiro and Gorock immediately peeled off to block the charging knight, opening the path for Tilly to slip in between. He pumped his legs in Sir Michael's wake while vaguely noting Hilbert, Amelia, and Franklin hanging back to start casting.

Sir Michael's charge must have been a gap-close *Ability* because as hard as Tilly had taken off, he had been left in the dust. The knight was almost instantaneously bashing his mace through the group of brawlers, like an Italian grandma attacking a lump of dough. The knight successfully locked down all four guards with his impact and follow-up strikes. Tilly took full advantage of his initiative to leap over the conflict, leaning into his now superhuman *Dexterity*. Sensing his intent, Kindle soared in behind him, matching velocity, and grabbed his back in the air, lending him a slight increase in lift to clear the dueling fighters. Mid-flight, Tilly finally regained a line of sight on the Black Market Trafficker . . . who had already reached the urn and was ripping off its lid with an expression of manic glee pulling tight at the skin of his face. The lid came fully away, and the markings around its surface flashed red and died, ending their containment of the thing within.

As soon as its prison was open, **Corruption** exploded out from the opening, a writhing mass of tentacles and teeth. This was especially unfortunate for Tilly, whose aerial momentum took him directly toward the center of the creature exploding out from the urn. A split second before he hit, **Identify** pinged, notifying him that it was not one large monster but hundreds of smaller things densely packed together in a stream of terror and hatred.

Level 12, Corrupted Splitter Collective

In a split second, Tilly activated **Wrath's Shroud**, a yell of anticipated trauma tearing itself free from his throat. His burning form crashed into the pillar of black writhing tentacles with a sizzling, meaty *thunk*. The impact disrupted the Splitter Collective's momentum as it attempted to branch out into dozens of attacking appendages. Kindle screeched from above and sent out a torrent of blue flames to follow up on the impact, multiplying the effect of Tilly's unwitting surprise attack.

The mouths near the impact site screamed as one, and their center mass exploded in a burst of fiery kinetic energy. Despite the caustic nature of his presence to the creature, the unmelted mouths now surrounding him furiously tried to latch onto his body, in some places succeeding before being burned away by the ongoing damage output of **Wrath's Shroud**. He waved his axes around wildly, cutting away huge swathes of the collective before falling through the creature to the other side of the urn and landing like a puddle of vomit at the feet of the Black Market Trafficker.

The Splitter Collective was utterly devastated by his attack, but it proved true to its name and divided what remained of its mass into hundreds of tentacled starfish with mouths. The little creatures scattered everywhere and rushed the surrounding knights, who were only just now charging into the fray, shocked at the turn of events.

Tilly looked up as manic laughter sounded above him, the greasy-haired human gloating in the chaos. A pillar of **Corruption** had grown up behind him, completely consuming one of the two guardian knights. It lashed constantly at the shocked queen, who had summoned a ruby shield just in time. Mallytza was by her side, whirling her daggers in complicated patterns, removing any offending appendages that came close to slipping past the queen's defense.

"Do you see, brother? Why fight it? A new world order is coming to this plane, and we are destined to be its rulers." His voice rang with that same velvety invitation he had used earlier. He cackled.

"Yeah, I'm going to have to stick with a no on this one," Tilly growled, then leaped to his feet and lashed out at him with two enflamed strikes. Unfortunately, the wild look in the man's eyes did nothing to slow his reflexes. Before Tilly's strikes could land, the man reached up to a pendant at his neck and activated an opaque faceted shield emblem, inset with a glowing gray gem. A spherical shield sprung up to protect the man, rendering him impervious to Tilly's attacks, which struck against the glass-like surface with dull thuds.

"Don't bother. Even she couldn't get through this easily." He smiled, wild glee glowing on his face as he gestured over his shoulder nonchalantly.

Behind him, the queen finished a series of arcane gestures and shouted, "Enough!" before loosing a surge of what could only be blood magic. The ruby streams of mana formed into a series of whirling blades and blurred through the creature in front of her, decimating it, then continued on to crash against the Black Market Trafficker's shield.

He didn't even flinch as the blades' impact thundered against the barrier. Instead, he leaned forward, a smirk secure on his face, and whispered conspiratorially over the din of battle, "See what I mean? Maybe her master could have been a threat, but he bailed on them as soon as he could."

The man didn't seem interested in actually fighting, so Tilly rearranged priorities and left him to gloat as he turned and focused on the small eldritch starfish flinging themselves at the surrounding knights. In a quick pivot, he shot back toward the thickest remaining group of creatures, choosing to ignore the human as a secondary threat.

"Why resist what is coming? Embrace it!" the black marketeer called after Tilly in a sing-song voice.

"**Absolute Blood Barrier**," echoed the shout of the queen's next spell. A ruby barrier rose between the pillars, closing in the room and sealing the chaos within. "Knights, remove this threat from our halls! When we are done, I will render the flesh from your bones, Weasel!" she called as Tilly released enflamed strike after enflamed strike, dropping **Wrath's Shroud** as his mana hit its bottom third.

"How many times have I told you idiots? My name is Wesley!" he shouted back, all of the laughter gone from his voice as it cracked into broken pieces.

Around the room, the Knights of the Round Table showed their skill at arms by easily dispatching multiple Splitters with every sweep of their weapons . . . But none of the creatures seemed to care that they were dying en masse for the chance to momentarily latch on to any exposed extremity. And, unfortunately, except for a few knights, none of the combatants were wearing their customary armor.

Tilly couldn't help but note how perfect the plan of attack was. No one who trained in a style of fighting that accounted for full plate would concern themselves with small wounds—that was the advantage of being fully armored—but that very mentality showed its drawbacks here when even the smallest wound had a chance to pass on **Corruption**. All of the unarmored knights were taking wounds as the creatures were quickly cut down, and Tilly could already see signs of infection spreading from some.

Arcane words rang out once again in the hall as the queen finished casting another longer spell, and the **Absolute Blood Barrier** exploded inward in a forest of spikes. Most spikes found a remaining Splitter and speared it through the center. While the majority of the spikes concentrated on the smaller creatures, the central portion of the attack concentrated on the Weasel's barrier, completely obscuring it from view, and crashed against the gemlike surface with a bone-shaking impact. The queen released a breath and the razor-sharp blood lances melted away, having dispatched the vast majority of the remaining Splitters. Unfortunately, the main target of the attack remained unharmed behind his barrier, leering at his surroundings.

The room became very still as the last of the Splitters were dealt with, and everyone's collective attention turned toward the man behind the seemingly impregnable barrier.

Through the stillness, the queen's voice rasped in fury. "Mallytza, I locked down all the doors. Find and destroy any of those disgusting creatures that may have gotten out before I raised the barrier. Knights, prepare your strongest *Abilities*. It is time the cur is punished," the queen ordered, her pale face livid.

The Weasel turned slowly to face her, his visage one of mild curiosity. His smooth, velvety voice once again echoed through the chamber. "I must say, it was painfully easy to topple what was left of your order. When they offered me the job, I was excited, to say the least . . . But I am sorry to say, this has turned out to be rather disappointing."

The queen's full, red lips pulled back in a hiss of fury, and she raised her hands once more as a dark red light began to build in her palms. The knights, despite sporting numerous infected wounds, lifted their weapons and readied *Abilities*, prepared to shatter whatever magic protected the confident saboteur.

"Looks like my time is up . . . ," the hook-nosed man said, then turned back to Tilly. "See you later, friend." He winked before snapping something hidden in his hand and beginning to glow.

"Destroy him!" the queen screeched, launching one of many salvos of mana-enhanced strikes and *Abilities*. The storm of power collided against the shield and shattered it, just as the figure within faded away like dew on a bright morning.

The queen's shriek of frustration tore through the room at the disappearance of their attacker. Then she collapsed into a boneless slouch on her ornate chair, as if the scream had held the last of her bodily energy. Her eyes, however, flicked around the room as she processed the implications of such an attack and ran through the possible outcomes.

After a moment of thought, she whispered into her hand and flung it out, releasing a bird that looked like a cardinal made of blood, which streaked by Kindle in the air and moved through the large doors as if they didn't exist. Then she issued orders to the rest of the room.

"Knights on vigil, find the rest of the Weasel's caravan and reinforce the gate! Send a report back to me at once. The rest of you, stay here. It seems this day's horrendous beginning will worsen before long," she said darkly, then released another arcane gesture and flung the large doors open.

All around the room, blades were sheathed, and about a fifth of the knights and guards hurriedly left the circular hall. Tilly noted that the dismissed knights were all the ones he had seen wearing armor, including the guard that had initially charged them. This group also included Sir Accolon, who refused to meet their eyes, sneering on his way out.

The rest of the knights in the room turned to the second set of intruders. Many sported wounds that they believed were unhealable, yet they remained alert, ready to respond to whatever the queen needed, wary eyes on this group of newcomers.

Mallytza materialized near the open doors and nodded to the queen in confirmation that the room and its surroundings were clear, and the queen let out a long slow breath.

"Tell me, human, how did you know?" she whispered, her quiet voice echoing through the chamber, its haggard tone complimenting the dark circles now shadowing her blood-shot eyes.

Tilly turned to face her fully and thought carefully about his answer, recognizing the terrible blow her faction had just received. "Your Majesty . . . ," he opened slowly, looking for the easiest way to explain who he was and what he could offer. "I am a deity's Champion, and my deity has set itself against this new threat. What you call Blood Darkness, we call **Corruption**. The Strigoi hordes on your border are using it as a new source of power, but really, it is only a set of chains."

Then, instinctually feeling it would lend the most immediate credibility to his words, he lifted his jacket to reveal his scarred side, where thick pulsating veins of **Corruption** reached out into the rest of his body. The surrounding knights once again reached for weapons at the sight of the ghastly scarred wound, and Tilly continued.

"Our faction, the Three-Fold Alliance, is beset now by a horde army, not because we are an easy target, but because we hold a power to cure all but the most terrible forms of this sickness, and we are searching out a solution for even that. Our patron has vested in me the power to remove this **Corruption** from any others that are still strong enough to resist. I cannot yet be free myself, but as long as I catch it early enough, I can remove it from others." As he finished, he dropped his jacket back over his torso.

"You must forgive me if I am slow to trust such an offer after my recent . . . interaction with your kind. Can you demonstrate this divine *Ability* of yours?" she asked slowly, her perfectly manicured hand cradling her chin as she resettled on her chair, displaying an impassive attitude.

Tilly nodded after peeking at his mana, which had ticked back above 32 percent. He turned a slow circle and found Gorock, who had, unsurprisingly, gotten covered in wounds in the recent conflict, his style of fighting similarly disadvantaged against an enemy like the Splitters. At Tilly's look, Gorock came forward without hesitating, bare arms covered with infected bite marks. He looked around the room as he approached with his teeth bared in an expression Tilly was still unable to decipher.

"My class *Ability* is activated through my breath. It multiplies a target's *Endurance* and makes them able to fight off any poison or infection. This is bolstered by the Champion's mantle I carry, which makes the effect several times more powerful against this specific kind of invader," Tilly explained before churning the flame at his center and exhaling it over Gorock's frame.

This time the Wall Breaker didn't flinch as his skin grew flushed and noxious steam rose from the myriad wounds on his body. In seconds, all of the black infected areas were clear and a cloud of dark smoke was gathering on the ceiling. Before Tilly even had time to say something, Kindle was there, bursting through the cloud with a body wreathed in blue flames, and dispersed it immediately.

The queen watched the process with a glint in her eyes as the **Corruption** was flushed from Gorock's body. Kindle's display at the end was icing on the cake, and the queen didn't stop the smile from curling her mouth, her two fangs pressing against her full bottom lip in a striking mix of hunger and beauty, as the cloud hissed into non-existence.

CHAPTER FORTY-ONE

The Queen's Gambit

The queen opened her mouth to speak but was interrupted by the scarlet bird she had released earlier streaking back into the room and fluttering around her excitedly. It passed on a silent message and then melted away. The queen's smile died on her lips, and she turned her eyes to the assembly, fury reigniting on her pale features.

"It is as I feared. This urn was not the only one containing one of those . . . *things*. The brawlers in the Weasel's caravan were forewarned and managed to open two more of the urns before we could lock them down. There were no casualties, but many more are reporting this sickness." After a moment's thought, her eyes narrowed in on Tilly and she continued. "They are now saying that the system notification is flagging it as **Corruption**. It has been tagged as 'Blood Darkness' for the last few weeks in our notifications, but with your arrival, it has changed . . . Just how connected to this substance are you?"

Tilly considered her question, looking for an answer that didn't involve sharing everything but still gave the gist of his credibility. This, of course, was made more difficult by the fact that even he hardly understood the forces at work in this conflict. Something big was happening all over Nephesh, and it seemed to reach through every echelon of power.

"I believe I have been set up as an opposition to this entity. My system calls it **Corruption**, and we have confirmation that it is appearing all over the plane. I don't know if it has a sentient center of control or if it is just the result of magical entropy. What I do know is that I have been granted a power set that seems to be uniquely suited to mitigate its spread. However, I am far from equipped to stop it alone. Honestly, I don't even know if I'll be able to clear it from my own body before it kills me," he declared heavily, the implications of his words dropping on the surrounding audience like stone weights.

"Look," he continued, gathering his resolve, "I still barely understand this world, but I know evil when I see it. I might not live through what's coming, but that doesn't change the fact that evil is at our door. If we let it, it will take everything from us. As you just experienced, no one is safe. **Corruption**, and whatever is behind it, is making a play for the whole plane. Its nature is voracious, and it will not stop until it has consumed everything. I, personally, would rather die than watch that happen," Tilly finished with a growl, some of the heat from his chest suffusing his whole body as he leaned into his conviction. As he looked around, he realized his words had been building throughout the chamber, echoing some unseen spirit of nobility that had once filled this room.

The queen watched Tilly as the ingrained magic of the chamber responded to him and washed through her order's greatest knights. Her eyes flicked back and forth in cold calculation before resting on the most senior of her knights. He moved forward at the unspoken command, and they exchanged a whispered conversation before he stepped back and to the side. Having made her decision, she sat up straight, exuding an effortless air of royalty as she pulled the attention in the room back to herself.

"Very well, I will need to know how often you can use this *Ability* and how costly it is to you. We will set up a rotation and move through all of those infected in the city, supplying you with potions and buffs. You will, of course, be reimbursed for your time, and I will personally offer you and your companions a sincere gesture of our gratitude for your services," she decreed, motioning for another knight to come forward and report to her as if the matter had been decided.

"Ugh, ma'am—" Tilly began, but Ichiro stepped in before he could continue.

"Your Majesty, we are here as ambassadors of a neighboring faction, and our interests are much greater than personal wealth. I am afraid our position necessitates that we leave in the next few hours. Your order is not our final destination. We came here in the hopes of brokering a temporary alliance of arms," he declared in a calm voice that did not have to fight to echo through the pillars of the room.

The queen froze at those words, then turned back to the group slowly, her lips thinning to a line at the apparent refusal. "I do appreciate your position and your timely intervention. But I am afraid I am similarly limited by my obligation to my people. Unless you can cast this *Ability* en masse, I must insist that you stay until we have cleared my population of this taint," she responded, mustering a reasonable tone that barely concealed the granite behind her words.

"Ma'am, I am more than willing to help as many of your people as possible. But our city is under attack as we speak. We need much more than money and gifts. We need an alliance," Tilly cut back in, not at all liking where this was going.

"Your Majesty!" Hilbert cut in before adding desperately, "They claim there are others in their faction who can cleanse this taint. I brought them here in the hopes that you would be willing to discuss a concerted effort to break one of the horde armies that has formed near our borders. Surely you can see now that we are their next target! Such an alliance would strengthen both of our positions."

At Hilbert's interjection, all reasonableness drained away from the queen's features, leaving only a mask of apathetic resolve. "It no longer surprises me just how far outside of your station you are willing to step, stable boy . . . I do not care that you think you are right or that you have found a small solution to our current problems. You have defied my authority for the last time. I will deal with you and *Sir* Michael when this is through," she snapped icily at the wizard's apprentice before turning back to Tilly and Ichiro. "Now, I am willing to speak of a martial alliance, but not until after you make good on your promise and cleanse my people. Until then, we have nothing more to speak of."

"No," Tilly said softly.

To his right and left, Ichiro and Gorock's hands fell back to their weapons.

"Ha! What happened to all of your grand words from a moment ago, human? As soon as things don't go your way, you sulk? Now, do as you said you would and cleanse those who are infected with this evil you claim to stand against," she hissed, ruby light beginning to flicker in her eyes.

"I will do exactly that, but not before we come to an understanding. I am not one of your subjects. I owe you nothing, but still, our offer stands," Tilly answered right back, his tone just as frosty.

"Well, we have ways of accommodating such a decision," she quipped, allowing her lips to curl up in a predatory smile, and leaned back into her chair. She magnanimously gestured with her right hand and the surrounding knights reluctantly drew their weapons.

"Actually, Your Majesty," Amelia declared in an easy tone, coming up from behind Tilly and drawing the attention of the room, "I may have a solution that meets all of our needs quite nicely." She reached back to her cloak and coaxed some of the inert Blood Weed there to shift into her hand. "I assume you are all familiar with this plant?" she asked as she held it before her and began to channel her mana.

The queen leaned forward in her chair, her curiosity piqued. "Yes, it is the vile weed that grows into the wounds of our soldiers if we let it. Like so much in the Strigoi lands, it sustains itself with blood alone. Why do you ask?"

Amelia watched it for a second and smiled as her magic finished imparting a verdant glow to the otherwise dead-looking grasslike stalks. "Mr. Tillman here is not the only one who is fighting an advanced infection of **Corruption**," she stated, taking a moment to look Tilly in the eyes before turning back to the queen. The

look had been filled with meaning that he would have to ask her about later . . .
But in the current circumstance, it might as well have been inscrutable. Nonetheless,
Tilly was glad for any idea that didn't involve them fighting against a group of
higher-leveled knights, or worse, being held prisoner as he was squeezed for every
last drop of magic he had.

Amelia stepped into the center of the room and raised her voice easily to present her idea to the room.

"My class revolves around plants, and I am able to imbue them with my mana
and impart specific commands that will last as long as my magic does. My own
infection has been contained but not eliminated by the same force that empowers
Mr. Tillman's *Abilities*, and this gives my magic a unique resonance with both
the fire that he carries and the **Corruption** that poisons so many of your wounds."
She looked back down at her newly imbued plant, excitement showing on her features. "Your Majesty, am I correct in assuming your command of blood would
allow you to hold a certain buff applied to it in stasis?"

"Theoretically, yes. I would have to build a ritual that would be able to act as
a target for his *Ability*. But if the magic takes hold, I should be able to lock it into
the blood for an extended period." The look of reserved interest on the queen's
face had bloomed into something altogether different as Amelia dived into her
explanation. Now she was leaning forward with something like eager fascination
enlivening her cold features.

It was then that he realized she was a leader facing the possible loss of the
majority of her power base. The harsh reality of her context was coloring her actions
to a strong degree. As that thought fell into place, he saw her unyielding focus on
the immediate restoration of her people in a new light. In her mind, she could not
risk anything less . . .

But now, speaking on a subject that she was passionate about, some of that
cold mask fell away. If there was another solution for her people, especially one
not centered around the whims of another faction, she would take it eagerly.

"We would need blood . . . ," the queen mused before turning to Tilly, all of
the earlier conflict absent from her features as she worked through the magical
problem. "It is my understanding you paid the blood tax, yes?"

"That is correct, ma'a—I mean, Your Majesty," Tilly said, not sure he understood exactly what these two were suggesting, but happy with the direction things
were going.

"That will do nicely. Your blood will be what I use to bind up the rest of the
volume into a metaphysical projection of an entity. That gives us our best chance
at capturing your *Ability* and imprinting its nature into the whole," she muttered
to herself, her eyes distant as she worked through the problem. Then, having rea-
soned what was needed to make the spell work, she called to the guards. "I need
the gate Blood Vessel brought here immediately." Then, less enthusiastically,

"Hilbert, come forward and assist me. I am confident in my ability to impart the meaning I desire into the spell form, but I want you to look it over . . . You remain *his* best student when it comes to theory."

Her subjects rushed to obey their commands, and Hilbert jogged forward, sneaking a small smile and wink at Mallytza as the queen turned to Amelia.

"What conditions will your weed need to propagate?" she asked as she rolled up the sleeves of her dress.

CHAPTER FORTY-TWO

Smoking Grass

An hour later, Tilly had cleansed all of the knights in the chamber with the assistance of two mana potions. During this time, Amelia and the queen had built a large circular spell around the magical Blood Vessel that had been carted up from the gate. Its top had been removed to reveal a two-foot-wide opening that exposed the large volume of blood within.

Some of the containment and transfer runes had been canceled so as not to interfere with the spell, and then the queen had drawn a triquetra around the enchanted container. She, of course, had used the blood from the vessel itself to mark the floors in the large open space in the center of the High Chamber. After marking out the shape with her finger dipped in blood, she had reluctantly called Hilbert over to consult on several points. They had talked through the concept of the spell and marked the edge of the shape with a string of runes, also drawn in blood from the vessel.

After all that was done, Amelia called Tilly back from the last of the cleansed knights. Despite his fears, none of their infections had progressed very far before he had had a chance to cleanse them, and Tilly realized that the armored class of knight must emphasize *Endurance* heavily as one of its primary stats. While it wasn't enough to stop or remove the infection, most of them had shown strong resistance to its spread. Regardless, he was glad he had been present to stop the spread of **Corruption's** influence through a faction that would hopefully become integral allies in the coming fight.

"Do you have enough mana to cast your strongest version of **Flame's Renewal?**" Amelia asked as he approached the outer edge of the spell, where she had been taking notes and preparing several Blood Weed shoots.

"I'm just above what I need to put out a maximum strength version of the *Ability*," he confirmed.

At his words, the queen waved him over to the third point of the ritual shape and had him stand at its apex while she and Hilbert marked out a few final touches on the spell. As they finished, a subtle snap clicked through the metaphysical space within the spell, linking Tilly to the vessel in a way he did not understand but absolutely felt, like a heavy rope had been tied to his chest and was subtly tugging him toward the vessel at the ritual's center.

"With that, we should be ready," Amelia called over, her eyes scanning over the runes, vessel, and Blood Weed, rechecking everything. "Tilly, once the queen says so, I want you to move to the vessel and cast your *Ability* at the surface of the blood. The queen's spell has been built with two functions. It should cause your *Ability* to affect the entire volume of blood, just like it would a normal target's body. Then, once your buff has settled in, she will enact the second portion of the spell and put the blood in stasis. I believe this is what they have done to the more severely infected knights to keep them from turning. Oh, and Tilly"—she found his eyes to emphasize her next point—"get out of the spell area before she casts the stasis portion, please."

"Got it," he said, feeling like the toddler invited to place the final block on top of a large tower.

After his acknowledgment, she looked back over the entire ritual one more time while explaining the rest to Tilly. "I have locked several simple commands into our Blood Weed test specimens. They should absorb your purifying ability in its stasis form as they feed off the blood. Then, once they are removed from the blood's surface, they will revert to their inert state. I theorize that they will be able to last days, if not weeks, in this state before my mana fades and they lose their effectiveness. However, I am not sure how long your *Ability* will remain intact in stasis within their simple mana path—"

"Wait, how will we use them once they absorb the blood?" Tilly asked, more to get her back on track than anything else. The queen looked on curiously now that she was finished building up her part in the plan.

"Oh! Yes, I believe they will behave just as they do in the wild when introduced to a wound. I have keyed their hunger reflex onto **Corruption's** resonance. They should seek out only infected blood and release the effect of your *Ability* once they have taken it in. I believe their rapid growth cycle brought on by the introduction of blood will allow a chain reaction that will keep new growth happening even as the old growth is destroyed by the reaction of the two opposing forces," she answered before giving Tilly a forced, bright smile. "Only one way to truly find out . . ." She then turned to the queen. "Are we ready?"

The monarch nodded, looking altogether relaxed, the sleeves of her dress pulled back and her fingertips stained a rusty red, as she said, "For what it is worth, Mr. Tillman, I do believe this will work. I have never used alchemy in such a . . . lively way, but the theories are sound, and from my experience with magic, strong intent can make even the strangest things possible." She lifted her hands to a ready casting position and nodded for him to proceed.

"Okay, here goes nothing . . . ," he said as much to himself as anyone else. He stepped over the edge of the spell and felt a strange sense of vertigo as if he were stepping into a familiar room. The sensation was not too different from what accompanied his **Spirit Walk** skill, and he did his best to ignore it as he carefully moved over the lines of the spell without disturbing any of the markings.

After several well-placed steps, he was at the lip of the Blood Vessel. He looked down into the still, dark mirror that the surface of the opaque liquid created. He saw his own wavy face looking back at him, his dark brows pulled down in focus as he began to churn the fire at his center and activate the pattern for **Flame's Renewal**. He took a deep breath and then exhaled, releasing shimmering heat waves through the air and rippling the surface of the blood.

The spell form all around him began to glow with a ruby light, and he quickly stepped back through the path he had charted for himself on the way in. The blood began to steam and then boil.

Just as Tilly exited the spell form, the queen called out in a loud voice, "Sanguine histasthai nocturnum!"

The spell laid out on the floor flashed once in a burst of power, then went completely dark. Tilly turned to look at the vessel and saw that steam was no longer rising from the top; all the activity that his *Ability* had caused had stopped immediately.

"Hilbert, what status effects are you reading?" the queen called across the ritual to the wizard's apprentice. He had a spell that formed a lens in front of his eyes through which he was watching the vessel intently.

"I see the **Flame's Renewal** reading on the vessel, and interestingly, it says the target effect is stacking with something that looks like a partial Title," he said, shooting a quick questioning glance in Tilly's direction.

"I have one that makes me more resistant to poison and infection. Probably the only reason I am still me and not a monster at this point," Tilly happily chimed in, attempting to ease the tension of the moment as the whole room waited to see if the spell would work.

"And . . . is it holding?" the queen asked.

Hilbert turned back to the Blood Vessel and watched it for several more seconds before answering, "Yes, Your Majesty. I see no change in status. Tillman, your *Ability's* effect is usually instantaneous, yes?"

"Yeah, I think so. It activates and then supplements the target's *Endurance*, increasing their ability to resist anything the system categorizes as an invader."

"Well, then, with no presence of poison or **Corruption**, I am happy to report that its continued effect means that the stasis has successfully held," Hilbert declared, looking up and smiling.

The queen schooled her focused expression back to something reserved, but Tilly could almost feel the satisfaction rolling off her as she said, "Mrs. Cooper, I believe it is stable. You may introduce the specimen."

Amelia moved forward, taking care to not disturb any part of the spell, and gently laid the Blood Weed on the still surface of the open container. As soon as the roots touched the surface, the plant started to shudder. New growth burst out in every direction, and it drank greedily from the surface. This wild growth continued until the plant was spilling over the lip of the vessel, then stopped immediately, most likely due to Amelia's influence. When it shifted into its active feeding mode, its color deepened to a rich red, as Tilly had seen before. But as it continued to spread, some of the original growth continued to change color, taking on a bluish hue before reverting to its inert state of rusty brown.

"Any change in the stasis?" the queen asked Hilbert.

"None, Your Majesty," he answered happily.

"Villers, come forward," she called to the surrounding crowd, which had grown precipitously. Through the audience stepped the same official that had taken Tilly's blood tax at the front gate. "Mrs. Cooper, Villers has agreed to be the first test of your solution. You may proceed."

The official moved forward, looking much worse than he had a few hours ago. His clothes were torn in several places, and Tilly could see a collection of wounds festering on his arms and chest from the second part of the Weasel's plan. Despite this, he presented himself calmly near the edge of the spell. Amelia carefully detached a piece of the Blood Weed from the carpet of flora that now covered the top of the open vessel. The hole made by its absence was quickly filled in by the surrounding plant, but as soon as it reached the lip of the container, it once again stopped expanding, held in check by Amelia's magic.

The Botanist Surveyor moved carefully out of the spell's effect and up to Villers, who regarded her stoically, manfully ignoring the black streaks of **Corruption** reaching out from each of his wounds and attempting to dig deeper into his body.

"Thank you for volunteering, sir," she addressed him as she checked over the plant with her magical senses, then lifted it in front of him. "This should only consume the **Corrupted** blood in your system. As it does, that blood should clash with the imbued *Ability* within the plant and destroy itself . . . But I am not sure what this reaction will look like. I am, however, prepared to pull it back at a moment's notice if you so desire. Simply say the word and I can stop its growth. Are you ready?"

The official, who had seemed bookish in their first interaction, showed a stern calm as he offered her a stoic nod in answer. He kept his face composed to a heroic degree as Amelia lifted the Blood Weed to his chest and placed the red-tinted roots against his largest wounds. The queen snapped her fingers and all of his scabbed-over wounds began to bleed freely, sending the Blood Weed into a frenzy.

The roots reached out to the source of new energy and burrowed deeply while the blades multiplied, sending new shoots in the direction of the other sources of free-flowing blood. Any place that wasn't actively bleeding was ignored as the plant covered all of the vampire's infected wounds in an eager explosion of manic growth.

In reaction to what must have been a horrendous experience, the official fully bared both fangs and allowed himself a long hiss at the pain. After about thirty seconds, the original part of the plant that Amelia had initially attached to his chest began to blacken and wither as the veins of **Corruption's** infection shuddered and shrunk.

Tilly watched in fascination as the growth charred before his eyes and eventually fell off the vampire, leaving a pale, uninfected wound behind. The shallow cuts began to heal immediately, and the intense expression on his face eased.

"Oh!" Amelia said in surprise. When Tilly looked over to smile at her success, he found her eyes looking into the middle distance, reading over some notification. Then his **Identify** pinged and her level changed.

Level 40, Botanist Surveyor

After allowing herself a happy smile, she read the prompt aloud to share it with the room. "The system has recognized this new use of Blood Weed as a discovery of significant proportions on the plane and hints that there is more to discover beyond this possible interaction."

CHAPTER FORTY-THREE

Quid Pro Quo

At Amelia's announcement, the queen scoffed, effecting a pained expression. "Of course . . . a crafting-martial hybrid class. I should have guessed from the name. I have always been a little jealous of your kind's ability to gain *experience* from advancing your craft as well as from combat," the queen said, her lips quirking in satisfaction at the success of their experiment. "Villers, did you bring the extractor?" she asked as she turned back to the test subject, her smile growing in eagerness.

The official looked up in distracted amazement as the Blood Weed withered and died over the rest of his wounds. It took him a moment, but then he registered her words and answered, "Yes, my queen." He reached into the folds of his torn petticoat and pulled out the same device that had been used to take the blood tax from them at the gate. He stepped forward smartly and presented it to her, and she took it in hand eagerly.

Turning to the Blood Vessel, she activated the portion of the enchantment that bonded the two devices and called absently, "Bring me a few of the most infected guards." The rest of the room watched curiously as she approached the vessel and tapped the extraction tube to its side, causing a ripple in the enchantment. "Hilbert, how is the stasis holding?"

"Unchanged, my queen," he answered, his tone rising in an unstated question.

"Your Majesty . . . If you don't mind me asking, what are you doing?" Amelia chimed in, watching as the sorceress fiddled with a dial on the side of the extraction tube. Several Dhampire Guardsmen shuffled forward, all looking much worse off than the official. Their torsos had been protected enough, but many had infected cuts and bites all over their arms and faces. It looked as if an army of feral rats had assaulted them, which actually would have been preferable to reality.

"My dear," the queen answered Amelia with a doting tone, "your method of transference with the Blood Weed is admirable and useful, as it is its own transfer vector and storage all wrapped up in one solution. But we are vampires, and as soon as you thought of this idea, another more direct method occurred to me." She looked up from the device in her hands as its runes lit up in a pattern reminiscent of a cup being filled with water.

She then turned toward the injured guards, and the senior-most man came forward silently as she continued to explain. "You see, each dhampire in our forces has a daily ration when on active duty, and that ration is doubled upon injury . . . This vessel was marked to cover the guards' ration for a few days. Now, Mr. Tillman, you have given me a way to pay out that ration and rid them of their taint at the same time." Seeming to understand her idea, the guard presented the inside of his forearm to the queen.

She laid the tip of the device against the dhampire's skin, and instead of the runes filling up with light, the glowing extraction tube pushed out its substance into the guard's body. He involuntarily shivered as the heat moved through his blood system and his wounds started to sizzle and steam. The injected blood cycled through his whole body, reacting with all of the guard's wounds and releasing that same noxious cloud. Immediately, the **Corruption** started to attempt an escape up into the ceiling, but the queen gestured lazily at the gathering cloud of roiling black smoke, and blood manifested all around it in an opaque ball. Then, with a clench of her fist, the sphere collapsed with a *pop*.

"There should be enough in this vessel to issue out hundreds of these *Ability*-imbued rations and grow enough supply of Blood Weed that we can travel with some form of immediate treatment for our people," she said as she turned toward Amelia and Tilly, her regal bearing slowly falling back into place now that a solution to her faction's problem had fully presented itself. "Now, if you don't mind, those that I have kept in stasis are in our sacred chamber. I would prefer it if you saw to them yourself while I discuss the details of our future military arrangement with your companion." She gestured over to Ichiro, a smile gracing her now serene features.

"You will break the siege on our faction?" Tilly asked excitedly, wanting to be sure he understood what she was hinting at.

"Contrary to what the young apprentice here has claimed," she said, raising her voice drolly as Hilbert winced, "I have not been holding back my forces out of fear or ignorance. Our faction and our arrangement with peoples further into the land of the living exist to curb the threat of the horde. We could never sit idly by and wait for them to ravage our lands and our people. But without a counter to this poison, my hands were tied. I would have been throwing away all of my forces in one attack, which would have been foolish by any measure." Hilbert's face screwed up in even greater discomfort over her shoulder as she revealed the rationale behind her actions. She seemed to sense his discomfort playing out behind her, and her smile shifted from serene to predatory in a blink. "Give us a day to marshal our forces and march. Your faction's emissary and I will work through the initial details while you fulfill the last of your promise.

"I am eager to see what future opportunities such an alliance can afford both our factions. But beware, what has shown up on your borders is far from the horde's main strength, and I am afraid the coming conflict will be decided over much more than a single battle."

The weight of her words settled on every soldier in attendance. Shoulders subtly shifted back, and brows lowered in understanding. Tilly realized she was speaking to them as much as to him.

"In the meantime," she continued, her tone lightening a fraction, "go revive the rest of my knights. Some of my best have been laid low by this sickness, and it would do our hearts well to have their number with us again. Villers, give Hilbert the tier-two extraction tube and set it to dispense a full ration allotment." The official stepped forward and handed Hilbert the silvery enchanted extractor that had caused Tilly such a headache earlier in the day.

"Now . . . Hilbert. You will take my errant Vigil Knight and our new ally to the Chamber of Repose. Your judgment has been postponed, but I do not wish to see your face again without a company of restored knights at your back."

"Yes, my queen," he said, smiling in relief after taking the object from the official. Then, as if his reprieve was time sensitive, he waved urgently over to Tilly, then gestured to a cleverly hidden gap in the round table at the rear corner of the hall.

I will fly over the gate. There is a chance they missed some of these creatures, and I want to hunt, Kindle sent from her perch on one of the doors.

Alright, send for me if you need anything.

I will not need you for such a small task, human, she sent back with the avian equivalent of a smirk. The image involved an artful flick of tail feathers. She leaped into the air and winged out of the chamber.

Tilly smiled as he moved toward Sir Michael, who was waiting on the other side of the table as if by magic. Tilly scanned the room one last time and found the queen dispensing healing to the worst of her injured guards and Ichiro stepping up for his audience with her. Amelia had wandered back over to the Blood Vessel and was collecting several samples of the Blood Weed and putting them in one of her pockets for later use.

"Well, that went better than I expected!" Hilbert said in a low cheerful voice to Sir Michael's faceless helmet as Tilly joined them, moving through the gap in the table.

"Yeah, about that. You left out a lot of details when you were trying to talk us into coming here," Tilly muttered, giving the apprentice a hard stare.

The object of Tilly's disapproval smiled demurely. "I knew it would work itself out somehow . . . Or at least, it always has in the past," he answered cheerfully.

On Hilbert's other side, Sir Michael shook his head slowly in disapproval as he moved toward the back wall. "Enough about what is done, let us get on to what still needs doing!"

Hilbert gestured to the small stone door Sir Michael had just reached. It was entirely made out of dark granite flecked with silvery granules of some other kind of rock. Its surface was carved in a relief of a knight kneeling with his sword pointed at the ground and a ring of coffins surrounding him. The artwork reminded Tilly of something he might see in a Catholic church.

"Just through here," Hilbert said lightly as Sir Michael pushed open the door. The hallway beyond was pitch black, and the knight moved into the darkness without hesitation. Tilly sighed and followed as Hilbert closed the door behind them and then clucked in disapproval at the pitch-black state of their environment. "My apologies!" Hilbert huffed, then snapped his fingers. A rosy pink light flared at the tips of previously unseen sconces and the small dark hall became slightly less ominous in the light of the flickering mana-infused flames.

Sir Michael continued to lead the way, seemingly unaffected by the presence or absence of the light. Eventually they arrived at a second stone door covered with another lifelike relief, this one of a long-haired vampire knight lying in the classic Dracula pose, with arms crossed over his chest.

Sir Michael paused at this door and placed his hands against the stone, waiting. After a few moments, previously invisible markings started to glow all over the surface of the door, and it opened soundlessly on its own.

The mana torches continued into a large cavern-like structure and their glow illuminated lines of stone coffins arrayed around a large central edifice. As Tilly's head wrapped around what he was seeing, he noticed that the walls of the cavern were also broken up with hundreds of carved shelves, their contents hidden in the flickering shadow of the torches. He didn't have to work hard at guessing their contents. This was a catacomb.

"Here is our resting place, eternal or otherwise," Hilbert breathed out beside Tilly. He sounded just like he had walked into his favorite bar, and Tilly couldn't help but smile at his clear comfort in such an ominous environment. At times, it was easy to forget that the unpredictable wizard's apprentice was partially undead . . . Or fully. Tilly didn't know how vampires were supposed to be classified.

Sir Michael moved forward into the lines of coffins and stopped at one with its lid askew. He shifted the stone slab to the side until it was completely open and turned back to the pair standing at the door.

"So, you keep your . . . dead here? I mean . . . the ones that no longer exist, or—" Tilly stumbled over his questions, not quite finding the right terminology to make it clear.

Hilbert turned to him and smiled, his eyes glinting in the torchlight. "Yes. Our original race, the Aos Si, has always enjoyed the feeling of being underground.

It is where we are most at rest. This became doubly true in our new forms, and we find great comfort in the presence of those who have gone before us. Many in this room have passed beyond this plane, but it is also where we keep those who are fighting this **Corruption**, as you call it," Hilbert explained, waving an open hand toward Sir Michael in a "Please, you first" gesture.

"Huh . . . Well, I guess that makes sense," Tilly said, shrugging, as he moved through the lines of stone coffins. As he entered into their uniform ranks, he realized that some were empty and others were closed. The group nearer to where Sir Michael stood all had their lids half open.

As Tilly approached the open coffin at Sir Michael's feet, he saw it held the body of a young blond-haired knight, lying as if sleeping with both hands folded over a plain, well-kept longsword.

"Good thinking, Sir Michael! Young Constantine is a wonderful place to start," Hilbert said as he walked up next to Tilly.

CHAPTER FORTY-FOUR

Silent Knight

Tilly stared down at the still body and began to notice several stretches of pale skin near the edges of his armor that showed black veins frozen in their insidious advance. His **Identify** pinged helpfully.

Level 71, Knight of the Sanguine Order

"So, he was one of the knights who went on the excursion?" Tilly asked.

"Yes, the name they chose for the venture was slightly more lighthearted than I would have liked, but the mission was serious. Several smaller roving bands of Strigoi were forming from the recent successful campaigns they had waged on other borders. We sent fifty knights on a scouting campaign with orders to disrupt and destroy any leadership they could find without getting caught in a full engagement. You have yet to see it, but a full contingent of armored knights on mounts is truly awesome to behold."

"What happened?" Tilly asked as Hilbert took out the extraction tube, which still glowed with active runes, its connection to the Blood Vessel seemingly unaffected by distance. The wizard's apprentice handled it carefully as he knelt beside the coffin, considering the body frozen in its near-**Corrupted** state.

"Upon contact with the enemy, they found the horde's numbers had grown far beyond our estimates. Somehow, the average Consumer's level had jumped significantly in the space of two months. So even against a smaller horde we lost five knights in a fighting retreat, and only ten in the entire force returned free of the Blood Darkness. We tried everything we could to cure it, but nothing worked, and while we do have a small Temple of Light based in our city, the holy magic and our natures do not mix well . . . When it was discovered that a cure was not available to our people yet, they volunteered to come down here, and the queen put them into stasis one by one to hold until the day we found a solution." He eased the tip of the device against Constantine's neck, then looked back up at Tilly. "Are you ready? The stasis will break when I administer a blood ration, and while I hope this is enough, perhaps for the first one you should add your active *Ability* to the one latent in the blood."

Tilly nodded and shot a glance up at Sir Michael. "Can you be on sludge duty? I don't know what form the manifestation will take in this situation, but hopefully, it's one you can smash with your mace." The faceless knight nodded easily and pulled his mace free from the latch on his thigh. "Ready," Tilly declared as he churned his mana and knelt opposite Hilbert over the lip of the coffin.

"Administering now," Hilbert said with quiet focus. Then he clicked something on the side of the device and the glowing light sank from its silvery surface into the knight's neck.

Steam started to hiss out from under his armor and the sleeping figure slowly bared his fangs in unconscious agony. Tilly took that to mean it was working and released his *Ability* in an exhale over the body. Once the second stack of the *Ability* took hold, the knight's body started to shake violently and thick black worms started to crawl out from under his armor, fleeing the newly hostile environment.

"Ah, Sir Michael, it looks like these will fall more into my purview," Hilbert breathed. Then he lifted his hands and flicked them through several arcane gestures before whispering, **"Abod's Gathering Hand."**

At those words, a large pink hand formed over the shivering body and began a slow pass down its length. Every place it went, the worms were sucked up into its form until the hand-shaped construct was packed with the black wriggling creatures. Eventually, the vampire's seizing stopped, his eyes flicked open, and his grip on the hilt of his weapon redoubled. Tilly could hear the leather of the finely made handle creaking.

"Sir Constantine! It is good to see you alive and well! . . . Or just well," Hilbert said brightly, accenting his greeting with a clenched fist. The motion was reminiscent of how the queen had dispatched the last manifestation of **Corruption**, and the black worms caught in his mage hand all disappeared with a *pop*, along with the hand itself.

In a much deeper voice than Tilly had expected from such an elegant-looking man, the knight asked, "It is done?" The words came out semi-garbled in a groan of pain as he slowly moved his head to examine the faces above him before groggily looking back down at his body.

"I believe so, but best query your character sheet to check," Hilbert answered.

The knight's eyes immediately glazed over as he took a few seconds to do just that. Then the urgency in his expression drained away, leaving him looking haggard, his skin drawn slightly too tight across his sharp cheekbones.

"I was never told you could dream in stasis . . . ," he mumbled distantly as he slowly sat up. "However long it has been, my time has been fraught with horrors.

I believe the sickness they carry is much more than it seems. Nonetheless, thank you, gentlemen. You have my sincere gratitude." He took another turn to look at the trio, lingering on Tilly the longest.

"You are correct in your conclusions, Sir Knight., it is much more. But a solution has been found for our people. Now, how does your status read? We have many more of your brethren to awaken and a strict timeline in which to get it done," Hilbert answered solemnly, some of the cheer bleeding from his tone.

They persisted in that room for hours and re-awakened and cleansed thirty-four knights in total. Tragically, two were too deeply infected for even the double stack of imbued blood and Tilly's *Ability* to cure. In a horrifying turn of events, the exhausted group had had to put down the two warriors as they began to sprout tentacles and scream in fury, attacking with abandon. The experience left even the most seasoned of the knights shaken, and by the time they reemerged from the catacomb, few looked much better than the walking dead they were.

The first failed cleansing had happened after only a few knights had been revived. For the rest of the attempts, Tilly couldn't help but be stressed to unbelievable levels, as each knight whose eyes flicked open had a small chance of immediately attacking. This was doubly true for the growing body of revived knights, who had to watch in tense readiness as each of their number was cleansed and awoken.

But as they filed into the chamber of the High Table, something about the sight of the pillars and the seven virtues inscribed into the central floor of the room revived them. Many had lingering debuffs from injuries and stasis, which would fade in the next few hours, but as they crossed through the stone door into the hall that enshrined their highest ideals, some of the shadowy doubt faded from their countenances and they stood a little taller.

Tilly was one of the last through the door, and he found the queen back in her chair, still speaking with Ichiro, who was now seated and flanked on one side by Gorock. Franklin and Amelia were absent, and there was a line of injured soldiers stretching out of the main doors. It ended at the Blood Vessel, which glowed much less brightly than it had when Tilly had left, and Villers stood at its side, carefully administering *Ability*-imbued rations to each soldier before waving to the next.

The knights who filtered into the room were diverse in their states of readiness, having been put in stasis from different posts. Some had been in full plate and some half undressed, but all looked drawn, like they could have used another couple weeks of sleep. The queen looked up from her conversation at their procession and allowed herself a grim smile.

"Report?" she asked, her tone somewhat gentler than Tilly had heard it at any point previously.

An elderly level eighty-two knight stepped forward, the one who had apparently led the doomed expedition in the first place.

"We lost two men completely to the Dar—**Corruption**. Seven more were cleansed but did not awaken when the ration was administered. There is a chance they just need more time, or they could have passed through to the final rest. At this point, we do not know," he announced solemnly.

The queen nodded. "Thank you, Sir Kay. I feared it would be much worse. I know from your perspective it seems you returned from the field only a day or two ago, but a campaign is being organized and Sir Cador is gathering all of the cavalry and knights the border forts can spare." She took time to look at the knights before continuing, paying homage to their strength as they stood before her, unbroken. "We have good information that the bulk of the Strigoi forces are committed on two fronts. We will be hitting the smaller of these armies with the intent to annihilate them before they overtake our new allies. I must ask you to be prepared to leave in a matter of hours. Do whatever you must, but be ready when the horn sounds at the gates . . . The Sanguine Order rides to war."

Sir Kay saluted sharply despite his clear exhaustion, and the knights behind him all did the same. Each of the men she addressed knew their duty, and even shaken, not one of them would hesitate to fulfill it.

After a moment of holding the queen's gaze, they turned and started moving for different exits from the chamber. Some were met by servants, others had squires rush up and greet them enthusiastically, yet the vast majority of the knights did not reply to greetings or inquiries. To a man, they wore an expression of budding wrath. Brothers had been lost, their sacred hall had been defiled . . . They were furious.

Tilly himself was exhausted. Even with his ridiculous *Endurance*, the last day and a half had pushed him for all he was worth. On top of that, his **Blood Loss** debuff was still active, adding its weight to the boulder of weariness that rested on his shoulders. He hoped that wherever Amelia and Franklin had gone, they were taking what rest they could.

The queen's eyes lingered on her exiting knights, concern breaking up the otherwise perfectly smooth porcelain skin around her eyes. As they all left, she made a beckoning motion, and Tilly along with Hilbert and Sir Michael approached the small conference area that had been set up for Ichiro and the queen.

Her eyes moved over to Tilly and did not miss his wrung-out state. The lines around her eyes eased up into a faint expression of gratitude. "You do not know, nor do I have time to tell you, the heroic and tragic history of our order. But suffice it to say"—she leaned in and lowered her voice—"we knew when we took on this new class that the power would come with a price. Each of our knights is irreplaceable, and our population can only support so many turned warriors before it collapses into . . . something else. I cannot let that happen.

"So, each year our strength fades, and still we do our duty, holding back the baser members of our dark heritage. With my husband gone and Merllyn off seeking a solution to some esoteric problem, it is easy to take on a level of fatalism." She admitted this last in a low voice. Her eyes, however, took on an intensity that belied her dour words. "But you have given us something today . . . Despite the traitorous blow leveled right at the heart of our order, the fire in our hearts burns again with renewed purpose. I will see this gift repaid. On my honor," she swore before leaning back and assuming the more impassive expression of royalty.

Just for that moment, Tilly saw the woman behind the mask. She was just as passionate as any of the knights about their place in the world and would do everything in her power to give them a chance to continue to achieve their noble goals.

CHAPTER FORTY-FIVE

Mounting Terror

The queen eyed their small group with a veiled air of respect.

"Lord Ichiro has informed me that your Three-Fold Alliance would be happy to enter into trade agreements with us once the siege is broken. I hope that many goods and resources will be made available to both sides that have otherwise been . . . difficult to obtain." At the vague summary of their discussions, Ichiro nodded formally, his face one of perfect serene decorum. They had hammered out something that would work well for both parties, but Tilly found his attention drifting to the third member of this small conference, who seemed to have sat in on the entire negotiation without saying a word.

Gorock was drooling slightly, his rhythmic breathing accompanying his middle-distance stare, as he stood behind Ichiro in silent support. After another second of watching, Tilly was rocked by the realization that the Wall Breaker was sleeping with his eyes open. Had he successfully slept through the whole meeting without anyone noticing?

"Uh . . . Thank you, Your Majesty," Tilly replied belatedly as he tore his eyes away from Gorock's large oblong irises, which seemed to leer at him even absent of their consciousness.

Ichiro broke in, covering over Tilly's stumbling response. "May I add, Your Majesty, that we would be honored to take you up on your offer of hospitality. We have precious little time to complete our mission, but in our state, I am sure a few hours rest will benefit us all."

"Your mission . . . Yes, of course. Mallytza will show you to some rooms, and I will see you at the gates before we leave." She dismissed them, leaning further back into her chair as she waved them away.

Mallytza, the Lady in Waiting who likely served in a role very similar to that of Mochizuki, the lapin washerwoman, materialized out of nowhere and waved them toward one of the many side doors in the chamber. Even as tired as he was,

Tilly didn't miss the look she shared with Hilbert as they moved to follow her. He also watched Gorock eagerly to see if he would startle as they got up to move, but the warrior just blinked a few times and seamlessly got to his feet, joining the group and moving toward the exit.

Damn, that was smooth . . . Tilly marveled internally at the warrior's well-honed ability to avoid any part of life that did not directly have to do with battle.

Mallytza led them through a series of smaller hallways that would have been a maze to any invader. As soon as they were out of the chamber, Hilbert joined her at the front of the group, and they fell into a whispered conversation that was impossible to hear despite its obvious intensity.

Soon enough, they arrived at the rooms, and Mallytza's conversation with Hilbert cut off as she turned to address the trio. "Your two companions are already settled down the hall. Take your rest in these rooms, and we will come to collect you in time to meet the queen before the main army marches off."

"Thank you, ma'am," Tilly said gratefully, already moving toward one of the doors as the thought of a few hours of rest sang sweetly in his ears.

"Your service is deeply appreciated," Ichiro added, and Gorock grunted in agreement.

As Tilly opened his door, his eyes barely noted the furniture or even the fire crackling gently in the room. His focus instantly tunneled onto the bed against the far wall. The door behind him closed slowly as he trudged over to the bed, and a few words of a heated conversation followed him to its inviting surface.

"What do you mean you *must* go with them?"

"Dearest . . . I have given my word—" Tilly recognized Hilbert's voice before it was cut off as the door clicked shut. Tilly didn't bother with covers or removing any clothes. If this was going to be as short as he thought, he wanted to take advantage of every moment of sleep he could get.

A soft knock sounded at his door, and he mumbled, "Wuh? Oh . . . Uh, come in."

A servant entered, then waved at a spot on the wall and activated some clever enchantment that filled the room with soft light from an alcove in the ceiling. For the first time, Tilly thought about how he was completely underground . . . No windows, no ventilation. But the keep hadn't felt stuffy or dark at all. They obviously knew what they were doing when it came to underground structures, and Tilly had found himself surprisingly comfortable for the most part.

"Sir, here is your pack and some provisions with which to refresh yourself. Your companions are being awakened as we speak, and an escort is ready to take you to the front gates of the city when you are ready," the servant said in a soft, respectful tone.

Tilly rubbed his eyes and spotted his pack, which he had embarrassingly forgotten outside the door during the urgent pace of events. The servant also brought in a tray laden with cold cuts of meat, fruit, bread, and cheese, along with a full pitcher. Even as Tilly was registering the contents of the incredible spread, the door closed, and the servant was gone.

Tilly groaned and stretched, more out of habit than any soreness. He once again reveled in the new condition of his body. Even after only a few hours of sleep, he felt restored. Not fully rested, but certainly ready to operate at full capacity. A quick glance at his health and mana showed them both at 100 percent, and the temporary **Blood Loss** debuffs had cleared.

He moved over to the platter and quickly ate his fill of the food provided, enjoying its variety and flavor. Tilly especially enjoyed the cheese, something that they had just started producing in the Alliance before he left. Most of what they had was something similar to mozzarella or feta. The block provided with his platter was a beautiful well-aged cheddar, and he mumbled happily to himself as he found a tightly woven cloth sack with a few basic enchantments on it under his tray.

I'm really beginning to like these guys! Tilly thought to himself as he tucked the remaining hearty portion of his meal into the small sack and threw it into his pack. He took one last long swig of watered-down wine and got up to leave, shouldering his pack and opening the door.

In the hall, Tilly found Ichiro nibbling absently on a piece of cabbage wrapped around assorted meat and vegetables, and Gorock stood next to him holding another comically large cut of meat.

Where does he keep getting those? Did he pack them?

Somehow, the image of Gorock's large pack being almost completely full of salted cuts of meat did not seem unfeasible. Amelia and Franklin emerged from down the hall and joined the group as Tilly eyed the heavy-looking pack on Gorock's back suspiciously.

"While supplies are understandably short in the city, I was able to secure us each some consumables with the reserve funds we brought. The queen had an agent purchase them for us at favorable rates," Ichiro announced as he handed out some red and blue vials.

Tilly got one red and two blue, Gorock got two red, and the other two got one each. He was about to just put them at the top of his pack when he felt something shift at his waistline on his lower back. He reached around under his jacket and found three small loops that were perfectly sized to slide the vials into.

How in the world do you choose when to be helpful and when to do nothing? he grumbled internally at his legendary armor set as he slipped the vials into the loops.

"I doubt that supply of imprinted blood will last them much longer. We should get moving before they decide they need Tilly to extend his stay," Amelia quipped as she dropped her vials into one of her pockets.

"Yes, it is best to get moving. Having a guide will save us some time, but I do not wish to tarry any longer," Ichiro declared, looking down the hall and finding the servant waiting a respectful distance away, ready to escort them.

"Let's go find our flower," Tilly said lightly, but the faces around him only nodded in grim agreement, not at all put off by the object of their quest.

As they met up with their guard escort at the gates of the keep, there was a noticeable difference in the feeling of the formation that surrounded them. It felt less like a prisoner escort and more like a "make way" kind of escort. The guards actively called ahead and cleared any obstacles before the group met them so that they were able to cross the city at an easy jog, passing both checkpoints without a pause.

Tilly reached for Kindle through his bond and felt her flying above the outskirts of the valley.

How was the hunting?

I have found and destroyed a score of the disgusting creatures. The last one I hunted had almost completely dissolved on its own before I ended it. It seems they cannot continue on this plane without the protection of a host.

*Yeah, that is consistent with what we have seen so far. Out in the open moving on its own, **Corruption** is violent and aggressive but does not last very long.*

I will return and meet you at the gate. There is quite a gathering of landbound outside the city, she replied.

The city itself was bustling with energy. People were moving everywhere, some hauling goods out of the city, others bringing in fresh supplies. Much of the traffic seemed to be flowing toward the city's transport hub, which lay far off the main road through the gate in the commercial district, and by the time they were nearing the front gates, Tilly was glad for the escort. The press became especially thick near the front gate, which was choked with traffic going both ways.

With a significant amount of shouting from the guards, they cleared the last gate and emerged out into the open field before the city. There, arrayed in neat groups of five, were almost seventy knights and a few hundred cavalry lined up loosely behind them. The fact that all of this had been mobilized in less than half a day was beyond impressive, and if the thousands of people still moving to and fro between the main force and the city were any indication, this rapid mobilization had been no easy task.

As the queen spotted them from the head of the formation, she turned away with a few of her knights and urged her mount toward them. Like everyone else in the formation, she was riding a Nightmare, but unlike everyone else, hers was massive, at least a third larger than any of the others. As she approached, belatedly followed by the first five knights in the formation, probably her honor guard, Tilly saw that her mount was formed entirely of blood.

"Our final preparations are being made, and I was informed you have gotten what you needed from our suppliers," she called as her mount cantered forward silently on the field. It didn't so much run as flow forward, covering ground in a manner that only faintly reminded Tilly of a horse.

"Yes, we are ready to head out," Ichiro answered. "Are our escort terms still acceptable?" He looked back at Sir Michael and Hilbert, who were just now coming through the gate with Mallytza leading the way, her face a storm of emotion.

"Yes, nothing has changed . . . But are you certain?" she asked as she eyed the approaching trio, then turned back to Ichiro and Tilly standing at the front of their small group. "We go to face the smaller of the two hordes, and you go directly toward the larger force . . . Would it not be prudent to join us in the campaign and then move on to yours as a united front?" Her authoritative visage softened slightly into a frown of concern as she finished.

"You are probably right, Your Majesty. But we have a quest, one issued to us from two different sources. There must be a way to complete it with the resources we have at hand," Tilly answered before leaning in and continuing in a softer voice, "and I worry that its completion is essential even to the success of your coming battle." Tilly eyed the approaching knights, resplendent in their full plate. Her eyes became hooded in response to his concern, but she did not contradict his words.

"Very well, I thought as much. It is best that we speed your way as much as possible, then." She leaned back in her saddle and reached into a pouch sewn into the side of her battle dress. From it, she produced a handful of silver pendants and reached down to offer them to Tilly. "These are the last of Merllyn's gifts. They each hold within them one of his personal contracts with a Nightmare. You can bind this item with a drop of your blood and then, once per day, summon a mount that will persist until you die or dismiss the bond," she explained as Tilly took the pieces of jewelry. There were five in all, each a differently shaped pendant hung on a silver chain covered in runes.

"Your summoned mount will not be friendly to any but you, and unlike our inborn *Ability*, you will not be able to pass on the bond while you live. However, the need is great, and your service to our faction has been exemplary, so here is our reward to you." She sat tall in her saddle as her own mount stood bearing her, absolutely still. It did not breathe or twitch, and its stillness was emphasized by the subtle flowing movement on the surface of its form.

Having received his pendant from Tilly, Ichiro bowed, clutching it tightly, and said, "Thank you, Your Majesty! This is an incredible boon."

"Yes, well, do me the favor of living long enough to enjoy the benefits of such a gift. I do not wish to throw away some of our people's greatest treasures on a fool's errand . . ."

CHAPTER FORTY-SIX

Strong Enough

Morning, the next day
Aurelia – Level 28 Priestess of Origin's Flame

The last day and a half of battle had easily been the most exhausting of Aurelia's young life. The closest thing she had ever experienced was the terrifying flight her family had undertaken before the advance of the naga army. The memory of those chaotic weeks played at the edges of her consciousness in shades of gray interposed by flashes of screaming color . . .

This was nothing like that. It was both far more terrible and somehow less overwhelming at the same time. The High Priestess remained on the wall night and day, handling each emergency as it came, and she had left Aurelia in charge of the healer's tent down below, well back from the fighting. She knew her job, and even as the initial panic of responsibility had faded into the dull grinding exhaustion of days of effort, she had done her absolute best to make sure everyone who approached them after their time on the wall received what they needed to recover.

She knew her younger self would have long since given up, but something was keeping her going, stumbling to her feet each time another rotation was called. She was not just a little girl in an adult body. Those years had not disappeared—she could feel their memories deep down, just out of reach. They undergirded her new strength of will, getting her to her feet even when she was convinced she had nothing left.

This is what she could do to protect her home . . .

"ROTATE!" the cry went out from above. She flinched as Watch members stumbled down the large rear stair, bleeding and broken. Erash had stopped healing and cleansing the centuries rotating off the wall a day ago. They were keeping her as a counter to the increasing numbers of elites coming with every wave.

That left Aurelia and the three acolytes to handle all of the healing needed for each rotation off of the wall. Depending on how heavy the press was above, they could be looking at two or three rotations in an hour. On top of that, the Rangers had run out of blessed projectiles hours ago, and several pallets were waiting for her as soon as she had another moment to spare.

Members of the Watch crowded down the stairs, some moving as fast as they could, as if chased, while others were almost completely incapacitated, carried by their brothers and sisters down to safety. The tide of enemies was endless, and at this point, they all knew they had yet to see the worst of the enemy's capabilities. Grim faces filed into the healer's tent, telling a story of hope dangling by a fraying thread.

"Please, ma'am! He can make it."

"He just needs a little help!" a pair pleaded with her from the front of the injured group.

Aurelia's stomach churned as she looked over and saw the dead satyr hanging on their shoulders. Wild eyes, bright with a potent mixture of desperation and fear, completely missed her defeated expression as they dragged the dead man up to her. Unable to muster any words, Aurelia just bit her lip, choking back a sob, and shook her head.

The two belatedly turned and looked at their burden, who might have been living before they had carried him off the wall. Aurelia tried to speak up, to repeat the orders she had received. She was the one they had left in charge here, and someone had to remind these tired soldiers of the best way to get help. They needed to make sure the most injured were at the front of the line.

But she couldn't squeeze the words past the blockage in her throat. She stood there, frozen in her despair, unable to look away as the two companions gaped in shocked disbelief at their lost friend. His empty eyes stared out into the middle distance as if he had forgotten something and was straining to remember it.

Then a strong voice called from behind her, breaking the dead man's spell.

"Check your debuffs and regen! If you are still able to gain health, however slowly, move on! If you are dropping, report to the healing station. Organize yourselves! The healers can't do everything, you need to put your worst brothers and sisters up front!" Linus called, approaching the healing station and gaining control of the situation with an efficiency that spoke of years in the field.

Aurelia and the overwhelmed acolytes glanced back in numb appreciation before turning to see the group of soldiers beginning to order themselves. They had already gone through this several times, but something about hearing the commander say it again helped the pieces fall into place for their tired, numb minds. Many stumbled past the station to find food and rest for as long as they could have it, but far too many remained lined up to receive healing, with the most severe cases finding their place before her.

She took a deep steadying breath, raised her hands, and cast **Flame's Warmth**, centering it on those in front of her but knowing it was a wide enough area of effect that it would cover many of the others. Creases of harsh worry and frantic hope eased slightly on their faces as the sensation of sitting down before the warmth of a fire washed through them, giving each target a 10 percent bonus to *Constitution* for their next two hundred breaths. Two of the three acolytes joined her area-of-effect *Ability*, casting on the group, easing pain, and disrupting **Corruption's** advance.

It was for this reason that they kept the lines so close, and she hoped it would give many the time they would need to have their turn at the front. She was even encouraged to see some at the back check their status screens and shuffle off after seeing that the buffs would compensate for their maladies until their native regen took over.

Fighting to straighten her shoulders, she turned to the first woman in front of her, one of their few minotaur fighters. Her impressive stature was curled in on itself as she shuffled forward holding a large wad of soaked cloth against her mid-section. The flesh was marred by several jagged wounds and filled with enough **Corruption** that the minotaur's healing had slowed to a deadly degree.

As had become her procedure, she raised her hands and cast the very first *Ability* she had received as a Priestess, **Cleansing Flame**. A stream of dancing blue flames leaped from her hands to bathe the wounds and consume the **Corruption**. Unlike Mr. Tillman's *Ability*, it did not expel the substance and create a manifestation. Instead, it consumed it completely, expunging its taint from the target's body.

A notification popped up, and she minimized it for a second while she went on to cast her second most powerful healing *Ability*. The wound began to close, and the minotaur's face went slack with relief.

"Thank you, Priestess. Praise **Origin**," she said as she moved past so that the next in line could come forward. Aurelia nodded back absently, recalling the notification screen as the next patient shuffled up.

***Congratulations!** You have cleansed 1000 targets in 24 hours. You have earned the Title [Fount of Purification]. All allies within a 100-pace radius of your position will have any infectious-class debuff potency reduced by 50%.*

There was no joy at the notification. She registered somewhere in her mind that it would make her role here that much more effective, but the majority of her attention was on the first number the screen had revealed.

One thousand in twenty-four hours . . .

Have there really been that many? she thought numbly.

She dismissed the screen and took in the next watchman to step up. He was holding his right arm close to his torso as he tried to stanch the bleeding of the nearly severed appendage. Aurelia immediately cast her most powerful healing. Any time there was a possibility of a loss of limb, she always took it seriously, knowing that the only one who could regrow them was Erash, and she didn't have any mana to spare for non-elite soldiers.

And just like that, they slowly cleared the lines. *And this time, thank **Origin**, we didn't lose anyone who had to wait in line.*

Actually . . . that wasn't entirely true. They had lost one right before he arrived. How could she have already forgotten?

Commander Linus had been standing with them throughout the rotation, saying nothing but somehow offering his support despite the silence. Aurelia could already hear the fighting above begin to increase in fervor as men and women began calling out the positions of enemy elites in the coming charge.

"It's time for you to take a break," Linus said simply, looking her over. She looked up at him in incomprehension, realizing she had unknowingly sat down on one of the pallets they needed her to bless. Her mind struggled to find the words needed to respond.

"I will, sir . . . After the next group of soldiers," she mumbled, squinting up at the scarred commander.

"It's an order, Priestess. Each of the acolytes has already rotated off for a few hours. You will take a full eight. We will find you when we need you." Those words cut through her fog slightly, and she was surprised to find bitterness welling up at the news.

"When you need me? You need me now, Consul! What are you going to do when the next century rotates off, let more die?" she questioned angrily, her bloodshot eyes narrowing blearily.

"We have our health potion supply up and running, and we will make sure Erash treats the worst injuries before they leave the wall," Linus responded, his face softening slightly.

"That won't be enough . . . We have lost too many as it is," she choked out, having to swallow down the sob that had returned to threaten its escape all over again.

"Aye. More will die. But that's not your fault. You need to trust me when I say that if you don't take a rest, the losses will be greater. The battle is far from over, and I am ordering you to take eight hours away from the wall," he stated with finality, his expression a strange mix of unyielding strength and a deep understanding.

The anger she had been using as fuel to push past the pain suddenly drained away, and all she had left was her weakness. Her body shuddered with the effort to hold back the sobs. Then the dam broke, and she lost the contest. Huge racking sobs shook her body as she cried like the little girl she no longer was.

A calloused hand gently cupped the back of her head as the commander pulled her into a simple embrace, holding her against his shoulder.

"I'm sorry . . . I thought I would be stronger," she stuttered out between sobs.

Then, in a quiet voice that somehow dampened the distant screams of battle, Linus answered, "Shhh. You've done more than we should've asked . . . I'm . . . I'm proud of you."

Four hours later
Pupienus – Level 45 Bureaucrat

There wasn't enough time . . .

The twenty-four-day boon was the only reason that they had anything resembling a working economy. And while it would grow on its own if given enough time, it seems they had run out of that as well.

Food and weapons production had barely covered the demand brought on by the challenge of fielding a few thousand soldiers at the drop of a hat, and now their three Alchemists were working day and night to produce some of the lowest-grade health potions Pupienus had ever seen.

I should have listened to my aunt and left with the rest of the family . . . , he fumed internally as another missive arrived on the table in his tent-office. He squinted up at the courier, but the man was already gone by the time the note hit his desk, joining the piles of paperwork all demanding his attention. He had been working on the mess all morning, and he probably wouldn't be able to leave his desk for hours yet.

"Hey! You can't . . ." Pupienus trailed off as soon as it was clear the messenger had truly left without issuing any sort of verbal report.

I am surrounded by idiots . . . How can I prioritize tasks if there is no input system? If everyone just stops by whenever they want to drop off something new, we will never make any progress.

He folded up the report the loud dwarfs had recently turned in. The quarry had uncovered a very rich vein of metals under the mountain, along with a large pre-dug tunnel. They had been able to produce stone and iron much faster than anticipated once they had discovered the hidden tunnel. They were asking for an increase in contribution points to reflect their higher output . . . and he would probably have to issue them. Their work was literally keeping the rest of them alive right now.

He picked up the dirty piece of paper the courier had flung at his desk. It had a note scrawled on it, and Pupienus had to squint at its contents through his spectacles, hardly able to make out some of the letters due to a large stain. Then a realization struck him through his exhaustion.

By the yawning Pits . . . is that blood? he thought in a mild panic. Holding it by its corner, he struggled to make out the message:

Councilmen, there is an urgent risk to the satyr element in the camp. We have discovered a conspiracy by some of the other races to displace our people and erode our position further. I fear that soon we will be little more than slaves in this "Alliance" they have formed. Meet us a third of the way up the mountain at midnight, and come alone. Not all of our people can be trusted . . .

CHAPTER FORTY-SEVEN

Mount Up

Jonathan Tillman – Level 23 Son of Flame

They departed along with the Sanguine Order shortly after receiving their enchanted pendants. The whole host shared the road, and Tilly's group rode up front with the queen on their new mounts until the first town, where they split off to head further north. From there Sir Michael and Hilbert led them through the rest of the day, only emerging back on the plains of the Deadlands as daylight faded.

Not that concepts like night and day had much meaning in these lands. The obscured sun and moon painted everything in similar shades of dusk and dawn. The difference in the time of day was more marked by yellow, orange, and silver hues than any increase or decrease in actual light.

As the soft pink and orange coloration of evening started to bleed across the cloud-covered sky, they passed by another of the order's forts, one that was now manned by a skeleton crew. They did not hail the gate, but the guardsmen atop the wall gave them a salute as they galloped by.

Tilly gratefully took in the momentary distraction of the fort, keeping his eyes on it for as long as possible before they were eventually dragged back down in morbid fascination to the forms his party's Nightmare mounts had taken.

Two were harmless enough, following logical lines that Tilly could easily parse out. Franklin's mount had taken on the form of an emaciated skeletal creature, which seemed to be more a husk than anything living. It gave off the feeling of living jerky, and Tilly took it to mean Franklin feared being without water. Ichiro's mount was covered in chains that seemed to wrap it tightly, and with his history of being held against his will by the **Corrupted** tree, that made perfect sense.

Even Tilly's own mount, while gruesome and nauseating, did not depart too much from the pattern. It showed veiny **Corrupted** infection all over its equine body, even producing several tentacles that undulated slowly with its galloping stride. The **Corruption**, however, was just an imitation. Sitting on the mount caused no reactions from the growing **Seed** within him.

Amelia's was the first of the mounts that he didn't understand. It was covered in an intentional pattern of thin cuts that always seemed to be bleeding but never left any trail behind the mount. He didn't know what it meant and felt like it was invasive to ponder it too deeply. At times he felt like they were warming up to each other. Then he would run headfirst into what felt like a huge invisible wall . . . Whatever her mount meant, he doubted it would be a good idea to ask.

That left the final member of their party. Almost against his will, his gaze swung back to Gorock, who rode what was easily the most horrifying of the Nightmares. The creature's body was sleek and muscular. Unlike his last mount, this one was proportionally sized, almost twice as big as the other mounts. In fact, it was the picture of anatomical perfection.

The Nightmare's head, however, was where it slipped from a bodybuilder's wet dream to something out of a bizarre European horror film. At the neck, it abruptly shifted into a ghastly caricature of a human head, the mane fusing into a shaggy head of hair and a terrified scream frozen on its face. Worse of all, it seemed to be able to feel whenever Tilly looked in its direction. Unable to look away, Tilly watched as it once again turned and leered over at him, bobbing along with the galloping motion of its body.

Unsuccessfully suppressing a crawling sensation that climbed up his back, Tilly whipped his head forward, feeling dirty for some reason. Each of them had steeled themselves as their mounts had manifested before them for the first time, but Gorock had squealed in fright when the summoned shadow had coalesced into a human-headed horse.

That particular part of the memory brought a smile to Tilly's face, and he replayed the sound in his head a few times before the awful urge to look back over at the creature returned. It was going to be a long ride . . .

Sir Michael raised his hand to call a halt an hour or two later, then brought his mount to a stop and jumped down, turning toward the rest of the group. Hilbert followed suit while pulling out his device and scanning the area in front of him, then gestured for them to come in closer so he could set wards around the group.

"The way ahead is choked with enemies, which is not surprising considering we are almost through the hills. A little further and we will clear them and have a full view of the Forgotten Plain and the mountain fortress known as Requiem. However, if we continue any further, we will be unable to avoid encountering any scouts. How do you want to proceed?" the wizard's apprentice asked as he finished establishing the ward around the group.

Tilly turned toward Ichiro, who nodded for him to go ahead.

"As it stands, the plan is for me to **Spirit Walk** into the city and hopefully make contact with an ally. We don't know how we are going to get in—or out, for that matter—but our priority is to make contact with the Facet and figure out how to obtain its patronage," Tilly said, attempting to sound more confident than he felt at how vague it all sounded. But with so little information, it was not like they could come up with much more. They would just have to stay flexible and hold onto the hope that this quest would be achievable.

"Uh, about that . . . I do have some news I can share on the escape front," Franklin added, speaking for the first time in quite a while.

He had been quiet almost the entire trip, and while they hadn't really had many opportunities to chat, something had felt off. Tilly didn't know him well enough to peg if that was just his personality around groups or something more, but he had worried about the honu's silence more than once.

Franklin readjusted his scarf and reached into his sleeve to pull out a conch shell covered with tiny glowing runes. "The elders gave this to me on my way out but cautioned that it might not be ready in time for us to use. I have checked it every few hours, and now, from the look of the spell link, it seems that they have succeeded. They have successfully tied it back to the platform in the village square, and now we will be able to activate it."

Hilbert's eyes widened, and a slow smile of relief crossed his face. "Ha! I told Mallytza this wasn't a suicide mission! Someone among your faction must be very talented in **Teleportation**."

"Any chance I can get the child's version of what you just said?" Tilly added dryly.

"Sorry, it's a teleport anchor keyed to our home platform. If I infuse the spell with my mana and break the anchor, every being within ten paces of my location will be pulled back to the platform instantaneously. It is the main way those without the use of a dedicated teleportation mage travel via the platforms. But with our platform broken, the elders didn't know such a thing would be possible in such a short timeframe. But with their new Way Finder classes, they seem to have been able to bridge the gap," he explained as he stowed the precious object back in the folds of his robe. Even delivering the good news there was something distracted about his tone. The timing was terrible, but Tilly was afraid it would only get worse from here.

"Hey, guys, would you mind giving us a moment?" Tilly asked, drawing away the honu until they were at the edge of the ward. He knew almost everyone would still be able to hear them, but it was the best he could do.

"Hey, man, are you okay? Something seems off . . ."

The honu returned his concerned gaze with a look of guilt, which slowly morphed into reluctant acceptance.

"I am sorry, Tilly. You are right to ask. You are not the only one who is wrestling internally on this journey. I am sure you have noticed I am the only honu with such a clothing item," Franklin said as he plucked absently at the blue scarf wrapped around his neck.

"Honestly, I just thought you were the best dresser of the bunch," Tilly quipped, evoking a ghost of a smile from the honu.

"That may be the case, but this isn't just any cloth . . . It was a gift from the oldest mage in the minotaur caravans. She said she was entrusting its care to me and that when the time came, I would know when to let it go."

"Let it go? Go where?"

"That is just it, I do not know . . . But it is an Epic-quality item that increases my *Wisdom* stat by fifty percent when I channel water mana. There is a real possibility that this item may be the only reason I got selected to go on this quest. Yet, I can't shake the feeling that it is trying to speak to me, urging me to move in the very same direction you have been leading. It . . . wants something. Something that lies just over these hills. But I fear that if I give it up, I will become a liability to the mission. Our people are depending on us— on me—to be strong."

"I see what you mean. I sure as hell wouldn't be in a rush to give up something that increased any of my stats by that much . . . Well, there isn't anything we can do about it until we know for sure. But I can say this: even without that scarf, you're not a liability. I trust you to make the right call when the time comes. You have been nothing but dependable since I met you. Hell, you should be doubting me! I'm the one—"

The honu began to shake his head firmly, an unexpected intensity gleaming in his eyes. "No, we will proceed as you say, but if you can choose to trust me, then I have the privilege to do the same, agreed?"

"Yeah, I'm clear on that." Tilly smiled roguishly, happy to receive the spirited rebuke from the reticent mage. He clapped the honu on the shell and turned back to the others, who all had the good sense to be looking in another direction. Except for Gorock and his horrifying mount, who were both watching them speak with bored expressions on their very different faces.

"Alright, Hilbert," Tilly stuttered, put off by the pair, "what can you tell me about this city and the siege it is under before I head out? I'm hoping I will be undetectable to the forces on the ground, but a little context about what I am going into won't hurt."

The wizard's apprentice perked up at his name but didn't answer right away; instead, he chose to look over at Sir Michael for a long moment. The knight slowly nodded in ascent, and Hilbert turned to Tilly, releasing a long sigh.

"Yes, well, the short version is that very few have ever been within the city, and everything I know is secondhand. It is a place of the dead, or, more specifically, a place for Whytes to exist in a state of rest, pursuing whatever it is they pursue in their semi-eternal state."

"And what exactly are Whytes? Ghosts?" Tilly asked, ready to finally get some clarification on this point.

"Not exactly. Ghosts are more like tortured fragments of a soul. They do not exist outside of the pain they are constantly forced to relive. A Whyte, on the other hand, is something much more complete. It is a memory construct formed from the impression that a remarkable individual can make upon the pattern of Nephesh itself. For that reason, they are often very powerful but also extremely limited."

"So, they are made of memories?"

"Yes, especially someone who has some unresolved desire or duty. If a person of considerable power or impact bent themselves toward a certain task for long enough, they would have a much higher chance of leaving behind a Whyte. They can think, feel, and often are indistinguishable from the originator, but they cannot gain levels. Every action they take is empowered by a certain memory from their originator and is therefore finite. Once all the memories are used up, they are unable to perform that action ever again. For this reason, they are known to spend months if not years in quiet stillness and are very uncomfortable amongst the living.

"They are also rumored to hold one of the greatest libraries on the plane, a collection of all the knowledge of their past lives. My master even visited the city once, paying in their currency for the knowledge to help create the very items you were gifted."

At this, Amelia spoke up. "Their currency? Is that code for more blood?"

Hilbert's mouth flicked up in a smile, revealing the points of his fangs in amusement. "No, madam, nothing so replaceable as that. They sometimes accept Standard, but their currency of choice is memory. They trade for what they do not have, to extend their agency on this plane. They trade with each other and, in times past, outsiders," Hilbert finished, his tone meandering, then he looked back at his companion and waved him forward.

At this, Sir Michael cleared his throat and moved forward, slowly pulling off his helm.

CHAPTER FORTY-EIGHT

Total Recall

Everyone turned in shock as the knight stepped forward into the center of the conversation and reached up to remove his ever-present helm.

"In a manner of speaking, this will be a sort of homecoming for him," Hilbert added theatrically as Sir Michael moved to uncover the features he had kept hidden.

The knight pulled back the front of the blank metal helm and revealed the gray, purplish skin of the Strigoi race, but in a form unlike any Tilly had seen. It was not the gaunt hunger of a Consumer or the emaciated skeletal structure of the even weaker basic warriors. Instead, Sir Michael's features were sleek and full. Something more akin to a well-fed predator than any sort of scavenger. His eyes smoldered steadily with a deep hunger undercut by an unyielding restraint.

"I was once known as Mikhail," he growled in a halting rumble, obviously having trouble forming the words. He turned to Hilbert and gestured for him to take up the explanation.

"The horde is led by something called the Prime Dirge. It almost never takes the field, and some say it is the progenitor of the Strigoi race. Sir Michael was once its second in command and the leader of its ground forces. I will not go into great detail for the sake of time, but he fought our king in a duel, and something about tasting Excalibur's blade freed him temporarily from the Prime Dirge's hold. Their forces retreated that day and Mikhail ran to find haven from his master's wrath.

"He found himself at the gates of Requiem, hoping that their hidden knowledge would be the key to his freedom and offered all of his memories in exchange. He does not know what transpired after that, but some time later, he emerged with a set of armor unlike any we had seen. While wearing it, he is in full control of his urges and can resist the once undeniable longing to obey the will of his master. He came to our order decades ago hoping to help end the Prime Dirge's reign in these lands. Arthur accepted him to the High Table at the advice of Merllyn, and the rest is history, as they say," Hilbert said, ending with a flourish and cheekily looking up to read the impact of his story.

Tilly took it all in with a raised eyebrow. He would never say this out loud, but to him, a vampire was still a vampire, and Sir Michael's race of origin changed very little. Hilbert's face fell as he took in the lack of reaction from the group. He turned back to his ward to fiddle with it in despair as silence hung heavy in the air. Finally, Ichiro stepped up to the stoic knight.

"You have treated us with honor, and this is a far greater measure of your worth in our eyes than your race of origin. Each of us carries the burdens of duty and failure, yet those things do not define us. Our choices do," the samurai offered before lowering his head in a small bow of respect. Sir Michael nodded in return before replacing his helm and facing out toward the Strigoi army somewhere in the distance, having said all he needed to say.

Kindle chose that moment to land amid their formation and look around while ruffling her feathers impatiently.

No, girl, we can't risk you being spotted. You will move forward with the rest of us as soon as I get back, Tilly answered her unspoken request. Turning to address the group, he continued aloud, "Alright, everyone, I'm going to scout in my spirit form. I will be back as soon as possible, hopefully with more information and a way past the enemy."

Ichiro nodded while pulling free his sheathed sword, then settled down in a kneeling vigil.

"We will watch and prepare for your return," Franklin added from behind Tilly.

Gorock unhelpfully slapped him on the back as Tilly sat down, distracting him momentarily from his breathing. "Don't take too long, Baby-Man. I don't know what I'll do if this trip does not liven up soon."

Turning with a grimace at the heavy-handed slap, Tilly deadpanned, "I'll try . . ."

The Wall Breaker nodded sagely and turned to take up his watch position. Tilly managed to keep a sigh from interrupting his breathing pattern, and breath by breath, he sank deeper into his meditation.

It was not necessary to activate his skill, but he had found that the better connected he was with himself before he went into his spirit form, the more mobility and strength he seemed to have.

So, he breathed through the pressures, the time crunch, and the overwhelming odds. He let each one surface in his emotional landscape and accepted it. The exercise had grown familiar over the last weeks, and he quickly found the simple calm he was working toward. The flame in his chest began to stoke merrily at the greater internal integration.

Just as he was about to activate the skill, the **Seed** wriggled distractedly, straining to reach deeper into his physical limbs. The sensation almost elicited a gag, and his eyes suddenly flew open in worry. His gaze flitted over his HUD.

Heath: 100%
Mana: 100%
Corruption's Influence: 36%

He hadn't taken much damage in the fight yesterday, so he hadn't paid much attention . . . But he had lost another 2 percent to **Corruption's** influence. He quickly closed his eyes again, attempting to regain focus, but bitterness began to bubble to the surface of his calm, signifying deeper worries that he was not ready to face.

He had missed it advancing again . . . And if there was anything like that red-eyed fucker here in this army, he might not even make it into the city. The more he ruminated over it, the darker his thoughts became. The flow in his internal environment was interrupted by these intrusive thoughts. They pressed in on him, heavy things moving ponderously over the surface of his mind like tanker ships in the night. He did his best to accept them and to let the feelings they carried move through him, but their weight began to overwhelm him, throwing off his rhythm and robbing him of momentum.

He had not sat down and taken the time to process the events of the last couple of days, the implications of the Weasel's scheme or his ominous mention of the "they" he had alluded to. Greater forces were working to advance **Corruption** across the plane on a scale that he could not imagine. The more that these realities sank in, the heavier he became until it felt like he was trying to breathe with hundreds of pounds pushing down on his chest.

Sure, there might be some crazy confluence of events to get them access to the Flower and then back to the Alliance . . . But what about after that? It was becoming clear that this stuff was everywhere. Who was going to stop it?

It seemed like most people were still ignorant of its existence, let alone had the power or willingness to do anything about it.

To top it all off, there had been no hint of **Origin** opposing **Corruption's** spread anywhere else on the plane. Did that mean it was all up to—

"Jonathan Tillman." Ichiro's voice floated quietly over to him from his kneeling position. The calm utterance broke through Tilly's downward spiral, and he realized he had lost his breathing cadence at some point, his breaths instead transforming into a rapid, panicky staccato. The tightness in his chest loosened at the sound of his name, and Ichiro's calm voice continued, shining a soft light in the dark corners of Tilly's reverie. "There is far more at work here than we can see. Do not drown in the waters of your ignorance. You have a path forward that only you can walk . . . It is up to you to choose it." His gentle chiding words cut through to the heart of Tilly's fears.

Tilly took a deep breath, feeling like he had come up for air, and thought about responding before closing his mouth and choosing to take another breath instead. There was nothing to say, no excuses, no apologies . . . He just needed to *do*.

So, he took another deep breath, then another, and returned to his rhythm with a force of will that he had not experienced since that first day outside the Temple. He could almost feel Ichiro's approval spurring him on as he crashed back into the waters of his despair, diving deeper than he had in weeks, searching out whatever was hidden in its depths.

For some reason, as he breathed and sank past the anxiety, the fear, and even the self-loathing, he found a memory floating up from his subconscious. It vibrated with a deep thrumming that shook his soul, and Tilly shied away from it at first, feeling the weight of its significance and fearing it. Then before the cowardly part of himself could choose to surface, he dived into the memory and surrendered to its overwhelming force.

He winced as he tried to shut the hospital door quietly, only for the stupid door latch to click shut thunderously. He turned quickly and found his daughter's eyes still shut, her breath coming in shallow watery gasps under her oxygen mask . . .

The news was worse than they thought.

This wasn't a virus at all.

He felt his chest constrict. Suddenly, not able to take a full breath, all of his desperate hopes came crashing down around him like the block tower that still lay all over the living room floor. She had knocked it over a few days ago when her coughing had gotten really bad . . .

Then, as if she could feel his entry back into the room, her eyes began to crack open, and he rushed to her side, stepping as quietly as possible around his wife's sleeping form.

Her eyes found him, and he reached forward and clutched her hand, holding it as tightly as he dared. She met his gaze with a small smile. Pain showed on her face with every effort-filled breath, but that didn't stop her smile as she caught sight of him.

Oh god . . . his baby girl.

He couldn't do anything to help. They had said there was nothing left to do.

But he could be here.

He could hold her little hand.

The memory faded, and he exploded forth from the depths as he activated **Spirit Walk**, rising from his physical body like a cloudless dawn on the horizon. He looked down at his spirit form and found himself wreathed in white flames, almost as if he had somehow activated an incorporeal version of **Wrath's Shroud**.

He may not have enough power to stop the end of the world, but there was something he needed to do here and now.

He looked around at the group as he shone with spiritual strength. His transition had once again gone unnoticed by most of them, but Kindle looked up at his emergence and met his gaze, sending a fierce mental image of a bird of prey in a shrieking dive.

I will get it done, girl . . . no matter what, he sent back as he turned and took off into the air.

His spirit responded to the command with shocking speed, and he found himself fifty feet in the air before he had even registered his extreme increase in velocity. He looked back down toward his body, which was now connected to him by a vibrant thread of woven fire.

Then he turned and looked forward, having cleared the sight line of the hills. From his new vantage, he saw a small mountain chain in the distance resisting the repeated crashing of an ocean of dark energy. It took Tilly a moment to register the immensity of the force crashing against the portion of the mountain chain that lay directly before them.

The scale of this enemy force dwarfed the one outside their own wall by an order of magnitude, and the density of its energy was significantly greater. Despite the enormity of the clash playing out before him, he immediately registered a faint sound dancing over and through the tumultuous conflict. The Flower's song, undaunted and undiminished, rang out through the air, continuing past the threat to touch the plane in incomprehensible ways.

The site of the conflict reinforced their need to reach the Facet, and Tilly shot forward, moving faster than he could have even at a full gallop on his new Nightmare mount. The flames covering his spirit form lent him incredible speed as he streaked past pickets of subtly hidden scouts and noted their positions.

Then he began to approach the main army, and even in his current empowered form the malevolent energy they exuded buffeted his flight, slowing his pace toward the embattled city significantly. As the pressure increased, he decided to stop short of the edge of their howling ranks. From the rear of their forces, he could now clearly make out the front third of the Strigoi army crashing endlessly against a wall that made the one the Alliance had hastily constructed look like a joke.

A pale ghostly energy crackled and snapped in the air above the edifice as projectiles and spells were hurled down by the defenders, mowing down the endless ranks of enraged enemies. The city that rose beyond the wall climbed the steep mountains of its backdrop until they both disappeared into the ever-present clouds.

Through it all, Tilly looked in vain for any way he could approach the wall without flying directly through the churning storm of mana that boiled above the conflict. He doubted he would survive such a flight in his current form.

In desperation, he scanned the sheer mountain faces, looking for some other way through. The closer he looked, the more he noticed some sort of subtle magic at play. An intricate weave of spellwork draped over the entire natural formation of stone, and the central root of the spell reached deep into the heart of the fortress city.

As he scanned west and then east, Tilly's eyes were drawn to a break in the flatlands that stretched out from the mountains in all directions. A river poured down from a great waterfall halfway up one of the mountains and wound its way through the flatlands, off into the distance.

The opportunity that the waterfall presented to his spirit form was as good a chance as he was going to get. He began to move in that direction, picking up speed and pulling away from the horde, when the malevolent cloud of energy hanging over the whole force shifted.

Tilly felt panic rise as he realized that the cloud of energy hanging over the enemy force wasn't just a mindless overflow from the creatures below it. He could suddenly feel its sentience as it shifted its focus to him as he tried to streak away. He felt a palpable weight withdraw from the wall and shift to his position as he fled the rear of the Strigoi force. Tilly poured energy into his flight, egging more speed from his form and burning off some of the flames that accompanied his empowered spirit state.

The weight of the cloud's attention rolled across the rear of the army, causing all of the creatures below it to flinch and howl in pain as their master swept its senses over them. Tilly raced just ahead of its rolling advance, pushing away in panic as it drew near. He looked back in dread and for the first time spotted his pursuer at the center of the vast hateful energy.

Floating amid the roiling cloud was a winged figure. Something about Tilly's attention changed the vague motions of the being's pursuit, and Tilly watched in horror as the thing looked up and met his eyes.

CHAPTER FORTY-NINE

Hammer Time

If he hadn't been in his spirit form, Tilly was sure his heart would have seized up from terror. The weight of the figure's attention surrounded him, blanketing his mind in numbness, and then began to squeeze, overwhelming his soul with instinctual fear. Tilly's flight stuttered to a stop as a silent scream tried to escape through his ghostly gritted teeth. The figure was still obscure, but as Tilly stared in growing dread, its eyes began to shine with a dark intensity.

Tilly couldn't tell if it was moving or not, but its indistinct features began to sharpen as the sounds of battle grew closer. Then the small part of Tilly that was still cognizant of his surroundings realized that he was involuntarily floating back toward the battlefield and the cloud roiling above it. The compulsion was as undeniable as gravity, and Tilly felt himself falling toward his doom. All the while, those eyes grew like twin stars of darkness, filling his vision . . . becoming his new reality.

Then a clarion call rang out from the wall, one so high and pure that it cut through the white noise of dominance that had fuzzed Tilly's mind and robbed him of all agency. Both his attention and, thankfully, the figure's shifted to the wall, whose gates exploded open in a surprise countercharge.

The gates reaped hundreds of enemy lives as they went from impenetrable to unstoppable in an instant, mowing down or flinging away anything in their path. Tilly couldn't help but flinch at the thunderous clang the three-story metal doors made as they slammed to a stop against the walls that barely held them on giant swinging hinges.

Behind them a stream of combatants took the field, charging through the recently made space and taking full advantage of the shock of their enemies to cut through their decimated front ranks and deep into the heart of the Strigoi offensive. Leading the charge was a wide variety of ghostly warriors, ranging from pale-looking humanoids to barely visible specters.

Simultaneously, the ranged attacks raining down from the wall suddenly multiplied, bursting forth with embedded magics. Fire, wind, and even spectral blades tore through the press of bodies just beyond the charging Whyte counteroffensive, softening their opponents further and removing the possibility of a rally.

With the weight of the figure's presence gone, Tilly could suddenly think again, and his fight or flight instinct redoubled. He had never been more sure of his need to flee a fight in his life. He poured everything he had into getting away from the battlefield, burning through whatever added spiritual agency the white flames had given him. There was no way he would survive that thing's attention if it bothered to look back at him.

In those moments when it had held his gaze, it had owned him, heart and soul. The loss of all of his control with just a glance from this new enemy filled him with a certainty of his own inferiority. Against something like that, he was well and truly in over his head. It hadn't been like last time with the red-eyed figure . . . There had been no struggle, just a silent, terrifying end to his *will*. Struck by a sudden thought, he desperately checked **Corruption's** influence on his HUD.

Corruption's Influence: 38%

It had barely been boosted by the other creature's *will* . . .

He released a silent sigh of relief as he tore through the air as fast as he could, following the face of the mountain range. Tilly wondered if the figure had even used an *Ability* or if the gap in their power levels was so overwhelming that someone with Tilly's low *Wisdom* was virtually helpless before it.

He risked another glance back, making sure to focus only on the wall and the conflict raging before it. The defenders had cut a huge wedge into the attacking army, killing thousands as they completely demolished the front ranks of the horde. But the Whyte offensive had slowed significantly as it approached the area covered by the chaotic dark cloud. Its influence rolled forward, pressing against the ghostly blue barrier attempting to hold it back. Under the returning corrosive influence, the effectiveness of the attacks from the wall halved.

His view was slowly blocked by the curve of the mountain range, and he turned forward hoping to still accomplish his goal before it was too late. Before him stretched the river, snaking off through the flat plains, and just up ahead were the powerful falls that fed it, thundering through a break in the mountains a couple of hundred feet up.

At this point, the white flames that covered Tilly's body had diminished to only a few patches, and his speed decreased incrementally as he approached the falls and ascended to its top. He angled his flight to meet the barrier where it hovered above the water and slowed to a stop, floating before it.

In his spirit form, the magic of the incredibly large spell was fascinating to see up close. He took a moment to marvel at what looked to be a tightly woven net of runes, exceedingly intricate and barely discernable even with his heightened sensitivity to mana in its base forms. The lines of arcane text slowly crawled through the pattern, causing a shimmering shifting in the ghostly blue lace of enchantment.

He reached out and touched the barrier and found it as strong as steel against his incorporeal hand. A little jolt traveled through his arm at the contact, and the faint song of the Flower became more audible for a moment.

He watched a faint ripple run through the magic in all directions and shoot off out of sight. Nothing else happened that he could see, so he decided to stick with his plan and slowly sunk into the deluge of water pouring out into the plain. His wince of hesitation relaxed into a smile as he entered the water and found that it passed through him with no resistance. In fact, as he fully entered its flow, the last pieces of flame burning on his form strengthened and grew, covering his shoulders and arms like a cloak. While the water was just water, hidden in its flow was something of significant spiritual weight that seemed to revitalize him.

The song had grown even clearer in the center of the water's outpouring, and Tilly suspected that the roar of the water would have been deafening in his physical form, but the way he was now, it was relegated to playing in the background. Surrounded by water and the growing sweetness of the song, he stretched out his hand a second time. His vision was obscured by the flow of the river, but as he reached forward, his hand was still arrested by the impenetrable barrier.

Even underwater? he thought to himself in disappointment. He was about to pull his hand away when he felt a ripple roll through the barrier and sink into his spirit form, mirroring what had happened when he had first touched the barrier but in reverse.

Come, little brother, we do not have much time.

Then the resistance before him was gone, and he hesitantly flowed forward, finding the way suddenly clear. As soon as he passed, he felt the barrier close in behind him, and it may have been his imagination, but the movement seemed sluggish and stuttering, like turning on the lights in an old building.

As he moved past the barrier, he felt the weight of another kind of attention close in around him. It felt distinctly fluid and wild, and Tilly suddenly got the impression that he was somewhere he did not belong.

Following instinct more than anything, he shot up out of the water and felt the weight of that unwelcome attention lift as soon as he removed himself from its domain. There, past the mouth of the falls, he found a curving path that cut through the mountains by the river. Without hesitating, he shot forward, following its curves and taking full advantage of his partially restored spiritual flames to streak forward as fast as his form would take him.

The river narrowed and broke off as he progressed, dividing up into the hundreds of different tributaries from which it received its water. After cutting around several bends, Tilly emerged through the mountain range and gained a view of the valley he had seen what felt like ages ago. He left behind the river, which cut back through the range at an angle, and floated forward, suddenly hesitant.

The song rang out here just as clearly as it had the first time he had visited this valley, and even with the terrifying pressures and obligations he now carried on his shoulders, he felt the weight of their urgency lighten slightly. He flew over the trees, skimming their tops excitedly now that he had finally made it back.

He cleared the top of the tree line in minutes, and the sight of his objective hit him like a physical blow. The Flower and the rising crescendo of its song were heady and overwhelming. He considered his recent bout with the leader of the Strigoi army and couldn't help but compare the two for a second.

The Prime Dirge's power had dominated him, crushing all resistance before he had even had time to realize what was happening. In contrast, the Flower and its song did nothing to snuff out his *will*. It was more than a force of nature, its power undeniable as it flooded the valley, yet it demanded nothing of its spectators and offered its gift freely. The Flower's beauty was continually being poured out and made even more alluring by the fact that it was . . . vulnerable.

Tilly longed to approach it, feeling deeply attracted to its physical presence, but at the same time, he felt a fiercely protective instinct rise up in him as he realized that the sole objective of the chaotic energy that suffused the Prime Dirge was to twist this power into something completely different.

Lost in the layers and nuances of the Flower's song, he found himself on the same hilltop he had visited the first time without realizing it. Revelations about reality itself seemed to be playfully hidden within its melodies and time took on a strange dreamlike quality in its presence.

Then the sound of a deep sigh drew Tilly's attention to his right and pulled him back into the present. Looking over, he found Thunder's Descent leaning on his hammer and wistfully taking in the same sight.

"When I united the tribes of my people, I was insatiable in my appetite for more. I wanted the greatest treasures of this plane for myself . . . I was arrogant and my pride spelled my doom. But my desire for great treasure lived on, and part of me continued in this form. I was looking for something I could not name but knew I had to find." He slowly pulled his gaze away from the Flower and met Tilly's eyes. "My new people found this place long ago, and to our wonder, we discovered that proximity to this Facet allowed us to act out memories of our predecessors many times before they faded. It has been the treasure of our culture for a thousand years, and each of us swore to protect it when we joined the city and learned of its presence." His smile fell as the solemnity of their situation sank in, even here at the heart of the hidden valley. "Now the time of our stewardship comes to an end. I heard the charge of my brothers and sisters and their courage calls to me. It is now time for me to break the pride of another arrogant heart." He straightened and looked back west, where the city lay on the other side of the mountains.

"Wait! How do I obtain the patronage of the Flower? How do I even get back here in my real body?" Tilly all but shouted as he realized this was going to be another abrupt end to a conversation with the huge Whyte.

Thunder's Descent rolled his shoulders as he looked off into the distance, his frown turning fierce as he considered his opponent.

"I believe one of your party has something that will grant you a boon from Old Man River. Take it to him, and he will help you to reach this place. As for the rest of your quest . . . ," he trailed off, then turned back toward Tilly and paused before continuing hesitantly, "I can't say I know. But there is a **Seed** in your party, and that is a good start." As he finished, he cracked a smile, as if that was everything Tilly needed to know. Then he hefted his hammer, and the sight of its sigil-inscribed head made Tilly's ghostly jaw ache.

"Now, I will send you back to save you some time. I do not think your presence has gone unnoticed, and the blood drinker has come to contest your claim. You must hurry," he stated, his eyes narrowing in concentration as the head of his hammer began to thrum.

"Wait, I need more information! . . . And what are you doing with your hammer?"

CHAPTER FIFTY

Old Man River

"This shouldn't hurt," Thunder's Descent muttered, concentration writ across his face as the head of his hammer shimmered and became incorporeal, matching Tilly's state.

Shouldn't? Tilly had just time enough to think before the hammer exploded forward and crashed into his abdomen. The impact transferred an incredible amount of kinetic energy to him, and he launched into the air, streaking over the mountains at unbelievable speeds. The thread connecting him back to his body tightened and began to pull him back, the flames woven into the connection flaring brightly with the strain.

Tilly choked off a belated scream as he realized that the impact hadn't actually hurt. His spirit form was fuzzing at its edges under the strain of taking on so much energy, but it did not cause him any harm, spiritual or otherwise.

After only seconds he had cleared the mountain range and gained a clear view of the battle raging below. The horde had made it through the gates and now had the upper hand in the battle. The Whytes, however, were exacting a high price for every advancing step, and Tilly saw at least half the attacking army had been destroyed in their reckless push.

He burned past the cloud of chaos and hatred, closing his eyes, hoping that it would make some difference. But just as his arc began its descent toward his physical body, he felt that same terrible awareness pass over him, attempting to latch on. It might have been because of the distance, Tilly's speed, or even due to some effect of Thunder's *Ability*, but whatever it was, the Prime Dirge's attention slid off him, unable to take hold. Tilly let out a sigh of extreme relief as his path shot him behind the hills. As soon as the line of sight was broken, Tilly felt the weight of its attention lighten considerably, but not disappear entirely.

Before he knew it, he was gasping for breath, once again fighting the feeling of vertigo that always accompanied his return to a physical state. All around him his companions stirred, getting to their feet.

"We have to go, now!" Tilly gasped as he rolled to his feet dizzily.

Ichiro rose from his sitting position smoothly and tucked away his sword. "We are ready. What is the plan? How do we get into the city?"

"The city is just a doorway into the valley, one that the horde will soon open, but I think there is another way," Tilly said while moving over to the embodiment of his fears and sticking one of his moccasined feet into the stirrup. As he stepped up and settled into the saddle, he looked around to find the rest of the group mirroring his urgency as they, too, mounted their Nightmares, looking to him for further information.

"I don't entirely know what this means, but we need to get to a river that pours down from the mountain range to the east of the city. The Prime Dirge is leading this attack directly and spotted me on the way in and out. My contact assures me that if we reach the river, we will be granted a boon and access to the valley. But first we need to clear these hills and then cut east to meet the river by the fastest line possible. Everybody ready?"

Everyone in the group nodded as they loosened weapons and prepared for what was to come. Kindle leaped into the air above them, crying out fiercely in anticipation. Tilly turned his mount toward the battle and the object of their quest.

"Let's go!" he called as he kicked his Nightmare forward into a gallop, not bothering to lower his voice.

The rest of the group followed, and they cleared the last of the hills in less than a minute. As they broke out into the plain, Tilly immediately felt the Prime Dirge's attention on him intensify, and he heard gasps and exclamations all around him as its weight settled down on the group. The battle was still too far away for them to make out any details of what was happening on the wall, but they did see a small contingent break off from the rear of the horde and start moving toward them.

Tilly cut to the east toward the distant river, urging his mount to move as fast as possible on the open ground. And move it did. Tilly could feel a slight tug of discomfort on his bond as the Nightmare pulled on his life energy even further to eke out more speed. The mount's feet were a blur as it pushed toward the river with all it had, followed closely by the others.

Turning back to measure the approaching group's relative distance, Tilly was shocked to see that they continued gaining even with the mounts at full speed. Even worse than that, Tilly could see the cloud approaching as well and felt the pressure on his mind increasing by the second.

He whipped his head over to Hilbert, whose nose was bleeding freely as he held an arcane gesture in one hand and the reins in the other. From his form, a shimmering shield had risen to cover over the group, interposing itself between the Prime Dirge's attention and the galloping group.

"I am doing all I can!" he snarled, the blood from his nose painting his teeth red as it continued to flow. The pinkish energy of his magic was thick above them, and it flickered ominously at the increasing pressure being levied by the distant pursuer.

Then the pressure redoubled and even the mounts began to slow under its weight, causing the pursuing contingent to gain on them even more. Tilly's group had a shorter path to the river, but whoever this group was, they possessed incredible speed.

Tilly looked back toward the battle once again, looking for any sign of the guardian Whyte. After a moment, he spotted something glittering in the sky high above the mountains. The distant object continued to grow until it resembled a meteor. It was then that the sound of a boom reached them, and a ring of concussive pressure exploded out from the object as it increased speed, hurtling down toward the battle.

As suddenly as it had fallen, the Prime Dirge's attention lifted again from the group, and they gasped in relief as the Nightmares picked up their speed in the absence of its pressure. Tilly, however, continued to stare back at the coming collision in awe. The cloud whipped around the Prime Dirge in a vortex before shooting up to meet the new threat like a lance.

As the cloud launched upward to meet the falling meteor, Tilly heard the shout of the guardian booming through the heavens.

"THUNDER'S DESCENNNNNT!"

Whether he was shouting his own name or he was named after his strongest *Ability*, Tilly did not know, but another boom, this time so loud that Tilly felt it in his chest, rolled off from the impact. The cloud was completely dispersed by the kinetic energy released as Thunder crashed into the Prime Dirge hammer first. Their collision with the ground below reminded Tilly of an artillery strike, and hundreds of the enemy army were caught in the resulting concussive blast.

It. Was. Epic.

Hell yeah, brother. Tilly grinned fiercely at the incredible opening move Thunder had used to lay into the Prime Dirge. Unfortunately, this had done nothing to slow the group pursuing them . . . And Tilly was dismayed to realize that they were still gaining. He turned forward in his saddle to try and measure their distance to the river and his heart sank further.

They wouldn't make it.

He sensed the formation of galloping mounts shift behind him and saw Ichiro in a tight conference with Sir Michael, speaking loudly enough to be heard over the gallop, but not loudly enough for his words to carry to Tilly. Whatever was said, the knight nodded and pulled back on his reins, causing the mount to slow.

"Gorock, with me," Ichiro called. Gorock looked back at the lapin and hooted with glee as he saw Ichiro's intentions. Tilly was about to slow as well, thinking that the group as a whole had a much better chance of defeating whoever had come to pursue them.

"No, Jonathan!" Ichiro called, slowing just enough so that he would meet the trailing attackers within sight of the river. "Do not forsake the mission! You must obtain patronage or this is all for nothing!" he shouted over the growing distance between their two groups. With him were Gorock, Sir Michael, and Hilbert. Kindle let out a fierce war cry, wheeling in the air and breaking off from the group to turn and face their pursuers.

Tilly's face fell, but he nodded in understanding and turned to fully focus on the approach to the river, which was coming up fast. Time was short and he would trust his companions' decision-making as much as they trusted his. To his right and left were Franklin and Amelia, both with complicated looks on their faces but appearing determined to continue.

Gorock's wild taunting echoed from behind them as they pulled up to the river's edge. Tilly dismounted, and the others hopped down just a moment behind him.

"Hey! Mr. River?" Tilly shouted at the flowing waters, urgency undercutting his attempt at a respectful tone. No answer came, and he looked at his two companions, feeling lost. Amelia returned his look with nothing to add, but Franklin ignored the look entirely and moved to the river with a strange mix of concentration and sorrow pulling down the lines of his face.

"This is it . . . This is the moment," he said quietly as he unwrapped the scarf from around his neck.

Tilly looked back to see the pursuing group almost upon the rest of their party. Ichiro's group had dismissed their mounts to regain the lost *Constitution* and were taking up a diamond formation with Sir Michael at its point and Hilbert at the rear.

"Well, whatever you are going to do, do it."

Franklin laid the blue length of fabric tenderly across his upturned hands, knelt at the edge of the water, and lowered it in. Tilly blinked in shock as the water rippled around the piece of clothing and formed the shape of a young girl with blue skin. She looked to be sleeping, but as Franklin lifted her back from the water, her eyes blinked open slowly.

The sound of a clash of arms and a cackling howl broke out in the near distance, but Franklin seemed to be immune to outside pressures as his face broke out in a brotherly smile at the appearance of the little girl.

"Hello, little friend, it is nice to finally meet you," he said as he settled her onto her feet. She looked around slowly and her eyes grew as big as saucers. Her location sunk in, and she rubbed the heels of her hands into her face as she fought back tears.

"Th-thank you for bringing me home," she stuttered through a hitching sob. Then behind her, the water began to froth and a man with a beard of flowing water and scales running along his upper body stepped up from its surface at a run.

"Daughter!" he exclaimed, throwing his arms open and rushing to the shore.

"Papa!" she cried as she collapsed toward the approaching figure.

He snatched her from her fall and twirled her around, laughing uproariously. Something in Tilly twinged at the sight, but something far deeper began to well up along with the pain, washing it in healing sorrow. He broke his eyes away from the sight and looked back at Ichiro's group, who were now completely enmeshed in battle with the pursuers. Now that they were much closer, Tilly was able to count around twenty Consumers being led by a huge Strigoi wielding a battle ax.

Even as the smaller group fought to keep them engaged, half of the Consumers broke off and continued toward the river. The water-bearded man looked up from his embrace and his smile fell.

"Ah, I see . . . ," he said, then set down his daughter and turned to address the three before him.

CHAPTER FIFTY-ONE

Face Tat

The physical personification of the river stood to his full height and surveyed the trio from several feet above their eye levels.

"You have my gratitude . . . I would ask what boon you would have of me, but given the circumstances, I imagine I already know the answer. It is within my power to bring you to the Flower and back. Simply step into my waters and I will carry you."

"Thank you, sir," Tilly said as he moved forward in a rush, every clang and shout from behind them instilling greater urgency into the moment. He couldn't stand the idea of them fighting to protect him while he just stood here.

"Honored Elder, I would request a different boon," Franklin said.

The river's look softened as he met the honu's eyes. "Yes, I see Little Brook's mark on you. It is no small thing to give up such a benefit to your magic."

The honu nodded, licking dry lips. "What I need most now is the strength to protect those with me. Will you grant me this?" he asked in a rush.

The battle raged a few hundred yards off and the smaller contingent of Consumers was almost upon them. Old Man River, however, took his time considering Franklin's request.

"My daughter's blessing would have followed you through every tier of growth, becoming something truly powerful if you survived . . ." He ran his fingers through his beard as he thought, and Tilly choked down a growl of frustration as he drew his hatchets and half turned to keep an eye on their approaching attackers.

The little girl tugged on her father's hand shyly, and he knelt down to hear her whisper before laughing in response. "Oh! Very good, child! I had forgotten all about her. That will do nicely!"

Tilly gritted his teeth at the pace of the conversation and finished turning to face the approaching group. They were now within his striking distance, and he would only be able to get in a few throws before they crashed into the riverbank.

Amelia was pulling several handfuls of something from her pockets, joining Tilly as he lifted his hatchets to ready a throw, when they heard a throat-clearing harrumph from behind them. Two huge vortices of water rose up from the river and crashed down on top of the sprinting Consumers with the weight of thousands of gallons behind them.

The force of the water was undeniable, but it did not push the attackers back the way they had come. Instead, it swept them to either side of the group and down into the river. And just like that, they were gone. Tilly suddenly felt a chill, and he belatedly looped his hatchets back on his belt. He looked back at Old Man River closely, but no identifier popped up above his head. The power he had just displayed, however, spoke for itself.

"Disgusting parasites if you ask me," the river sniffed absently as he turned his attention back to the three of them. "Now, to your boons. You two, pass through my waters, and I will grant your companion a gift worthy of his deed."

Amelia looked over at Tilly and raised her eyebrows, and he nodded. Whatever was to come, they had to get to the Flower first. Without hesitating, she dismissed her mount, and Tilly turned to do the same. With a flex of his *will*, the mount faded, and 10 percent was restored to his *Constitution*.

Then they turned together toward the water and stepped off the shore into a surprisingly deep drop-off. Before Tilly could even shout out in shock, he was slipping into the river's depths joined by a twin splash to his left.

The water swallowed them, and Tilly felt the invisible grip of a mighty hand encircle him and launch him forward. It felt as if they were slipping between the flow of water, and Tilly felt no resistance as they shot upriver.

His lungs constricted, and he fought panic as they moved in a way that confounded his comprehension until, suddenly, he was breaking the water's surface. He looked up, wiping water from his eyes, to find himself on the small rocky bank of a shallow mountain stream at the base of the hidden valley.

Franklin – Level 35 Tundra Caller

Amelia and Tilly disappeared as soon as they stepped into the river, and he could feel his mana stirring in response to the wild application of water and teleportation magic that Elder River had employed.

The presence of the being before him vibrated in his senses, and he did not think either of the other two had a grasp on what they were dealing with. This wasn't a river. This was a manifestation of all rivers . . . His power suffused Franklin's water-attuned senses as he tried to maintain calm before what might as well have been a deity.

The figure in question turned from watching the two disappear and looked Franklin in the eyes, his expression becoming more frank with the others gone.

"You know who I am?"

"Yes, Honored One," Franklin answered quickly, attempting not to choke on his own nervousness. His great uncle had spoken of such beings. Creatures that bridged the gap between the Land and the Divine realm, standing with one foot in each. He had said he had only met two in his time, and both had been as wild and unpredictable as a summer storm. They lived by their own code of conduct and had very little regard for the wants or cares of the sentients who subsisted off their bounty.

"Good. Keep that to yourself. As much as I would like to help, I am bound to my domain, but your actions have allowed me to tip the scales slightly. So, as my daughter suggests, I will grant you a contract with something not seen on Nephesh for Epochs. She will be scaled down to your power level, but I think you will find her a more than suitable reward," he said, his eyes beginning to glow.

Franklin was about to thank the being but was distracted by two glowing tendrils of water rising from the river before him. They moved toward him almost hesitantly, as if considering, their glow matching the light coming from the river's eyes.

"Now, you need to hold still . . . ," he muttered as the tips of the tendrils tapered off to razor-sharp points and shot forward. The movement was so fast and shocking that Franklin only had time to blink as a pattern of pain erupted from his brow. They punctured him thousands of times in the space of a breath, moving faster than thought, and Franklin bit back a shout as their movements danced a hair's breadth from his eyes. Then, as quick as they had come, the tendrils misted away, and the river leaned forward to admire his work.

The girl clinging to his side smiled encouragingly at Franklin as he lifted his hands to his face. He felt no physical change, but he could feel a new *Ability* available to him, though he did not pull up his screen in front of the elder—he feared such a thing would be rude.

"I think it is a fierce reminder of what she is," he said absently while turning to his daughter. "What do you think, Little Brook?"

At his side, the little girl's smile turned mischievous, and she spoke for the first time since entering the water.

"Auntie Fjord will love it!" she exclaimed. Her father clapped in delight, then turned back to consider the scene playing out just beyond his reach.

"Your friends have shown a surprising amount of resilience, but I am afraid they will be overwhelmed shortly without your help," he said, waving a dismissal.

"Thank you, Honored One!" Franklin said while sketching a respectful bow, then turned quickly to find Ichiro's group a few hundred paces out, surrounded by harrying attackers as the huge Strigoi at the front hammered down blows on Sir Michael's crumbling shield.

At the sight, Franklin jerked forward, caught the neck of his skeletal mount and climbed up into the saddle, then kicked the Nightmare into a gallop.

"Too many in these milder climates have forgotten what we can do, young Tundra Caller!" the river shouted after him. "Remind them!"

Franklin nodded and clung to his mount as it charged forward with a speed inconsistent with its emaciated leathery frame. Franklin sent his senses through his magic and discovered the new frigid place that housed his gift. He pulled up its description in the moments he had before arriving at the battle.

> ### *Summon Elemental of the Primordial Ice:*
>
> *At the cost of 45% of your mana, you may summon the elemental once a day, and she will persist until destroyed or a thousand breaths have passed. Her Strength and Endurance will be scaled to 2x your Intelligence and Wisdom, respectively, and she will be granted control over her element equal to your highest ice-related skill. She may manipulate that element using her own mana but doing so will shorten her summon time.*

Franklin sensed that he could begin the summoning anywhere in his line of sight, and he immediately activated the *Ability*, causing whatever had been done to his face to suddenly ache with cold.

He centered the summons right behind the Strigoi leader, and a whirling vortex of icy winds began to spin in that place. The leader reflexively jumped back from Sir Michael's crumpled form and turned to take in the new threat.

Gorock looked like he had bathed in blood, most of it his, but the attackers on his side of the surrounding group were all wounded in some way. Ichiro's robe was glowing with a strange pattern, and he seemed to be untouched, having struck down several foes far above his level, but his eyes were bleeding profusely, and his movements showed an uncharacteristic sluggishness.

Hilbert had simply done all he could to hold back the thin group that had come around for a full rear flank. He had his same barrier up again, but Franklin watched it shatter on the next blow from one of the Consumers. Kindle dived in between the wizard's apprentice and the Strigoi and released a gout of flame that bathed the oncoming attackers.

They surged forward into the gap despite the flesh melting from their frames as Franklin's *Ability* fully activated. The icy whirlwind snapped to a standstill and then exploded with a powerful roar. The sound parted the blanket of snow that had manifested, allowing a huge ursine creature to walk through, its pure-white fur showing intermittent patches of frost.

As soon as it emerged from the portal, its presence blanketed the area in a sudden freezing cold, and all the attackers paused and pulled back to take measure of the new predator entering the field. Franklin could feel the elemental's savage satisfaction at the enemies presented before it, and it let out another huge roar. One layered with notes of challenge and defiance.

The Strigoi leader did not hesitate to charge the elemental after releasing a shout *Abilitiy* that froze Franklin and the others in place. The elemental rose on its hindlegs, unaffected, and slammed them down to release a rolling wave of icy spikes against its charging attacker and most of the Consumers surrounding the group.

The ax-wielding leader jumped out of the way, breaking off his shout as he did so, and Franklin lurched into action launching ice spikes at the backs of the distracted Consumers charging Hilbert's position.

The whole fight erupted into chaos as the thin balance of the conflict was completely disrupted by the emergence of the new combatants on the field. Gorock bellowed in unimpeded joy as he dived into the midst of his attackers, who had been scattered by the ice-spike attack.

Ichiro wove through the new obstacles, his white eyes ablaze with a piercing silver light as he removed any stray appendage that appeared in the field of death. Several of the Consumers tried to break through the icy barriers, but as soon as their bodies made physical contact, they were slowed and immediately grew frosty patches of ice all over their skin.

The leader turned to see he was losing the initiative and roared again, activating some sort of overdrive. His body swelled with engorged muscle and ropy black veins of **Corruption**. His fanged mouth began to pour out a mixture of black ichor and blood as he screamed in part outrage, part pain, "Mikhail, this is the last time you escape!"

Enraged, he tackled the elemental, ignoring the patches of ice that formed all over him, and viciously cut into the ursine creature's side with his huge serrated ax. The elemental roared in response and began to gore the flesh of its attacker, even as it continued to reform with ever-increasing layers of engorged muscle.

The remaining Consumers also went into a full rage, their forms bulging as they shrugged off the slowing effect of the Primordial Ice.

CHAPTER FIFTY-TWO

Lay It Down

Amelia Cooper – Level 40 Botanist Surveyor

She dragged herself up from the rocky stream, gasping for breath. Jonathan had arrived with her through the strangest transport magic she had ever experienced, and they both stumbled to their feet on the other side of the mountains.

Something prickled all along her skin and Amelia quirked her head. Her growth-aspect mana stirred interestingly as she bent her internal senses to find the source of the sensation. Jonathan had explained to them what this Facet was like, but she had not expected it to resonate with her mana so . . . profoundly.

Then the sound of screeching metal followed by a concussive boom reverberated through the mountains. Amelia looked up to see something crash into the far mountain range, chased by the malevolent creature that had almost destroyed them in their flight to the river.

"The barrier is down, we have to hurry," Jonathan noted grimly beside her, his eyes following the trajectory of the impact.

"Let's get moving, then! You lead and I'll keep up," she replied, running her hand through her wet hair to get it out of her eyes. She had some Drinking Dust stored away somewhere, but they didn't have time for something as petty as drying off.

"Alright, let's go," he said, distracted by the fight occurring in the distance. Then, as if jolted by electricity, he lowered his head and moved straight for the forest at a jog. Amelia jumped to follow, fighting a grin at his sudden shift into action.

After all this time, she was still bemused by the man. He could be exceedingly short with his words and direct in his manner one moment, then playful and clever the next. Below all of it lurked deep waters that she would catch glimpses of in the strangest moments. That being said, she hadn't exactly been the best version of herself with him either. She had left behind her kind decades ago, writing them off and doing her best to embrace this new life.

Then he had shown up, just as everything she had built had begun to crumble. She had been running herself ragged trying to beat this infection in the children, and he had just showed up and done it . . . At first, she had been frustrated that someone else had stepped in to solve her problems. Then as she saw him cleanse people until he was comatose, she had grown a grudging respect for him, but that respect had not removed the tiny seed of bitterness that continued to whisper in her ear, *Look, you are still not good enough.*

As he moved through the trees ahead of her, she lengthened her stride to keep up. Her feelings toward him were still in constant flux. He was proud and hated to see others sacrifice themselves in his place. Yet he insisted on doing so for everyone around him. His martyr complex was truly impressive . . . And yet, she could not deny he was honest and courageous when it mattered.

Actually, he probably leaned into those virtues more often than was prudent, charging in without thinking, sharing secrets without hesitating . . . Amelia shook her head ruefully as she ducked a low-hanging branch.

Whatever his failings, he had been good to the people he had promised to help. He might not be much of a leader, but she now fully understood that his intentions were in the right place. Even if he drove her crazy with his bullheadedness. For just a moment she allowed herself to imagine what life would be like if they survived whatever conflict was washing over the entire plane. Forgotten wounds ached again at the thought of possible companionship with another of her race, at the risk of her disappointing someone else . . .

Even as old pain rose to the surface, the sensation around her deepened. The feeling of goosebumps on her skin spread from her arms down to her back, like warm water flowing down from a hot shower. A shiver of delight and relief suffused her senses as she moved deeper into the valley and the warm reality of endless possibilities seeped into her soul.

You are holding him back.

What part did she have to play in all this? Was she just here to get her **Corruption** cleansed? Or was there something more? The feeling of lightness danced just on the edge of her hearing, growing clearer with every step. It was the ringing of bells . . . No, that wasn't it, although it had that quality. There was singing there, too, and some sort of rhythm present as well.

It's music! she finally realized.

Her steps became lighter, and the chains of guilt and condemnation that so often bound her heart began to loosen. Emotional weights so familiar to her that they had become a fact of her existence began to lessen, and a small smile tugged at her straining face as she plowed after Jonathan through the ancient forest.

Then a jarring staccato of violent crashes echoed through the valley followed by a symphony of screams that sounded as if they had been ripped from hundreds of mouths. Whoever was fighting that thing had to be extremely strong. She hoped it could hold it off long enough for them to accomplish their quest.

"The only thing you will find in this valley is your end!" the voice of their temporary protector shouted in the distance.

"You are almost forgotten, shade. Then the power of Endless Life will be mine, and my children will wash over the Land like the tide."

Jonathan looked back at her with a desperate question left unspoken on his lips. She sighed internally and called forward to him, "If you are holding back for my sake, don't! I'm here to help, not hinder!" She was suddenly furious that he was going slower than he had to for her sake. They had a mission to accomplish!

He picked up the pace significantly, moving directly toward what Amelia now recognized as the Flower's song. The forest started to thin again, and she began to notice another growing sensation in the pit of her stomach. Something that started as a painful cramp and grew with every step into a halo of stabbing pain surrounding her core. She stifled a groan as the pain redoubled.

The **Corruption** . . . It had never done anything like this before. Instead of trying to integrate with her body, it had begun to attack her internally, as if finally realizing its end might be near.

She glanced up to see her health now falling with every step as the sensation of repeatedly being stabbed reached further and further into her torso. The **Origin Seed** within her also seemed to be reacting to the song, but not in a way that counterbalanced the damage being done by the now furious parasite.

They cleared the trees and the song grew louder, as did the discordant notes of her agony. A few steps ahead of her, Jonathan was grunting in his own pain, his gait hitching oddly as he continued forward. It was then that she noticed the blood he was leaving behind with every step.

Health: 72%

She reached under her shirt and found that her abdomen had also started weeping blood. The pain was now lancing into every nearby area of her body with violent disregard for function. It was getting desperate, and part of her hardened in the face of this inescapable opposition. If it wanted to kill her, so be it. She would rather die than quit while so many were counting on her.

Her insides wrenched, dropping her health another 5 percent, and she bit back another scream. Out of long habit, she palmed her health potion, ready to down it as soon as she became unable to keep up with the dogged pace he was setting.

She knew his infection was far more pervasive than hers and she refused to be the reason they slowed down. If Jonathan could continue, then so would she.

They stumbled to the top of a low rise, and the sight of **Origin's Bloom** at the center of the valley was almost enough to make her forget her pain. It was nothing more than a simple blue flower, yet for some reason it felt more real and vibrant than the breath in her lungs. The sight of it did nothing to lessen her agony, but it did give context to the pain. They were almost there. Almost done.

Ahead of her, Jonathan grunted and slowed for a moment as they both took in the sight. She moved the last couple of steps to catch up to him and saw, to her horror, that his mouth was pouring dark blood. Before she could say something, he stumbled down the rise in an almost mindless motion, as much through stubbornness as will. In that glimpse of his face, she had seen death. She tightened the grip she had on her health potion and moved to follow, focusing all of her attention on keeping up.

We are so close!

Health: 41%

That symphony of screams echoed through the valley again, this time much closer, and Amelia heard a sad but friendly voice carry over to them on an invisible breeze.

"This is all the time I can give you, little brother, little sister. Spend it well."

Before she could process those words or their source, the sky boomed and shook the entire valley as lightning descended out of the ever-present clouds and crashed down out of sight. Those same screams of outrage warped further into wails of pain as the lightning continued in a seemingly endless bar of energy. It was as if heaven itself was pouring out the entire cup of its wrath in one violent judgment.

They both continued toward the sweet song; its source poured forth unbridled joy, uninterrupted by the conflict around it. Jonathan coughed wetly a few steps ahead of her and released a guttural groan before falling over. They were ten feet from the Flower, which swayed softly just beyond their reach.

She stumbled over to him and pressed her potion into his hand, and the sharp sensation of pain at the action almost caused her to keel over as she straightened.

"Don't stop . . ." He coughed, then gasped, his eyes fixed on the Flower, "One of us has to make it."

He isn't going to make it . . . The reality slammed into her, almost driving her to the ground as hot knives of pain wriggled and reached further into the cavity that was vainly attempting to protect her organs.

Health: 28%

Her jaw was clenched too tightly to answer him, but she forced her body to take another step and then another.

What's the point?

You'll both be dead in minutes.

Just sit for a second and catch your breath.

That same sickly-sweet voice kept bubbling up through the pain, promising her the relief of no longer caring. Step after stumbling step, she answered the voice. Not with malleable arguments that only gave it more power. But with the iron finality of action. She had no clue if the Facet could save them or not. But she was done being ruled by fear.

She wasn't going to give up this time.

The sensation in her midsection boiled over into a frothy orgy of pain as she collapsed in front of the Facet and reached out her hand to gently touch the edge of a petal. It was so blue that it drank in her vision, drowning her in its azure vibrance. Its song was so clear that even through the pain she felt her tense body relaxing in relief. At her touch, the song coalesced around her, somehow forming words in her consciousness.

This Facet's Champion has fallen.
Eligible candidate for Bloom's Guardian detected.

Smiling spitefully in the face of the gut-wrenching pain attempting to scramble her insides, she sent her assent to the music-formed notification, and the song roared into a crescendo, causing all kinds of flowering plants to erupt from the ground around them.

Then something changed in the midst of the song; an order rippled through the wild melodies that intertwined the Flower and its new Champion.

Emergency Quest Initiated.
Transport compatibility identified.
Relocate Facet to a safer location.
Reward: Patronage of Origin's Bloom
Do you accept?

In for a penny, in for a pound . . . Amelia thought grimly as she accepted the notification.

CHAPTER FIFTY-THREE

Death's Doorway

Jonathan Tillman – Level 23 Son of Flame

Tilly's insides were boiling over in an exquisite mixture of burning flesh and agonized organs. As soon as he had begun to approach the Flower, the **Corruption** within him had started to struggle, resisting his movements and causing him pain, but it was nothing his crazy *Endurance* couldn't counterbalance.

But as he cleared the trees, the warnings turned into waves of frenzied attacks that increased in intensity the closer he got to the Flower. He started to wheeze, then cough up blood as the **Corruption's** internal network of branching feelers flexed and pierced his internal organs. Even with Tilly's mana-reinforced internal structures, the damage moved from dangerous to severe to catastrophic as he attempted to push through the last fifty feet to their goal.

He felt Kindle's consciousness blaze into his mind, taking in the damage he was experiencing along with its source.

Do not die, Bonded! I am coming. I have just remembered something important!

Tilly sent back a vague assent as more and more of his *will* was demanded in the struggle to keep moving forward.

Step after grinding step, he pushed, picking up the **Internal Bleeding** debuff and watching it slowly stack until **Organ Failure** joined it on his HUD. None of that mattered to Tilly . . . His mind's eye was fixed on the fight going on just past the mountains. He would not waste their sacrifice!

After an eternity of agony, he attempted to clear his blurry eyes of the film of free-flowing tears to see the Bloom just a few feet away. **Massive Hemorrhaging** appeared next to his other debuffs, rounding out the trio. As soon as it locked into place, strength drained from his limbs like water from a tub, and he stumbled to the ground, struggling to breathe, his eyes still fixed on the Bloom barely out of reach. His torso was a mess, his abdominal muscles shredded in their attempt to contain the fury of the **Corrupted** tendrils. He tried and failed to pull his legs under him, finding some essential connection missing . . .

A wet gurgling gasp sounded next to him, reminding him that he was not alone in this agony. Straining the mostly intact muscles of his neck, he looked up to see Amelia still stumbling forward, a grim scowl pulling down the corners of her mouth as her own invader attempted to keep them from their goal.

"Don't stop . . . One of us has to make it," he wheezed through needle-filled lungs. The fire flowing through his mana pathways burned the **Corruption** where it could and attempted to combat its mindless attacks, but this only resulted in further internal damage to Tilly's ruined organs. He blinked as a blurry shadow passed him by, and he felt something small and cold settle into his hands. He uncorked the object and lifted it to his lips, the motion more a memory than a conscious decision.

He coughed wetly as it went down, and his focus returned a few moments later as he watched in some satisfaction when Amelia fell to her knees and lifted her hand to touch the Flower. At that moment, as the unnatural healing rushed through his body and attempted to combat the massive damage being leveraged against him, he thought of his ex-wife. Not the woman he had known near the end, when their relationship had devolved into a bitter, shriveled ghost of itself. No, watching Amelia fight tooth and nail to do what no one else could reminded him of Laura at her best. Tough as old leather, yet relentless in her support of those in her care.

The Flower's music rose victoriously at her touch, and Amelia sat there for a breath or two before the melody began to fade, whispering into silence. Then, to his dismay, the Flower dissolved into motes of light. Tilly managed a grunt of shock as he watched the Facet disappear. In an almost comical mirror of this turn of events, the temporary spike in his health ran out as the potion's magic waned before the furious onslaught of his internal enemy. The fact that he had any health left at all was truly a testament to the stubborn nature of his *Endurance-*infused body.

Through the gut-wrenching pain, Tilly watched the motes of light dance through the air and swirl into a vortex that centered on Amelia's core. As the song faded in its entirety, the motes completely vanished into their chosen vessel.

Ha! Tilly thought triumphantly, cracking a bloody smile at the sight. If that wasn't a good sign, he didn't know what was.

Then a new sound arose, completely replacing the sweet music that had only just faded. A multitude of screams tore through the air toward them. The brutally disfigured Prime Dirge appeared over the near horizon and crashed into the ground before Amelia, tearing a huge furrow in the previously vibrant carpet of grass and clover.

"**What have you done!?**" the cacophony of discordant voices screamed from hundreds of mouths all over the muscular gray and purple skinned creature. Its fight with Thunder's Descent had obviously not been one-sided, and the waxy molting of severely burned skin covered its once sleek form. Yet, even wounded, its presence completely overwhelmed Tilly. The Prime Dirge struggled to its feet, looking around in momentary confusion, and centered its attention on Amelia.

Tilly's health ticked down to 1 percent, and he desperately activated [Resolute] as he fought against the mental weight that had settled over him like cement. Darkness crept in on all sides, surrounding the scene of their failure like the curtain closing on the final act of a play.

The Title kicked in, and all the damage he was receiving from his internal trauma ceased just as Kindle's burning presence entered his peripheries, high in the sky.

Bonded, I need your mana! Kindle sent urgently as Tilly hovered dangerously close to the edge of death. The horrifying slurry that was now his internal organs had somehow been stabilized by [Resolute], muting the battle between his flame and the juvenile Seed of Corruption, yet it had all been for nothing. The Prime Dirge stood before them gravely injured—but still far beyond their power to resist.

Kindle's words stoked what little *will* Tilly had left and revealed a minute avenue of opposition, a final desperate hope flickering back to life in Tilly's mind. A glowing sigil lit up on the back of his right hand, and in it, Tilly could feel the straining need of his bond. Tilly raged against the aura that blanketed the area, pulling on his wild desperation, then lifted his arm and threw every bit of mana he had into the link before launching it toward the phoenix.

Far above them, Kindle wheeled into a dive, her distant speck bursting into a startling brightness.

Warning! Your Bonded Phoenix has activated the Sun's Final Descent. This has a 77% chance of severing your connection forever.

Do you accept?

Y/N

A scream seemed to scrape Amelia's throat raw as the Prime Dirge's claws began to dig into her abdomen curiously, its voice a mellow, warm chuckle. "**Ah, I see. You tucked it away. Unfortunately, dearest, flesh is something of a special—**"

Its words cut off as it whipped its head around in search of the sudden feeling of danger.

Tilly slammed "Yes" mentally and felt his bond swell dangerously as it drew in all of his flame and demanded more. Even as he watched the horror unfolding before him, he shoved everything he had into the connection: his manic need to do something, his longing to live, even his overwhelming desire to be finally free of the **Corruption** that had poisoned almost every moment of his new life. All of it became fuel for the righteous sun of anger bearing down on them.

The Prime Dirge narrowed its eyes and jerked its bloody hand away from Amelia's torso, then glared up as it found the source of the impending attack. Kindle plummeted through the air like a shooting star, burning with azure intensity. Its disdainful frown turned into a grimace as Kindle's burning intensified into a supernova-like blaze only a few feet from impact. Her fierce cry tore through the valley in defiant opposition.

At that moment, having poured all of himself into the bond, Tilly understood Kindle's nature. No phoenix died of old age; they burned ever brighter until a suitable end was found, then they crashed against that end with the full explosive weight of their fire.

[Resolute] snapped and withdrew whatever system-governed protection it had leveed against Tilly's grievous injuries. His health ticked down to zero, the final chime on an old clock, and his perspective careened downward as the final vestiges of strength left his body. The Prime Dirge tensed to dash away from the suddenly deadly attack, recognizing its end.

Tilly! Do not give in! Kindle screamed into his soul through their straining bond.

He fell face-first as thick roots surged up from the ground in front of him and snared the Prime Dirge's clawed feet as it attempted to push away from the impact site.

There was no collision as Tilly hit the ground. It was almost as if he kept falling, plunging ever deeper into an endless darkness . . .

Behind him, worlds away, there was an earth-shattering roar followed by a burning heat. That burning plunged deep into Tilly's body, chasing his soul into its darkness, and reached across the seemingly endless divide to establish a tenuous but vibrant connection.

Amelia Cooper – Level 40 Botanist Surveyor

A scream tore itself from her lips as the most terrifying being that she had ever seen casually reached into her flesh and began digging around. It was just on the verge of grasping the explosive energy that was hidden away in her core when it narrowed its eyes and pulled its hand free with a wet sucking sound.

If Amelia had not been held fast by the overwhelming aura that poured off the injured Prime Dirge, she would have collapsed in a boneless heap. The trauma of her badly damaged midsection being violated in such a way almost pushed her over the edge.

But as the creature looked up, the disdain on its face morphed into something resembling fear. She felt the faintest glimmer of defiance shine out from her core to connect with the vibrant energy of the Facet, flooding her pathways with power. Time slowed to a crawl as her senses expanded to an extraordinary degree, and she began to absorb the primal energy spinning in her center.

An awful heat bloomed above her, and she found herself grinning as she vindictively channeled the torrent of energy into the ground below herself and the Prime Dirge. The many rooting plants lying hidden underground instantaneously mutated into monstrously thick versions of themselves and shot out of the ground to tangle the horror's legs, even as it attempted to jump away and dodge whatever judgment had come to claim it.

Oh no, you don't. Whatever this is, it's here for both of us, she mentally exclaimed. Satisfaction washed through her battered soul as time shuddered back into motion and a white supernova crashed into the creature, vaporizing Amelia's world and incinerating the center of the valley.

The blast washed over her, strangely pleasant to most of her senses. The area of her body that had been ravaged by **Corruption** sizzled as white-hot fingers of fire traced their way through the twisting paths of its infection, violently cleansing the area.

Almost before the pain could register, the energy overflowing from her core rushed in to fill the space left by the burning furrows through her flesh. A furious itching filled the blackened voids and her body reknit itself in a spontaneous and incredible burst of regrowth.

Her eyes popped open to find her surroundings completely changed with ash falling all around them like a gentle snow. She urgently patted her body, surprised to see that even her clothes had gone unsinged, but as she lifted her shirt, she saw that the messy handprint that had covered over the site of her infection was completely gone. Instead, the area over her stomach showed only restored pink skin.

She looked up in wonder and saw that the Prime Dirge had been reduced to a ruined husk in the middle of the impact site. She almost spat on the thing in vindictive triumph before a thought struck her, shattering her moment of victory. Her eyes widened, and she urgently scanned the area until she spotted him lying face down under a pile of ash.

"Jonathan!" she shouted as she rushed over and collapsed to her knees next to the body, then grabbed his shoulder and hauled him over to lay on his back. His lifeless eyes stared blankly into the cloudy sky. "No, no, no!" she sputtered in confusion.

She lifted his jacket to find his own gristly scarring wide open and charred, revealing a large amount of gore and burned tissue. The **Corruption** had been burned out of him too, but without the growth energy of the Bloom, he had nothing to save him.

"This can't be the end . . . You were so close!" she cried, refusing to believe her eyes. Her core was already full to bursting again, and she took all that energy and shoved it out through her hands into the ruined body before her.

She was shocked to see the flesh start to regrow as networks of fat, muscle, and skin were rewoven, pulling deeply on the seemingly endless energy of the Bloom. Hope burst through the damn of her denial, and she eagerly watched his face for any flicker of movement. But even as his body regrew from its terrible wounds, his eyes remained empty.

A gasping sob escaped her as the reality of the situation hit her. The power of the Bloom continued to sing in her blood, flooding her pathways with possibility, but even with all of that, she could do nothing to reach wherever he had gone . . .

She gently took his hand, looking down sadly at his slack expression, almost peaceful in its emptiness. The tears came quietly after the first sob . . . All of that, and in the end, the voice had been right.

She hadn't been enough.

A strange itch started to tingle under her palm as she took a final moment to mourn her friend. Then the sensation flared painfully, and she snatched her hand away to find a glowing rune shining on the back of Jonathan's hand. Belatedly, she realized that something had been pulling the Facet's energy from her.

As soon as her strained mind caught up with what had just happened, she grabbed at the hand glowing with the strange rune. Again, the Facet's power began to flow into the mark, completely outside of her control. Ignoring the pain that this was causing, she pushed more of the foreign power into the mark, which seemed to be able to drink in the energy like water on parched sand.

The pathways down her arms began to burn with the constant strain of handling such huge amounts of power, but she pushed on without hesitating and watched in morbid fascination as the distinct shiver of a heartbeat reverberated powerfully through the once still body.

Jonathan Tillman – Level 23 Son of Flame

Tilly had no idea what death would feel like, but he hadn't expected it to be so *painful*.

None of his senses were functioning, and even his ability to think was gone. He had been reduced to a singular experience of suffering. Burning fingers reached deeply inside him, rooting out everything that didn't belong, and he lost himself to the agony of being cleansed.

Thump.

Thump.

Thump.

Thump.

Thump.

Tilly was yanked up from the dark, comforting embrace of unconsciousness and thrust back into the world of screaming sensations and harsh light.

He moaned in pain as nerves were brutally reconnected and the essential pathways of life restored through his shattered body. A relieved sigh sounded somewhere nearby.

"—too stubborn to die . . ."

With the voice came the faint tinkling of music keeping time with the heavy thumps of his beating heart. He blacked out moments after awakening, his mind completely overloaded by the cacophony of wild electrical signals flooding his recently silent brain.

Awareness flashed again briefly to the sensation of his feet dragging on the ground and the majority of his body lying on something pliable with two rigid poles compressing the sides of his shoulders.

His body was still a ghastly mess but was slowly, miraculously clawing its way back from ruin. Moments later, mercifully, darkness crashed down on him again.

Tilly jolted back into consciousness as his body hit the ground.

"You are every bit . . . as heavy as you look," Amelia declared above him between gasping breaths.

Tilly groaned in response, a million pieces of information hitting him at once even as he lay face down in the rocky dirt.

First and foremost, the sensation of unspent stat points hovered at the edge of his awareness. However, unlike other times, when it had sat patiently like a paperweight in the back of his mind, the heaviness of the amount of stats that he had to allocate lodged itself in his psyche like a piece of Stonehenge.

His eyes flicked open to the notification bell at the top of his HUD and another revelation struck him like a slap to the face. His debuff line only held a single entry . . . **Resurrection Sickness.**

Corruption's influence was gone.

It was gone.

The thought attempted to register again and again in his mind but just would not land. Despite his entire body feeling like a giant bruise, a distinct feeling of wholeness pervaded his physical form. It wasn't that he felt good. Actually, he felt like he had just been run over by a truck several times. Rather, he felt singular. Like his body was wholly his again.

It's gone.

Somewhere around the seventh or eighth try, it finally started to sink in, and up from the depths of his being came an overwhelming response. Joy.

"It's gone," he choked out through a parched throat.

Those words, uttered from exhausted lips, elicited a gasp from above him, and he felt long graceful fingers reach under one shoulder and roll him over onto his back.

"You're awake," exclaimed a beaming Amelia. She stood looking out over the bank of a small rocky stream near where they had arrived earlier.

"Yeah . . . But I need a moment, if you don't mind," Tilly whispered breathlessly, weighed down by an extraordinary exhaustion. She nodded, the skin around her eyes tight, betraying some lingering concern.

Kindle? he sent out.

No answer.

He tried to feel internally for the bond and found it . . . It was strained, but present. Yet, as he reached through it to find his partner, the connection seemed to disappear into a void.

Tilly considered lifting his jacket to see what had become of his side, but even thinking about the motion caused his bone-deep weariness to push him further into the ground. So instead, he mentally pinged open the notification window and his vision was filled with a torrent of messages.

CHAPTER FIFTY-FOUR

Crashing to a Head

Linus – Level 66 Consul

The last transition off had been rough. Despite what he had said to the young priestess, she had become invaluable to the system they had developed for enduring the almost constant waves of enemies.

Linus checked the gnomish device they had in the corner of the large healer's tent and saw that she still had an hour left on her leave. Erash had done her best to heal the worst cases before they came down, but they were losing too many in the wait to be seen by the few acolytes. The non-combatants' growth had been shocking in the last couple of days, but it was nowhere near enough to keep up with the strain of the constant inflow of injured and near dead. The now-exhausted supply of health potions had made a difference, but they were gone.

Erash had blessed everything the fletchers and smiths had sent a few hours ago, but those supplies had run out as well. Linus thought about going up to check on her again, and while the tempestuous High Priestess was hard to read, the last time he had seen her, Linus would have bet that she was about to collapse. They all were.

None of the leadership had slept and they were all showing it. They had used every trick in the book to keep the soldiers as fresh as possible, but the wear of the battle showed deeply on everyone's face . . . Well, besides Hiro. The Guardian Daimyo had stayed near Erash's side making sure she only spent mana on healing or on essential counters to certain enemy pushes, and he seemed unaffected by the days he had spent on his feet guarding their most precious resource.

"Watchman," Linus called to a passing soldier who looked every bit as haggard as he felt. The satyr was joining a century about to head back into the city for a few hours' rest.

"Consul!" He turned and saluted.

"When you get back to the camp, I need you to find the priestess and send her back here."

The soldier nodded sharply and then jogged off to join his century. They were down to twenty-four units . . . Yet every surviving man and woman had seen an increase of at least twenty levels in the last days . . . He once again winced at the lost opportunity. If they had had true military classes and Unit Magic, they could have benefited so much more, but as things stood, they were holding on.

When Aurelia returned, he would need to find a way to get Erash a rotation off the wall, and maybe—just maybe—they could hold another day.

A distant horn sounded.

A million things shot through the Consul's mind as he dashed from the tent and up the main stairs. Stalling tactics shattered in his mind as his days-long suspicion was finally confirmed. These tactics of attrition had grated on him. Not because they weren't valid, but because they seemed to be completely in contrast to the nature of their enemies. His commander's instinct had itched in anticipation of the whole balance crashing down and the enemy throwing forward all of its reserves at once.

Whatever reason held the main body of the horde back, it could not last. He had known this as surely as the setting of the sun. So he had done his best to balance the scales for this moment, holding what little they could in reserve, preparing.

"Bastions! With me! Marcellus, get your ass on this wall and fill out the first rank!" Linus shouted down at the unofficial Bastion transition area near the stairs, where the surly veterans had waited days to face the enemy as a unit. They had all gained many levels on the wall while leading their respective centuries, but there was not a man among them that didn't long to show the enemy the true strength of the line.

Linus kept up his shouting even as he topped the wall. "I want three more centuries up here! Form second, third, and fourth ranks behind the Bastion line. I want two more units in reserve on the stairs! The rest of you, form behind the wall! We are all in the fight now!" Men and women started to rush in different directions at his commands.

He found Erash leaning heavily on her staff and muttering an incantation as he approached. She finished and gestured forward tiredly as she formed a circle of glowing runes that magnified the enemy forces enough to see clearly.

"Is it wise to use this again?" Hiro asked at her side, his ear twitching as the distant horn sounded again.

"I don't think many of them are looking our way at this moment," she replied tiredly as she used the divination spell to scan the horizon until it hit on a distant glint. Night had fallen hours ago and the horde could barely be seen in the dark, but something about the spell made its targets plainly visible.

There, moving forward at a trot and building into a canter was a line of heavy cavalry. As Linus watched, the spell began to populate classes and levels. The first rank all had the Knight of the Sanguine Order class, and their average levels looked to be in the upper seventies. But more importantly, they looked to be charging directly at the horde's rear.

As soon as he saw this, a fierce smile cut Linus's face. This was somehow tied to the human's actions . . . He could feel it. They stood little chance of surviving the night, but at least now there *was* a chance.

Erash quickly panned back to the enemy mass and revealed disarray and infighting beginning amongst the chaotic groups that formed the enemy force. The monsters' mysterious discipline was gone, and Linus's hope flared further. Then a fierce barking call resounded through the milling chaos, echoing so powerfully that even Linus felt the pull of some of its magic.

In response, the entire horde split to meet their opponents on both fronts. Their heavy units moved into a countercharge against the knights, followed by thousands of support. The rest of the main body began to amble in a charge directly at the wall. Erash pulled back the scope of the magnification to sweep the entire mass.

Linus wasn't sure of the count, but his gut told him there must still be ten to fifteen thousand coming in the charge against the wall. The average Flame's Watch level was now in the forties, but it wouldn't be enough to face what would likely be at least a thousand of the enemy's elites at once. The mass movement built into a frenzied charge as the enemy army committed itself in its entirety to the attack.

"BASTIONS!" came a booming shout to the right of the lens Erash had created. Linus couldn't keep the death's-head grin from forming on his face as he looked over to see the last of his old unit filing into the first rank of defenders on the wall, Threstus at their center. The waiting was over. It was good to finally, honestly lay all the cards on the table.

"Vacation's over!" Threstus, the new Bastion commander shouted theatrically up and down the formation. "It's time to show these dogs what it means to HOLD THE LINE!" As one, the empire's finest soldiers slammed down their shields on the edge of the wall and began to emit the familiar glow of their Unit Magic. "SHIELDS UP! Let our enemy come and crash against us! DON'T GIVE AN INCH!"

The familiar notifications washed over him as Linus's soul brimmed with nostalgia and not a small amount of pride. The centuries that filed in behind the first rank, however, had never seen the unit in action. They only knew these men as commanders, a role his men had chafed under just as much as he had.

The effect of the magic taking hold was unmistakable. The shuffling stopped, murmuring quieted, and the top of the wall became unnaturally still, facing the sea of approaching enemies unmoved. Spears bristled over the heads of the first rank, who stood with stoic, almost bored expressions. These were soldiers who had elevated indifference in the face of death to an art form. Linus would know . . . He had trained almost all of them himself.

He didn't know what that cavalry was capable of, or if the status of the quest was even close to being complete. But none of that mattered . . .

They would hold for as long as it took.

Cog – Level 0 Gnomish Child

A little sigh of relief escaped his mouth as Cog considered their closing window of opportunity. They wouldn't have even had a chance if those overbearing tree huggers hadn't been so busy constantly checking the plant barrier for bad guys trying to sneak in. The two oldies seemed to have eyes in the backs of their heads.

But even with the oldies busy, no one was just leaving them to their own business. No matter how many times Cog snuck into the Alchemists' burgeoning workshop, someone would always come for him before nightfall to collect him back to the "safety" of the oldies' house near the forest. Well away from the city, the refugee camp, and the wall.

Away from anything that mattered.

Mrs. Amelia asked us to watch you! You need to be grateful and mind her wishes.

Running messages is plenty important! Do what you can now, and soon enough, you will be able to help in other ways!

The adults kept repeating these stupid sayings over and over. The original fifty that had hung around Mrs. Cooper's shop may not have been adults, but they sure as Pits weren't kids. To make matters worse, the youngest of their number had snuck off and somehow become full-grown, with a class and everything!

It wasn't fair, and no matter how many times he asked about it, they just kept stonewalling him.

He was sick of it.

Everyone else gets to fight! It's not like keeping us penned up at night will save us if they get through . . .

These and other more intrusive thoughts had made Cog what the adults called "surly." Well, they could think what they wanted . . . He and the rest of the originals were going to find out just how Aurelia had done it, and to do that, they needed to make it to the Temple without any more of the adults' meddling.

So, they had hatched a plan. Earlier that day, Cog had run messages with the rest of them before getting away as soon as possible to the Alchemists' workshop. He liked the three haggard crafters, who seemed to do little besides work and sleep. As long as he wasn't in the way, they treated him like another of the assistants hoping to unlock the class and never mentioned his age, or his current lack of class.

He spent the last few hours till evening crushing leaves into powder in bulk, running out to get more wood for the cauldron fire, doing whatever they needed, but all the while, he kept an eye out for a few of the more "useful" ingredients. He didn't feel that bad about pocketing a few things; they weren't that valuable and probably could be counted as payment for all his hard work, anyway.

But just as the sky started to change hues, he snuck around the back of the workshop and started rolling zip rocks in along with spark leaves, twisting the edges of the water-tight packet just like his favorite uncle had taught him . . .

"Cog! What have you got there?" one of the farmhands said as she came up on his not-so-hidden spot, trying to catch a glimpse of what was in his hands. Cog slipped the packet into his pocket, not bothering to hide the guilty look on his face.

"They gave me some sweets for the rest of the kids . . . I just wanted to try one!" he wheedled.

The farmhand's eyes softened, and a knowing smile quirked the edge of her mouth. "Oh, alright. I won't tell, then. But it is time to come along."

Idiots, Cog thought, disgusted at how quickly she had bought that load of Auroch crap.

"Everybody ready?" he whispered into the large room where they usually bedded down for the night. Milas sat straight up as she threw off the covers to reveal her fully clothed form, her horns glinting in the moonlight. If he was the brains of the outfit, she was the brawn.

"Yeah, we are all ready to go. You got the goods?" she whispered back. Cog nodded slowly in response, his teeth glinting in sharp anticipation.

"What's the status on Flavian?" she turned and whispered to the little form at the door.

"He's out!"

"Alright, let's move. And for Pit's sake, everyone keep quiet!" Cog said up, barely keeping his own voice down in his excitement.

The whole group filed out into the short hall and past Flavian, the farmhand who had watch duty tonight. He liked to sit for the first part of his watch and would almost always be asleep by the time his shift was up.

They eased through the outside door and past the farmhands' house, where the rest of the workers slept. Both George and Edna had been called away almost every night as stray bad guys pressed the barriers at different points near the wall.

If they were ever going to make it to the Temple, tonight was their night. The moon shone brightly as they moved through the quiet fields, staying as close to the river as possible.

This was the trickiest part of their plan. The newly built stone bridge was guarded and not an option . . . But the old ice bridge had held up surprisingly well, showing as a sparkling ruin just above the water upstream from the stone bridge. It was almost completely gone, but it could still be crossed if they were careful . . . and small.

Milas had perfected this over the last few days, and she helped each of their group over the uneven, mostly melted structure. Once they were all over to the other shore, and quite a bit wetter, they followed the riverbank until it met the base of the mountain.

It would take about an hour or two to climb in the dark, but they would be halfway up before the next farmhand woke Flavian at midnight and found them missing.

Too late to stop them.

CHAPTER FIFTY-FIVE

Bring Back Vine

Jonathan Tillman – Level 35 Son of Flame

The scroll of notifications zipped by him at an enormous speed, and his mind quailed at the thought of pulling out the pertinent information while his friends were dying on the battlefield.

But he refused to rush on and leave resources on the table that he could use to help their cause. So, he settled for a quick and dirty review of the high points. In a flash of inspiration, he mentally instituted a filter that combined all of his level-up notifications into one line, and after another moment's thought, he got rid of all the notifications concerning *experience*. Instead, he asked the system to display his percentage of *experience* gained until the next level, saving him a headache as those numbers grew exponentially.

The changes took place immediately; the math was nothing to whatever operating system governed the backend of his user interface. The notifications blurred together and left him with a final result.

> ***Congratulations!*** *You are now level 35.*
>
> *You have earned 60 stat points to distribute plus 24 points in Endurance and 12 points in Dexterity.*

Tilly hurriedly pulled up his stat spread and did some math to make sure he kept [Resolute]. He added to his stats as evenly as possible, shoring up some weaknesses while keeping the insane imbalance he had committed to.

> ***Stats:***
>
> *Constitution: 23 > 26*

> *Endurance: 145 (159.5) > 150*
>
> *Dexterity: 52 (57.2)*
>
> *Strength: 13 > 23*
>
> *Wisdom: 28 > 30*
>
> *Intelligence: 16 > 18*

Despite the injuries and debuff, the stat distribution made an immediate difference. As the points hit, energy rushed through his body, easing strain and strengthening muscles and ligaments. Tilly groaned as he sat up and looked over to see Amelia catching her breath, lost in concentration. Concentric circles of plant growth flowed out from her body rhythmically in time with her breathing.

"Are you doing that on purpose?" Tilly asked, turning to look the way they had come and seeing their path marked by a verdant streak of wild growth through the forest.

"I am afraid not . . . My pathways are overflowing with the Facet's energy. Even in its dormant state, it is constantly pushing my mana past a hundred percent," she said, then screwed her eyes shut as a particularly large burst of greenery surged out around her and washed the area in a riot of spontaneous growth.

Taking that as one more sign that he needed to hurry the hell up, he zipped through the rest of the notifications, rapidly taking in just how many multipliers were involved in Kindle's last strike. [Divine Wind] and [**Origin's** Champion] had affected her final attack, and he smiled in pride at how fiercely she had struck down the Prime Dirge . . .

Then his smile turned back downward as he reflexively reached along their bond and found nothing. He quickly shoved that worry down, promising himself he would return to it as soon as this was all done.

Finally, he found the end of his notification scroll and caught sight of two new Titles.

> ***Congratulations!*** *You have died and been reborn due to the intervention of a Facet of Origin connected to growth and rebirth.*
> *You have been awarded the Title: [**Verdant Rebirth**].*
>
> *[**Verdant Rebirth**]: Power from one of the Land's key nexus points was used to restart your nonfunctioning heart and regrow essential bodily systems damaged in your cleansing. This has fundamentally marked you. You are now a part of the Land's deeper tapestry and will be recognized as such by its fellow denizens.*

> ***Congratulations!*** *You have struck down an enemy over 5 times*
> *your level while emptying yourself of all internal resources to do so.*
> *You have been awarded the Title: [**All or Nothing**].*
>
> *[**All or Nothing**]: Once a day, you may choose to channel*
> *all of your mana into a single Ability.*
> *This Title is limited by Intelligence.*

After that last notification, Tilly glanced up hopefully at the other side of his HUD before sighing in disappointment and stumbling to his feet while his body screamed in protest.

Health: 38%
Mana: 22%

The first Title was another nebulous one like [Scarred Heart]. He wouldn't be able to measure its effect, but judging by the events that had just unfolded, he was sure his most mysterious Title must have been operating on an unseen level. He took another moment to collect himself and stumbled forward to the edge of the stream. Amelia looked over at him inquiringly, and he just smiled, completely unaware of the dirt and blood that was caked all over his face.

"I'm good . . . Let's do this. River, we are ready!" Tilly called, and Amelia shuffled beside him, now clutching at her midriff and attempting to school her breathing.

He was about to call again when the water began to froth, and a very different being stepped forth from its depths. Where Old Man River's features had been marked by a neatly defined beard and balanced symmetrical features, the thing that stepped out of the water was distinctly more chaotic in its visage.

It still resembled a large man covered in scales, but it had wild spray dancing around its head for hair and churning waters flowed down from its chin. Its back was stooped, and its eyes were different hues of blue and green.

"It would be my pleasure to carry you . . . Cousin?" it said, looking at Tilly curiously, as if trying to identify an interesting bug. "And you as well, blessed one," it said to Amelia.

Before Tilly could utter a hesitant thank you, the thing struck fast as a snake, elongating its arms and yanking them into itself. Tilly didn't even have time to scream as a thunderous churn of water pressed in on him from every side and caused his body to flip end over end. Water invaded his mouth, and he barely kept himself from gasping in surprise as his lungs immediately began to spasm in response to the tumultuous experience.

Then, as quickly as it had begun, he felt the distinct impression of being shoved from behind, and his body violently broke the surface of the water, arced through the air, and landed with a thud on the riverbank.

Gasping for air in between coughs, Tilly looked back at the waters that had just spat them out and saw the crazy being's head just above the water leering at him. As soon as it noticed Tilly's gaze, it winked and sank back down into the river. Then Tilly noticed the new growth bursting forth on the shore. He looked over at Amelia in growing concern. Her breathing was labored, and her eyes were screwed shut in concentration. Tilly spotted small flowering vines poking out from the sleeves and collar of her coat.

"How much longer can you carry it?" he asked, his voice tightening.

"I don't know, but the music is deafening. I can barely think," she replied in a murmur.

Tilly hauled himself to his feet and moved over to help Amelia as he took in the mayhem playing out on the plains before them. The once focused might of the horde was now scattered over miles, consuming itself. Everywhere he looked, Tilly could see creature fighting creature in a frenzy of gore and animalistic fury.

Ahead of them, fighting in a shambling retreat, were their allies. Tilly pulled Amelia's arm over his shoulder and started to shuffle forward, partially supporting her and partially leaning into her for balance as his own body slowly recovered from its greatest trauma yet.

Franklin voiced a distant exclamation upon spotting the pair, but his words were lost in the tumult of battle. The chaos had not yet made it to the river, but Franklin's group continued to gain the attention of a steady flow of enemies looking for something to consume.

Tilly drew one hatchet as he and Amelia neared the edge of the conflict, and the ragged formation of his friends continued to retreat toward the river. A deep bestial roar drew his attention to the front line of their formation, and he was surprised to see a giant gore-soaked polar bear. It was covered in gashes and lacerations that bled a glowing blue substance, yet its ferocity seemed undiminished.

A smile cracked Tilly's concerned visage as he realized that Old Man River had not skimped on his reward to Franklin. The honu himself seemed more or less uninjured and was helping along an uncharacteristically drunk-looking Ichiro, who had blood running down from his eyes like tears. Hilbert shuffled behind them clutching a broken arm, the left side of his robes stained a sopping red.

Gorock held the left side of their formation and was an absolute mess of wounds. While he didn't seem to be slowed by any of them, blood puddled on the ground every time he stopped moving to block a strike with his shield or ward back an attacker with a sweep of his spear. Sir Michael held the other flank, his shield buckled into a misshapen concave bowl and his enchanted armor covered in dents.

None of the group was missing, and for that Tilly was thankful. He hobbled to meet them, trying to stay ahead of the threat of being surrounded by a growing tide of enraged enemies. Both groups would have been overwhelmed in seconds if not for the fact that most of the horde were busy fighting themselves, having broken into thousands of small conflicts of dominance.

"It is good to see you, my friends!" Franklin exclaimed tiredly as they neared enough to be heard. "Did you do it? Do we have the Facet's patronage?"

Tilly winced, and Amelia answered in a tense voice, "Not yet. We have to deliver it to the Temple." She followed her answer with a groan, and Tilly felt power rush out of her and into the ground as a wave of explosive growth shot out in all directions.

The growth hit the other group, and they momentarily stumbled over the now waist-high wild grasses flowering with exuberant blooms. They soldiered on through it and finally met about a hundred yards from the river.

Franklin disentangled himself from Ichiro and produced the glowing conch shell, then began to whisper over it. Amelia likewise pulled away from Tilly and eyed the surrounding enemies threatening to press in on their group.

She arduously produced her staff from one of her pockets and called, "Everyone, try not to move!" Then she whipped her other hand from another pocket and threw vine cuttings out into the crowd of enemies. She followed up the movement with a thump of her staff into the grass, and green light exploded from the crystal on its tip. The vine cuttings she had scattered around their group shot into the ground and emerged again with ropy, thorn-covered thickness to entangle the closest enemies while continuing to grow so fast that they combined to form a macabre wall of thorn-pierced enemies. The thicket continued to grow, becoming denser at the formation's perimeter, and fanned out deep into the milling chaos that was now the horde.

The rest of the group looked over at Amelia in awe. Strangely enough, her face relaxed into relief as a fierce green light continued to shine from her staff.

"I am carrying the Flower within me now . . . The power is overwhelming, to say the least," she explained.

Tilly's smile at her relief soured quickly as he noticed that the growths emerging from under her jacket had continued. Now the vines creeping up her neckline had mingled in with her hair, dotting her dark brown locks with blooming flowers.

"It is ready," Franklin added as he lifted the conch, which was now vibrating with potential energy.

"Do it," Tilly responded urgently, unable to take his eyes off the vines that seemed to be growing out from her body.

Franklin threw down the shell and it shattered. The reaction was far greater than Tilly had anticipated; the enchanted object had seemed to be much more fragile than the grassy soil. The glowing script that had covered it, however, did not break along with the shell. In fact, it hung in place above the broken object and began to whirl and expand, now free to accomplish its purpose.

"Hold on!" Franklin called as the entire group was drowned in deep blue light.

CHAPTER FIFTY-SIX

Running Up That Mountain

Jonathan Tillman – Level 35 Son of Flame

A wave of azure energy swept them up and slammed them down. Except, as they hit the ground, it shifted from rusty grass to stone. The bottom of Tilly's moccasins landed easily on the hard surface, and he opened his eyes to find himself once again in the old village square.

A shout of surprise followed by a gasp of disbelief greeted them as Tilly spun around to take in the state of his faction's city. His ragged allies joined him, scanning their surroundings with weapons drawn. Looks of relief softened the harsh lines of concern on their faces as they found the city intact and undamaged. One of two honu elders rushed forward, having waited to meet them.

"Thank **Origin** . . . We felt the spell activate . . . I got here in time!" she exclaimed.

At the look in her shining eyes and the familiar sight of what had once been a simple village square, Tilly could not hold back a tide of comfort that rolled over his battered psyche. After such a harrowing journey of completely new environments, returning to something vaguely familiar lifted a weight off his shoulders. Unlike the Twilight Lands, the moon hung in the sky in full view, and Tilly relished the scene of the moon-washed city as they all got their bearings.

The faint sounds of battle reached his ears as his mind fully adjusted to his new environment.

"Are you well? . . . Did you complete the quest?" she asked, her voice quieting slightly as she belatedly took in the sight of the polar bear covered in gore.

"We are close, Mother, but some of our number must be delivered to the Temple," Franklin answered for the group. Tilly looked over to check on Amelia and found her on her knees, dazed. He quickly got an arm under her shoulders and hauled her to her feet as she struggled to adjust.

The honu elder nodded at Franklin's answer and waved her sextant-topped staff over them, washing them in cool magic. "This is a small . . . blessing . . . One that should . . . help you find speed along your path."

"What is the situation at the wall?" Ichiro asked in a slurred voice, rivulets of blood still leaking from his eyes.

"The enemy . . . has launched its . . . full force against us . . . We are holding . . . But barely."

Tilly looked up from Amelia to the others and said, "I think I need to be the one to take Amelia to the Temple. Are you all able to fight?"

The others nodded, and Gorock even smiled at the question as he swayed unsteadily on his feet. "We are at your disposal until this is done," Hilbert answered with a tired conviction as he shook out his recently broken arm. He took a deep pull from his flask, and Sir Michael took the opportunity to use his injector.

Tilly smiled grimly at them. "Good. See you on the other side."

Then he slung Amelia's arm over his shoulder and started to hobble away as briskly as he could manage. If time was as short as he believed, he didn't have another moment to waste. She leaned heavily on him, and her staff dragged behind her. Wild growth followed its path over the hard-packed dirt, marking Tilly's line through the expanded square. The others moved off in the opposite direction in a steady jog toward the wall and the battle that waited there.

Marcellus the Elder — Level 56 Corrupted Aristocrat

It had been simple to grab the priestess brat as she slept, gagging her and removing any chance of her activating one of those disgusting *Abilities*. Then things had become complicated.

He had gathered a pitiful fifteen men in his time in this wretched camp, encouraging the small amounts of **Corruption** he had found in each of them to grow, making them more malleable to his will until they were little more than puppets. In that time, he had received instructions and learned of the critical weakness of the power exalting itself in the Temple.

The gift inside him squirmed in response to the thought, and he looked back in frustration at the men tasked with moving the girl. She had been wrapped in cloth and thrown in with supplies on a hand cart. One with a ghastly rusting wheel hub that was distracting. As annoying as it was, the noise drew the attention of anyone they passed to the wheel of the cart and away from any pitiful mewling that emerged from under the piles of fake supplies. This had worked like a charm as they passed through the camp and to the base of the mountain.

The idiot pulling the cart, however, looked like he was going to be sick and moved at an increasingly slow pace.

"What are you doing?" Marcellus the Elder whispered fiercely, dropping back to berate the bumbling fool. The closer he got to the cart, the more his insides clenched in discomfort.

"Sir . . . It's the girl," the supposedly strong portly man in a butcher's smock whined pitifully. "Being near her hurts something dreadful."

Marcellus the Elder screwed up his face in disgust, making sure to show none of his own discomfort. "You have a simple task with an extraordinary reward, but it is plain to me that you are too weak to achieve it . . . You can and will be replaced," he threatened with all of his menace, even allowing his hood to fall back slightly and show some of his glorious new form.

The man flinched back, moaning in terror. "I'll do it. Please, just let me change out with one of the others when we meet up."

Marcellus the Elder scowled as he pulled his hood back into place with some of his new appendages. "You will do as I command, or you will die. Now, stop squealing like a pig and pick up the pace!"

Even with his motivating presence, the trip took twice as long as it should have. Instead of arriving with plenty of time to set up the space for their meeting with the Bureaucrat, they arrived at the chosen spot barely ahead of him.

The rest of his men had arrived in twos and threes over the last hour, with the exception of those he had shadowing their target. He had been forced to switch out the ones pulling the cart multiple times as their complaining grew to unbearable levels. Marcellus looked forward to killing all of these imbeciles.

"Hurry up, you fools! It is almost time!" he spat out in annoyance, having to force himself to keep from shouting.

They had set up at a flatter portion of the trail, with lots of low bushes covered in little blue berries. The path here ran parallel with a creek bed, which gave his men ample places to hide for the initial part of the meeting. The cart rolled into place to block the path just ahead of him, and the one pulling it immediately edged away. Marcellus fought to not do the same as proximity to the girl turned his stomach.

"You and you, stay in plain sight. The rest of you, conceal yourselves just like we discussed!" he commanded as he gestured to his two most intimidating flunkies to flank the cart and their cargo.

Just as they hid, a skinny one-armed satyr raced up the path, the gaps in his teeth visible in the moonlight as he pulled to a stop, huffing, before Marcellus.

"Out with it!" Marcellus growled.

"Two with him, and two hidden following behind," the man gasped, his face screwing up as the girl's presence washed over him. "Gods . . . What is that?" he moaned, the flushed color of his face draining to something pale and sickly.

"Do the ones I sent to follow know what to do?" Marcellus asked, absolutely disgusted by the weakness on display before him.

The man hesitated to answer, looking like he was about to vomit. This ratcheted Marcellus's fury to a new level, and before he could even consciously consider his actions, part of his new form had whipped out from behind his layers of robes and wrapped around the insect's neck.

Snap.

He could not stand incompetence. The men behind him flinched at the display of power, and a rich syrupy feeling of pleasure rose up from his center. This was true strength! They would see . . .

They would all see.

Then, the thing that used to be Marcellus the Elder casually launched the corpse into the woods, keeping his hands comfortably at his sides.

Cog – Level 0 Gnomish Child

Things had been going so well until they started climbing the mountain. Before they had even hit the halfway point, someone had come behind them, huffing loudly.

"Get off the path!" he whispered desperately down the line, and the small figures vanished into the forest on either side of the trail. Everyone disappeared without a sound.

He would like to see what the adults thought of that . . .

No one in the originals had arrived at the old empire's capital on vacation, and every one of them knew what was at stake when the call came to hide. Cog ducked around a tree, hunching his already small form, and Milas slid into a dip nearby before going completely still in the deep shadows cast by the canopy. The moon was full, and no clouds hung in the sky, but that did not mean it was bright in the forest.

Soon enough, a one-armed satyr who Cog did not recognize jogged past, clearly struggling to make it up the mountain. He moved through their position none the wiser, and Cog slowly shifted to find Milas's eyes shining in deep shadow.

She raised her thick brow in a silent question, and he answered with a shrug. They both knew enough to wait until they could no longer hear him before slowly approaching each other, waving to the others they could see to remain in place while they figured out what to do next.

"Who was that, and what is he doing heading toward the Temple?" she asked.

"Pits if I know. But he sure as the Six Princes wasn't one of the Watch."

"What shou—"

Something crashed in the forest up ahead, and both of the young conspirators shot uncertain looks up the path. Then, before they could discuss what was happening, another nasally voice sounded, moving up the path.

"Did you hear that, Aticus? Whoever they are, these men must be buffoons. Keep your weapons at the ready! I have no patience for fools."

Milas sunk down, and Cog knelt back at the base of the tree, hoping to catch a glimpse of the new group moving up the mountain. The sound of constant murmured grumbling approached, interspersed with the heavy hoof clops of armed satyrs.

Suddenly, the man stopped right as he was passing Cog's position and turned. Cog's silent breathing hitched in his throat at the unprompted stop. Turning to look past the two watchmen, the man said in a steady but carrying voice, "Make sure to stay out of sight until I call for you, and for the gods' sake, keep quiet, we are almost there." He spoke to two shadowing figures further back, who Cog only now noticed due to the direct address of the satyr in charge.

Wait, I know this guy. He's the one with the funny name in charge of the camp . . . What in the Deep Pits is going on here?

The satyr in question smartly turned on his heel and continued up the mountain, and his two guards made sure to make what Cog now saw was an obvious amount of noise. Once they were out of sight, along with the two other watchmen with cloth stuffed into their armor, Cog almost stood back up, but Milas's heavy hand snaked around his ankle and squeezed desperately.

Cog froze in response, his prey instinct taking over as he heard a faint rustle of leaves from the path. He slowly moved his eyes to the young minotaur and saw her nostrils flaring as her dim eyes flitted up and down the path.

He followed her gaze and spotted two more figures covered in rags and dirt, bloodshot eyes shining in the dark. They crept up the path following after the strange procession. Both held naked blades in their hands, and their intentions were broadcast clearly by their almost silent movements and expressions of hungry anticipation.

Finally, they passed, and Cog hurried over to Milas's position, whispering desperately, "I don't know what is happening, but it can't be good. We can't bring the rest any further."

She nodded at him seriously, then crawled over to the next original's position, and said, "Plan's changed. Stay here. Cog and me will check ahead. Pass it along."

She turned to Cog, determination shining in her eyes, as gentle whispers continued down the line of hidden orphans. "We gotta do something," she declared softly in the shadowy light of the moon.

"Yeah," Cog said, fingering his emergency plan in his pockets. "We do."

CHAPTER FIFTY-SEVEN

Taken

Aurelia – Level 28 Priestess of Origin's Flame

It seemed impossible to take a full breath under the pile of dirty fabrics they had tossed on top of her after tying her up. All she could do was squirm uselessly, furious at herself for being used in this way. Her gag was so tight that every time she tried to open her mouth to scream, it seemed like more of it was pushed into her mouth. Tears leaked from her eyes as she moaned again and again trying to call for help without throwing up. Meanwhile, the constant whining grind of the wheel near her head drowned out her ability to hear anything outside of her own personal Pits of Despair.

After what felt like hours of bumping along an uneven path, they finally came to a stop. The indistinct mutterings clarified into garbled words as the grinding wheel hub ceased, and she heard a cruel voice begin issuing commands. Wherever she was, her captors were no longer concerned about being discovered.

Then a crash sounded off to the side of the cart, and silence reigned amongst her kidnappers, lasting the space of a few dozen shallow breaths through her nose. The smell of the used fabric scraps and her own sweat mingled in her nostrils as she fought to push down the rising panic that battered against the doors of her self-control.

In desperation, she again reached within and attempted one of the meditation techniques Erash had taught her. The movement and whining of the wheel hub had been too distracting before, but now that they had stopped, she tried again. Without her voice, she couldn't activate any of her class *Abilities*, but at this point, that didn't matter. She needed something, anything, to distract from the indistinct voices outside of her prison deciding her fate. Breathing as deeply as she could through her nose, she dived into her center, focusing on the small flame there and somehow managing to shove her panic into its burning heart. Fear and impotent fury drained away with every shallow breath, and soon, she had moved from being overwhelmed to regaining some control of her thoughts.

The cruel voice started up again, this time answered by a nasally one. The words were just beyond her ability to make out under all the layers of intervening material, so she kept focusing on feeding her flame, fighting to be ready for anything.

They needed her for something or else they would have already killed her. She refused to be a tool in the enemy's hands, and if they made the mistake of giving her a chance to fight, she would, even if they killed her. Breath by breath, she continued to shove her panic into the flame. The mana-generating connection at her core grew hotter and hotter as it slowly integrated with her soul on a deeper level under the pressures of her situation.

She did not know what it was accomplishing, but any progress was better than just lying there helplessly. Shortly after the voices began speaking, the materials above her were pulled away to reveal a leering, dirty face. The leer became a choking gag as the man yanked her into a sitting position, loosening the cloth that had bound her, but kept her gag intact.

She was yanked to her feet out of the cart, and a knife was shoved up under her throat, carelessly nicking her skin. She felt a dribble of blood trickle down her neck, joining the cold sweat that already covered her body.

Finally out of the cart, her attention was quickly drawn to the others crowding the small forest path. There was a man in crumpled official's garb, flanked by two watchmen. His face screwed up in outrage at the sight of her, and hope bloomed in her chest.

"What is this? She is barely more than a child!" the official snarled. The guards on either side of him drew their weapons.

"Now, now," the cruel voice demurred to her right. She slowly shifted her gaze over to him, trying to not disturb the knife at her throat, and saw a figure draped in many layers of grimy, dark cloth. "Do not be so hasty to dismiss your salvation. Sometimes, to protect one's people, a leader must do distasteful things . . . You have been lied to and used, just like the people you serve." An incredible feeling of foreboding radiated off of his figure. Aurelia had to suppress a shiver at his proximity.

The knife at her throat wiggled painfully as its holder suddenly retched, vomiting to the side behind her.

"Distasteful! This is the path forward you spoke of? This is nothing! Now, let her go, or I will be f-forced to take d-drastic action," the official said, his voice quavering.

The robed figure chuckled and gestured. At the signal, men stood up from the surrounding forest, all clutching weapons. "Perhaps the presence of your men has emboldened you irrationally . . . Let me help you with that."

Barely contained panic shattered what little confidence the official had, and his voice cracked as he screamed, "Now!" and desperately looked back the way he had come.

A flurry of motion rocked the night as weapons clashed, and grunts of effort erupted around Aurelia. She tried not to flinch as the watchmen were both overwhelmed and summarily executed, taking down several of her captors in the process.

The official backed away from the melee, shooting looks desperately behind him all the while, but out of the shadows, two more thugs emerged wielding knives already dripping with blood.

"Let me ask you again," the robed man's voice cut through the melee. "Will you do what is necessary to ensure the survival of your people? One death will prevent tens of thousands. Be a man and do what you must to save your constituents!"

The official swallowed and looked at Aurelia again, weighing his options. Hope died in her chest as the flame struggled to hold back the tide of despair that threatened to drown her. The sight of her would-be rescuers getting cut down in moments had cut her to her core, and a pang of deep guilt began to build even as she watched the man in front of her struggle to come to a decision. He licked his lips, eyes darting between her gagged form and the rest of her captors, who now outnumbered him eight to one . . .

"Why are you doing this? Why me?" he blurted.

"I represent the interests of the opposition. We are not at all what you have been told. You simply have to prove your sincerity with this small task, and when our forces take the city in a matter of hours, you will be spared."

At those words, something in the official's gaze shifted, hardening, and his eyes settled heavily back on the robed figure—broken, but not in the way Aurelia had expected.

"Ah, earlier you mentioned saving the whole camp. Now you specify me . . ."

The robed man spread his arms in a theatrical gesture. "No matter what, the first step is to take hold of your salvation!" he declared magnanimously, urging the man before him.

The official sighed, then reached into his robes and pulled out something that looked like a letter opener. "Very well. Where must it be done."

The robed figure laughed richly and the thugs around the official relaxed. "We will head up to the Temple and finish this unfortunate task," the robed figure answered, lowering his arms.

Aurelia quailed at the turn of events but saw the moment when the official's hand clenched down on the handle of his pitiful weapon. Eyes shining with unshed tears, he lurched into the nearest thug and plunged his letter opener into the thug's neck. The thug screamed, spurting blood all over the shocked face of his attacker, and the others fell on him, stabbing and bludgeoning the official until all that remained was a bloody pile of ruined clothing and bruised flesh and one pair of shattered spectacles.

"A pity . . . I thought for sure he was our best option for desecrating the Temple." The robed figure sighed in disappointment, then turned to Aurelia and let his hood fall back, revealing a horrifying visage. Something that might once have been a distinguished elderly satyr face looked back at her. Yet the strong angles of his sneering face were now intersected by thick, dark roots that dived in and out of the flesh of his jaw and scalp in a seemingly random pattern. "Nonetheless, the **Seed** assures me that your blood spilled in the sanctuary will be enough to cut off the flame's influence for now. We can find another innocent to pervert its power later."

Aurelia bit back a moan of terror even as the flame within her blazed in resistance to the mind-numbing emotion blanketing her thoughts and making her feel pitiful and small again.

I'm all alone . . . It's my fault they are dead—

"Man, you guys are really stinking up this mountain!" a high-pitched voice called from slightly down the path. The whole group turned in surprise to see a comically small figure casually step out from the forest. "You know there is a river right next to camp? No charge or anything," he continued, stepping into the moonlight. His voice warbled in false bravado, and his hands shook as he clenched something in both his fists.

*Oh **Origin**, it's Cog!* Aurelia thought desperately, her teeth clenching on her gag.

"Who are you, little boy? And how did you find us?" the **Corrupted** satyr hissed, unconcerned. The thugs all raised their weapons and began to move toward him.

"Not so fast, Stink Gang, or whatever you call yourselves!" he sputtered as he raised his fist dangerously. He was terrified, yet the absolute impossibility of this confrontation made the thugs hesitate at his threat. "I have two fistfuls of gnomish explosives right here, ready for anyone who wants to take them. Now, Give. Me. Back. My. Sister!" he finished with a shout, actually stepping forward with his threat. Aurelia's insides twisted in fear for him even as his words bolstered the flame in her chest to an inferno.

"You idiots! The boy is bluffing. Kill him and then search for any other rats hidden on this Pit-cursed mountain!" the robed figure yelled.

"Have it your way!" Cog shouted back as he lobbed the contents of his fists at the oncoming thugs. He immediately dived away and caused the rush of individuals to flinch as the small objects he had thrown scattered before them.

Everyone was staring down, confused, at the point of impact, when a disorienting series of flashes and bangs exploded from the ground, one after another, in a rapid staccato of light and sound. The thugs screamed, and even Aurelia had to blink back tears as her vision was filled with afterimages.

The knife at her throat suddenly vanished, and she heard the man behind her cursing vehemently.

"Kill the boy!" the robed figure screeched in frustration.

The blazing stars faded from her sight as she slowly reached to remove the gag from her mouth, not wanting to alert anyone with a sudden movement. The cursing behind her suddenly ceased, and her hand froze, hovering above her gag . . .

Had he seen her?

Then the flame within her roared over her fear, and she realized she would rather be stabbed in the back than used in this ploy to destroy her people. In one motion, she yanked the wadded cloth from her mouth and whipped her head around, ready to ward off the blow she knew must be coming.

But it didn't. Instead, she found a scared-looking young minotaur standing over her unconscious captor.

"Milas?" she whispered, her voice horse and dry. The girl smiled for just an instant before the commotion behind them demanded their attention. The group of thugs had caught Cog, and he was now struggling uselessly, shouting in defiance with a courage that belied his small form. They began pounding into his little body with punches and kicks, punishing him for his impudence. Milas moaned in fear, but the sight did something altogether different inside Aurelia. Her flame, already blazing, exploded from within her.

One of the thugs grew tired of the game and pulled back his knife to end it.

Something inside Aurelia broke.

Her limits, her place in this world, her self-doubt . . . They all shattered along with it.

"Get away from my brother!" she screamed as the forest around her began to dance with blue and white light.

Her words thrummed with power, and a new *Ability* lit up her mana pathways as she instinctively reached for something, anything, to save him.

Jonathan Tillman – Level 35 Son of Flame

Amelia's weight had shifted more and more onto his shoulder as they moved through the camp at a hobbling jog. To make matters worse, greenery kept sprouting all over her form, adding even more weight to the awkward movement.

But Tilly soldiered on, listening to each gasping breath issuing from Amelia's mouth with mounting worry. By the time they started climbing the mountain, she had lost the ability to walk and was sucking in air desperately as she tried to lift her feet so they would not drag and slow them further.

With a grunt of exertion, Tilly squatted down and threw her body across his shoulders, then straightened up and picked up the pace. Amelia groaned—whether in pain or protest, Tilly could not tell, but seeing the vines now completely covering her exposed skin had done it for him.

Somehow, he pushed his jog into a sprint. He squeezed everything he could out of his new stats as his patchwork of injuries and debuffs did their best to tear apart his only recently restored body.

Thankfully, the moon was bright enough that even well into the night, he could make his way up the worn path without much trouble. He pumped his legs over and over, sucking in as much breath as his cramping torso would allow.

Bang, bang, bang!

Bang!

Bang, bang, bang, bang, bang!

Tilly almost tripped at the sudden interruption as a staccato of small explosions sounded further up the path.

No way this is anything but more bad news.

He growled down at his legs, urging his thrusting knees to increase their pace.

"Get away from my brother!" a screaming voice demanded from above.

As Tilly ran up the path, he saw little figures standing in the forest to either side. He almost dropped Amelia and grabbed his weapons before realizing they were all children . . .

The kids Edna and George were taking care of.

That's when the voice fell into place in his memory. Tilly rolled Amelia off his shoulders to the ground and called his hatchets into his hands as he burst into an all-out sprint. Blue flames lit up the forest ahead of him as he ran up the mountain.

CHAPTER FIFTY-EIGHT

Tree, Part 3

The sound of multiple screams egged him on as Tilly topped an upward bend in the path and emerged into a scene of fiery conflict. Seven or eight satyrs were arranged in a writhing circle around a little lump of clothing. A familiar blue fire was everywhere, originating from another confrontation still playing out twenty yards beyond the initial scene of destruction.

Tilly's eyes momentarily struggled to make sense of the twisting mass of root-like appendages surging toward the source of the flames. In the middle of the inferno was Aurelia, the priestess. Her whole body had been set alight as she pushed out wave after wave of fire.

"YOU THINK THIS IS ENOUGH TO STOP ME?" a screaming voice cajoled from the center of the root creature's mass. It rolled forward, attempting to push through the waves of fire being released by Aurelia. The priestess held up both hands in a warding posture, screaming in effort. The roots were constantly being burned away but regrew at an equal rate, offsetting the damage and allowing the thing to inch closer to the girl.

As soon as he registered the enemy, Tilly's body whipped into action. He engulfed his weapons with his mana and sent them whirling toward the enemy. They each hit with a wooden-sounding *thunk* as they cut deep into the cloth-bound center of the creature, evoking a caterwauling scream before the thing turned away from the object of its wrath.

"Hey, you overgrown shower clog! Roll your ass over here and try me on for size!" Tilly called as he stepped over the pitifully mewling bodies on the path before him to stand unobstructed before the thing. As the expanding mass of dark, ropy roots rotated to face him, Tilly saw that nested in between the tightly bound layers of dirty clothing and writhing appendages was a face. One rendered almost unrecognizable by the roots diving in and out of its flesh.

But the eyes, filled with icy hate and brimming over with cold superiority, were a dead giveaway. Behind the creature, Aurelia collapsed, her fire sputtering out as the last of her mana was used up.

Level 56, Corrupted Aristocrat

"Ah! The cockroach himself! What a happy coincidence to meet you here at my ascension. I am eager to snap your neck myself before I cut off this pitiful excuse for a faction from its benefactor!" The speaker's original body seemed to be gone, now lost in layers of cloth suspended by hundreds of roots.

Tilly recalled his hatchets, trying not to reveal his dismay at how ineffective the attacks seemed to be. The place where his hatchets had lodged in the creature's side had burned away and detached from the whole before quickly being replaced by new growth. If he was going to take this thing out, he would have to bypass the shifting mass of wooden roots and hit this guy in the face.

Trying to buy time, he called, "I didn't see it before, but man, the resemblance is uncanny! You are the spitting image of your son. The apple really doesn't fall far from the tree . . ."

Marcellus the Elder chuckled in reply as he advanced slowly, roots tearing up the ground in front of him like a hundred-legged spider. "You did me a favor getting rid of that weakling . . . My true heir was always the eldest. After this, I'll bring that pup to heel, and we will take our place at the front of this glorious revolution."

Tilly peeked behind him as he considered a short retreat to draw this thing further away from Aurelia and did a double take. The little lump in the middle of all the bodies had rolled over and was struggling to get to its feet.

Cog . . . Shit, looks like it's here and now, he thought to himself desperately as he turned back to the slow, confident advance of the monstrosity. His patched-together internal healing felt like it was ripping at the seams, but Tilly bore the sensation with a scowl, shifting his weight to try something else.

"Ah, how the bravado of the ant dies before my stomping hoof," Marcellus the Elder sneered out spitefully. Tilly responded by spinning in place, then releasing and calling back his hatchets in a fiery whirlwind of rapid attacks and feints to try and make it past the layered guard. But the curtain of roots rose seamlessly, absorbed the hits accompanied by small blue explosions, then fell away and were replaced.

Even the lingering embers that would typically do damage over time were shed along with the dead roots, removing their effect on the whole. As disturbing as Marcellus's new form was, he was now a perfect counter to Tilly's burst damage area-of-effect and damage over time. **Flame Expulsion** would not work, and neither would his thrown axes—not until he got past that guard . . .

The roots parted mockingly before him in a twisted game of peekaboo. Marcellus's leering face peeked out from in between his myriad appendages, and he crooned, "Let me show you what true power feels like!"

Then, almost moaning in ecstasy, he shed any guise of sanity, and the many feelers of his new form quivered in anticipation before he suddenly shot toward his prey. Tilly's weapons twitched as he tried in vain to figure out how to get out of this one.

His only chance was to get as close as possible and activate **Flame Expulsion**, hopefully before Marcellus raised his guard back up. Tilly adopted a mask of hopelessness—something that wasn't much of a challenge in his current circumstance—and dropped his hatchets in defeat. Marcellus's root-pierced visage pulled up short of his charge and paused to lean toward Tilly through his curtain of defense, black ichor dribbling like drool from a too-wide smile.

Internally, Tilly steeled himself . . . Kid or no kid, as soon as that thing grabbed him, he was going to activate his new Title [All or Nothing] in tandem with **Flame Expulsion** and see if he couldn't take this bastard out.

Then the trees all around them groaned and the ground undulated like a quivering mass of jelly. For a moment, Tilly was afraid that it was some sort of new *Ability* from his opponent, but Marcellus's leer fell into a grimace, and he plunged more roots into the ground to stabilize himself.

Tilly's mana pathways had lit up in preparation to take advantage of the surprise when the surrounding flora erupted in a flurry of growth. The ground all around the Corrupted Aristocrat exploded as roots native to the mountain burrowed in amongst their invading counterparts, and tree limbs shot in to tangle the floating curtain of appendages that fanned out around Marcellus the Elder's transformed body.

"What is this?" he cried as he tried to pull away from the entanglement. Then the combined force of all the new growth simultaneously went taut, pulling away all of his additional protections, and left his center of mass exposed.

He cried out in impotent frustration and the beginnings of fear.

A strained voice rose from behind Tilly, ringing with a finality that sealed Marcellus's fate.

"Get away from my kids, you piece of shit!"

Not one to waste the opportunity before him, Tilly shifted the Title's focus to his first and simplest *Ability*. He enflamed the hatchet in his right hand with twenty to thirty times the normal amount of mana, and an immense *WUMPH* went off at his side as he felt the very nature of his Soul-Bound weapon shift in response to contain the new power. Tilly lunged forward, swinging his weapon in a simple downward chop, and delivered a strike like a blue solar flare into the face of his opponent.

For just a moment, Marcellus the Elder's **Corruption**-infested expression was brightly illuminated in stark blues, a caricature of shock, then the concussive blast of the overcharged *Ability's* impact turned Tilly's world white and blew him back through the air. A series of branches attempted to arrest his flight, which ended decisively as he hit the thick trunk of a tree. He fell to the ground, his body finally giving out after hours of relentless abuse.

There on the ground, he groaned incoherently as he tried to muster up the strength to get an arm under him, a knife-like ringing cutting through the center of his head. The blast had addled him, and his thoughts fell through his mental fingers like sand as he fought to impose his will on his disjointed extremities. They refused to answer his confused mental urgings, and he lay there in a heap like a puppet with cut strings.

"Amelia . . . Temple . . . ," he muttered to himself, his lips dry and cracked, half of his face dug into the ground he had collapsed in. His thoughts swam in lazy circles, utterly refusing to form a linear plan.

At the periphery of his awareness, many small hands grabbed his limp body, then pulled him up and dragged him forward, advancing arduously up the mountain path. Tilly's consciousness flashed in and out as unknown debuffs fought against his will to stay awake. His regen struggled to balance out the toll they demanded as his battered body clung to consciousness with the rigid stubbornness of a two-year-old.

Blink.

Some children moved past holding Cog's small, weak body between them.

Blink.

A young minotaur dragged a tangle of vines and branches larger than her body up the obstacle-strewn path. She was crying and others were walking behind the mass of greenery, lifting and pushing where they could.

Blink.

High-pitched voices argued about what to do next as an ornate wooden entrance stood open before the group. Then they all went silent as a groggy voice muttered, "Oh Cog! Are you okay?"

Blink.

Warmth flooded Tilly's body as ligaments and muscles that had been operating on sheer will for far too long knit back together. The muddled soup that was his mind clicked back into operation and his eyes snapped open.

He was surrounded by the same kids he had seen outside Amelia's shop months ago. At the front of the group stood a frazzled Aurelia, tears streaking down her face, and behind her rested a huge messy tangle of still-growing plants.

Tilly looked around in confusion as he found himself in the crystal chamber of the Temple, its steady glow offering comfort to the distraught group.

"I'm sorry, Mr. Tillman! This isn't something I can fix. I can barely sense her in the middle of all that strange mana," Aurelia cried, waving hysterically at what used to be Amelia. The whole of the situation crashed into Tilly's rebooting mind, and he lurched to his feet, his body wobbling uncertainly.

"Come on, we have to get her to the central chamber," he said confidently, not at all sure if that was all they needed to do, but hoping desperately, nonetheless. He stumbled over to the car-sized mass and grabbed onto a few sturdy-looking branches, then started hauling it toward the inner hallway, which was just barely wide enough to accommodate Amelia's increased size.

He groaned in effort as his healing body attempted to leverage the full extent of his newly increased *Strength*. The children quickly scampered in around him, grabbing anything they could, and lent their collective effort to the endeavor. The mass began to move, scraping along the walls and floor as they pulled and pushed for all they were worth.

After a long thirty yards, they arrived at the central chamber. The fit through the last door was the tightest yet, and the effort to get the tangled knot of vegetation through caused the whole group to tumble out into the slightly sloped chamber as they pulled her free of the impediment.

Tilly, who had been hauling backward and pulling with both hands from an almost seated position, landed flat on his back as the resistance vanished and Amelia's flora-choked form entered the central chamber of the Temple.

A roaring flash erupted from the altar in response to their arrival, and Tilly, from his position on the ground facing Amelia, saw a subtle green flash answer it, originating from the center of the mass.

A jet of blue fire shot out from the altar, and the vegetation all around Amelia began to wither and die, meeting the flame as dry tinder, ready to be consumed. Tilly almost cried out in distress before seeing the flame immediately pull back as the vegetation was consumed, leaving an unharmed Amelia surrounded by a cloud of ash.

Her eyes opened, and she smiled in relief as green motes of energy so potent that they set Tilly's teeth on edge emerged from her core and drifted by him toward the waiting flame. Along with every other person in the chamber, he turned to watch the gentle shivering of the flame on the stone surface as music bubbled up all around them.

As soon as they appeared, the motes orbiting the flame shifted in time with the melody that was just beyond Tilly's ability to comprehend. As the song built they drifted nearer, until the chamber was flooded with an energy so rich in potential that Tilly felt his very soul start to vibrate in harmony with the song.

Tilly saw a thousand ends and ten thousand new beginnings as all of the universe expanded in an ever-evolving pattern of sound and light.

Amidst the crescendo, a small ember, brighter even than the surrounding flame, rose up from the center of the altar. The green dancing motes swung around in their orbit and crashed into the ember one by one, combining to make something new, adding to the depth of its multi-hued vibrancy.

Tilly's next breath seemed to take a lifetime as he watched the motes finish joining with the central ember and transform into a tiny, perfect **Seed**. The riot of energy flooding the chamber dampened and steadied along with the **Seed's** formation, and the urgent vibrancy of the moment faded, eliciting a sigh of loss and relief from its audience.

The **Seed** floated back down into the flame and slowly cracked open, then shot forth a delicate sprout with two little leaves. Then, as if the entire event had been a whisper designed to draw in their attention, a booming notification exploded out from the altar in a tidal wave of green and blue energy.

Congratulations! You have obtained the patronage of
Origin's Bloom and completed a Hidden Quest.
Quest Rewards incoming . . .

CHAPTER FIFTY-NINE

Glow Way Up

Jonathan Tillman—Level 36 Son of Flame

The wave of green and blue energy washed over Tilly and instantly cleared away his remaining debuffs and soothed his strained mana pathways. As his vision cleared, he saw that all that was left of the immense wave of energy was a dancing blue and green flame hovering before him. It floated there expectantly, and, not entirely sure what to do, Tilly followed his instincts and lifted his hands to the flame as if receiving a gift.

It split obligingly; its green nature moved toward Tilly's left wrist and its blue nature moved toward Tilly's right, and the flames elongated and cooled to form two silver bracelets. They were a matching set, one with a vibrant green crystal set in the midst of carved flames and the other with an electric-blue gem set in an intricate scene of interlaced flora.

Celestial Bracelets of Substitutional Might

Celestial . . . Isn't that the highest grade in existence? Tilly thought to himself as he pulled up his notification log to see just what these items were capable of. All around the chamber, the vibrant energy of change thrummed as Amelia and every member of the originals were transformed.

Linus – Level 69 Consul

Linus thrust his borrowed spear right into the eye of an oncoming Consumer that had leaped over the first rank using the hill of crumbled bodies as a springboard. With its momentum arrested on his spear, a soldier to his right screamed and chopped deeply into its neck even as it was still fighting to disembowel those in the second and third rank.

"PUSH THEM BACK!" the new Bastion commander called from somewhere down the wall. The Bastion's Unit Magic sent a concussive burst outward that cleared the top of the wall momentarily, buying the whole formation a few breaths of room.

"Second rank, fall back! Third, fill-in! Reserves, UP!" Linus called in a hoarse voice, his commands echoing up and down the wall as they took their moment of reprieve to refill the ranks supporting the stalwart Bastions on the front of the wall.

Incredibly, they were holding. The roiling mass of enraged enemies had been stopped, unable to clear the obstacle before them. For days the enemy had tested the stopping power of the soldiers on the wall, and repeatedly, the units stationed at the top had barely held. They had stood fast, taking minor but, over time, significant losses facing just a fraction of the enemy's might.

But this was a calculated risk, one that had finally paid off. From his time as their commander, he knew that even with the increase in average level, the Bastions would run out of Unit Magic to spend in the next couple of minutes, but they had successfully stopped the full weight of the charge against the wall, and now much of the enemy was clamoring over itself in confusion at the sudden halt in the attack.

In the distance, he heard the sound of inhuman roaring followed by a crash so loud that it rattled the sword sheathed on his hip. Whatever that cavalry was, their **Charge** *Ability* was like nothing Linus had ever seen.

His attention was drawn back to the battle before him as the Strigoi regrouped and sprinted up the mountain of their own dead to take running leaps at the Alliance's front line all over again, crashing like waves of enraged flesh against the bulwark of the Alliance's finest soldiers. Erash, guarded by Hiro, was down on one knee as she channeled all of her mana into the enchantment that spread her heal over time to the entire front line. Green energy sparked subtly around the Bastions' boots as her buff plus their own Unit Magic gave them everything they needed to stand fast.

The enemy died in the hundreds and then the thousands as the previously dominant Consumers met their match in the stalwart front-line defenders. If the Flesh Bags had been allowed to charge, it would have been a massacre. But the Consumers and lesser Strigoi alone were all strength and speed. With their momentum arrested against the immovable shields of the Bastions, they fell like so much wheat before the scythe, feeding the entire formation's *experience* at an incredible rate.

A screaming call was taken up at the center of the enemy's mass, one that spread to the entire back half of the forces that had come to take the wall. Linus's burgeoning hope came crashing back down as half of the charging enemy turned toward the surrounding cliffs and split their forces down the middle preparing to try and climb in order to circumvent the wall altogether.

"Rangers, Tide Callers, and third rankers! Get everything you have on those cliffs. Now!" Linus bellowed urgently before hefting his own spear and hurling it with incredible accuracy at one of the front-running Consumers.

He watched just long enough to see his throw find its mark among far too many misses from his still unskilled soldiers. Then he turned and shouted down into the logistics area, which was choked with all of their remaining soldiers in different states of injury or resupply.

"Reserves! Fall back and sweep the nearby forests! We have flankers incoming!"

Unfortunately for their plan, almost all of the unit's leaders were up on the wall holding the first rank against the horde, but he did hear one all too familiar voice start to rise above the chaos down below.

"Alright, you worthless slugs! Nap time is over! Get equipped and get into the trees! Kill anything that moves!"

That woman deserves a commendation, Linus thought wryly as he rushed to the units on the stairs. They would need to pass up their spears to replace the ones just lost in the initial volley . . .

Igor – Level 86 Vampiric Mesmer

An ear-splitting screech of frustration ripped itself free from between his teeth. This was not how it was supposed to be! The stubborn cattle had displayed a surprising amount of resilience in the face of their charge, and while Igor was confident he could break their cowardly collective *Abilities* himself, doing so would embroil him in hand-to-hand conflict.

That was less than ideal if he wanted to be the first to reach the succulent prize at the heart of this little faction. He flexed his *will* in fury against Father's commands before once again finding them completely gone . . . He had already forgotten he was now free.

Why play by the rules? Why delay?

He layered *Command* over his voice and called for a change in the attack. Any of the horde too far from the wall to make themselves useful were to pull away from the frontal assault and take to the cliffs.

Then, using even more of his dwindling mana, he shrouded himself in **Plain Visage**, siphoned off as much mana as possible from the surrounding fodder, and started scaling the cliffs along with thousands of his weaker brethren. He could have pulled ahead but knew it would be easier to pass unnoticed amid the flood of his kin.

A pitiful few projectiles and *Abilities* swept along the vertical surface, removing hundreds of those around him but leaving thousands more untouched. They would flood the surrounding forest and sow chaos, providing the perfect distraction for Igor to pluck the prize he had so readily earned from this low-hanging branch.

As he joined the flow of fodder over the lip of the unnaturally tall cliff face, he became aware of something strange happening along the route that most of his inferiors had taken toward the cattle settlement. Howls of surprise and the sound of snapping wood greeted his senses as he followed the flow a little further into the forest until he found that many of his kin were locked in combat with . . . plants.

Igor growled in frustration at his own faction's stupidity. They continued to throw themselves into the carnage, not nearly as disciplined as they had once been under the heavy shackles of Father's *will*. He thought for a moment about redirecting them, but then he spat in disgust and left the idiotic conflict behind, choosing to range further laterally until he found a gap in whatever protection this was. Their purpose was chaos, and they were accomplishing it just fine.

He moved through the forest like a ghost, leaning into all the advantages that his respectable *Dexterity* gave him in this obstacle-strewn environment. Now that he was away from all the noise and stink that unfortunately always accompanied the horde, he was able to pick up a sharp, bitter smell about twenty paces closer to the settlement. It stung his nostrils and reminded him of burning metal.

His combat instincts, honed over decades of fighting every day for every scrap of power he had gained, kept him from pressing the mysterious protection multiple times. They prickled up and down his back as he attempted to approach the barrier. It was no enchantment—Igor would have tasted it on his tongue— but something had been set in place around the settlement that was dangerous to his kind.

His limited experience in magic was not enough for him to investigate further, and he honestly didn't care. He knew he didn't understand what was at play here, and that made him worry. He had not survived this long by being reckless . . . But his new strength gnawed at his insides, salivating for him to move in for the kill and take the prize hidden within. The **Hunger** he had won at the Bloodwells was not a patient force, and his rows of sharpened teeth cut fresh lines of blood in his gums as his jaw clenched in internal conflict.

Finally, the desperate part of his nature won out and he used half of his remaining mana and 20 percent of his health to summon **Blood Armor**. Wounds opened all along his body and blood gushed out, then immediately hardened into dozens of shell-like carapace plates that would block almost any strike, but shatter in the process. He was not too worried about the mana loss—he was sure there would be plenty of snacks on the way to find his unguarded prize.

Now fully armored, he changed the direction of his run like a striking snake and dived into the bitter-smelling line of magically fortified plants. They immediately reacted to his presence and whipped toward him with mana-enhanced speed, attempting to snare him in vines, branches, and roots.

He leaned fully into his build and dodged as many of the grasping plants as possible while making sure to only take hits on armored areas when he couldn't avoid the plants' touch. Blood carapace shattered around him as he burst through the hostile zone and left the reach of the animated guardians.

He sneered back at the inept defensive measure, then turned to orient himself and froze.

There, leaning against a tree, was one of the cattle. He looked gristly and seemed not to have noticed Igor crashing through the forest. Instead, he was entirely focused on lighting a pipe before taking a deep pull from its stem and releasing a smoke ring with a grunt of contentment.

Igor smiled, happy to take his meals raw or smoked. He sprang forward, clawed fingers extending to rip out the vermin's wrinkled neck, when the creature looked up and met his eyes.

There was no surprise there, not even concern, and Igor's combat instincts screamed at him. He broke off his lunge, strafing sideways, and lowered into a crouch as he eyed his surroundings warily for some trap.

"You were right again, wife," the elderly swine called as he looked down at Igor in amusement. His identifier read,

Level 58, Agriculturalist

Igor snarled in fury at his casual dismissal, especially when this was so clearly a weakling, but his instincts continued to scream at him to flee. Something about how they smelled did not match up with the low levels shown to him by the system.

"George, it's been three Epochs and you are still so quick to doubt."

Igor's head whipped to the side as another bony specimen stepped out from in between some trees.

Level 52, Arborist

Looking back and forth at these two, Igor began to feel an itch at the back of his mind. A lifetime of pushing against Father's influence had sharpened his *will* to a razor's edge, and his eyes narrowed in suspicion as the system-produced identifiers started to waver, as if covered in a haze.

"Not so fast, little monster," the elderly male rebuked as he shook his pipe stem at Igor in mock chastisement. That final dismissal of his superiority was enough to break Igor's caution. The **Hunger** screamed in him to kill, and he obliged. He lurched for the female in the blink of an eye, and his eyes lit up with **Mesmerize** as he strained toward her jugular with his claws.

Something like a vice clamped around his extended arm and arrested all of his momentum, nearly ripping his arm out of its socket. He looked up from the easy smile of the female to find the bony male's hand around his arm. Acting on instinct, he channeled all his remaining mana into his *Ability*, pouring weaponized hate out through his glowing red eyes.

The man stared back, his dull gray eyes slowly developing a multi-hued glow of their own. "You want into my head, do you? Suit yourself . . ." he muttered around his pipe stem.

Igor's *Ability* crashed into the man's soul and dissipated like a drop in the ocean. He tried to pull back, but the connection was already made, and the weight behind those eyes crushed his soul with barely a thought. The Vampiric Mesmer's body collapsed in a boneless heap as he screamed internally, locked away from any agency over his soon-to-be-ended life.

"That doesn't count, does it?" George asked, looking over at Edna, a few creases of worry forming around his eyes.

"I'm sure it doesn't. This is just saving us a little mess down the line. It doesn't change anything major," she answered as she moved over to pat him reassuringly on the shoulder.

A boom of energy sounded in the distance, and a light flashed near the top of the far mountain. Both of the elderly satyrs glanced in that direction, eyes reading through the many layers of reality with long practice.

"Oh, good! The dears made it. I knew all that trouble with little Cog would be worth it!" Edna said with a smile.

"Right again, dear," George replied as a slow easy smile stretched the corners of his mouth, forming a familiar network of lines that reached up to his eyes. "Right again."

CHAPTER SIXTY

Ends and Beginnings

Hiro Matsumoto – Guardian Daimyo of the Three-Fold Alliance

His charge had finally succumbed to her exhaustion, and with her, the enchantment bolstering the Bastion rank had flickered out. Hiro had been planning his next move for hours and instantly took her unconscious body and slung it back behind the wall with all his strength. He wanted her well clear of any enemy combatants while he was gone. She filled too important a role in the faction at present to let anything happen to her.

He watched as she crashed into a few tents before rolling to a stop over two hundred paces away. He was no longer surprised at what he was capable of with his newly bolstered *Strength*, and with her *Constitution*, such an impact would be negligible . . .

Once he was sure of her safety, he turned to the flagging front line. Behind them, the thinning second and third ranks barely held on in their support role as waves of enemies continued to crash against their formation. Linus had sent out the reserves as soon as the enemy's attack had shifted in nature, but now with no replenishment available and the healing gone, the first rank would soon break. Thousands of the enemies sprinted up the mountain of their own dead, using it like a morbid siege ramp as they attempted to bury the soldiers in bodies. The Consumers among the rolling charge focused on landing as many strikes as possible in the chaos before being rebuffed. The only goal was the slaughter, and all thought of strategy had faded from their collective attack.

Iron thigh muscles flexed as he took this all in and crouched down, gathering the new strength in his body and focusing it into his legs.

On the outside, he still looked the same except for his eyes, which now gleamed a crystalline green. But internally, his stats were completely transformed, and while he no longer could gain levels from combat, he had grown much more accustomed to this form over the multi-day battle they had fought defending the wall. He had not tired, and no wound he took remained for long. His greatest limitation now was that he could only be in one place at a time, and the defensive nature of this conflict did not play to the strengths of his build. So, he had hung back and helped keep their main magical support in the fight for as long as possible.

But that had just changed.

A booming *clap* sounded as he exploded from his crouch and launched into the air under the power of his applied *Strength*. The path of his jump took him high above the center of the enemy formation, and for the first time in days, he allowed himself a grim smile. Sword in hand, he reached back and extended its midnight blade fully behind him, perfectly timing the motion to coincide with the top of his flying arc.

"**Waxing Shadow**," he whispered, unnoticed by the masses of creatures below. His blade's weight suddenly multiplied, layering on metaphysical significance that began to pull him to the ground along with gravity.

He held the blade back as he began to fall like a meteor, its weight continuing to increase. This *Ability* was an aspect of the special nature of his Legendary blade and was scaled to match its wielder's *Strength*. A stat that had recently doubled for Hiro upon his resurrection as a guardian.

His fall picked up speed, and he brought the blade around, straining against its reality-warping significance. It ripped through the fabric of space as Hiro swept it forward, aided by the full momentum of an object crashing down from the heavens. As he completed his swing, the energy that had been building was expelled forward ahead of his fall at an angle designed to hit a large portion of the horde before the wall. Much of his kinetic energy was canceled out by the unleashing of the *Ability*, and he felt all of his built-up momentum transfer seamlessly into the attack's release.

A cataclysmic roar sounded in the air around him just before the *Ability* crashed into the enemy below. The first rank of enemies to be hit by the expanding arc were obliterated by the concentrated epicenter of the weaponized darkness.

Hiro landed with a crouch in the recently cleared area, surrounded by enemies. Ahead of him, his *Ability* continued to expand, mowing through enemies at an incredible rate, clearing fifty, then a hundred, then two hundred of the Strigoi from the rear of their chaotic formation. By the end of its expenditure, some of the Consumers were able to block the arc of dark energy, breaking bones and weapons, but by that time, Hiro had created an immense gap in the roiling mass of creatures. The collective weight of the horde's attention turned as one toward the newly created gap in their midst, howling in frenzied challenge at their new attacker.

Scanning his surroundings calmly, Hiro took in a deep breath, held it, and then exhaled. The Land was now attuned to him in a way he could not express to the others. It was a part of him, and here, defending it against invaders, he felt at peace. He was completely one with himself, and as easily as putting on an old pair of boots, he entered **Battle Trance**. His son may have evolved this technique into something new . . . but he had learned it at Hiro's feet.

As enemies charged in from all sides, Hiro shouted back in defiance and activated **Waning Light** and **Cascading Strike**. An umbral darkness exploded out from him and eagerly drank in the charging enemies as they flooded the gap his first attack had created.

Breath steady, Hiro began to move through his sword forms. **Cascading Strike** caused every consecutive strike in a battle to increase his *Strength* by 1 percent. The second passive *Ability* of his weapon activated along with this, increasing the weight of the blade by 1 percent with every consecutive strike. Both of these effects worked in tandem to create a vastly overpowered damage output for very little mana expenditure, and Hiro simply focused on adjusting his steps and posture with every swing to accommodate the change in the weapon. The motions were so familiar and the effects of his *Abilities* so well practiced that Hiro's meditative state only deepened as the world around him became a chaotic storm of blood, fangs, and claws.

Not a step was wasted, not a swing misplaced as he leaned into the darkness of his environment like an old friend. The Land beneath him augmented the combination of *Abilities* like never before, giving him an even greater understanding of his surroundings.

He danced between the enemy's frenzied forms, whirling around and through tightly packed bodies desperate to vent their long-suppressed fury on an enemy. The carnage grew so thick that blood began to mist the air and offal sprayed out in concentric circles from each of Hiro's strikes, showering the blinded combatants. Then his trance was almost broken in shock as the Strigoi nearest to his sword strikes lost any semblance of control in the presence of so much blood and rent flesh.

Enveloped in complete darkness, they seemed to give up altogether on telling friend from foe, and an orgy of slaughter began to grow from the epicenter of Hiro's *Domain*. He stilled and crouched down as he attempted to center himself again, an island of calm in a sea of madness. He had hoped to buy the wall some time . . . But as the screams of combat grew from the midst of his *Domain*, more and more enemies charged in from all directions, collapsing the press against the wall and drawing in its weight to the center of the new killing field like a black hole.

Just as he was about to enter back into the fray, a deep reverberation echoed through the Land. His head whipped up, peering unimpeded through the umbral *Domain* toward the mountain. Something had just happened to the Sovereign Crystal. A rippling tide of energy was washing over the Alliance's land, touching every member and imparting some of its bounty as it expanded inexorably over the entirety of the faction's holdings.

Hiro stood smiling as the wave of azure light was accompanied by a new verdant counterpart. He could feel it restoring and empowering as it washed over those on the wall. That was not all: the energy not only touched those defending its domain, but also spent a small portion of its wrath upon each enemy combatant. It laid them low with some sort of debuff he did not understand, though they were not killed . . . No, instead it cleansed them of the darkness that was using the monsters as hosts and rendered the bodies comatose from the sudden loss of animating energy.

As the wave washed over him and moved to the boundaries of their allotted portion of the Land, he felt it grow outward, pushing the boundaries of what had once been theirs, expanding and transforming their faction's influence, and along with it, his *Strength*.

Canceling his umbral *Domain* to reveal a shocking field of eviscerated bodies, Hiro called to the wall in a booming voice, "Attack now, defenders of the Alliance! Your enemy has been delivered to you. Now reap them for the *experience* they offer!"

His voice echoed supernaturally past the wall, deep into the forests and valleys, and spurred every newly empowered member of the Three-Fold Alliance to charge forward and finish the work that the faction's transformation had begun.

Deep below the mountain, at the epicenter of a network of tunnels that had only just begun to hear the ringing of mining picks once again, something stirred. The energy of the faction's transformation had reached deep below the bedrock of the Holy Temple to touch an ancient magic of binding and sleep. The contact stirred the enchantment, and a series of if–then logic statements began to unravel as the spell unwound itself around its target, beginning a process of reanimation. The supernatural slumber that had held it for Epochs began to fade . . .

Wesley – Level 59 Black Market Trafficker

Wesley couldn't help but sneer at the posturing fool next to him reporting on what had happened on their assignment. He had set everything up perfectly and this fool had to go and ruin it by bringing in some unknown variables at the last minute.

"—because of the ineptitude of this slimy human, the trap was sprung too early, allowing many of my brethren time to respond. That, along with the presence of this unknown warrior, caused much of the infiltration to die in its infancy. We still gained dozens of new agents at every level of the order, but it was not nearly what we had planned," the dark-haired knight said, smoothly shifting the blame for the failure to Wesley.

Wesley could not allow those to be the last words of the report . . . So, with scorn dripping from every word, he rebuffed the accusation.

"And who, *pray tell*, gave entry to this warrior in the middle of our operation? Perhaps you are not as loyal as—"

"**Silence**," came a hissing cacophony of voices from one of the thrones. Wesley flinched as if struck. There were six gigantic thrones arrayed before them, each holding a figure of unbelievable power cloaked in darkness. Wesley's eyes darted across the line of thrones as he knelt immediately, trying to parse out which figure the voice had come from.

The command hung over the gargantuan chamber like a leaden weight. The Hall of Fallen Princes had not been occupied in millennia, and even Wesley knew that the thrones were no longer being held exclusively by classic figures of demonic strength. Power had shifted in the Pits just as it was shifting everywhere. Times were changing, and a new empire was rising, one that would drown the current system of hierarchies in its own arrogance.

"**Tell me of this warrior and the power he wielded to expunge our influence.**"

Epilogue

40,000 years ago
Epoch of Gods and Heroes

B rokenridge breathed in the scent of his *Domain*, letting the heady layers of aroma enter into his ridged nostrils to be parsed into a thousand pieces of information and sorted by his superior intellect.

He had set the green two-legs that were scattered all over the surrounding forests to look for tribute worthy of their master, and it smelled like they had returned. They stank of anticipation and fear . . . Good, perhaps they would have something worth adding to his treasure chamber this time.

Gleaming piles glittered around him, as if doubtful that such paltry trinkets could improve on their beauty . . .

"Do not worry, darlings, only the best will be allowed to join you," he breathed out in a smug rejoinder to their cute self-assurance, smoke dancing lazily between his arm-sized fangs at the cleverness of his response.

He also detected the tangy bitterness of subterfuge from the hairy ones he had caught burrowing under his mountain. When he had first discovered them, they had pled ignorance, and he had shown them mercy. A few hundred dead were nothing to the thousands that still infested the area below his mountain.

Their few petty enchantments were no impediment to his fire . . .

His jowls rose in excitement at the memory of the smell of so much burning meat. It had been a while since he ate one . . . Perhaps it was time he had another snack and reminded them who the ruler of this *Domain* was, above and below ground.

Their offers of tribute had been . . . acceptable. He found them much better sources of treasure than the tribes of nomads infesting the surface. While it was always enjoyable to start huge forest fires, collecting loot and carrying it back to his lair was arduous. He much preferred to create a tribute system, which was slower but steady.

His slit pupils dilated as he imagined growing his hoard until it rivaled even the greatest of those peacocks roosting in the Council Peaks. They ruled over a system of their own devising, growing fat off the labor of others, and he would snap its mechanisms between his jaws before he served under it again.

Soon it would be time to slumber again and absorb the strength of his chamber, adding to his not inconsiderable might. The journey would be long, but without the punishing burden of fattening those above him, he would grow strong enough to take what was his by right.

He breathed in the Scorch-marked magic that permeated the cave, indicating to all who knew to look that this was his *Domain* and connecting the treasure within to his soul. Its strength was his strength.

Remaking a Soul-Bound chamber had been very difficult, especially after those pretenders had destroyed his last chamber and stolen all the treasure within, robbing him of much of his unprocessed strength. With nothing left, he had been able to tear his soul free from the destroyed chamber in an act of desperate cunning. What he had done was almost unheard of, and none would expect him to reforge a new chamber in this place, so far away from his enemies and the center of things.

They thought him exiled and weak . . . They would see.

He eyed the piles that seemed a little less impressive at the memory of what he had lost. Gold to increase his strength, jewels to increase his magical output. Weapons and armor for his claws, teeth, and scales. It was all here . . .

There was just far too little of it. Perhaps he needed to take a visit down to the hairy ones' kingdom and see what other baubles they possessed. However, that raised the question of those copper-cursed tunnels . . .

Brokenridge huffed out a smokey sigh.

A problem for another time. Soon he would sleep and take in his gains from the last five hundred years of conquest. Then he would loot, pillage, and burn to his heart's content. Tongues of flame danced past his snout and his blood ran hot at the thought of the coming glory of further conquest.

On his next inhale, he pulled in the mixed aroma of the green skins and the hairy ones approaching together. They had entered the opening to his lair at the base of the mountain and were advancing cautiously down the long ramp deep underground that led to his Soul-Bound chamber.

He had made the mistake of choosing a high abode once before, where many of his enemies could approach at once. Now only one dragon at a time could advance on his *Domain*, and he could rend them each, tooth and claw. Plus, there was an unpleasant smell near the top of this peak that he could not stand to approach. He was hoping it would ward off any others in the chance that they came looking for him during his slumber.

But the smell was not the only advantage to this location. It also contained a startling density of Fate, which had made bonding his new chamber possible, if not easy.

"Lord Dragon!" one of the hairy ones called, asking permission to enter. This was followed by the guttural call of the green skins' mana user, who used his tribal title instead.

"Burning End!"

He quite liked the name they had given him, not that he would ever tell the meat that.

"**Approach**," he uttered, layering his voice with *Authority.*

The small group advanced down the appropriately sized tunnel pulling a large cart behind them piled high with tribute.

Just what he needed before a long nap.

He rose up on his forelegs excitedly, flames leaking out of his clenched jaws as he beheld a rather impressive pile of gold, weapons, and even a few magical artifacts. One in particular caught his eye at the top of the pile. It was a perfectly round sphere of crystal, which exuded a strange, almost hypnotic power. He flicked out his tongue to taste the magic but was unable to identify exactly what it did.

His curiosity rose . . . Unknown could mean powerful, and powerful was always welcome.

"**What have you brought your master?**" he asked, making sure to keep the greed from his voice. It would not do to let the peasants think they had pleased him. Fear was the only reliable motivator for one's servants.

"Your Deadliness! Our king sends his tribute to your growing kingdom, long may you reign!" the hairy one declared loudly as that same tangy stink of betrayal rose off him in cloying waves . . . But the crystal sphere glittered invitingly, and he found himself too intrigued to care what little scheme they were running.

He would eat this one later.

"Burning End, our conquest of the local elves has succeeded with your leadership. We have brought you the finest of their weapons and treasures," the greenskinned mana user said, his scent oddly muted to Brokenridge's senses.

His eyes narrowed as he scrutinized the pile. Whatever these "elves" were, they were no crafters . . . There were some small magics on the weapons and armor, several enchantments for sharpness and durability.

Trash.

Then his eyes wandered back to the top of the pile, and he breathed in the magic of the sphere all over again, finding it intoxicating. His disappointment was forgotten as he beheld the powerful artifact.

"And where did you get this lovely bauble?" he asked, unable to keep the pleasurable chuckle from escaping his throat.

"Your Greatness, that is something our king found deep in the under dark . . . He fought through fearsome magics, defeating terrible foes called Beholders to obtain it. They called it a Foci. Does it please you?" the hairy one asked, beginning to exude the heady scent of satisfaction.

Brokenridge decided to allow him his small victory at satisfying his master. More and more of his attention was consumed by the sphere, which seemed to pulse and throb with alluring power.

What does it do? What will I gain from such a treasure?

Absorbing an artifact like this would accelerate his timeline greatly. This was the kind of power he had been searching for. The power to dethrone pretenders and take what was his.

"Leave," he said quietly, gazing upon the sphere. The two-legs glanced at each other, passing some meaningless silent message, then scurried away like the little mice they were.

Brokenridge reached forward with one of his claws to hook the end of the cart and pulled it close to the mound of treasure he lay upon. He lowered his snout to the newest addition to his hoard and took another exultant inhale, breathing in the magic of the artifact deeply.

His eyes narrowed for just a moment as he detected the faintest thread of magic anchoring the sphere to some distant point. Just as he was about to snip the little strand with an *Authority*-tipped claw, the sphere flashed and flooded the chamber with a magic so heady that it overwhelmed Brokenridge's senses.

His eyelids grew heavy, and his head dipped past the cart to rest gently on the stone floor.

And why not? he thought tiredly to himself.

He had already intended to absorb the power locked away in his chamber, why not start a few months early?

4,000 years later

Brokenridge's eyes flicked open as he sneezed out a gout of flame. His internal clock instantly told him how long it had been, and he gazed around his chamber suddenly alert as he found the entire cavern empty.

He urgently thrust his senses inward to check if he had already absorbed it all in such a short time.

But no.

He had not advanced in any of the categories he should have. His mana well had actually diminished, and his scales had lost much of their luster. His adamantine claws clicked dully in frustration against the stone floor as he struggled to come to terms with his situation.

Flame churned in his chest and his blood began to boil in his veins as the betrayal took full shape in his memory.

He roared, flooding the front of his lair with dragon flame. Its intensity was so great that it thrust out through the front entrance and burst into the sky, announcing to all his kingdom his great fury.

He tried not to think about how much of his well that display had just used, and his claws tore into the stone supporting his immense weight as he leaped forward, charged up the tunnel out of his chamber, and launched himself into the air.

THEY WILL PAY! he thundered internally, breathing in deeply to find where the little rats were hiding . . .

Nothing.

None of the musky scent of the green skins or the sweat and metallic odor of the hairy ones.

Gone.

They were gone and they had taken what was *HIS*.

He roared again, his fury thundering across the landscape, when he finally caught a new scent. Rather, something old . . . Layered and complex but also simple. He took in another breath and detected something that smelled vaguely like food and dead wood fashioned together in a rudimentary manner.

His pulse quickened and he wheeled in the air, diving toward the source. His fury demanded destruction, and whatever lonely few they had left behind would tell him where the others had gone . . .

Air howled past him as he pushed his speed, wings grasping huge quantities of atmosphere and launching him forward with every beat. In a few moments, he had crossed the breadth of his Land and dived through the canopy to crash into the narrow dirt track hidden beneath the leaves.

Earth exploded outward from the force of his impact, and he dug his claws deep into the ground to arrest his incredible momentum. He roared again in fury, and liquid flame dripped from his gaping jaw as the rain of detritus settled and the object of his rage was revealed.

There before him, placidly chewing on some grass, was a long-eared four-legged food, attached to a cart with a single occupant . . . and absolutely no treasure. A female two-legs draped in all sorts of cloth sat on the front bench of the cart, her chin held in her hand as she hunched forward.

The sight of what was clearly not his quarry sent Brokenridge over the edge, and without consciously deciding to end these pathetic creatures, his eyes narrowed to slits and a geyser of dragon's flame bathed them and all their surroundings in the hottest substance known to the plane.

The nearby trees were vaporized and those beyond them burst into flame, instantly creating a barren wasteland of destruction and ash . . .

That is, except for the four-legs, the two-legs, and the cart.

Unbelievably, they remained untouched, now backed by a landscape remade in the image of his wrath.

"Very impressive, if misplaced . . . Something I believe you have consistently failed to correct over your lifetime," the clothed two-legs drawled as she straightened on her seat and stretched.

"How dare y—" It finally hit him as his *Authority* was choked out by a weight greater than his. This was no average two-legs. She must be one of the new spawn that had emerged with this Epoch . . .

"Go on, you are getting close to the truth," she said, watching his thought process play out over his draconic features.

"Little Godling. What business do you have in my *Domain*?" he tried again, this time baring his teeth in a minor acknowledgment of her power.

"Not quite, but it will do," she answered, confusing Brokenridge even further. "I am here to make an offer. You desire the Council Peak throne, and you seek to try and take it using the same system of power that you hate . . . This will fail. In fact, your scheme failed before it even began."

Brokenridge did not bother to quiet the rumbling growl that vibrated through his chest at the being's mockery. Godling or not, he would see just how well that cloth could hold up against the snap of his fangs.

"Now, now." She waved him down in a conciliatory manner. "Your ambition is laudable, though impossible unless you are willing to change. Like will never change like. You must be different if you want to supplant that which you hate."

The rumble died slowly in his chest at her words, and he breathed in her scent again, attempting to gain some grasp of the being that dared suggest anything besides the superiority of his race. Strange scents floated in amongst the ash and char. Images flashed through his mind as he attempted to place them: a balanced scale, silver . . . old paper? Pervading it all he sensed the *Beginning* on her, something that he recognized by instinct, not experience.

Dragons were some of the first creatures on the plane, and some memory of that explosive time remained locked deep in their blood.

Nonetheless, Brokenridge refused to be some pawn in the convoluted games the "lords" of this new Epoch played.

"I refuse. I will defeat my enemies with my own strength or not at all. I will never serve another."

"Ah . . . But you already serve a master you do not know," she answered, quirking a smile.

Brokenridge roared at the insult. "Dragons serve none but ourselves!"

"You are truly a poor servant to yourself if you have sought your benefit. From where I am standing, it looks like you are worse off than you have ever been."

Brokenridge's mind blanked in rage. He lunged forward in the blink of an eye and snapped his jaws closed on her relaxing form.

The clack of empty teeth cracked through the forest, and his eyes narrowed even further. He pulled back and refocused on his prey, who had bent down to pick up something at her feet that positively thrummed with mana. The movement had looked slow, but it put her upper body just below where his strike should have torn her in two.

More trickery . . . He hated trickery.

"Look, I know you are an honest dragon, so I have gone to great trouble to shape what I propose in Scorch. You may look it over and see the complete intent."

That caught Brokenridge's attention. Very few outside his race understood the draconic equivalent of writing. Many thought that because dragons could read, they simply used an inferior form of communication when they were not speaking face to face. That this godling claimed not only to understand Scorch but to be able to write it as well was truly intriguing . . .

Seeing her opportunity in his hesitance, the two-legs unwrapped the object to reveal a perfect triangle of dragon glass etched all over with the unmistakable glowing symbols of the dragon language.

He breathed it in deeply, taking in its sight and scent as he unraveled the dense symbols and smells, unpacking the layers of enchantment they represented.

It was an augmentation of the magic he used for his Soul-Bound chamber, an inborn ability of all dragon-kind. Yet this augmentation was tailored to his exact mana signature. Some of the concepts were foreign to him, which was the most impressive thing he had seen yet from the godling. Where had she gotten this information?

Some things, however, he understood immediately. This would radically expand the boundaries of his soul chamber, and the list of unprocessed treasure he would be able to benefit from would grow exponentially. There was mention of the activation of some object of power to initiate the transformation, but no such object existed to his knowledge. It seemed to reference Land allegiance being held by some other entity or being.

"This is interesting, but nonsense . . . This makes use of things that cannot and do not exist. In fact, the fifth and third principles are based on laws that have not been established," he said with a sigh, disappointed at the waste of what was obviously the work of a master.

"Yet," she answered as she covered up the dragon glass, then tucked it away.

Her single-word answer stuck in his mind like a splinter, and understanding slowly lodged its way into his brain. All of the unknowns about this encounter fell into place, forming a single cohesive conclusion.

"Fatewatcher," he muttered, then ducked his head low and bared all of his fangs in the closest thing a dragon could show to respect.

"Correct." She smiled, emphasizing his revelation with a pointed finger. "He who took everything from you will not sit on the throne forever. Your time to challenge him will come, but this is the only path that moves toward that end." She lifted the covered object. "Furthermore, your opportunity will not come for Epochs yet. Now, tell me, Dragon, are you willing to wait to obtain your greatest desire?"

Brokenridge redid the calculations on how long it would take him to reascend to his previous heights, before he had been cast out, and then surpass them enough to challenge the King of the High Mount . . . Millenia at least.

"I can wait," he breathed, allowing lazy, contented smoke to coil up from his nostrils. "Tell me where the **Weave** is going, Fatewatcher."

Author's Note

I hope you have enjoyed reading *Son of Flame* as much as I enjoyed writing it! I am still recovering from the mild shock of having real-life readers like you, and it has been an honor to be able to share this story with so many. The dream of dreams would be to support my family with writing income alone, which would mean many more stories like this one. There are so many ways you can help me get there, but by far the most important thing you can do is rate and review this book. You literally have the power to change my life, and it would mean the world to me if you shared your opinion with the rest of the internet.

Regardless, stop by my website: www.jjhutto.com. I would love to hear from you!

About the Author

J. J. Hutto is the author of the Son of Flame series, originally released on Royal Road. He moved often as a kid and became a fixture at various local libraries as a result. There, he studied under fantasy's greatest authors and became obsessed with the hero's journey, which likely inspired his career as a firefighter/first responder. Hutto currently resides in Atlanta, Georgia, and is pursuing writing full-time . . . among a few other dubious professions.

9 781039 479814